KEY LIME PIE MURDER

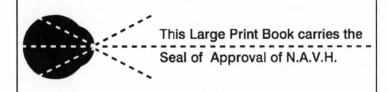

This Large Print Book carries the
Seal of Approval of N.A.V.H.

A HANNAH SWENSEN MYSTERY WITH RECIPES

KEY LIME PIE MURDER

JOANNE FLUKE

THORNDIKE PRESS

An imprint of Thomson Gale, a part of The Thomson Corporation

THOMSON

GALE

Detroit • New York • San Francisco • New Haven, Conn. • Waterville, Maine • London

THOMSON
GALE

LIBRARY OF CONGRESS CATALOGING-IN-PUBLICATION DATA

Fluke, Joanne, 1943–
    Key lime pie murder : a Hannah Swensen mystery with recipes / by Joanne Fluke.
        p. cm. — (Thorndike Press large print mystery)
    ISBN-13: 978-0-7862-9541-8 (alk. paper)
    ISBN-10: 0-7862-9541-4 (alk. paper)
    1. Swensen, Hannah (Fictitious character) — Fiction. 2. Women detectives — Minnesota — Fiction. 3. Bakers — Fiction. 4. Minnesota — Fiction. 5. Large type books. I. Title.
PS3556.L685K49 2007
813'.54—dc22   2007003679

Published in 2007 by arrangement with Kensington Books, an imprint of Kensington Publishing Corp.

Printed in the United States of America on permanent paper
10 9 8 7 6 5 4 3 2 1

This book is dedicated to Tooni,
who truly knew how to love.

ACKNOWLEDGMENTS

For Ruel, my in-house story editor and research team. And for the kids, who've learned not to count carbs out loud whenever I serve dessert.

Thank you to our friends and neighbors: Mel & Kurt, Lyn & Bill, Gina & the kids, Adrienne, Jay, Bob, Amanda, Dale, John, Trudi, Dr. Bob & Sue, Laura & Mark, Richard & Krista, Barbara & Val, Lana from Baltimore, and Mark Baker, who always shows up, sometimes twice.

Thank you to my editor-in-chief, John Scognamiglio. Without you, this wouldn't be nearly as much fun and I'd probably fall flat on my face. The same goes for Walter, Steve, Laurie, Doug, David, Joan, Maureen, Magee, Meryl, Colleen, Jessica, Justin, Robin, Lydia, Lori, Mike, and Barbara.

Thank you to Hiro Kimura, superb cover artist, for the original cover design of the yummy key lime pie. And thanks to Lou

Malcanji for designing such a delectable dust jacket.

Thanks also to all the other talented folks at Kensington who keep Hannah sleuthing and baking up a storm.

Thanks to John for fixing all the computer tech stuff I don't understand and can't spell.

Thank you to Dr. Rahhal & Trina for all that you do.

Big hugs to Terry Sommers for trying out all the recipes in this book and never once bringing up the subject of calories.

Thank you to Jamie Wallace for her superb work on my Web site **MurderSheBaked .com**

And many, many thanks to everyone who e-mailed or snail-mailed. I'm baking key lime pie for dessert tonight. How about you?

CHAPTER ONE

At precisely eight forty-five on the second Monday morning in June, Hannah Swensen took a number from the deli-style dispenser mounted on a pole next to the secretary's desk and plunked herself down in one of the nondescript chairs in the nondescript waiting room to wait her turn.

It was hot and muggy, standard fare for this time of year. While other states boasted of fish that jumped, living that was easy, and cotton that was high, summertime in Minnesota was just the opposite. The muggy heat caused fish to lurk at the bottom of the lake, totally unmoved by even the tastiest bait, and the living was far from easy, especially if you owned a family farm. The corn might be knee high by the Fourth of July, if it was a good year, but the only thing that was high in the second week of June was the humidity.

A low rumble made Hannah frown. She

hoped the sound came from one of the big trucks she'd seen delivering carnival rides to the midway and not from gathering storm clouds. This was the first day of the Tri-County Fair and the gates opened at noon. The coming week would be like a holiday, with hundreds passing through the turnstiles to look at the exhibits, enjoy the rides on the midway, and attend the rodeo that was held every afternoon.

Hannah brushed several orange cat hairs from her tan slacks. They landed on the seat of the orange plastic chair next to her. Although she vacuumed every weekend, it was a losing battle. Her orange and white tomcat, Moishe, contributed twice as much hair as she collected in the bag of her vacuum. There were times when Hannah seriously considered installing an orange and white carpet, buying orange and white furniture, and eating only orange and white food during the shedding season. It wouldn't cut down on the cat hair, but it would be camouflaged. At least she wouldn't be aware of how many strands she was walking on, sitting on, and ingesting.

This type of chair would work. Hannah couldn't even see where the cat hairs had landed. But spending more time in a chair like this was something to be avoided. It was a clone to every other molded plastic chair in every other waiting room in the state. Perhaps it was true that form followed function, but in this case it was horribly uncomfortable and as ugly as sin.

Rather than glance at her watch for the third time in as many minutes, Hannah thought about why so many businesses bought these chairs for their waiting rooms. The plastic was impervious to spills and scratches, and they did add a splash of color to an otherwise drab room. The chairs were bolted to rails that conjoined them as sextuplets. Hannah supposed that this was meant to discourage theft, but she seriously doubted that anyone would want to steal them anyway.

Sitting up straight didn't help to relieve the strain on her back, so Hannah tried slouching. That was even worse. A little notice stamped on the back of the chair in front of her said that it had been designed to fit the average body. And that brought up another question. Was anybody truly *average?* Average was a statistical tool that took tall people over six feet, added them to short people under five feet, and came up with an average of five and a half feet. Hannah knew from bitter experience not to buy slacks marked *average.* They were too short for tall people and too long for short people. Perhaps somewhere there might be a handful of people the slacks would fit, but Hannah had never met them. And if these chairs were designed for an average body, it was clear that the model the manufacturer had used bore little resemblance to Hannah. Looking around her, Hannah suspected that she wasn't alone. Everyone who was waiting to see the secretary at the Tri-County Fairgrounds looked just as uncomfortable as she did.

"Swensen?" the secretary called out, and Hannah walked over to take the seat in front of the secretary's desk that had been recently vacated by a man in work clothes and a hardhat. "I need some information from you before I can issue your pass."

Hannah waited while the woman opened a drawer and pulled out a book of bound and printed forms. She flipped it open, retrieved her pen, and looked up at Hannah. "Your full name please?"

"Hannah Louise Swensen."

"Marital status?"

"Single."

"Age?"

"Thirty." Hannah gave a little sigh. This was June and her thirty-first birthday was in July. When did a woman become a spinster?

Had it happened last year when she hit thirty? Or would the women's movement grant her a reprieve so she wouldn't enter the old maid's category until she reached forty? This was a question she could ponder by herself, but she certainly wouldn't discuss it with her mother! Delores Swensen wasn't reticent about reminding her eldest daughter that her biological clock was ticking.

"Street address?"

"Forty-six thirty-seven Maytime Lane," Hannah replied, smiling a bit as she gave the address of her condo complex. Maybe she *was* a spinster but she owned her own home and business.

"City and state?"

"Lake Eden, Minnesota."

"And your reason for applying for a pass?"

As usual, she'd probably bit off more than she could chew. But what else could she have done when Pam Baxter, the Jordan High Home Economics teacher, had called her in a panic at six o'clock this morning to say that Edna Ferguson had been taken to Lake Eden Memorial Hospital for an emergency appendectomy? Pam had practically begged Hannah to fill in on the judging panel, and of course she'd agreed. "I'm a last-minute replacement on the panel to judge the baked goods at the Creative Arts Building," she said.

"Lucky you!" The secretary looked up with a smile that instantly humanized her.

"Really?"

"You'd better believe it! That's a job I wouldn't mind having. I love desserts and I need to lose a few pounds."

Hannah blinked. "You want to judge the baked goods contest because you need to lose a few pounds?"

"That's right. My aunt lost thirty pounds when she took a job at a chocolate factory. They let her eat all the candy she wanted, and after the first couple of days, she stopped eating it. She's been retired for ten years, and she still can't stand the sight of chocolate."

"That wouldn't work for me," Hannah told her.

"How do you know?"

"I own a bakery and I still love desserts."

The secretary sighed as she handed Hannah her pass. "It probably wouldn't work for me, either. Say . . . is your bakery called The Cookie Jar?"

"That's right."

"Then I'm almost positive you're going to win blue!"

"Blue?"

"A blue ribbon. I don't mean you personally, but the man who took your picture for the photography exhibit. I saw it last night and it's the best in the show."

Less than five minutes later, Hannah was staring at the entry that the secretary thought would take first place in the photography exhibit. It was a candid picture, she hadn't even realized it was being taken, and it was undoubtedly the most flattering photo anyone had ever taken of her.

Hannah felt the smile begin in her mind, spread out to her face, and flow right on down to the soles of her feet. She felt as if she were smiling all over as she gazed at the photo. It was a wonderful picture, and she could hardly believe that she was the subject! First of all, her hair wasn't sticking up in wiry curls the way it usually did, and it looked more auburn than red. And if that weren't enough to please her, she appeared at least ten pounds thinner than she actually was. Both of her eyes were open, her pose wasn't awkward or contrived, and the half-smile on her lips was intriguing. This photo was a miracle, and Hannah knew it. Any photographer who could make her look good deserved a blue ribbon and then some!

Norman Rhodes had taken it, of course.

Hannah's sometimes boyfriend divided his time between his vocation of dentistry, his avocation of photography, and his habit of being a prince of a guy Hannah knew she should probably marry. Unfortunately, she couldn't seem to do it, even though her mind told her it was the smart choice. She'd come to the conclusion that she simply wasn't ready for marriage, and reminders from her mother about biological clocks shouldn't force her into walking down the aisle until the time was right for her.

Hannah shook herself mentally and glanced at her watch. It was nine-thirty and she had to meet Pam and her teacher's assistant, Willa Sunquist, at ten. She didn't have time to think about marriage now.

She turned her attention back to the photograph. It was huge, two feet by three feet, and Norman had taken it at The Cookie Jar. The sign painted on the window was clearly visible in the mirror behind the counter, and that must be the way the secretary had recognized her. Hannah was standing behind the counter, looking off into the distance, and there was a very loving, almost beatific expression on her face. It was clear she was thinking about someone or something she loved, and Hannah wished she could remember who or what it was.

16

There was a calendar on the wall to the left of the counter, and Hannah noticed the date. Norman had taken this photograph when Ross Barton and his movie crew were in Lake Eden. The clock on the wall told her that it was almost noon, the time when Ross and his crew arrived to have lunch at The Cookie Jar. Hannah guessed she could have been thinking about Ross, her old college friend who'd turned out to be much more than that.

Then there was Mike Kingston. She could have been thinking of Lake Eden's most eligible bachelor, the best-looking detective in the Winnetka County Sheriff's Department. Thoughts of Mike always put a smile on her face and made her heart race harder in her chest. Or perhaps she'd been thinking of Norman. While he wasn't heart-stopping handsome, he was kind, and sweet, and sexy, and gentle, and . . .

"Good heavens!" Hannah exclaimed under her breath. Since she didn't remember why she'd been smiling, her smile would just have to remain a mystery. She gave one last look and turned to head for the Creative Arts Building, reminding herself that no one knew why the Mona Lisa had been smiling, either.

Hannah took a shortcut through the food court, an area with picnic tables that was ringed by food and snack stands. Some of them were getting ready to open, and Hannah stopped in front of a sign that read, DEEP-FRIED CANDY BARS.

One glance at the description that was written in smaller type near the bottom of the sign and Hannah's mouth started to water. The candy bars were impaled on sticks, chilled thoroughly, dipped into a sweet batter that was a cousin to the one used for funnel cakes, and then deep-fried to a golden brown. The booth was called Sinful Pleasures, and that was entirely appropriate. There should have been a warning sign that read, NO REDEEMING NUTRITIONAL MERIT WHATSOEVER, but Hannah doubted that would stop anyone from ordering. The choices of candy bar were varied, and she was in the process of debating the virtues of a Milky Way over a Snickers Bar when she heard a voice calling her name.

Hannah turned to see her sister Andrea running toward her across the food court. Her face was pink from exertion, and wisps of blond hair had escaped the elaborate twist she'd pinned up on the top of her head. She was wearing a perfectly ordinary outfit, light blue slacks with a matching sleeveless blouse, but she still looked like a fashion model.

"Amazing," Hannah muttered under her breath. "Totally amazing."

"What's amazing?" Andrea asked, arriving at her side.

"You look gorgeous."

"You need glasses. I'm wearing my oldest clothes and my hair's a mess."

"It doesn't matter. You still look gorgeous."

"It's nice of you to say that, but I don't have time to talk about that now. I tracked you down because I need your help and I'm in a real rush." Andrea stopped and stared as someone opened the shutters on the fried candy bar booth from the inside. "I read about those deep-fried candy bars in the *Lake Eden Journal.* You're not going to order one, are you?"

"They're not really open yet," Hannah hedged. "None of the food booths open until noon."

"Well, that's a relief!" Andrea fanned her face with her hand. "I don't have to tell you that they're loaded with calories, and you still haven't lost the weight you put on over Christmas, do I?"

"Absolutely not," Hannah said. Wild horses wouldn't get her to admit to Andrea that she was sorely tempted to come back when the fair officially opened and order one. "Why do you need my help?"

"Let's sit down and I'll show you."

Andrea led the way to one of the picnic tables that sat in the shade of a huge elm. She brushed off the top and opened the file folder she was carrying.

"Photos for the Mother-Daughter contest?" Hannah stated the obvious as Andrea laid out four different poses of her and Hannah's oldest niece, Tracey.

"That's right. Norman dropped them off last night and I can't decide which one is the best. I have to turn it in at ten this morning," Andrea frowned as she glanced at her watch, "and I've got only twelve minutes to take it to the secretary's office."

Hannah looked at each photograph in turn. They were all good, but one was a smidgeon better. "This one," she said, pointing it out.

"Why that one?"

"Because your heads are tilted at exactly the same angle."

"That's true," Andrea said, but she didn't

look happy. "How about the one on the end?"

"It's a good picture, but the resemblance isn't as striking. Tracey's looking straight at the camera, and you're looking off to the side."

"I know. I noticed that. It's just . . ." Andrea's voice trailed off, and she gave a little sigh.

"It's just what?"

"My hair looks better in the picture on the end."

"True, but it's not a beauty pageant. It's a mother-daughter look-alike contest."

"You're right, of course." Andrea gathered up the photos and put them back in the folder. "I'll use the one you picked."

Hannah's sisterly radar went on full alert. Something was wrong. Andrea was worried about how she looked, and she'd mentioned her hair twice in the past three minutes. "What's wrong with your hair?" she asked, forgetting to even try to phrase the question tactfully.

"I knew it!" Andrea wailed, and her eyes filled with tears. "You noticed and that means everyone in town will notice. Bill said he couldn't see any more, but he must have missed one."

"One what?"

Andrea took a deep breath for courage and then she blurted it out. "A gray hair! I'm going gray, Hannah, and I'm only twenty-six. It's just awful, especially since Mother isn't even gray yet!"

She would be without the wonders of modern cosmetology, Hannah thought, but she didn't say it. She'd promised Delores she'd never tell that an expensive hair color called Raven Wing was partially responsible for her mother's youthful appearance. Wishing for the wisdom of the Sphinx, or at least that of a clinical psychiatrist, Hannah waded in with both feet. Her goal was to make Andrea feel better even if it took a little white lie to accomplish it. "Oatmeal," she said, remembering the extra bag of cookies she was carrying in her large shoulder bag.

"What?"

"Mother swears oatmeal prevents aging. She eats it every day."

"I know it's supposed to be good for your cholesterol, and some people use it for facials." Andrea looked thoughtful. "Does Mother really believe that it keeps her from going gray?"

"Absolutely. But whatever you do, you can't mention it to her."

"Why not?"

"Because we're not supposed to believe

she's old enough to have gray hair. If we mention it, she'll take it as an insult."

Andrea thought about that for a moment. "You're right. I'll never mention it."

"So are you going to try it?"

Andrea made a face. "I *hate* oatmeal. Remember how you used to try to trick me into eating it by sprinkling on brown sugar and making a face out of chocolate chips on the top?"

"I remember. And it worked because you always cleaned your bowl."

"You only *thought* it worked. I ate off the brown sugar and the chocolate chips, and then I gave the bowl to Bruno when you weren't looking."

"You did?" Hannah was disillusioned. She thought she'd been so clever in getting her sister to eat oatmeal, and the Swensen family dog had gotten it instead.

"Maybe I shouldn't have told you," Andrea said, watching the play of emotions that crossed Hannah's face.

"That's okay." Hannah began to smile as she thought of the perfect ploy. She'd get Andrea to eat oatmeal now, every single day, to make up for her deception! "Bruno was a gorgeous dog. I used to wish I had hair that color."

"I know. And his coat was so soft. I still

get a little lump in my throat every time I see an Irish Setter."

Hannah took a deep breath. She was about to drop the other shoe. "I'm glad you told me about the oatmeal."

"Why's that?"

"Because now I understand why Bruno never went gray. It must have been the oatmeal you gave him. Too bad *you* didn't eat it."

Andrea groaned. "If I'd known, I would have. And now I suppose it's too late!"

"Not necessarily. Mother never used to eat it when she was young."

"Really?"

"You were probably too little to remember, but all she used to have for breakfast was coffee. She said she never got hungry until noon, but I think that was just an excuse."

"For what?"

"For not admitting that she was on a diet. Mother put on a little weight after Michelle was born and she had a hard time taking it off."

"So when did she start eating breakfast?"

"It was after I went off to college. I'm not positive because I wasn't there, but I think she started eating oatmeal for breakfast right after she got her first gray hair."

Andrea shuddered slightly. "Okay, I'll just have to do the same thing. It's close to a tossup, but I'm pretty sure that I hate gray hair more than I hate oatmeal."

"Atta girl!" Hannah reached into her purse and pulled out a bag of cookies. "And just to make that oatmeal more palatable, here's a present for you."

"Cookies?"

"Karen Lood's Swedish Oatmeal Cookies. They're authentic and they're absolutely delicious. Mother got the recipe from Karen before she moved out of town."

"Thanks, Hannah. I don't usually like oatmeal cookies, but they're bound to be better than eating oatmeal in a bowl."

"Taste one."

Andrea pulled out a cookie and took a bite. She chewed and then she smiled. "Good! I like these, Hannah!"

"I knew you would. They're a really simple cookie, and sometimes simple is best."

"Maybe this is crazy, but these remind me of your Old-Fashioned Sugar Cookies."

"It's not crazy at all. Both of them are buttery, crunchy, and sweet. Just make sure you have three a day, and come down to the shop for more when you run out. We bake them every day in the summer. There's no chips to melt and they hold up really well in hot weather." Hannah glanced down at her watch and started to frown. "You'd better get a move on, Andrea. You don't want to be late turning in that photo."

"Right." Andrea stood up and took a step away from the picnic table. Then she turned to smile at Hannah. "Thanks, Hannah. No matter what's bothering me, you always make me feel better."

Hannah smiled back. Andrea could be a pain at times, especially when she went into a tirade about the unfashionable way Hannah dressed, or the fact that she was a bit too plump. But on that giant tally sheet sisters kept in their heads, she'd won this round hands down.

Swedish Oatmeal Cookies (Karen Lood)

Preheat oven to 350 degrees F., rack in middle position.

1 cup butter *(2 sticks, 1/2 pound)*
3/4 cup white *(granulated)* sugar
1 teaspoon baking soda
1 cup flour *(no need to sift)*
2 cups oatmeal *(I used Quaker Oats-Quick)*
1 egg yolk

Melt the butter in a microwave safe bowl on HIGH for approximately 1 1/2 minutes. Let it cool to room temperature. Mix in the white sugar.

Add the baking soda, flour, and oatmeal. Stir thoroughly.

Beat the egg yolk with a fork until it's thoroughly mixed. Add it to the bowl and stir until it's incorporated.

Grease *(or spray with Pam or other nonstick cooking spray)* a standard-sized cookie sheet. Make small balls of dough and place them on the cookie sheet, 12 to a sheet. Press them down with a fork in a crisscross pattern the way you'd do for peanut butter cookies.

Bake at 350 degrees F. for 10 to 12 minutes or until they're just starting to brown around the edges. Let the cookies cool for a minute or two on the sheets and then transfer them to a wire rack to complete cooling.

Yield: approximately 5 dozen, depending on cookie size.

CHAPTER TWO

"Did I say thank you for the cookies?" Pam Baxter, the head of the three-woman judging panel, reached for another cookie.

"You did. About six times."

"And did I?" Willa Sunquist asked, reaching in right after Pam.

"Seven times, I think."

"What did you call them again?"

"Pineapple Delights. We got the idea from Lisa's aunt, Irma Baker. She uses dried apricots too, but Lisa changed it to all pineapple because Herb's crazy about pineapple."

"Well it's a cinch you'll win the cookie competition!" Willa declared.

"No, I won't. I run a bakery and coffee shop, and according to the rules, I'm not allowed to enter."

"That's a break for the rest of the contestants," Willa said with a laugh. A nice-looking woman in her late twenties, Willa had just finished the school year as Pam's classroom aide. The job hadn't paid much, but Pam and George had given Willa a break by renting their basement apartment to her at a ridiculously low price so that she could finish her teaching degree at Tri-County College.

"Do you have any questions about the rules, Hannah?" Pam asked, closing her slim booklet titled, *Guidelines for Judging Baked Goods.*

"I don't think so. The score sheets spell everything out. We just rate each entry on the variables, using a scale from one to ten."

"And when we're finished with an entry, Pam collects the score sheets," Willa said. "At the end of the night, we add up the numbers, enter them on the master score sheet, and Pam authenticates it by signing her name."

Pam glanced down at the sample score sheet that had come with the booklet. "Do you have any questions about the variables?"

"Just one," Willa said with a frown. "What's the difference between presentation and appearance?"

Pam gave her a quick smile. "I asked the same thing! Presentation is how the entry looks when we first see it on the plate or platter. Appearance is what it looks like when it's sampled."

"That makes sense," Hannah said. "The decoration and frosting on a cake would be judged under presentation. We don't judge appearance until we actually cut the cake and see how it slices and looks inside."

"How about pies?" Willa asked, still looking a bit confused.

"We rate the top crust or the meringue under the presentation variable. And we don't rate appearance until we actually dish out a slice and see if the custard slumps, or the berries are too juicy."

"Got it," Willa said. "How about breads and coffeecakes? That's what we're judging tonight."

"If it's been baked in a pan, we judge presentation on how evenly the top crust and the sides are browned. If it's a coffeecake and it's frosted or studded with fruit, we rate how that's done. The same goes for sweet rolls, sticky buns, and doughnuts."

"Okay." Willa glanced down at her booklet again. "Muffins and quick breads would be exactly the same, but how do you judge cookies on presentation *and* appearance? It's not like you slice them or anything."

"Hannah?" Pam turned to her.

"It'll be harder, but it can be done. Some cookies are frosted or decorated with sugar.

That would be presentation. Others might be decorated with nuts and dried fruits. And if the cookie isn't decorated at all, we'll have to judge the presentation on how expertly the baker browned it in the oven."

"How about appearance?" Pam asked, looking almost as puzzled as Willa.

"We'll have to bite into the cookie or break it apart to judge appearance. If it has a filling, we can judge how well that's placed in the cookie. If it's chocolate chip, or chopped nuts, we can judge how many there are and whether the cookie might need more, or less. With cookies I think we'll have to take it on a case-by-case basis."

"Good thing you're filling in as a judge," Willa said. "Judging cookies sounds really tricky."

"Maybe, but it'll be fun. What time should we meet tonight?"

Pam glanced down at the schedule. "It has to be after six. That's the cutoff for the day's entries." She turned to Willa. "You're through at eight, aren't you, Willa?"

"Yes. I can come right over here after the pageant. Once the curtain closes, the girls are free to go home."

Hannah's ears perked up. "Are you talking about the Miss Tri-County Beauty Pageant?"

"Yes, I'm the chaperone."

"My baby sister's a contestant," Hannah told her. "Michelle Swensen?"

"I saw her name on the roster."

"If you get the chance, say hello from me and tell her I'll be by to see her at Mother's when I'm through judging. She came in on the bus early this morning."

"From college?" Willa guessed.

"Macalester. She's a theater major. I wonder if she's got a chance of winning."

"Everybody's got a chance. Your sister's pretty. I saw her picture. But the judging covers a lot more than that."

"Talent? Personality?" Pam looked puzzled when Willa shook her head.

"We have those, too, but they're a part of *any* beauty contest. Just like the rest, we have one night for evening gowns, one for swimsuits, one for the talent showcase, and one for the interviews with the announcer. The fifth night is just for fun, and the girls perform a couple of musical numbers for the audience. And then on Saturday night, we have the pageant parade, and the judges announce the winner and the runners-up, along with the special awards."

"So what makes Miss Tri-County different?" Hannah wanted to know.

"We also assess a girl's character. Just take

a look at my grid," she said, pulling a clipboard out of her backpack and handing it over so that Hannah and Pam could see. "The girls are expected to get here by noon and check in with me at the auditorium. They have to make themselves available at various venues, hold interviews with the press and the beauty contest judges in the afternoon, and take part in the formal pageant in front of the audience every night from seven to eight. That's a lot more than just looking good in a bathing suit."

"It's an eight-hour day," Hannah agreed.

"It's meant to be. The pageant organizer retired to Arizona, but I talked to her by phone. She told me that the activities planned for the contestants are a test of their maturity and reliability. They're judged on those categories, too, and that's why I have the grid."

Hannah glanced down at the grid again. "I see the names of the contestants. They're written here in the left margin. But what are the numbers in the columns at the top?"

"Each number represents an attribute. They're coded so if someone sneaks a look at my clipboard, it won't show how any individual contestant is doing. They'll see checkmarks, but they won't know what they represent."

"I know you can't tell us the code," Pam said, "but could you give us an idea of the categories?"

"Sure. One number stands for complaints. Every time a girl complains about going to a venue, or talking to the press, or how she's sick to death of smiling and she wishes she hadn't entered the contest in the first place, I put a checkmark in the complaint category."

"That makes sense," Hannah said. "Nobody likes a whiner. What are some of the other categories?"

"Another number stands for being tardy. If a girl is late to any scheduled activity, I put a checkmark in that column. There's another code for breaking the rules."

"For instance?" Pam asked.

"Like swearing. The girls aren't allowed to swear while they're wearing their contestant ID badges. That's because younger girls look up to them and we don't want our contestants to set a bad example. If they forget and get five checkmarks in the swearing category, I have to disqualify them."

"So some checkmarks are weighted more than others?" Hannah asked.

"Definitely. If a girl does something illegal, she's immediately disqualified. That one's a no-brainer. But she gets more than one chance with things that aren't so serious, like being late and not showing up for a planned event."

"Sounds complicated," Pam said.

"Not really. It's just like life. The consequences for some things are worse than the consequences for others."

"So you think it's fairer than other beauty contests?" Hannah asked, reading between the lines.

"I think so. As a rule, I don't like beauty contests, but this one's the best I've seen. Each girl gets marked in exactly the same way. If her total adds up to the wrong number, she's gone."

"Do you have to tell a contestant when she's disqualified?" Hannah asked.

"Yes."

"That must be tough."

"It must be, but I agreed to do it when I took the job. I'm hoping that I won't have to disqualify anybody. I'm giving every girl a copy of the rules, so it's not like they won't know. And I'm planning to tell them that I'll be keeping track of their behavior on my clipboard. I'm even going to warn them when they're one checkmark away from disqualification. I don't think it can be any fairer than that."

■ ■ ■ ■

"I have to stop by the Cookie Nook booth and see if they need more supplies," Hannah said as they walked out of the Creative Arts Building.

"Is that Mayor Bascomb's booth?" Willa asked.

"Technically it's the Lake Eden Chamber of Commerce booth, but Mayor Bascomb's the one who's running it."

"Must be an election year," Pam said, grinning.

"It is," Hannah confirmed, "but he's running again, unopposed."

"Do you think anyone will ever challenge him?" Willa asked.

Both Hannah and Pam shook their heads.

"Never?" Willa persisted.

"I doubt it," Hannah answered. "Everybody agrees that he's doing a fine job running Lake Eden."

"And nobody else seems to want the job," Pam pointed out.

"I can understand that!" Hannah gave a little laugh. "If something goes wrong, the first person people call is Mayor Bascomb."

"You're right," Willa said. "Remember when the power went out in our classroom and I went to report it to Mr. Purvis? The first thing he did was to ask Charlotte to call Mayor . . ."

Willa stopped in her tracks. She gave a strangled gasp and her face turned so pale, Hannah reached out to grab her arm. "What's wrong?"

"I . . . I . . ."

"Are you in pain?" Pam asked, grabbing Willa's other arm.

"No! I just . . . have to sit down."

"Help her around the corner to the food court," Hannah said, taking charge. "I'll get her some water."

Hannah rushed up to the nearest booth and got a cup of water. On her way back, she looked to see if she could spot anything that might have startled Willa. The only thing happening was a roping demonstration on one of the outdoor stages. Several cowboys from the rodeo were doing rope tricks and teaching them to the 4-H kids.

"Thanks, Hannah," Willa said when Hannah got to the table and handed her the cup of water. "I'm not sure what happened. I just felt a little faint there for a second."

"Did you eat breakfast?" Pam asked.

"No, but I had lots of Hannah's cookies and I'm not a bit hungry. I think it was the sun. It was beating down on the top of my head, and I started feeling a little woozy."

"That could do it," Pam said, nodding quickly. "We'll just sit here for another couple of minutes, and then I'm taking you to the booth that sells hats."

"But really, Pam. I don't need . . ."

"Yes, you do," Pam interrupted her. "And I'm going to buy it for you. No way do I want one of my judges quitting because of sunstroke!"

"So we all got hats," Hannah wound up her story and handed Lisa a bag. "I got one for you, too. They're cute and they were really cheap and they had a two-fer going. The second one was only a dollar."

"Thanks, Hannah," Lisa said, and she looked absolutely delighted as she opened the bag and pulled out the white straw hat with red flowers around the brim. "It's just great."

Hannah smiled. Once she'd left the hat booth, she'd checked in with Mayor Bascomb and agreed to deliver ten dozen more Pineapple Delights. Then she'd driven straight back to The Cookie Jar to help Lisa handle the afternoon rush.

"So where is everybody?" Lisa asked, lifting her coffee mug to take another sip of the strong coffee their customers called

Swedish Plasma. "Not that I'm complaining, of course."

"Me neither," Hannah said, lapsing into a colloquialism she seldom used. They were sitting at their favorite table in the back of the coffee shop, enjoying the fact everyone in town seemed to think that it was too early for a lunch cookie and too late for a breakfast cookie.

"So do you want to stay out here to wait for customers while I mix up more Pineapple Delights? Or would you rather do it yourself and make me sit on the edge of my chair out here?"

"Huh?" Hannah blinked hard as she stared at her petite partner. She hadn't gotten much sleep last night, and she was having trouble keeping her eyes open. Lisa was wearing one of their serving aprons with their logo printed on the bib, the ties wrapped twice around her waist. Hannah blinked again. The cookie in their logo, the one with the bite missing, was shimmering like a mirage.

"You'd better stay here, Hannah. Put your head down on the table and take a snooze. Everybody's out at the fair anyway, and if friends come in, they'll help themselves to coffee and leave the money on the counter."

Hannah knew that Lisa was right. She

hadn't slept well last night because she was worried about Moishe. Her feline roommate usually came to bed with her, snuggled for a second or two, and then moved down to his favorite place at the foot of the bed. But last night Moishe hadn't come to bed. He'd stayed out in the living room all night, and Hannah had gotten up several times to check on him. Since she'd found him staring out the window and he hadn't seemed to be in any distress, she'd gone back to bed and slept fitfully for the rest of the night.

"Deal," Hannah said, giving her partner a grateful smile. "Have I told you lately that you're a gem?"

"Only last week, and I hope I'm a sapphire."

"Why?"

"Because that's my gemstone. I just love the blue ones. They're so pretty."

And with that, Lisa headed off to the kitchen, leaving Hannah to gratefully comply with the urge to rest her head on her folded arms. It was exactly what she'd done in her eight o'clock geography class during her first semester at college. The professor had used slides of maps to illustrate his lectures. He'd dimmed the lights and Hannah had immediately nodded off. She'd slept through every lecture, and it was only by the kind intervention and last minute cramming from a classmate who liked the cookies she brought for their study sessions, that she'd managed to pass the course.

Pineapple Delights

Preheat oven to 350 degrees F., rack in the middle position.

2 cups butter *(4 sticks, one pound — melted)*
2 cups brown sugar
2 cups white *(granulated)* sugar
4 eggs — beaten *(just beat them up in a glass with a fork)*
1 teaspoon baking powder
1 teaspoon baking soda
1 teaspoon salt
2 teaspoons pineapple extract *(if you can't find it, you can use vanilla)*
4 cups flour
2 1/2 cups chopped sweetened dried pineapple *(measure AFTER chopping — if you can't find pineapple, you can substitute any dried fruit chopped in chocolate chip sized pieces)*
1/2 cup chopped coconut flakes *(measure AFTER chopping)*

3 cups rolled oats *(uncooked oatmeal — I used Quaker Oats Quick 1-Minute in the round paper can that you save, but you don't know why)*

Melt the butter in a large microwave-safe bowl. *(About 3 minutes on HIGH.)* Add the sugars and let it cool a bit. Then add the beaten eggs, baking powder, baking soda, salt, and pineapple extract. Mix in the flour. Then add the chopped pineapple, chopped coconut, and rolled oats, mixing them in thoroughly. The dough will be quite stiff.

Drop by teaspoon onto a greased cookie sheet, 12 to a sheet. *(I roll mine in a ball so the cookies turn out nice and round.)*

Bake at 350 degrees F. for 12 to 15 minutes. Cool on the cookie sheet for 2 minutes and then remove them to a wire rack to cool completely.

These freeze really well if you roll them in foil and put them in a freezer bag.

Chapter Three

Uh-oh! There was Mike Kingston and there was Norman Rhodes, and they were both waiting for her at the altar! There was going to be a fight right here in church, and it was all her fault. She must have done something incredibly stupid and accepted both of their proposals!

They didn't *sound* angry. She could hear them talking, and they seemed perfectly friendly. Mike said something and Norman laughed. They were getting along like best buddies, and that was fine with her. At least she wouldn't have to choose between them. The laws must have changed so that she could have two husbands instead of just one.

Norman said something about coffee, and he walked over to the counter that had replaced the front pew. It was where Priscilla Knudson, the reverend's grandmother, usually sat, and Hannah hoped that she was all right. Even a summer cold could be dangerous for a lady in her eighties.

There was a coffee pot behind the counter, and Hannah wondered how the church elders felt about that. Coffee in the basement or at the very back of the church might be welcome, but this was up at the front and it was sure to disrupt Reverend Knudson's sermons. Of course it could have been installed specifically for her wedding. Everyone knew how much she loved coffee, and Holy Redeemer Lutheran had made exceptions for brides before. Just last month Reverend Knudson had given Annice Borge permission to hold her little teacup poodle when she took her vows.

The coffee smelled wonderful. Hannah felt her nose twitch, and her mouth began to water in anticipation. Coffee was one of her favorite things, and she could really use a cup about now. Would it be a terrible breach of etiquette for the bride to make an early appearance, just so she could get a cup of coffee? Or should she ask Mike and Norman? Except they didn't sound like Mike and Norman anymore. One of them sounded like a woman, and the other one sounded like a man. They must be joking around about something.

"Hannah? I brought you some coffee."

Norman's voice was still high-pitched, but

she didn't care about that. He'd actually read her mind! Somehow she'd managed to communicate with him without words. She had coffee, and now the only other thing that she craved was chocolate. If she could have chocolate, she'd be perfectly content.

"And I brought you a couple of Black and Whites. I figured you could use the chocolate."

Mike sounded different than he usually did, but that didn't concern her. This was a miracle. She'd obviously communicated with him, too. No wonder both of them had been waiting for her at the altar! It was only right that she marry them both, since both of them could read her mind.

"I do," she said, opening her eyes wide to smile at them. And that was when she noticed that she wasn't in a church at all. She was sitting at a back table in her own coffee shop. Lisa was sitting across from her, right next to her husband, Herb. There hadn't been any wedding. She'd caught forty winks while Lisa had been mixing up the cookie dough, and she'd dreamed the whole thing.

"You do what?" Herb asked.

Hannah looked at him blankly. She didn't have the foggiest idea what he was talking about.

47

"When you woke up you smiled at us and said, *I do*."

"Oh." Hannah thought fast. "You said you figured I needed chocolate and I said *I do*." And then, before Herb could think about it and ask more questions that might prove embarrassing, Hannah turned to Lisa. "What time is it?"

"A little after two-thirty. I closed because we haven't had a customer since noon."

"All the stores on Main Street are closing early," Herb informed her. "Nobody's doing any business, not even Rose down at the cafe. Everybody and their cousin's out at the fairgrounds."

"That figures." Hannah took a gulp of her coffee and bit into a cookie. It was just as good as she thought it would be. Nothing could beat the winning combination of chocolate and coffee.

Lisa reached out to take Herb's hand. "There's no traffic in town, so Mayor Bascomb told Herb he could have the rest of the afternoon off."

"I can help you and Lisa mix up cookies," Herb offered. "Or I can make deliveries if you've got any. Or maybe you just want to go home for the day?"

Hannah noticed the hopeful look in her partner's eyes. Lisa and Herb had been married for only four months, and they didn't get much time alone together. They both worked six days a week, and they spent almost every Sunday with his mother and her father.

"I do have one delivery," Hannah said, turning to Herb, "but you'll have to take Lisa with you."

"Sure. Where do you want us to go?"

"To the fair. You can take the Pineapple Delights Lisa just baked to the Cookie Nook." Hannah gave her partner a smile. "And since all of our customers are already at the fairgrounds, you can pack up all the cookies we have left here at the shop, and take them with you. They're not going to eat them here, so they might as well eat them out there."

"Okay. I'll leave a box for you to use for samples and load up all the rest."

"Perfect." Hannah was glad Lisa had remembered. Unless they completely sold out, she usually packed up the leftover cookies and put them in her cookie truck. There was almost always an occasion to give out samples, and Hannah was convinced that they created a lot of new business that way.

"It should only take us about forty-five minutes," Lisa said, glancing at her watch. "We can be back here by three-thirty at the latest, and then we can mix up the cookie dough for tomorrow."

Hannah shook her head. "We'll do that in the morning. We don't have any cookies on the menu that need to be chilled before baking."

"Well . . . if you're sure . . ." Lisa hesitated, and Hannah could tell she felt guilty about not putting in a full day's work.

"I'm positive. I'll just finish up a couple of things here and go home."

Hannah had another cup of coffee while Lisa packed up the cookies. Then she helped them pack the boxes in Herb's cruiser. As they drove away, Hannah noticed that Lisa had slid across the bench seat and was sitting close to Herb. If anyone had been foolish enough to give her odds, Hannah would have bet that the two lovebirds would be doing some billing and cooing before the night was over.

An hour later, Hannah opened the door to her condo and braced herself for the greeting ritual that Moishe had initiated on the first day he'd moved in with her. The pattern hadn't varied in over two years. Once she opened the door, Moishe hurtled himself into her arms, landing with a thud that rocked her back on her heels. Hannah's catapulting feline reminded her of an old picture she'd seen at the Lake Eden Historical Society. Her grandfather and some of his cronies were standing in a circle on the beach at Eden Lake, tossing a medicine ball around. According to some research her mother had done, the ball they'd used had weighed over twenty pounds. Since Moishe had tipped the scales at twenty-three pounds the last time she'd taken him to the vet, Hannah considered their greeting ritual part of her daily exercise regime. If the truth were known, it was the *only* part of her daily exercise regime, unless she counted the aerobic benefits of lifting giant bags of sugar and flour in her bakery kitchen or walking several miles across the coffee shop floor to refill coffee mugs and deliver orders of cookies.

Hannah stood there waiting for the onslaught, but absolutely nothing happened. The door was open, and Moishe was nowhere in sight. Heart in her throat, Hannah rushed in and tossed her purse on a chair. "Moishe?" she called, fearing the worst.

There was no answer, and Hannah felt a chill of foreboding. She should have taken Moishe to the vet this morning when she'd found him staring out the window at nothing. Animals couldn't tell you when they were sick. Their humans had to watch for signs of illness, and one sign was atypical behavior. He'd tried to tell her, and she was a bad kitty mommy for ignoring the sign!

Relax, she told herself and took a deep breath. It would do no good to panic. She had to stay calm and think clearly. The first thing to do was to find Moishe and check for other signs of illness.

Hannah headed for the kitchen. Perhaps Moishe had his head buried in his food bowl and he hadn't heard her come in. But there was no orange and white cat ear-deep in his kitty crunchies. Instead, Hannah found something even more alarming. She'd given him his breakfast before she'd left for work this morning, and her normally ravenous cat hadn't touched a morsel!

"Uh-oh," Hannah groaned, staring at Moishe's full-to-the-brim Garfield bowl in disbelief. Moishe always emptied his bowl and was yowling for more by the time she came home. There had to be something drastically wrong.

Hannah checked the usual places, but Moishe wasn't there. There was nothing furry under the Formica kitchen table that was only a few years short of becoming antique, and no inquisitive orange and white head peeked out from behind the kitchen wastebasket. Moishe was not in the kitchen, not unless he'd morphed into one of the dust balls that was hiding in the two-inch-high space under the refrigerator.

The laundry room was next. Hannah checked the space behind the washer and dryer, even though she thought it was too tight a squeeze for him. There was a smattering of gravel outside his litter box. He must have used it since she'd swept the floor this morning. That was a good sign, wasn't it?

Hannah went down the hall toward her bedroom, but she stopped as she noticed that the guest room door was open. She always kept it closed so that Moishe couldn't chase after the appliquéd butterflies on the expensive silk coverlet Delores had given her for Christmas one year, but perhaps the latch hadn't caught. She'd have to be more careful in the future or her mother's butterflies would meet a force even more dangerous than the rigors of migration.

Hannah poked her head in, but Moishe wasn't on the bed and the coverlet looked untouched. Since the butterflies were intact, she was about to pull the door shut behind her when she saw movement out of the corner of her eye. "Moishe?" she called out.

"Brrrowwww!"

It was a loud, healthy yowl and Hannah gave a huge sigh of relief. Moishe sounded just fine. But why hadn't he come to greet her? And why wasn't he eating? She stepped inside the room and began to frown as she saw what her cat was doing.

Moishe was balanced, rather precariously, on the guest room windowsill. He was staring out at the condo next door, where the Hollenbeck sisters lived. There was no one home. Today was Monday, and the two sisters spent all afternoon out at Lake Eden Memorial Hospital, working as volunteers. The Hollenbeck sisters were both retired. Marguerite had worked for forty years as a kindergarten teacher, and Clara had put in forty-two years as a court reporter at the Winnetka County Courthouse. They'd told Hannah that they were devoting the rest of their lives to doing good works, and they were active church members. Hannah had met them the day she moved in. They'd invited her over for dinner that night, and they'd dined on Clara's Mexican hotdish, a casserole of hamburger, corn, mild green chilies, shredded cheese, and spicy tomato sauce. It was topped with more shredded cheese and some crushed corn chips that formed a delectable crust. Marguerite had provided the beverages, and she'd made her namesake Margaritas with white wine instead of tequila, since the sisters didn't drink hard liquor. They were delicious, a perfect complement to the hotdish. Hannah had downed two, and she'd been very careful navigating the thirty feet that separated their second-floor condo units.

"What are you doing, Moishe?" Hannah hurried over to steady her cat on the narrow windowsill. She looked out, but she saw only windows with curtains drawn at the unit next door. "There's nothing there. Clara and Marguerite are out at the hospital today."

"Yow!" Moishe said, as if to contradict her, but he let her pick him up and cuddle him. He even licked her chin, which only happened when he was feeling affectionate.

"Thank you," Hannah said, giving him a scratch behind his ear. Then she carted him out of the room, shut the door tightly behind her making sure that it latched, and took him off to the kitchen. But when she put him down in front of his food bowl, he turned around to look at her ruefully, as if to say, *What are you trying to do here? I don't want this stuff.*

"Okay. Just let me change clothes and I'll get you something you'll like better," Hannah promised, heading off to the bedroom with Moishe following in her wake.

It took a few minutes, but at last Hannah was dressed in an outfit that her mother would deem appropriate for an older sister of a Miss Tri-County contestant. She brushed her hair, secured it with the clasp Michelle had given her for her birthday, and turned to face Moishe.

"Okay?" she asked him. She was wearing the lightweight summer suit that Delores had bought her several years ago. The pants and top were made of a crinkled material that reminded Hannah of the pinstriped seersucker pants and jacket that her father had worn. Hers was navy blue with a white stripe, and her father's had been tan with a white stripe. Now that she thought about it, Delores had bought her father's suit, too. And her father had always hated it. Hannah thought about that for a split second, but time was flying and food was more important than rejecting her mother's fashion guidance. "No time to change; it'll have to do," she said, leading the way to the kitchen.

Once she'd arrived, she put Moishe down on the floor. "Tuna?" she asked the cat, who loved Chicken of the Sea. But Moishe wasn't even looking at his food bowl. He was sitting in the doorway, watching her with a hopeful expression that Hannah interpreted to mean, *I don't really care what you eat as long as it's good and I get some.*

"A Denver sandwich?" Hannah asked, smiling when her cat's ears perked up. "With or without onions and peppers?"

Moishe's expression changed slightly, something that only Hannah could interpret. At least she thought she could interpret it. Moishe wanted his portion without peppers or onions, and he'd appreciate it if she'd double the ham.

"Okay. I'll call you when it's ready. If you're still interested in watching for the neighbors, you can see their unit from the back of the couch. It's a lot more comfortable up there, and you won't slip off the windowsill."

Hannah spent the next few minutes chopping ham, green peppers, and onions, and wondering why a Denver sandwich was named after the mile-high city. She whipped up eggs in a glass with a fork, the way her Grandma Ingrid had done, and poured them into a buttered, preheated frying pan. She sprinkled chopped ham, minced green peppers, and finely chopped onions over the top, except for the section that would be the penumbra if her frying pan were a full moon. In that sickle-shaped portion, she put only ham and she made sure there was plenty of it.

In less than five minutes, Hannah's sandwich was ready. She cut it into fourths diagonally, the way her grandmother had done to make it "special," and arranged it on a green Fiestaware luncheon plate with the tips pointing out like a star. Then she dished up Moishe's portion on a turquoise blue plate that set off the yellow of the eggs perfectly.

Hannah carried the two plates out to the living room. Using a Fiestaware plate for Moishe would have garnered her mother's objections on two fronts. Delores believed that pets should have their own food bowls and never be fed from "people" dishes. She didn't even think they should be mixed in the same load in the dishwasher. Hannah's mother also loved antiques and family heirlooms. Letting Moishe use one of the six plates that Grandma Swensen had left Hannah would have positively horrified her.

Once their food was placed on the coffee table in front of the couch and the television was tuned to KCOW for the local news, Hannah called her cat down from the back of the couch.

Moishe's ears swiveled forward at the sound of his name, but he didn't move. Hannah fanned his plate with her hand so that he could catch the scent, but that didn't do it either. As a last resort, she lifted the plate and held it in front of him, so he could see what was there. "What's the matter, Moishe? Aren't you hungry?"

"Rowww," Moishe said, something that Hannah interpreted to mean she'd hit the nail on the head.

"Okay," she told him. "I'll leave your plate right here and you can have some when you're ready. Be careful, though. If you break that plate, Mother will kill us both."

The sound Moishe gave was more growl than comment. As Hannah watched, his eyes narrowed to slits, his hair puffed up to make him look larger to an opponent, and his tail switched back and forth. Mentioning her mother's name always had this effect. Moishe hated Delores. Hannah figured it had started when they'd first met and Delores had tried to pick him up despite Hannah's warning that he was still skittish around people. It had been a case of stubborn cat versus determined human, and stubborn cat had won. Delores had finally stopped trying to pick up Moishe, but it had taken a half-dozen pairs of shredded pantyhose to dissuade her.

"Sorry," Hannah said, reaching up to smooth the hair on his back. "We won't talk about her now."

Moishe gave a sigh that convinced Hannah he understood and settled back down to stare out the window. As she ate her sandwich, Hannah divided her time between watching the news and watching her neighbors' window, but she still didn't see anything moving in Clara and Marguerite's apartment. Was it possible that something was wrong and Moishe could sense it?

Hannah imagined a dire scenario. Clara hadn't felt well this morning, so she'd sent Marguerite on to the hospital alone. And as the hours passed without her sister, Clara had become very ill, so ill that she couldn't even get to the phone. Was she calling for help in a voice so weak only Moishe could hear it?

Just to make sure, Hannah picked up the phone and called the hospital. Yvonne Blair, Doc Knight's secretary, answered.

"Hi, Yvonne," Hannah greeted her. "I just wondered if the Hollenbeck sisters were there today."

"They were, but they just left. I can probably catch up with them in the parking lot if you need me to."

"No, that's okay," Hannah said quickly. "It wasn't that important. I'll catch up with them at home."

"Okay. You're going to the Miss Tri-County contest tonight, aren't you?"

"Of course. Michelle's one of the contestants."

"I know. She was out here this morning with flowers for Edna Ferguson. Of course you probably know that since your name was on the card."

"Right," Hannah said, making a mental note to reimburse and thank her baby sister for something she should have done herself. "Is Edna on any kind of restricted diet? Or can I bring out some cookies?"

"Hold on and let me check the computer."

While she waited for Yvonne to check, Hannah glanced over at the unopened computer boxes that sat on the floor under her desk. She'd been forced to buy it when she lost a bet last month and Norman had helped her pick it out. He'd offered to give her a crash course in computer technology right after the Tri-County Fair was over, and Hannah had accepted gratefully. She knew the basics, but she hadn't used a computer since her college days and things had changed a lot since then. The computer industry was continually evolving. Her computer was aging right there in its box, and by the time she learned to use it, it would probably be several generations away from a state-of-the-art model.

"Doc's marked her down for a normal diet," Yvonne said, coming back on the line. "No restrictions at all. Feel free to bring cookies, Hannah. And if Doc's directions change and Edna can't have them, I'm sure they'll find a good home."

After promising to drop by with goodies, Hannah hung up the phone and turned to Moishe. He was still staring fixedly at the window next door. "There's nobody home. I just checked."

But that didn't seem to make any difference to Moishe. He just kept staring as if the most fascinating thing was happening behind the curtains. Hannah stared, too, doing her best not to blink. For a minute or two that seemed like hours, absolutely nothing happened. And then Hannah gave a little gasp as she saw the curtain wiggle slightly.

"I saw it!" she told Moishe. "Was that what you were waiting for?"

Moishe gave her his Sphinx look, the one that said, *I am the font of all knowledge, and I am inscrutable to a mere human person like you,* and Hannah gave up. She wasn't even sure she'd seen the curtain move, but if she had, there was probably a perfectly reasonable explanation. Marguerite and Clara had an attic air conditioner that had been installed when their unit was built. Clara suffered from chronic allergies, and Doc Knight had suggested it as a means of filtering out some of the pollens and allergens that turned her nose red, made her eyes water, and stuffed up her sinuses.

"See you later, Moishe," Hannah said, after she'd carried their plates to the kitchen and scraped his uneaten food into his bowl. "You can watch their curtains wiggle while I go out to the fairgrounds to cheer on Michelle."

CHAPTER FOUR

Hannah was so proud of her sister she was glad she hadn't worn anything with buttons to pop. Michelle had looked truly gorgeous in the dazzling white satin, Grecian-style evening gown that Claire Rodgers, The Cookie Jar's Main Street neighbor, had chosen for her to wear. According to the full-page acknowledgment in tonight's program, Claire's shop, Beau Monde Fashions, was selling the gowns that had been seen in tonight's contest on a silent auction basis. If the contestants wanted the gowns they'd worn, they could buy it at a fifty percent discount. But if a contestant didn't want it, it went in Claire's window to be auctioned off to the highest bidder.

"Genius," Hannah said, catching Claire by the arm and pointing to the page in the program.

"I think so, too." Claire, a gorgeous blonde in her thirties with a svelte figure that Hannah would have done anything except diet to replicate, gave a little a laugh. "It was Bob's idea."

Hannah knew the *Bob* in question was Reverend Robert Knudson, Holy Redeemer Lutheran's bachelor minister. Claire and Reverend Knudson wanted to get married, but there were complications. Most Lake Edenites, or whatever they wanted to call their collective noun, suspected that Claire had spent several years as their mayor's mistress. No one could prove it, but that didn't stop the tongues from wagging.

"Your mother already called me and said she wanted to buy Michelle's dress," Claire said. "It was gorgeous, wasn't it?"

Hannah nodded. She was almost positive that Claire's expertise was one of the reasons her sister had come in first in the evening gown competition. "It was absolutely wonderful. You couldn't have chosen anything more perfect."

"I thought so, too." Claire gave Hannah a smile. "So do you think Michelle is going to win the Miss Tri-County crown?"

Hannah shrugged. "I don't know. That's almost as much of an unanswered question as yours."

"Mine?"

"That's right. When are you going to let

Reverend Knudson announce your engagement?"

Claire gave a little sigh. "I think we might do it in the spring. Maybe people will have forgotten by then."

"You're kidding!" Hannah stared at her in total disbelief. "Lake Eden's a small town. People in small towns are like elephants."

"You mean they never forget?"

"Not unless it's their last promise to their wife," Hannah said. And then she wished she hadn't. This wasn't the time for joking. "I think Reverend Knudson should announce it this summer, Claire."

"Why this summer?"

"Because summer is the most popular time for weddings, and people have love on their minds. They're so busy with weddings in their own families, they won't have time to think about yours."

"You're sure?" Claire looked doubtful.

"No, but it's worth a try. And if there's gossip, you'll ride it out." Hannah thought about it for a moment, and then she played her ace in the hole. "Which would you rather . . . announce it now? Or have somebody accuse you of having an affair with Reverend Knudson?"

"They wouldn't!" Claire looked shocked.

"They would. If I were you, I'd head them

66

off at the pass and make the announcement soon."

Claire thought about it for a long moment, and then she sighed. "You're right. I'll let Bob do it at the end of August. That's when a lot of people go on vacation. If we do it the last Sunday in August, you'll be there, won't you?"

"You got it," Hannah said, thankful that this was only June and she had over two full months to figure out how to get Reverend Knudson's congregation to embrace Claire with open arms.

"Stop in tomorrow," Claire said. "I've got in a new shipment, and there's a matching pants and top set that's absolutely perfect for you."

Hannah wavered. She really couldn't afford any new clothes, but when Claire said something was perfect, it was. And since Claire always gave her a generous discount, she caved in. "Okay," she promised. "But this hasn't been a really flush month."

"When have I ever overcharged you?"

"Never," Hannah hastened to say. "It's just that Doug Greerson down at the bank is getting ready to rip out the rest of the checks in my checkbook so I won't be tempted to bounce one."

"It's that bad?" Claire looked concerned.

"Well . . . not quite *that* bad."

"Come in tomorrow and try on that outfit. If you like it, I'll give it to you at my cost. When you opened The Cookie Jar, my business doubled. People walk up the street to have cookies and coffee, and they look at the display in my window. You have no idea how many of your customers come in to try on something they've seen after they leave your place."

"Really?"

"That's right. And I'm not even counting your mother. Every time she comes in, she buys something."

"Mother can afford it." Hannah glanced at her watch and slipped into a faster gear. "I've got to run, Claire. I'm judging the baked goods contest tonight."

"Good luck," Claire said, taking her cue. "I'll see you tomorrow, Hannah."

After Claire left, Hannah glanced around. People were still filing out of the auditorium, and it was time to make herself scarce. There was somewhere she had to go, and she had to do it fast. If she hurried, she'd have just enough time for the clandestine treat she'd decided to enjoy before she joined Willa and Pam at the Creative Arts Building.

■ ■ ■ ■

Less than two minutes later, Hannah rounded the corner by the deep-fried candy bar booth. She was slightly out of breath, and she stopped to let her breathing return to a normal rate. There was a friendly-looking woman sitting on a stool behind the counter, and her nametag read RUBY in bright red block letters. No one else was in line at the moment, and Hannah stepped up to place her order.

"What'll it be, Ma'am?" the woman named Ruby asked. And that meant Hannah had to come to a decision. She'd been debating the merits of a Milky Way and a Snickers Bar all day. She knew full well she shouldn't indulge in a deep-fried candy bar, especially since she'd be sampling coffee-cake, cinnamon bread, and sweet rolls in less than fifteen minutes. But all day long she'd been dreaming about a deep-fried candy bar. It was driving her crazy, and the only way to stop thinking about it was to have one.

"Ma'am?" Ruby prodded her back to the present, and there was a knowing smile on her face. "It's hard to choose, isn't it?"

"Does the Milky Way have the original

milk chocolate? Or is it the kind with the semi-sweet dark chocolate?"

"It's the original with milk chocolate. I wouldn't have it any other way."

"You like the milk chocolate best?" Hannah asked, interpreting her comment.

"You got it right. I don't understand why they wanted to mess with something that was already perfect."

"Neither do I."

"I felt the same way when they came out with peanuts in the M&Ms. And I really hate the new Hershey's Kisses with fruit and nuts. They're supposed to melt in your mouth without chewing, you know?"

"I know." Hannah felt she'd found a kindred soul. "I really shouldn't have a deep-fried candy bar at all. I'm judging the baked goods contest in less than fifteen minutes."

Ruby threw back her head and laughed. "You're right. You shouldn't. These things are loaded with calories and you can't take just one bite. Once you taste it, you have to finish the whole thing. It's addictive."

"How many calories does it have?" Hannah asked, hoping that if she didn't eat anything except lettuce for the next two days, she could have one without gaining weight.

"Believe me, you don't want to know!"

"That bad?"

"Worse. I started to figure it out once, but I quit when I got up to a thousand. I figured it wasn't a real good selling point."

"You're right," Hannah said, hoping it wasn't quite as bad as Ruby was making out. "I've got to taste one, though. I've been dreaming about it ever since I walked past your booth this morning."

"Okay. What kind of candy bar do you want?"

"I'm still trying to decide between the Milky Way and the Snickers. Which one do you . . ." Hannah stopped speaking and whirled around as she heard someone calling her name. "Uh-oh!" she said with a groan. "It's my mother!"

"Caught in the act?" Ruby asked, and something about her smile told Hannah that the same thing must have happened with other customers and other mothers.

"That's right. She's always after me to lose weight, and . . ."

"Say no more," Ruby interrupted her with a wink. "I'll take care of it for you."

Hannah remained silent. It seemed that Ruby was a pro in situations like this.

"I think I saw her," Ruby said when Delores was within earshot. "She came past here about five minutes ago, and she headed off toward the Ferris wheel."

Hannah winked back, and then she turned to face Delores. "Hi, Mother. Did you happen to see Lisa?"

"Not tonight." Delores had looked as if she were loaded for bear, but her eyebrows settled and Hannah knew she was biting back a lecture on saturated fats, empty calories, and elevated cholesterol levels. Ruby had effectively defused the Mother-bomb, and Hannah owed her at least a dozen cookies in return for the favor.

"I'm glad to see you, dear. But for a minute there I thought that you . . . never mind."

Hannah turned back to Ruby. "Thanks for the information. Those deep-fried candy bars look like real killers."

"They are, but there's no way I could make a living selling deep-fried lettuce."

Hannah burst into laughter, but her mother looked intrigued. "I wonder if it would be good."

"I'm not sure," Ruby said. "Maybe not, because lettuce is mostly water. That's what makes it such a great diet food."

Delores stepped a bit closer to the counter. "That's true."

"I've had deep-fried broccoli, and it's delicious," Ruby continued. "Carrots and sweet potatoes are good, too."

Delores nodded quickly "You're right. Are you with the carnival? Or do you live around here?"

"I'm with the carnival. I'm married to Riggs. He's the announcer at the rodeo."

"I heard him this afternoon on my way to the Lake Eden Historical Society booth," Delores said. "He has a wonderful voice."

"I think so, too."

"Then you travel with the show?" Delores asked.

"Yes. We have our own trailer. Riggs is the rodeo manager. He announces and he also runs the show."

"That must be a big job, with all those cowboys and animals. I hope he's well-paid for . . ." Delores stopped suddenly and looked uncomfortable. "I apologize. I shouldn't have broached such a personal subject."

"That's okay, I don't mind." Ruby turned to Hannah, who was staring at the two of them in absolute amazement. She'd never known her mother to be so friendly with an absolute stranger before. "You'd better get a move on," Ruby said to her. "You've got that contest to judge."

"Right. I'll see you later, Mother."

"Fine, dear." Delores dismissed her with a wave and then she turned back to Ruby. "So tell me about life on the road. I've never traveled anywhere to speak of. Do you find that all these little towns look alike after a while?"

"If I have to taste another coffeecake, I'm going to die!" Willa declared, leaning back in her chair and rubbing her stomach.

Pam laughed. "I know what you mean. There were ten of them. But you're in luck now. The next six entries are sweet rolls."

"Tell me they're not all cinnamon," Hannah said, taking a swig of the bottled water that had been provided as a palate cleanser.

Pam looked down at the listing of entries and gave Hannah a thumbs-up. "There's only one, and we'll test it after the orange rolls. That should give your taste buds a break."

"My taste buds thank you," Hannah said, meaning every word of it. They'd only gone through three-quarters of the sweet bread entries, and she was firmly convinced that cinnamon was the most overused spice of them all.

"Moroccan Delight," Pam declared, cutting small wedge-shaped pieces of the sweet roll on her plate. "According to the recipe, the predominant flavors are supposed to be coconut, honey, ground walnuts, and dates."

Hannah gasped as she bit into the incredibly sweet concoction. "This is sugar overload."

"You're right." Willa made a face. "It's almost as sweet as the chocolate baklava I had in California."

Both Pam and Hannah turned to look her, but Pam was the first to speak. "I didn't know you went to California."

"It was a long time ago, when I thought I could get along anywhere," Willa said. And then she gave a rueful laugh. "I was wrong. I found out I never should have left Minnesota."

Pam looked a bit confused. "I didn't know you left Minnesota."

"Well, I did." The color came up on Willa's cheeks, and Hannah knew she was uncomfortable. "It was a big mistake. You probably noticed that I dropped out of school for a little over a year."

"I saw that in your transcripts," Pam said.

"It took me that long to realize that I wasn't going to get anywhere unless I finished school. But when I enrolled at Tri-County College, I found out that a lot of my credits didn't transfer. I had to start my major all over again." Willa stopped to smile at Pam. "And you hired me as a teacher's aide so that I could finish and get my degree."

"How long do you have to go?" Hannah asked, hoping that Willa would make it.

"Only one more semester. All I have to do is student teach for Pam until Christmas and I've got it!"

"You'll make it," Pam said, turning around to face the long table where the remaining entries were lined up to be judged. "Only one left. After that we'll tally up the scores and declare a winner. And then we can all pick out a couple of our favorites and take them home."

Hannah was surprised at this news. "I didn't know we got to take anything home!"

"Well, we do. That's why the contestants are required to use disposable pans. We get to take what we want, and we leave the rest for the cleaning crew. It's one of the perks they get for cleaning this building."

"I'll bet they never have any trouble finding people to clean up," Hannah commented.

"Probably not." Pam picked up the last entry and set it in front of them. As with all the other entries, there was a card giving the name of the recipe, but the contestant's name had been concealed with removable tape. A number was written on the front of the tape, and the scorecards were numbered accordingly. "This is chocolate cherry coffeecake," Pam said, reading the card. "The contestant describes it as, *Bite-sized morsels of chocolate and cherry in a tender buttery sweet dough. Drizzled with melted dark chocolate and cherry icing, it's the perfect accompaniment to a strong cup of coffee.*"

Hannah's mouth started to water. "Sounds yummy!"

"Chocolate and cherry is a traditional combination," Willa stated the obvious. "What kind of cherries did she use?"

Pam flipped the card to read the list of ingredients on the back. "Dark cherry pie filling. She rolled out the sweet dough and spread out the cherry pie filling. Then she sprinkled on the chocolate chips, and folded the dough over the top."

"How about the cherry frosting?" Hannah wanted to know. "Did she use part of the cherry pie filling for that?"

"No. It says that she used cherry liqueur and a drop of red food coloring."

Hannah watched as Pam cut bite-sized pieces for all three of them. She wasn't that wild about using food coloring, but she had to admit that the combination of drizzled chocolate and pink cherry icing was pretty.

"Any more questions?" Pam asked after they'd tasted their sample. When Hannah and Willa shook their heads, she passed them the numbered scorecards. "Let's mark our scores and go on."

Hannah had just turned in her scorecard when she had a thought. Delores loved the combination of chocolate and cherries, and Pam had said they could take some of the baked goods home. "If nobody else wants it, I'll take the rest of that chocolate cherry coffeecake."

"Fine by me," Pam said.

"You got it, Hannah," Willa agreed. "I'm taking the rest of the raised cinnamon doughnuts. I thought they were great."

Hannah didn't comment. She hadn't given the doughnuts a high mark. She'd thought they were a bit greasy, and the contestant had used too much cinnamon for her taste. "What are you taking, Pam?"

"The sticky buns. They're George's favorites. And I think I'll take one of the apple coffeecakes, too. George's sister loves apple coffeecake. I'll just pop it in the freezer and take it with me the next time we visit."

The next few minutes were spent tallying scores. Hannah read them off, Willa punched them into the calculator that had been provided for them, and Pam marked them down on the master score sheet. They were nearing the end when Pam gave a little gasp.

"Good heavens!" she exclaimed, staring at the master score sheet as if it couldn't possibly be right. "Mrs. Adamczak only got an honorable mention?"

Hannah was every bit as shocked as Pam looked. "You've got to be kidding! She's never come in lower than second place!"

"And that was right after she had her hip replacement and she couldn't stand for more than five minutes at a time," Pam said with a frown. "There's got to be some mistake."

"Which entry was hers?" Willa asked.

Hannah glanced down at the master sheet. "Number thirty-two, the cinnamon raisin bread. It was the only one entered. Nobody wants to put their cinnamon raisin bread up against Mrs. Adamczak's."

"Are you sure you tallied her score right?" Pam asked Willa. "I didn't think Mrs. Adamczak's bread was quite as good as last year, but I still gave her nines across the board."

"And I gave her almost all nines," Hannah said.

Willa looked highly uncomfortable. "Her score's right. I gave her threes and fours.

When I added all the marks together, her score averaged out to a little below seven, and there were three other entries higher than hers."

"You gave her threes and fours?" Hannah had trouble believing that Willa hadn't liked Mrs. Adamczak's bread. "But that's below average."

"I know. I thought it had too many raisins. And I didn't like the golden ones mixed in with the regular."

"Okay," Pam said. "What else was wrong with it?"

"There wasn't enough cinnamon and it was mixed with some spice I didn't care for. I think it was . . . cardamom?"

"That's right," Hannah said, glancing quickly at the list of ingredients. "Was there anything else you didn't like?"

"I thought it was overbaked."

"I agree that it was a bit too brown on top," Pam said, turning to Hannah.

"So do I. I gave her an eight on presentation for that. But it was still moist, so it didn't hurt the texture or the internal appearance."

Willa looked a bit regretful. "I suppose Mrs. Adamczak's going to be really disappointed." And when Pam and Hannah nodded, she gave a deep sigh. "She's the lady that lives in the yellow house right across from the school, isn't she?"

"That's right," Pam answered her.

"I wonder if . . . I mean, it's probably not allowed, but . . . do you think I should change my scorecard?"

Hannah and Pam locked eyes. It was a tough question, and Willa was clearly struggling with it.

"Let's put it to the test," Hannah said at last, after Pam had failed to speak up. "Do you still feel the same way about her bread?"

"Yes, I do."

"Then your objections are valid. You didn't think it deserved to win before, and you shouldn't change your score now that you know who baked it."

"Absolutely right," Pam agreed, giving Willa a smile. "It's like the student you hated to flunk. Remember?"

Willa turned to Hannah. "I really liked him, but I graded his final project and it was awful. He had to make breakfast, and he chose pancakes, bacon, and eggs."

"He didn't drain the bacon, and it was grease central," Pam took over the story. "The eggs were incinerated, and I thought we'd never get the sulfur smell out of the room."

"And the pancakes?" Hannah asked.

Willa gave a rueful little smile. "Raw inside. And he tried to heat the syrup in the microwave without taking off the metal cap, and it sparked like fireworks. I still feel bad, though. Because of me, he has to go to summer school to take another class."

Pam passed over the final tally sheet for all three of them to sign. Then they packaged the sweet breads they were taking with them and parted ways at the bottom of the steps to the Creative Arts Building.

As Hannah headed off across the fairgrounds, slapping at mosquitoes and juggling her sweet burdens, she decided that the first day of judging hadn't been so bad. She'd tasted some very fine sweet dough treats, and she was going to her mother's house with the chocolate cherry coffeecake to congratulate Michelle on winning the evening gown competition.

Hannah was about to head for the turnstile at the exit when she thought about Sinful Pleasures, the deep-fried candy bar booth. She was alone. Pam and Willa had already left. Delores had driven Michelle home, and Lisa and Herb were gone. This was her perfect chance. She could have a deep-fried Milky Way with impunity.

Life is good, Hannah thought, as she freed up a hand and slapped at another mosquito.

The only thing that would make this moment better was if she'd remembered to wear insect repellent.

CHAPTER FIVE

She had to wait in line for several minutes because there were at least a half-dozen people in front of her, but at last she reached the counter. And since there was no one in line behind her, she had time to chat with Ruby for a moment.

"This is for you, Ruby." Hannah handed over the cinnamon raisin bread she'd snatched up at the last minute. "It only took an honorable mention, but it should have placed higher. I've had it before, and it's great for toast in the morning."

"Well, that's really nice of you," Ruby said, sounding both surprised and pleased.

"It's just a little thank-you for defusing the situation with my mother."

"No problem. Parents are always pulling their kids away from my booth."

"Yes, but I'll bet those kids are usually a lot younger."

"That's true. But some mothers just can't

seem to let go, even when their kids are grown up. I'm that way myself."

Hannah stared at Ruby in surprise. She'd assumed Ruby was about her age, but if she had a grown child, she had to be older. "I can't believe you have a child that old!"

"She's not really my child. She's my half-sister, but I raised her when our mother died."

"How old were you?" Hannah couldn't help asking.

"Almost eleven."

Hannah gave a little sigh. When she was eleven, she'd done something similar. Michelle had been a cranky baby and she'd helped to take care of her when Delores had needed a break. But that had been only for an hour or so, a couple of times a week. Hannah couldn't even imagine shouldering the sole responsibility of motherhood at that age. "How old was your sister?"

"Two and a half. It wasn't easy, but all the rodeo wives helped. The ones who had kids used to invite Brianna over to play so that I could get some of the housework done. And they were always inviting us over for meals. There was one barrel rider, Missy Daniels, who used to bring us tuna casserole."

"That was nice."

"No, it wasn't. It was the worst tuna casserole I ever tasted. My stepfather, Sam, said we had to be polite and tell her we liked it, so we did. But that backfired."

"She brought you even more of it?" Hannah guessed.

"That's right. We had it every Friday night. I still can't stand the sight of a can of tuna. Anyway, between the wives and the single gals who wanted to pick up on Sam, we got along all right. Of course when we wrapped up the season, it was a lot easier."

"Why?" Hannah asked, curious about what it would be like to travel with a rodeo.

"We wintered in Florida with Sam's parents. Bri and I lived with them in Fort Lauderdale. Gram took care of Bri so I could go to school, and Sam spent the winter booking skeleton shows." Hannah must have looked as confused as she felt, because Ruby hurried to explain. "It's a pared down show, just the bones. That's why we call it a skeleton show. It's really more of a demonstration, and you can put it on in a park, or even a vacant lot."

"So your stepdad was the booking agent for the show?"

"That and everything else. Sam owns the Great Northwestern Rodeo and Carnival. He finally gave up Brahma riding last year after he broke his arm twice, but he still keeps his hand in by doing some trick riding. See that Winnebago parked at the edge of the trees?"

Hannah looked in the direction Ruby was pointing. There was a large Winnebago parked behind the midway, just to the left of the Ferris wheel. "I see it."

"That's where I grew up. Of course I don't live there now. Riggs and I have our own trailer. But Sam still lives there with Brianna. She just got engaged to one of the cowboys. He's a Brahma rider and his name's Tucker Smith."

"It must be a very different sort of life," Hannah mused, wondering how it would feel to travel with a rodeo.

"Oh, it is. We don't stay anywhere for more than a week, and that means we have to be really self-sufficient." Ruby stopped talking and gazed over Hannah's shoulder. "So how about that deep-fried Milky Way? Your mother's nowhere in sight."

Hannah laughed. She didn't know how she could possibly manage it after all the sweet dough breads they'd tasted, but the thought of getting to taste one at last made her mouth start to water. "Well . . . I really shouldn't but I guess . . ." Hannah stopped in midsentence when a voice called her name. She turned to see Norman hurrying across the food court toward her, and she gave a little sigh. She was glad to see him. It wasn't that. But this was the second time she'd been thwarted in her attempt to taste a deep-fried candy bar.

"You can't eat one right now?" Ruby guessed.

"You got it," Hannah said, and then she turned to give Norman a smile as he arrived at her side. It had been several days since she'd seen him, and it felt good to be with him again.

"Are you going to eat one of those?" he asked, as he arrived at her side.

"No," Hannah replied. Norman didn't sound censorious, the way her mother had, but it would be wise to play it safe.

"I need your help, Hannah." Norman took the pan from her arms and steered her away from the booth, barely giving Hannah time to wave goodbye to Ruby. "I've got a problem with my dishwasher."

Hannah was confused. " 'I'm sorry to hear that, but I don't know anything about fixing dishwashers."

"I know you don't. And I wasn't asking you to. All I want you to do is help me pick it out. The brochures for the kitchen appliances came today, and I can't make up my mind between two models."

"No problem. I'll be glad to help you."

"Thanks, Hannah. I was afraid I'd pick the wrong one." Norman looked down at the pan he was carrying. "I heard you were filling in for Edna. Is this tonight's winner?"

"No, it's part of the third-place entry, a chocolate cherry coffeecake. I'm taking it to Mother."

"Now?" Norman asked, looking disappointed.

"Now. I'm going to deliver the coffeecake, congratulate Michelle on her win in the evening gown competition, and then I'm going straight home. I think Moishe might be getting sick."

"What's wrong with him?"

"I don't know. It's probably the heat, but I'm a little worried. He didn't touch his breakfast."

"How about dinner?"

"Only a sniff and a lick. And I made him a Denver sandwich without the onions and the bell peppers. I even put in double ham and he still wouldn't touch it."

"That sounds serious. How about if I stop at my house to pick up the brochures, and head over to your condo to check on Moishe? Maybe I can get him to eat. When you get home, you can take a quick look and tell me which model is the best."

Hannah didn't have to think twice about that. "Great," she said, giving Norman a grateful smile. He always came through when she needed him. And that was one of the things she loved most about him.

"Hi, Hannah!" Michelle greeted her oldest sister at the door. Her face was devoid of makeup, and she was wearing cut-off jeans and a Macalester College T-shirt. "What have you got?"

"Chocolate cherry coffeecake. Where's Mother?"

"In Dad's old office. She's using it now. She said she had some work to do on her computer."

"What work?"

"I don't know. I asked, but she said it was personal."

Hannah frowned as visions of e-mail romances with prison inmates danced through her mind. "Is she on-line yet?"

"No. The cable company's going to have free installation on their high-speed Internet access next month. She told me she's waiting until then."

"Good! I mean . . . I just didn't want her to start something with . . ." Hannah stopped, not quite sure how to phrase what she'd been thinking.

"Weirdos, perverts, and creeps?" Michelle asked. "With a few con artists thrown in?"

"Exactly."

"I wouldn't worry too much. I think Mother learned a lot from what happened last spring."

"I *hope* so! It just makes me so mad that somebody tried to take advantage of her!"

"Me, too. But it's over now, and Mother's smart enough not to fall for somebody like that again." Michelle gave Hannah a little shove toward the office that Delores was using. "Do me a favor, okay?"

Hannah knew better than to agree without knowing what Michelle wanted. "That depends on what it is."

"It's snooping. I tried to see what Mother was working on, but she's got one of those privacy screens. One keystroke and all you can see is a bouquet of flowers, or pine trees in a snowy forest. See if you can find out what she's working on. I just hate it when people say that it's personal and they won't tell you what it is."

"Okay, I'll do it," Hannah agreed. And then she headed down the hallway to see if she could figure out what secret their mother was hiding.

"Mother?" Hannah called out, tapping on

the door and then opening it without waiting for an invitation.

"Hello, dear." Delores looked up when Hannah came into the room. "Sit down and wait just a moment, will you? I really need to finish this paragraph."

"Sure. Michelle said you were working on something personal." Hannah sat down in the old leather chair that had been moved to a spot near the window. It had been her dad's desk chair, but Delores had replaced it with a smart-looking model upholstered in blue tweed. It was clear at a glance that her mother's new chair rolled, reclined, and swiveled, while the old leather chair merely sat there.

"That's right."

"I'm curious. What is it?"

"Nothing you'd be interested in, dear."

Delores went right back to typing, and Hannah gave a little sigh. She'd struck out. So much for being forthright. She'd have to think of some other way to find out.

"You were always the best speller in the family," Delores said, pausing with her fingers poised over the keyboard. "*Recommendation* has one *c* and two *m*'s, doesn't it?"

"Recommendation?" Hannah repeated, not sure she'd heard her mother correctly.

"That's right. Yes or no, dear."

"Yes," Hannah said, and then she spelled it out. "Are you writing a letter of recommendation for someone?"

"No, dear. Just give me a moment more and I'll be through."

Hannah's curiosity reached new heights. Her mother had told Michelle it was "personal," and it wasn't a letter of recommendation. Asking politely hadn't worked, and she'd promised Michelle that she'd snoop if she got the chance. Feeling a bit like someone cheating on an exam, Hannah craned her neck to try to see her mother's computer screen. Unfortunately she was off-axis, and all she saw was a faintly lighted screen. She inched slightly to the side to get a better view, not an easy task with a heavy desk chair that didn't roll, but the only thing she could make out was faint lines of double-spaced type. It was definitely not a letter. Letters were single-spaced.

"Almost through, dear," Delores said, her fingers beating a staccato rhythm on the keys.

Hannah gave a lurch, and the chair slid another inch to the side. That was better! She could almost read something! She was leaning forward, squinting to make out the words, when a huge bouquet of flowers replaced the words on the screen.

"It's time for a break," Delores stated, leaning back in her chair. "You looked a bit upset when you came in the door, dear. Does it make you sad to see me using your father's office?"

"A little," Hannah admitted.

"That's what I thought. You spent a lot of time in here with him."

"You got a new desk chair."

"Yes. I tried using his, but it just wasn't right for me. So I ordered a new one, and then I kept thinking of what he'd say if he saw me replacing his desk chair. I was going to give it to charity. It's really too big for this small room. But . . . I couldn't just throw it away. He spent so much time in here, sitting in that chair. Sometimes when I'm working late, I'll turn, and for just a second I think I can see him there. Is that crazy?"

"No, that's love. And memories."

Delores blinked several times, and then she gave a little smile. "You're right. But I really do need to put a file cabinet in here, and there won't be room with that chair. Would you like to have it?"

Hannah was tempted. She'd always associated that leather desk chair with her father. Then she thought of her condo and how it was already full to the brim with other things that Delores had given her. "I don't think so, Mother. I'd like it, but I don't have anywhere to put it."

"That's what I thought. I'll ask Andrea and Michelle, but I don't think they'll want it, either. And I really hate to just . . . toss it."

"I don't want you to just toss it, either. Do you think it'd help if we found it a good home?"

Delores thought about that for a moment. "I think it would. Do you have any prospects in mind?"

"Not really, but I'll think about it and . . . Norman!"

"Norman?"

"He might want it. His new house has an office, and as far as I know, he doesn't have any furniture."

"Oh, that would be perfect!" Delores looked delighted. "I'd like to give it to Norman."

"Even if I don't end up marrying him?" Hannah couldn't help asking.

"Even if you don't. When can you ask him if he wants it?"

"I'll ask him tonight. He's waiting for me at my condo. I'm going to help him pick out a dishwasher."

"That's wonderful, dear."

Delores gave another smile that rang alarm bells in Hannah's mind. Her mother seemed much too pleased about the fact that she was helping Norman pick out kitchen appliances. "It's just a dishwasher, Mother. It's not any more than that."

"That's all right, dear. Good marriages aren't made overnight. Your father and I dated for several years before we married."

Hannah bit her tongue. Sometimes it was better not to say anything.

"Is that for me, dear?" Delores asked, glancing at the foil-wrapped package Hannah still held in her arms.

"Yes. It's the chocolate cherry coffeecake that took third place at the baked goods competition tonight."

"It sounds marvelous! I'll have some when I take my next break. And that reminds me . . . you don't have anyone staying in your guest room, do you?"

"No." Hannah readied herself for a major imposition. Her mother had mentioned something about a cousin three times removed who'd wanted to visit Lake Eden.

"Oh, good. Would you mind terribly if Michelle stayed with you?"

"You mean . . . our Michelle?"

"Yes. It's just that I'm so busy right now. I

really don't have much time to spend with her, and poor Michelle must be lonely with only the television for company. I thought it might be more fun for her if she . . ."

"That's fine, Mother," Hannah agreed, before Delores could continue. "I'd love to have Michelle stay with me."

"Wonderful! Go out there right now and have her pack up her things. Tell her she can use my car for the week. Then she'll have her own transportation, and you won't have to drive her around."

"But won't you need your car?"

"No. The only place I'm going is out to the fair, and I can ride with Carrie. We signed up for the same hours at the booth."

"All right, Mother."

"Tell her to come in and say goodbye before she leaves. I'd come out, but I still have several more pages to write before I'm through, and then I need to get some sleep. I'm burning the candle at both ends to get everything done."

"Okay. I'll tell her." Hannah stood up, but before she could take a step, her mother stopped her.

"It's not that I don't want her, dear. Make that clear, will you? It's just that with working at Granny's Attic and supervising the booth at the fair, I don't have time to get things done around here. And that reminds me . . . you *are* going to be at the Historical Society booth from eight to closing on Saturday night, aren't you?"

Hannah took a deep breath and stifled the complaints she wanted to make. She'd agreed to help out in the Lake Eden Historical Society booth when her mother had asked, assuming she'd be passing out literature and taking contributions. But Delores had tricked her. What Hannah had really agreed to do was sit on a stool in a frilly dress while contributors threw balls at a target that would open a trapdoor and dunk her into a vat of cold water.

"Hannah?" Delores prodded.

"Yes, Mother. I said I would and I'll be there."

"Thank you, dear. And thank you for the coffeecake. I'll have a piece when I take my next break. Chocolate and cherries are my favorite combination."

"I know," Hannah said. And then she headed out the door to tell Michelle that she was being transplanted from her mother's guest room to Hannah's guest room in the condo, and she didn't have the slightest idea what their mother was writing.

CHAPTER SIX

Hannah woke up with a cat on her head. Moishe had climbed up in an attempt to wake her so she'd shut off the alarm. When she didn't sit up quickly enough, he batted at several unruly curls that were sticking out over her ear. And when *that* didn't work, he gave an ear-splitting yowl that made his wishes abundantly clear.

"Okay, okay," Hannah groaned, reaching out with one sleep-leaden arm to depress the alarm button on the clock. But the clock wasn't where it was supposed to be, on the table right next to her bed. The bedside lamp wasn't there either, and Hannah encountered a perfectly smooth surface. What was going on?

Moishe yowled again, and Hannah realized that what she'd heard wasn't her alarm clock at all. It was coming from the television, and the clock belonged to a starlet whose face she didn't recognize.

Hannah watched for a moment through partially closed eyes. She'd fallen asleep on the couch last night during *Casablanca.* Since this wasn't a young Ingrid Bergman, Hannah figured she was at least one, probably two features past her bedtime.

The starlet reached out to turn off the alarm clock and climbed out of bed with the sheet wrapped around her like a toga. As she walked across the bedroom set and disappeared through a door, Hannah wondered if anyone had ever pulled the sheet off the bed for modesty's sake while they were alone in their bedroom. It seemed silly. You'd just have to remake the bed from scratch.

After one glance at the time, which was subtly displayed at the lower right-hand corner of the screen, Hannah clicked off the television with the remote control. It was almost four-thirty in the morning. Since she always set her alarm clock, the one in her bedroom, to go off at a quarter to five, it seemed silly to go to bed for fifteen minutes and count the seconds she had left before it was really time to get up.

A compelling scent wafted in from the kitchen to help Hannah make up her mind. The timer on her coffee pot had activated, and her morning brew was ready.

"Coffee," she pronounced in a voice that was midway between a groan and a prayer. She needed caffeine, and she needed it fast, before the specter of another hot, muggy day would drive her to turn on the window air conditioner the former owners had installed in the bedroom and sleep until the unseasonable June heat wave headed east, or west, or anywhere far away from Lake Eden, Minnesota.

Hannah stood up and shivered slightly. She'd fallen asleep in her favorite summer sleep outfit, an extra-long, extra-large tank top in such an eye-popping shade of magenta that she hoped Moishe's vet, Dr. Hagaman, was right and cats truly were colorblind. Not only was her sleepwear the wrong color choice for anyone with red hair, it was plastered to her skin in a manner her mother might call decidedly unladylike.

"Okay, I'm up," Hannah declared to the orange and white tomcat who still wore the scars of his former life on the streets. She tugged her tank top back into place, got to her feet with what she thought was a minimum of groaning, and headed off to the kitchen. "Just let me pour a mug of Swedish Plasma and then I'll get your breakfast."

But Moishe didn't follow her into the kitchen as he usually did. He didn't even move from the back of the couch where he'd perched. And then everything came back in a rush of memory, and Hannah recalled why she'd been sleeping on the couch. She was worried about Moishe. He wasn't eating. And she'd wanted to wake up and take note if she heard him crunching his food in the middle of the night.

Hannah had just poured her first, life-giving mug of coffee when she heard a voice that seemed to be coming from inside her condo.

"Is Moishe okay?" the voice asked.

Even in her sleep-deprived state, Hannah recognized that voice. It was Michelle, and she was staying in the guest room.

"Don't know yet. Want coffee?" she managed to say, anything other than Pidgin English eluding her.

"I'll get it. Just sit there and drink yours. Do you know your eyes aren't open all the way?"

"No."

"What time did Norman leave?"

"No numbers." Hannah took a giant swig of coffee and felt it burn all the way down. It was worth it if it lifted the curtain of fog from her mind. "Never good at math in the morning."

"I'm sorry I asked. Take another sip of

your coffee. I won't bother you again until you finish that mug."

Hannah finished her coffee in several large, near-scalding swallows and held out her mug for more. By the time Michelle had set it on the table in front of her, the mists of sleep were starting to depart and she had glimpses of clarity. "Okay," she said, giving her youngest sister a little smile, mostly because Michelle's sleep outfit, a green cotton nightgown with miniature cows grazing all over it, was even more ridiculous than hers. "What did you ask me before?"

"I asked if Moishe was all right."

"I'm not sure. I think I heard him eating something in the middle of the night, but that could have been wishful thinking."

Michelle set her own mug down on the table and walked to Moishe's food bowl. "How full was it last night?"

"It was up to the brim. It was even mounded a bit in the middle. I wanted him to have plenty if he got hungry and wanted a midnight snack."

"Well, it's not mounded on top anymore."

"Really?" That information got Hannah out of her chair to join her sister at the food bowl. "You're right. He definitely ate some kitty crunchies."

"So you can stop worrying?" Michelle followed Hannah back to the table and sat down across from her.

"I'm not sure. He didn't eat very much. He usually cleans his bowl during the night and yowls for more in the morning."

"How about water?"

"He's drinking. His water dish was full, too. He drank about half, and that's what he usually drinks."

"That's a good sign, isn't it?"

"I think so. It's just not like him to turn down food. You saw what happened when Norman tried to give him fried chicken last night. He *loves* fried chicken, but last night he just sniffed it and walked away."

Michelle leaned to the side so that she could see into the living room. "I think you'd better take him to the vet, Hannah. He's sitting on the back of the couch again, just staring out the window. Maybe it's just the hot weather and he doesn't feel like eating much, but you'll never forgive yourself if it's something serious and you didn't have Dr. Bob check him out."

"You're right. This is Tuesday, isn't it?" When Michelle nodded, Hannah glanced at the clock over the table. It was five-fifteen, much too early to call for an appointment. "I'll take my shower now, and I'll call Sue at home at six."

"Isn't that kind of early?"

"Not really. Tuesday's their half day and they're open from seven to noon. That means they're bound to be up if I call them at home at six. If I can get Moishe in right away at seven, I can run him back here and still get to work by eight-thirty."

Michelle shook her head. "You can get to work by seven-thirty. I've got Mother's car and I'll follow you to town. I can bring Moishe back here with me and you can go straight to work."

It was six-twenty when Hannah pulled up in the parking lot behind the Lake Eden Pet Clinic. When Michelle pulled into an adjoining parking space, Hannah picked up the bag of cookies she'd brought, grabbed Moishe's leash, and got out of her cookie truck.

"Do you want me to carry something?" Michelle asked.

"All I've got is Moishe and the cookies. Moishe would rather walk on his own, and since you haven't had breakfast yet, I'm not sure I should trust you with the cookies."

"What kind are they?"

"Walnut-Date Chews."

Michelle rolled her eyes heavenward. "I remember those! You used to make them for Dad. They taste almost like date nut bread, right?"

"Right."

"I haven't had them for so long!" Michelle looked at the bag hungrily. "And dates and nuts are so good for you."

"They are?" Hannah asked, tugging a bit on the leash to get Moishe moving forward.

"They're both heart healthy. Dates are especially good for your muscle tone, and walnuts prevent cellulite."

Hannah's eyes narrowed. Michelle sounded just a tad too convincing to be believed, and she *was* a theater arts major. "You just made that up, didn't you?"

"Yes, but I *love* those cookies. And you haven't made them in ages. Can I please have one, Hannah?"

"May I. And no, you may not. They're for Dr. Bob and Sue for letting me bring Moishe in so early."

"Not even one? They're my all-time favorite cookies!"

"Absolutely not. But when you get home, there's a bag just like this on the kitchen counter. You'll find another two dozen in there."

Michelle was grinning as Hannah knocked on the back door of the clinic. When she'd called, Sue had answered the phone from the clinic and she'd told Hannah that they always arrived an hour early when they had overnight patients.

"Hi, Hannah," Sue said, opening the door. She spotted Michelle standing behind Hannah and gave her a friendly smile. "You looked really wonderful last night in the evening gown competition. Bob and I talked about it on the way home, and we're so glad you won."

"Thanks," Michelle said, and Hannah noticed that her sister was blushing slightly. There were big differences between the three Swensen sisters. Andrea knew she was beautiful and took compliments in stride, Michelle didn't realize how gorgeous she was and was still slightly embarrassed when someone complimented her, and Hannah had looked into the mirror enough times to know that if someone said she was beautiful, they probably wanted something from her. Except for their differing hair colors, Andrea and Michelle had inherited the gene for beauty from Delores. All three of them were petite with lovely features and figures that would not be out of place in a string bikini. Hannah had inherited her looks from her father, who had been tall with curly red hair and the tendency to put on more than a few extra pounds around the middle.

"What's wrong with Moishe?" Michelle asked, bringing Hannah out of her musing.

Hannah looked down at the cat and began to frown. Moishe's fur was bristling, his ears were down flat, and he was making a little growling noise in his throat. "I don't know. He's never been like this before."

"Is he afraid of Dr. Bob?"

"No. He doesn't absolutely love coming here, but he's always walked right in before." Hannah gave a little tug on the leash. "Come on, Moishe. Let's go."

But Moishe wasn't going. He dug in his claws and refused to move, stopping dead at the threshold. No amount of coaxing or tugging would budge him, and Hannah was about to pick him up and carry him bodily into the building when Sue stopped her.

"Wait a second, Hannah. I think I know what's wrong. Moishe's never come in the back way before. Walk him around the building and I'll let you in the front."

"Okay, if you don't mind. I hate to pick him up when he's this rattled."

Michelle slipped inside with Sue. Hannah was amazed to see that the moment the door closed, Moishe's fur smoothed down and his ears perked up. The low growl he'd been giving subsided as she walked him around the side of the building. Was it possible Sue was right? This was the way they'd entered in the past when he had a regular appointment, and he didn't seem to mind it at all.

"Here we are," Hannah said, opening the front door the way she always did. And to her surprise, Moishe marched straight in and rubbed up against Sue's ankles.

"This is really strange," Hannah said, puzzled at his behavior.

Sue shook her head. "Not really. Pets are creatures of habit. They feel safe when their routine stays the same. Coming in the back way was a change in routine, and that made Moishe nervous." She reached down to pet him, and Moishe started to purr. "Take him right in to examining room one, Hannah. Bob's waiting for you."

Less than fifteen minutes later, Moishe was in the car with Michelle on their way back to the condo, and Hannah was driving to The Cookie Jar. She was somewhat reassured when Dr. Bob hadn't found anything wrong in his physical examination. All that remained was the lab work.

Since the patient didn't speak English and Dr. Bob didn't speak cat, Hannah had assumed the role of interpreter. Yes, Moishe was eating a bit of food, but much less than usual. And he'd been turning down treats that he loved like tuna, salmon, and fried chicken. No, she hadn't seen any signs that his stomach was upset. Yes, he was drinking water. Yes, he was using his litter box. And no, she hadn't switched his food. It was the same brand of kitty crunchies she'd always fed him. Her main concern was his odd behavior. He'd shown very little interest in looking out the windows before, but in the past two days he'd spent hours balancing on windowsills, staring fixedly out at nothing.

Hannah pulled up in her parking space, right next to Lisa's old car, and hurried to the back door. But before she could reach for the knob, Lisa opened it.

"How's Moishe?" she asked.

"I don't know yet. Dr. Bob examined him, and when he couldn't find anything wrong he took a blood sample."

"When do you get the results?"

"I'm supposed to call in at noon. He said he should have a fax from the lab by then." Hannah stepped inside and hung her purse on one of the hooks by the back door. She glanced at the baker's racks and gave a little groan when she saw that Lisa had baked all the cookies without her. "I'm sorry you got stuck with all the baking. I'll come in early tomorrow and make it up to you."

"Don't be silly. I know you'd do the baking alone if Herb got sick and I had to take him to the doctor."

Hannah was about to tell her that it wasn't the same thing, but she reconsidered. Perhaps it was.

"You look beat, Hannah. Sit down and I'll get you a cup of coffee."

"Thanks," Hannah said, sinking down on a stool at the work island. She'd polished off a whole pot of coffee with Michelle, but she'd only gotten four hours of sleep and she could use a little more caffeine.

"Here you go." Lisa placed a mug of coffee in front of her. "Do you know what Herb calls it?"

"Coffee?"

"No," Lisa replied with a giggle. "I called it Swedish Plasma this morning, the way you always do, and he said we should call it Vitamin V."

Hannah sifted through the possibilities in record time, but she couldn't think of an appropriate word beginning with the letter *V.* "Okay, I'll bite. What does the V stand for?"

"Vertical. Herb says it's the only thing that gets him up on his feet in the morning."

Walnut-Date Chews

Preheat oven to 350 degrees F., rack in the middle position.

1 cup melted butter *(2 sticks, 1/2 pound)*

3 cups brown sugar *(pack it down in the cup when you measure it)*

4 eggs, beaten *(just stir them up in a glass with a fork until they're a uniform color)*

1 teaspoon salt

1 teaspoon baking soda

1 Tablespoon *(3 teaspoons)* vanilla extract

2 cups finely chopped walnuts *(measure AFTER chopping)*

1 cup chopped dates***

4 cups flour *(don't sift — pack it down in the cup when you measure it)*

*** *You can buy dates already chopped at the grocery store if you don't want to chop them yourself.*

Melt the butter on **HIGH** in a microwave-safe container for 90 seconds, or in a small saucepan on the stove over low heat.

Transfer the melted butter to a large mixing bowl and add the brown sugar. Mix it well and let it cool to slightly above room temperature, just enough so that it won't cook the eggs when you add them!

Mix in the beaten eggs. Stir until they're thoroughly incorporated.

Add the salt, baking soda, and vanilla. Mix it all up together.

Mix in the walnuts and let the dough rest while you chop the dates.

You can chop your dates by hand with a knife, but it's a lot easier in a food processor or blender. Just pit them first *(of course)*, cut each one into two or three pieces with a knife, put them into the bowl of your food processor or blender, and sprinkle a little flour *(approximately 1/4 cup)* on top. The flour will keep them from "gumming up" when you process them.

Measure one cup of chopped dates and add them to your mixing bowl. Stir them in thoroughly.

Add the flour in one-cup increments, mixing after each addition. This dough will be fairly stiff.

Form the dough into balls with your fingers. *(Make them the size of a walnut with shell.)* Place them on a greased cookie sheet,

12 to a standard sheet. *(They will flatten a bit and spread out when they bake.)*

Bake at 350 degrees for 10 to 12 minutes or until lightly browned. Let them cool on the cookie sheet for two minutes and then remove them to a wire rack to complete cooling.

These were my father's favorites. Delores liked them, too.

Lisa says her dad likes these best with a dish of vanilla ice cream.

CHAPTER SEVEN

The display jars behind the counter in the coffee shop were filled with the day's cookie offerings, tables were set up with napkins, sugar, artificial sweetener, and cream, and the thirty-cup coffee pot was perking merrily in preparation for the customers they might or might not have on this, the second day of the Tri-County Fair. Hannah and Lisa had just finished packing up the massive order of cookies for the Cookie Nook booth at the fairgrounds, and they were sitting on stools at the kitchen workstation, going over their weekly supply order.

"Another cup?" Lisa asked Hannah, gesturing toward the pot in the kitchen.

"Sure. One more and I might feel human." Hannah smiled as Lisa fetched the pot and filled her mug. "Anything else we need?"

"I'm not sure. How are we doing on nuts?"

"We get more than we used to, but you really shouldn't talk about our customers that way."

Lisa stared at her for a split second, as if she'd lost her mind, and then she gave the giggle Hannah loved. "That's *funny!*"

"Thank goodness. I thought I'd lost my sense of humor, but this last cup of coffee must have brought it back. Did you happen to notice how much oatmeal we have left? I promised Andrea I'd make her some more Swedish Oatmeal Cookies."

"I thought Andrea didn't like oatmeal."

"She doesn't, but she's eating it now." Hannah began to grin, relishing in the fact she'd tricked her sister into eating it at last.

"There's a story here."

"Yes, there is. Remind me to tell you when we've got more time. Just remember that if she ever asks you, oatmeal is really good for your hair."

"Your *hair?*"

"That's right." Lisa looked uncomfortable, and Hannah knew why. Her young partner hated to lie. "You don't have to come right out and lie about it."

"Okay. I'll just smile, or not, or . . ." Lisa stopped talking as the back door opened and Andrea came in with Bethany in her arms. "Hi, Andrea. We were just talking about . . ."

"Bethany." Hannah saved Lisa in mid-blurt. "And there she is now! Lisa wanted to know if she was crawling yet."

"She's crawling, I guess. If you can call it that."

"What's she doing?" Lisa asked, bringing Andrea a cup of coffee and a plate filled with cookies.

"I'll show you." Andrea set Bethany down on the floor.

Hannah began to smile. When Tracey was a baby, Andrea was convinced that she shouldn't be in any environment that wasn't antiseptically clean. She hadn't even put her down on a clean blanket in her own living room. She hadn't allowed any visitors except family for the first three months for fear baby Tracey might "catch" something. She'd sterilized everything, boiled the washcloths she used to bathe Tracey, and cried gallons of tears when she hadn't produced enough milk to nurse her. She'd read all the cautionary books and exhausted herself trying to do everything the baby gurus had advised. And when anything went wrong and baby Tracey came down with a cold or didn't finish her dinner, Andrea had felt she was a failure as a mother.

It was different this time, and Hannah was

glad to see it. Andrea and Bill had a live-in nanny, Grandma McCann, who took care of Bethany while Andrea worked. The results were nothing short of remarkable. Andrea was able to have a good time with Bethany and relax around her.

"I don't think she's going to crawl," Hannah said, gazing down at her perfectly beautiful, perfectly immobile niece.

"We'll fix that." Andrea pulled a stuffed rabbit, from the diaper bag and set it a few feet in front of Bethany. "Go get it, Bethie. Show Aunt Hannah and Aunt Lisa how you crawl."

Bethany sat there staring at her toy for a moment, and then she gave the sweetest smile Hannah had ever seen. It wasn't clear if the smile was for the stuffed rabbit or them, but it didn't really matter. Her youngest niece was simply adorable.

When Bethany moved, it was fast. She tucked one leg under her, leaned on it, and pushed off with the other leg. She repeated it several times, scooting toward the stuffed rabbit in spurts.

"See what I mean?" Andrea asked, smiling when her daughter reached the rabbit, grabbed it, and chewed on the ears. "It's not really a crawl, but it works. Grandma McCann thinks it's because we have hardwood floors. Crawling would be hard on her knees, so she scoots. It cracks me up every time I watch her. The way she tucks her leg up reminds me of something, but I don't know what."

Hannah thought about that for a moment, and the swimming classes she'd taken as a child flashed through her mind. They'd learned all sorts of swimming strokes and kicks, practicing them on the shore of Eden Lake and then in the lake itself. It wasn't a flutter kick or a scissors kick, but there had been another that she'd never quite mastered and that one had been . . .

"The frog kick!" she said aloud.

Andrea turned to beam at her. "That's exactly what it reminds me of, a sort of crooked frog kick. Mine were always crooked."

"So were mine," Hannah admitted. "And Michelle's, too. It must be hereditary."

"You'd better not let your mother hear you say that," Lisa warned. "I don't think she'd like being compared to a mother frog."

"Right," Hannah said, and gave a little wave as Lisa headed off to the coffee shop to open for business.

"I almost forgot why I drove over here," Andrea said. "I've got news that'll rock your world."

"What?" Hannah asked, not believing it for a moment. Andrea tended to exaggerate when she had some juicy gossip to tell. Her news might be interesting, perhaps even mildly startling, but it certainly wouldn't rock anyone's world.

"I got this straight from Bertie at the Cut 'n' Curl." Andrea reached down to pick up Bethany, who'd managed to propel her way over to the work island. "Up you go, Bethie."

"Let me hold her." Hannah held out her arms and was rewarded by a wide, open-mouthed grin from Bethany.

Andrea handed the baby over, and then she retrieved a bottle of juice from the diaper bag and put it in front of Hannah. "She can have this. Bethie loves apple juice."

Hannah settled the baby in the crook of her arm and uncapped the bottle of juice. When Bethany had the bottle and she'd begun to drink, Hannah turned back to her sister. Andrea didn't look as if she'd just had her hair done. "So what were you doing at the Cut 'n' Curl?"

"The Mother-Daughter look-alike luncheon is today, and I thought it might influence the judges if Tracey and I had the same hairstyle. Bertie's doing Tracey's now. Then she's going to give Willa Sunquist a comb-out. She just had a cut and a color weave. When she finishes with Willa, she'll do me."

Hannah was surprised. Willa didn't have much money, and a color weave was expensive. Perhaps her job as the chaperone for the Miss Tri-County contestants paid well. "Do you want me to keep Tracey and Bethany here while you have your hair done?"

Andrea shook her head. "Grandma McCann's down at Bertie's with Tracey. I just wanted to bring Bethie up to see you and give you the big news."

"All right. Give."

"Well, Bertie got it straight from Carrie. She's the one who got the phone call."

"What phone call?" Hannah asked, and she felt her frustration level jump up a notch. Andrea loved to drag things out when she had some juicy gossip. "Is it something about Norman?"

"It sure is. The secretary from the fairgrounds called Carrie this morning to tell her that the picture Norman took of you won first place in the photography competition."

"That's great!" Hannah exclaimed. This time Andrea's news really was important. "Does Norman know?"

"He does, now. He was down at the café, and Carrie called him on his cell phone to tell him."

"Thanks for coming here to tell me," Hannah said. And then, because she just couldn't resist, she followed it up with, "I'm really happy Norman won, but it didn't exactly rock my world."

"That's because I haven't told you the rocking-your-world part yet."

With that, Andrea stopped speaking and grinned at her older sister. The only sound was Bethany sucking on her bottle of juice. Hannah let the absence of conversation go on. It was a test. The sister who spoke first lost.

Long moments passed without a word, and Hannah was amazed at her sister's restraint. She really wanted to know Andrea's news, but there was no way she was going to give in and ask. Just as she was beginning to waver, she had work to do and they couldn't sit here like this all day, Andrea caved in.

"All right. I'll tell you." Andrea leaned forward as if she were about to impart a state secret. "Mike was sitting next to Norman when Carrie called and he heard the whole thing. And he bought Norman's picture for five hundred dollars!"

"What?!"

"I told you it would rock your world!" Andrea looked smug.

"But . . . but why did Mike buy it? And why did he pay so much? I'm sure Norman would have made him a copy if he'd asked. And . . ."

"That's all I know," Andrea interrupted what promised to be a barrage of questions. "If you want to know more, you're going to have to get it from the horse's mouth."

"Okay. I guess the horse's mouth would be Norman. If Mike really did pay five hundred dollars for a photo of me, that makes him another part of the horse's anatomy."

"So what did he say?" Lisa asked, when Hannah got off the phone with Dr. Bob.

"The blood test was normal, right across the board," Hannah reported. "More coffee?"

Lisa nodded, and Hannah filled a carafe with hot coffee and carried it to the back booth where they'd been sitting. Yesterday's lack of customers was repeating itself today. They'd had only a few local businessmen in the morning, and a couple more for what usually was their noon rush. Now that noon had come and gone, the coffee shop was completely deserted.

Lisa reached for the carafe and poured

more coffee for both of them. "What does he think you should do?"

"Nothing, at least for now. I'm supposed to change the food and water in his bowls every day so when Moishe starts eating again, it'll be fresh. He says it won't kill Moishe to lose a few pounds, and I shouldn't worry. Pets sometimes go through periods of not eating. Just like humans, they lose their appetites for one reason or another."

"Not me."

"Me, neither," Hannah said, reverting to the vernacular of her childhood.

Hannah was manning the counter in front while Lisa packed cookies. There was only one table filled at The Cookie Jar, a young couple who'd told Hannah they were just passing through town on their way up north. She'd already wiped down the counter and straightened the display jars, and now she was sitting on the tall stool by the cash register, looking out the window and wondering whether Mike had really purchased Norman's photograph of her.

Hannah supposed it was possible, considering the changing dynamics between Mike and Norman. When Ross Barton had come to Lake Eden to film *Crisis in Cherrywood*, the two rivals had banded together to keep her from getting too serious about him. But now that Ross was gone, Norman and Mike were rivals again and each one was trying to outdo the other. Norman's picture of her had won a blue ribbon. That was one point for him. And Mike had purchased it for more money than most people would spend. That tied the score. Just as Hannah was wondering what shenanigans would be next, the two men in question came in the door.

"Hi, Hannah!" Norman took a seat at the counter while Mike hung up his sheriff's department windbreaker on the coat rack by the front door. "Did you hear that the picture I took of you won a blue ribbon?"

Hannah gave him a warm smile. "I heard. Congratulations!"

"And did you hear about the new artwork I'm going to hang over my couch in the living room?" Mike asked, taking the stool next to Norman's.

"I heard that you bought Norman's photograph, if that's what you mean," Hannah said. "Coffee for both of you?"

Hannah busied herself behind the counter, filling mugs and delivering their cookie orders. Once that was done, she took up a position behind the counter, midway between them, and waited to see what would happen.

For a moment all they did was crunch their cookies and sip their coffee. Mike had two Chocolate Highlander Cookie Bars, and Hannah was glad. The endorphins in the chocolate might take the edge off his tendency to challenge Norman.

Norman had ordered two Peanut Butter Melts. No help there. Hannah didn't think that peanut butter had endorphins, but it probably wouldn't make much difference. Like oil and water, Norman and Mike needed an emulsifier to mix, and that emulsifier was friendship. They truly did like each other. But both of them had a tendency to play one-upmanship whenever she was around. And when they started that particular game, Hannah felt obliged to referee.

The tension grew right along with the silence until, at last, Mike cleared his throat. "Did you hear how much I paid for your picture?" he asked, dipping his paddle into the waters first.

"Andrea told me it was five hundred dollars. Did you really pay that much?"

"You bet I did."

Hannah turned to Norman. "And you charged him that much?"

"I didn't charge him. That's the price the judges set. All the photographs get auctioned off on the final day of the fair, and the money goes to charity. If you want to buy an entry before that, you have to pay the price the judges set."

Hannah turned to Mike. "Why didn't you wait for the auction? You might have gotten it cheaper."

Mike shook his head. "It's a silent auction and you only get one bid. Somebody could have outbid me and then I would have lost you."

"Then you would have lost a *photograph* of me," Hannah corrected him, "a photograph that your friend Norman took. I'm sure he would have made you a copy if you'd asked him."

"I didn't want to ask. You really look good in that picture, Hannah. You've got this . . . I don't know . . . kind of dreamy expression on your face. I know you were thinking about me."

Norman shook his head. "No, she wasn't. She was thinking about me."

Uh-oh! Hannah thought, *Let the games begin.* She had to stop them both in their tracks and there was only one way to do it.

"Wrong!" she exclaimed. "I wasn't thinking of either of you. I was remembering how Grandma Ingrid's chocolate cashew pie tasted and wondering if I could make it."

"It must have been really good," Mike said, and Hannah could tell he didn't completely believe her.

"It was. Unfortunately, she didn't write down the recipe and I'm still trying to recreate it."

"Let us know when you get it," Norman said, giving her a look that told Hannah he hadn't bought her explanation either.

Hannah mentally kicked herself as she wiped down the already immaculate counter. What on earth had possessed her to rave about a pie her grandmother had never baked? Was there such a thing as a chocolate cashew pie? Hannah had never heard of one, but now that she'd stuck her foot in her mouth, she'd better come up with a recipe.

"Did you buy it?" Lisa asked when Hannah came back from *Beau Monde.*

"Of course."

"Are you going to wear it to the fair tonight?"

Hannah shook her head. "No. I'm going out there at seven to watch Michelle in the bathing suit competition, but nobody's going to pay any attention to me. And later, when I judge the pies, I might spill something on it. It's gorgeous, Lisa. When Claire says she has something that would look great on you, she means it."

"I know. She picked out the dress I wore for the wedding. And that reminds me of Marge. Just so you won't be surprised, Marge submitted a pie for the baked goods contest tonight."

"She did?" Hannah was surprised. Marge baked wonderful cakes, but she wasn't known for her pies. "What kind of pie did she bake?"

"She used one of Mom's apple pie recipes. I couldn't do it myself because I'm your partner and that makes me a professional baker. But Marge tasted it, and she thought it was so good she wanted to enter it."

"I can hardly wait to taste it. But Lisa . . . I can't give it any special consideration just because it's your mother's recipe."

"I know that, and so does Marge. We just wanted to tell you that it was coming."

"Thanks, Lisa."

"Herb and I are going out to the fair at six with Marge and Dad. Do you want me to take the boxes of cookies to the Cookie Nook booth?"

"That would be great." Hannah was glad to be relieved of the task. "Then I'll have time to stop by the hospital and bring Edna some cookies."

"I'll pack them up for you. How many do you need?"

"Six dozen assorted ought to do it."

Lisa's eyes widened in surprise. "That's a lot of cookies for just one person."

"Oh, it won't be just one person. I told Doc's secretary I'd bring cookies, and she's probably told the nurses by now. They'll be in and out of Edna's room until the whole six dozen are gone. Edna's going to get round-the-clock nursing care, even if she doesn't need it."

CHAPTER EIGHT

Hannah couldn't seem to keep the smile off her face. Michelle had taken second place in the bathing suit competition, and she was proud of her baby sister. That was enough to make anyone smile, but she had a second reason. Hannah was having a great time tasting pies. She liked them almost as much as she liked cookies.

All in all, it had been a good day. Hannah cut off the tip of an entry, a piece of peach pie with a little vanilla custard in the filling. The crust was tender and flaky, the peaches still held their shape and weren't overbaked, and the custard was so rich and creamy it could have gone solo and starred in its own pie.

"I take it you like this one?" Pam asked, pulling Hannah out of her reverie.

"Yes, it's delicious."

"We could tell. You were practically purring when you tasted it." Pam turned to

Willa. "What do you think?"

"I'm still deciding. I need another taste to be sure." Willa ran one hand through her hair, a gesture Hannah had seen her make before when she was considering the merits of a particular entry. But instead of causing her hair to tangle, as it had in the past, Willa's new layered haircut bounced right back into place.

"Have I told you I like your new haircut?" Hannah asked.

"Yes. I told Bertie I wanted a new look, and this is what she came up with. I really like it, too. And it's a good thing I do, because I'm going to be eating nothing but peanut butter and jelly sandwiches for the next month and a half."

"That's a new outfit, isn't it?" Pam asked, turning from the sideboard, where she was cutting into the next pie, to look at Willa.

"Yes. Everybody down at the Cut 'n' Curl said my new look wouldn't be complete without a new outfit. I bought it this morning right after I got my hair done."

"It's a gorgeous dress," Hannah said a bit enviously, "and it's perfect for you. Claire has something like it down at *Beau Monde*."

"Not anymore. I bought it."

Hannah was surprised. Clothing at Claire's boutique was expensive, even if you got a good neighbor discount the way she did. And everything Claire carried was classic. Willa's new summer sundress was a throwback to the fifties with a circle skirt and a sleeveless top with a matching bolero jacket. It was made of polished cotton in a gorgeous shade of light coral that Hannah wished she could wear.

"New hair *and* a new dress?" Pam looked very surprised. "Did you come into some money you didn't tell me about?"

"No. I put this on my credit card, and I'll have my check from the beauty contest organizers before the bill comes in. I really hated to max out my card, but . . . I just had to do it."

Pam cocked her head and gave Willa a scrutinizing look. "There's got to be a man involved," she said. "How about it, Willa?"

"There's *always* a man involved, isn't there?" Willa gave a little laugh.

Hannah could see that Willa was embarrassed. Her cheeks were turning pink. But Pam didn't seem to want to let it go.

"Remember when we went to see Madame Zaar at the school carnival?" she asked Willa.

"Of course." Willa looked a bit relieved, and Hannah could tell she thought that Pam had changed the subject. "I thought

Mrs. Purvis was perfect as a fortune teller."

"It was a great outfit," Hannah agreed. The principal's wife, Kathy Purvis, had looked so different in her costume that hardly anyone had recognized her.

"She predicted that a tall, dark, handsome stranger would come into your life," Pam reminded her with a grin. "I'll have to tell her that she was right."

"She wasn't right. He hasn't come into my life . . . at least not yet."

Hannah watched as the color rose in Willa's cheeks again. She was trying to be flippant, but it was obvious she didn't want to discuss the man in question. To save her the discomfort of further probing by her supervising teacher, Hannah decided to change the subject. "Whoever he is, he's going to love the color of your dress," she said. "I wish I could wear that color, but my dad won't let me."

"Your dad?" Pam looked confused. "But . . . didn't your father die a couple of years ago?"

"He did, but his red hair lives on through me. I can't wear red, pink, maroon, coral, or peach unless I want to cause traffic accidents. I guess I'll just have to eat my heart out. And speaking of eating . . . I'm ready for the next entry. How about you, Willa?"

"I'll be ready just as soon as I fill out this scorecard." Willa filled it out quickly and handed it to Pam. "Okay, I'm ready. What's the next pie?"

"Key lime."

Willa gave a little sigh. "I *love* key lime pie, but I bet it's not made from real key limes."

"Then you lose," Pam said, flipping over the card. "It says so right here . . . key limes, freshly squeezed."

"But are they really?" Willa wanted to know.

"Yes. Here's a letter from the contestant. She says her daughter flew to Mexico on vacation and brought the key limes back with her."

"Mexico?" Willa sounded surprised. "I thought key limes came from Florida."

Hannah shook her head. "Not so much anymore. There are still a few growers down there, but key limes aren't an easy crop to produce. They're susceptible to all sorts of things. They grow much better in Mexico. If you see key limes in a grocery store, that's probably where they're from."

"Here's a photo," Pam said, passing it over to them. "The little ones are key limes, and they're right next to a lemon so you can see how small they are."

"They look like Rainier cherries before they turn color, except they're a little bigger. And I bet they're harder to pick."

"You've seen cherries growing?" Pam turned to look at her in surprise.

"Oh, yes. I learned more about cherries than I ever wanted to know when I was in Washington."

"D.C.?" Hannah asked.

"Washington State. We picked cherries in the Yakima Valley for a couple of weeks. A Rainier cherry is a cross between a Bing cherry and a Van cherry. It was developed at Washington State University over fifty years ago, and the mother tree is still there."

"I've heard of Rainier cherries," Hannah said. "They're sweeter than Bing cherries, aren't they?"

"A lot sweeter. Washington State won't let you sell cherries that aren't at least seventeen brix. The orchard we worked for didn't pick them until they were at least twenty brix."

"Bricks?" Pam asked, looking totally puzzled.

"Brix with an *X*," Hannah explained. "It's a measure of sweetness. Peaches are around thirteen brix."

Pam still looked puzzled. "What were you doing in Washington State?"

"Working. I took some time off and traveled with . . . a friend. And whenever we got low on money, we worked. Can we have that sample now, Pam? I want to see how sweet it is."

"Okay," Pam said, carrying the samples to the table and setting them down. "Let's see if those key limes really make a difference."

Willa looked down at hers and frowned. "Are you sure this is the right pie?"

"It said key lime on the entry form. Why?"

"I saw a lot of key lime pie when I was in Florida. I think it's the state pie, or something like that. But those pies were green."

Pam looked surprised. "You were in Florida, too?"

"Yes. We went down south during the winter and we stayed a while in Florida. Almost every restaurant has it on the menu down there."

"It's supposed to be only as green as key lime juice," Hannah said, examining her slice. The key lime filling under the meringue was yellow with just a hint of green. It was exactly the way key lime pie was supposed to look.

"If you see a slice that's green, the baker used food coloring," Pam told Willa. "Some restaurants do that."

Willa looked thoughtful. "That makes

sense. It's probably so the waitresses can tell at a glance that it's not lemon meringue. The restaurant where I worked had both. I might have mixed them up if the key lime pie hadn't been green."

"This one's a little more yellow than the others I've seen," Hannah said, glancing down at her piece again. "I wonder how many egg yolks she used for the filling?"

Pam flipped the card over to read the recipe. "Two whole eggs plus three yolks. No wonder it looks so yellow."

"I'll bet it's good," Hannah said. "Let's taste."

For a long moment all was silent and then Hannah gave a blissful sigh. "Wonderful!"

"It's real key lime pie," Willa said, licking her lips. "It's not quite as sweet as the one we served, and I like that."

Pam agreed. "I'd say this is almost perfect. And the contestant's made a little note here. She says that if you can't find key limes, you can also make this pie with regular limes. The lime flavor won't be quite as intense, but it'll still be delicious."

"Too bad she didn't bake one with regular limes," Willa said. "I'd like to taste the difference."

Pam went back to the table and picked up three more plates. "She did. This one has regular lime juice."

Again, there was silence as all three of them tasted. Hannah was the first to speak. "She's right. The flavor from the regular limes isn't as tangy, but it's really delicious."

"Agreed." Willa gave a little nod. "I like her crust, too. It tastes like shortbread cookies."

Pam looked up with a smile. "And the meringue is perfect. I'm giving it perfect scores right across the board."

"Me, too," Hannah said, handing over her scorecard.

"I'm with you two." Willa handed in her scorecard. "It's the best pie I've tasted tonight. How many more do we have to go?"

Pam got up to check. "The key lime was the last of the meringue pies. We've already done the one-crust pies with crumb toppings and the one-crust with whipped cream toppings like the pumpkin and the sweet potato."

"Right." Hannah leaned back and took a sip of water. "We did the latticework crust pies, too. The blueberry won, remember?"

"It was good," Willa said. "Usually they're much too sweet. And the first group we tasted was the two-crust fruit pies. Does that mean we're through?"

"Not quite," Pam answered her question.

"We still have to taste the novelty pies."

Hannah began to frown. "Wait a second. Lisa told me that Marge Beeseman entered an apple pie. I don't remember tasting it."

"Neither do I," Willa said. "We tasted five apple pies, and none of them were hers."

Pam glanced down at the packet she'd received from the judging committee, and then she looked up with a frown. "It's on here as a novelty pie."

"Novelty?" Hannah was surprised. "But novelty pies are pies that don't fit into any other category."

"Or pies that have unusual ingredients," Pam reminded her.

Willa thought about that for a moment. "Well, it certainly fits into the two-crust fruit pie category, so it must have an unusual ingredient. Why don't you check the recipe, Pam?"

"I can't. We don't get the novelty pie recipes. They don't want us to know what's in them until we judge them."

"Because if we knew the unusual ingredient, it might prejudice us?" Hannah guessed.

"That's right."

"But what could be *that* unusual?" Willa asked.

"I'm not sure." Pam turned to Hannah.

"Any ideas?"

"Several. Have you ever eaten my Mystery Cookies?"

"Lots of times. I love those cookies," Pam stated.

"They're the best spice cookie I've ever had," Willa echoed the sentiment.

"If I'd told you the mystery ingredient, you might not have tasted them in the first place."

"We already said we love them," Pam said, "and we're not about to change our minds. Right, Willa?"

"You can tell us the mystery ingredient now," Willa said.

"Tomato soup," Hannah said. And when they just sat there stunned, she got up to slice the first novelty pie.

KEY LIME PIE

Preheat your oven to 325 degrees F., rack in the middle position.

THE CRUST:

Make your favorite graham cracker or cookie crumb crust *(or buy one pre-made at the grocery store — I used a shortbread crust.)*

THE FILLING:

5 eggs
14-ounce can sweetened condensed milk
1/2 teaspoon lemon zest *(optional)*★★★★
1/2 cup sour cream
1/2 cup key lime juice★★★
1/4 cup white *(granulated)* sugar
  *** Key limes are difficult to find. If your store doesn't have them, look for frozen key lime juice. If you can't find that, just buy regular limes and juice those.*
  **** If you don't have lemon zest, DO NOT*

142

substitute lime zest, especially from regular limes — it can be very bitter and the little flecks of green aren't very appetizing.

Crack one whole egg into a medium-sized mixing bowl. Separate the remaining 4 eggs, placing the 4 yolks into the bowl with the whole egg and the 4 whites into another mixing bowl. Leave the bowl with the 4 whites on your counter. They need to warm a bit for the meringue you'll make later.

Whisk the whole egg and the egg yolks until they're a uniform color. Stir in the can of sweetened condensed milk. Add the lemon zest, if you decided to use it, and the sour cream. Stir it all up and set the bowl aside.

Juice the limes and measure out 1/2 cup of juice in a small bowl.

Hannah's 1st Note: Key limes aren't easy to juice. They're very small and a regular lime juicer won't work very well. I just roll them on my counter, pressing them down with my palm, until they're a little soft. Then I cut them in half on a plate, (so that I can save any juice that runs out,) hold each half over a measuring cup, and squeeze them with my fingers. It's a little messy, but it works.

Add the 1/4 cup sugar to the key lime

juice and stir until the sugar has dissolved. Now add the sugared lime juice to the bowl with your egg mixture and whisk it in.

Pour the filling you just made into the graham cracker or cookie crust.

Bake the pie at 325 degrees F. for 20 minutes. Take it out of the oven and set it on a rack to wait for its meringue.

DON'T TURN OFF THE OVEN! Instead, increase the oven temperature to 350 degrees F. to bake the meringue.

THE MERINGUE: *(This is a whole lot easier with an electric mixer!)*

4 egg whites *(the ones you saved)*
1/2 teaspoon cream of tartar
a pinch of salt
1/3 cup white *(granulated)* sugar

Add the cream of tartar and salt to the bowl with your egg whites and mix them in. Beat the egg whites on HIGH until they form soft peaks.

Continue to beat at high speed as you sprinkle in the sugar. When the egg whites form firm peaks, stop mixing and tip the bowl to test the meringue. If the egg whites don't slide down the side, they're ready.

Spread the meringue over the filling with a clean spatula, sealing it to the edges of the crust. When the pie is covered with meringue, either "dot" it with the flat side of the spatula to make points in the meringue, OR smooth it out into a dome and make circular grooves with the tip of your spatula from the outside rim to the center, to create a flower-like design.

Bake the pie at 350 degrees F. for an additional 12 minutes.

Remove the pie from the oven, let it cool to room temperature on a wire rack, and then refrigerate it if you wish. This pie can be served at room temperature, or chilled. It will be easier to cut and serve if it's chilled.

(To keep your knife from sticking to the meringue when you cut the pie, dip the blade in cold water.)

Hannah's 2nd Note: Key lime juice is a very pale green color, midway between green and yellow. The eggs and egg yolks added to the filling will color it more yellow than green. If you see a key lime pie that's green inside, the baker added green food coloring.

CHAPTER NINE

They'd tasted three out of the four entries in the novelty pie category, and they were equally divided. Hannah liked the peanut butter cream pie with the chocolate crust the best, Willa preferred the vanilla ice cream pie with caramel sauce, and Pam was intrigued by the four-layer concoction with peach jam, baker's custard, vanilla wafers and M&Ms.

"I can't believe you really like it," Hannah said, once Pam had told them her favorite.

"I can't either, but I think the contestant deserves some sort of consideration for making something completely different."

"Let's see if we can agree on the apple," Willa said, getting up to cut them a sample.

"How does it slice?" Hannah asked.

"Beautifully. And it maintains its shape on the plate."

"It looks good," Pam said when Willa had

brought their plates. "And it smells wonderful!"

"Cinnamon, lemon, and . . . nutmeg?" Hannah did her best to identify the scents for them. "Pass me those coffee beans, will you?"

Pam passed over the canister of coffee beans the head judge at the rose competition had given them. He'd told Pam that sniffing coffee beans or freshly ground coffee between other scents refreshed the nose.

"Does that actually work?" Willa wanted to know.

"It seems to," Hannah answered her. "That third scent is definitely nutmeg. I can smell it now."

Again the room was silent as Hannah and her companions tasted Marge's pie. Pam took a sip of water and tasted again. "I'd say the spices are perfect."

"Agreed," Willa said, "and the crust is flaky and a little sweet. I like that."

Hannah gave a little sigh. "I'd be happier if the apples had a little more texture, but other than that, it's a winner."

"So you think it takes the novelty pie category?" Pam asked.

"Yes," Hannah said.

"Definitely," Willa agreed. "It's even better than my grandmother's pie, and that's going some."

"So it takes first in the category?" Both Willa and Hannah nodded, and Pam held out her hand for their score sheets. "Okay. We've got the winners in all categories. Now all we have to do is tally the scores, pick the best pie of them all, and we're through."

With Willa on the calculator and Hannah reading the scorecards aloud, it didn't take long to tally the results. The Key Lime Pie took first prize overall, Marge's apple pie took second, and a delicious pineapple custard pie took third.

Once the goodies were divided, the three judges headed for the door. Pam went to hand in the master scorecard, and Hannah and Willa lingered at the top of the steps.

"Are you sure you don't want this?" Hannah asked, glancing down at the Key Lime Pie she was carrying. "I know you loved it, and it's not like I need it or anything."

"I'd love to take it, but I'm not going straight home. I have to meet someone and I don't know how long that'll take."

"Okay," Hannah said, glad that she'd asked and even gladder that Willa hadn't taken the pie. Michelle had a date with Lonnie, and she'd share it with them when they got back to the condo. "See you tomorrow, then."

"Yes. Tell Michelle . . ." Willa stepped a little closer and lowered her voice. "Tell her that I hope she wins. She's the nicest of all the contestants. Of course I can't say that directly to her."

"I understand." Hannah smiled as Willa walked away. It seemed the youngest Swensen sister had made another friend. She could hardly wait to tell Michelle that Willa was pulling for her.

"Hannah?" a voice called out.

Hannah turned to look and she gave a little wave as she saw Lisa and Herb walking through the crowd of 4-H kids hanging around the entrance to their building. "I didn't know you'd be at the fair tonight."

"We came with Marge and Dad," Lisa explained. "I know you probably shouldn't tell us, but how did Marge's pie do?"

"I shouldn't tell you, but the results will be posted tomorrow morning, so it doesn't really make any difference. It took second place."

"Fantastic!" Lisa did a little high-five with Herb. "Then you must have liked it?"

"It was a really good apple pie."

"But?" Herb caught the hesitation in her voice.

"But . . . I thought the apples were just a bit overcooked. I wish they'd had just a bit more texture."

Hannah watched in amazement as Lisa let out a whoop and dissolved into laughter. Herb laughed right along with her, and then they exchanged another high-five.

"What?" Hannah asked.

"The apples couldn't have more texture," Lisa said, grinning at her.

"Why not?"

"Because . . . they weren't apples!" Herb finished the explanation.

"What?!" Hannah was astounded, and it took her a full minute to recover. When she did, she posed the obvious question. "If they weren't apples, what were they?"

"Soda crackers," Lisa and Herb said in unison. And then they held on to each other and collapsed into gales of laughter again.

Hannah gave them a minute. They were obviously deranged. "Soda crackers?" she asked at last.

"Saltines, to be exact," Lisa told her. "And Marge owes us ten dollars. She thought you'd guess, but you didn't."

Hannah gave a little groan. Both Lisa and Jack had mentioned Lisa's mother's Mock Apple Pie with soda crackers instead of apples, but she'd fallen for it anyway. "Okay. You guys win. I really thought they were apples."

"I think it's the lemon juice," Lisa said, giving her an out. "Mom always said it tickles the taste buds into believing you're eating apples. And the spices help, too."

"Your mother was right. I never suspected that the pie wasn't made from apples."

"I can hardly wait to collect our bet," Herb said, giving Lisa a little hug. Then he turned to Hannah. "Do you want to tell Mom that she won a red ribbon? We're meeting them at the Ferris wheel in five minutes."

Hannah glanced at her watch. It was past nine-thirty, and she had two stops to make before she was through for the night. "You two tell her. It'll be official any minute now. I still have a couple of things left to do and then I'm heading home."

"Did Moishe eat anything yet?" Herb asked her.

"Not much. He crunched a little dry food, but that was it."

"Lisa and I bought this for him." Herb handed her a white plastic bag with the words THANK YOU FOR YOUR PATRONAGE printed on the side in green script.

"What is it?"

"A Paul Bunyan burger," Lisa answered. "We had them leave off the onions and the steak sauce, so it's mostly just meat. It's

151

really good beef, and Herb thought maybe Moishe would eat it if you warmed it up a little in the microwave."

Hannah was touched. It was very sweet of Herb and Lisa to be so concerned about Moishe. "I'll try it on him the minute I get home," she promised. "Thanks from both of us."

After Lisa and Herb had left, Hannah hurried in the opposite direction. She was going to stop by the Lake Eden Historical Society booth to assess the possibility of contracting swimmer's ear during her scheduled stint on the dunking stool. Delores had said the bull's eye was small and difficult to hit, but Hannah wasn't sure she believed her mother. After all, this was the same mother who'd tricked her into donning a frilly dress and sitting on the stool in the first place!

"And here she is now!" Delores called out, as Hannah approached the booth. "Now we can get it right from the horse's mouth."

Hannah felt like giving a loud whinny, but of course she didn't. She might have if she'd known all the customers gathered in front of the counter.

It was obvious that Delores was playing queen bee again. She was dressed in a bright yellow pantsuit that highlighted her perfect figure like a beacon. With her dark, beautifully styled hair, perfect makeup, and a tan that Hannah suspected came from hours under a sun lamp, Delores looked closer to forty than sixty. Norman's mother, Carrie, a plump bleached blonde, appeared to be several decades older in comparison.

"Hi, Mother," Hannah said, stepping up as the crowd miraculously parted for her. It was a little like Moses parting the Red Sea. Hannah almost made a crack about that, but she reminded herself that her mother might make the bull's eye larger if she was upset with Hannah's attitude, so she didn't do that, either.

"We were just talking about the pie judging, dear." Delores reached out to pat the shoulder of a rail-thin woman with lovely white hair. "This is Cora Gruman. She lives across the street from the lady who baked the Key Lime Pie. Did you like it?"

Hannah knew her mother was fishing, but there was no reason not to tell her. "We all liked it . . . a lot. We gave it the blue ribbon."

"Marvelous!" Delores and Cora looked absolutely delighted, just as if they'd baked the pie themselves. "How about second place? Can you tell us that?"

"Marge Beeseman's Mock Apple Pie."

"Mock apple?" Delores looked puzzled. "Is that a new type of fruit?"

Hannah just smiled. "It's a very special pie, Mother. It's Lisa's Mom's recipe, and I'll bake it for you sometime. And a lady from Browerville came in third with her pineapple custard pie. Her first name was Doreen, I think."

"Oh, my!" A heavyset woman with frizzy brown hair began fanning herself with a Lake Eden Historical Society brochure.

"That's her pie," the lady standing next to her explained. "She told me she didn't think it could win because she put in too much pineapple."

Hannah laughed. "That's one of the things we liked about it."

As the ladies wandered off by twos and threes, Hannah walked around the corner of the booth to see precisely what she'd be facing when she assumed the position of dunkee on Saturday afternoon.

Florence Evans, the owner of the Lake Eden Red Owl Grocery, was sitting on the stool. She looked happy enough, and Hannah noticed that her clothing was dry, so perhaps this wouldn't be as bad as she'd thought.

"Hi, Hannah!" Florence greeted her with

a smile. "Want to try to dunk me? Only five dollars for three balls, and it goes to a good cause."

"Sure. Where do I buy the balls?"

"Right around the corner from your mother, or Carrie."

Hannah retraced her steps. Her mother was still knee-deep in conversation with two ladies who hadn't gone to see the posted results of the pie contest, but Carrie was free. Hannah told her she wanted to buy three balls and forked over a five-dollar bill. A moment later, she was standing in front of the target, wondering how close she could come to hitting it.

"Ready, Florence?" she asked.

"I'm ready."

"Okay. I'll give it my best try."

"Make it your second-best try," Florence said with a laugh. "I'm through in twenty minutes, and I'd like to stay dry."

Hannah threw three balls, missing with each by a country mile. "You're still dry," she said when she'd finished.

"And I'm grateful. Did you miss on purpose?"

"No. I've never been any good at pitching balls. And I figured that if I tried to miss, I might just hit the bull's-eye. So I just aimed for it and hoped my natural nonexistent talent would keep you dry."

"Whatever. It worked." Florence looked over Hannah's shoulder and groaned.

Hannah turned around to see a tall, lanky young man approaching. He waved at Florence, and then he went around the corner of the booth. "What's the matter?" she asked Florence.

"That's Bernie Fulton."

Hannah let that sink in, but the light failed to dawn. "Who's Bernie Fulton?"

"He's a pitcher on the Twins farm team. Everybody says they're going to bring him up from triple A by the end of the season. He's pitched three no-no's, and that's practically unheard of."

"No-no's?"

"No runs, no hits."

"Then he's very good!"

"The best." Florence gave another little groan. "He's dunked every single woman volunteer at least once."

"But why?"

"For the publicity. At least that's what he told the other women before he dunked them."

Both Hannah and Florence waited breathlessly. Was Bernie going to do it again, or had he gone on to another booth? A few seconds later, their question was answered as he reappeared, juggling three baseballs in one hand.

"Ready?" he asked Florence.

Florence sighed in resignation. "I'm as ready as I'm ever going to be."

"It's nothing personal. I'm just trying to get publicity so they'll bring me up early. And don't forget that my publicity is your publicity, too. Delores just told me that contributions tripled since they ran that television spot on the sports news last night."

Hannah glanced around. Sure enough, there was Wingo Jones with his cameraman, ready to capture Florence's dunking for the KCOW sports news. "Hang in there, Florence," she said, giving the object of Bernie Fulton's publicity a sympathetic glance. "I'll go get you a towel."

As she hurried around the corner of the booth, Hannah heard three sounds in rapid succession: a thud, a shriek, and a loud splash. Bernie Fulton was impressive. It sounded as if he'd succeeded with his first pitch.

"Take this to Florence, will you, dear?" Delores handed Hannah a fluffy bath towel without being asked, and Hannah got the impression she'd known exactly what was going to happen.

"Thanks." Hannah grabbed the towel and rushed back to Florence to help her dry off. It was only after Florence had resumed her place on the stool and Hannah was walking away that she realized Bernie "No-No" Fulton had called her mother *Delores.*

Hannah's eyes narrowed, and she turned back to give her mother an assessing look. Delores waved and assumed a perfectly guileless smile that didn't fool Hannah for a second. Bernie obviously knew Delores. And Delores knew the evening news crew at KCOW Television, including the sports commentator, Wingo Jones. She'd also expected that Bernie would dunk Florence because she'd had the towel ready and waiting. Was it possible that her mother had set everything up to garner more publicity and more donations for her favorite project?

"Uh-oh," Hannah said with a sigh, turning on her heel and heading off in the direction of the Sinful Pleasures booth. She needed a deep-fried Milky Way, and she needed it now. There was no doubt in her mind that Delores intended to sacrifice every one of her frilly-dressed volunteers, including her eldest daughter, to the huge tank of water that was positioned beneath the dunking stool at the Lake Eden Historical Society booth.

Mock Apple Pie

Preheat oven to 450 degrees F., rack in the center position
Yes, that's four hundred and fifty degrees F. and not a misprint.

Use your favorite piecrust recipe to make enough pastry for an eight-inch double crust pie.★★★

Assemble the following ingredients:

20 salted soda crackers
1/4 to 1/2 cup softened butter
1 1/2 cups cold water
1 1/2 cups white *(granulated)* sugar
3 Tablespoons lemon juice *(freshly squeezed is best)*
1 teaspoon cinnamon
1/2 teaspoon nutmeg
1 1/2 teaspoons cream of tartar

★★★ If you're in a hurry, you can use two frozen pie shells — just thaw them and use one for the bottom and one for the top.

159

Butter the soda crackers, *(I ended up using just a bit over a quarter-cup of butter to do this,)* put the buttered crackers in the saucepan, and break them up into fairly large pieces with a wooden spoon.

Add the water, sugar, lemon juice, cinnamon, nutmeg, and cream of tartar. Give everything a good stir with your spoon and bring the mixture to a boil over medium to high heat on the stovetop.

Once the boil has been reached, turn down the heat and simmer for exactly two minutes.

Set the saucepan aside on a cold burner.

Divide your piecrust dough in half and roll out the bottom crust large enough to line an 8-inch pie plate.

Pour the soda cracker mixture into the lined pie plate and cover it with the top crust. Crimp the edges together. Cut a couple of slits in the top crust to let out the steam while the pie bakes.

Bake the pie at 450 degrees F., for 15 to 20 minutes, or until the top crust is nicely browned.

Cool and serve.

Jo's Note: This pie has fooled everyone every single time I've served it!

Lisa says she likes this pie best with vanilla ice cream. Herb prefers it with cinnamon ice cream. Lisa's dad likes to accompany it with a slice of sharp cheddar. Herb's mom likes hers with sweetened whipped cream.

CHAPTER TEN

Hannah set her Key Lime Pie down on the counter and waited until Ruby had finished waiting on three giggling girls and an overweight man who kept glancing over his shoulder.

"Hi, Hannah," Ruby said when everyone had left. "Are you ready to try that candy bar yet?"

"I'm ready. I need a dose of carbs and chocolate."

"What's wrong?"

Hannah gave a deep sigh. There was no doubt in her mind that she'd be getting a dunking in the historical society booth on Saturday. "I just found out that my mother set me up again."

"I'm sorry to hear that. And I can understand why you need something to cheer you up. Did you decide which candy bar you want to try first?"

"First?" Hannah gave a little laugh. "I like

the way you think, Ruby! I'll have the deep-fried Milky Way and then, if I can still waddle, I'll have . . ." Hannah stopped in midorder as she heard someone call her name. "Oh no! Not again!"

"This one's real cute," Ruby said, glancing over Hannah's shoulder. "Tall and handsome with a great body on him. If he doesn't work out, I'll be surprised."

Hannah turned around and put a smile on her face. "Oh, he works out, all right. He's got a minigym at his apartment complex, and there's a full one out at the sheriff's department."

"Bet he looks good in his dress uniform."

"Oh, yes," Hannah said, and turned to greet Mike. "Hi, Mike. Meet Ruby. She runs the most intriguing booth on the midway."

"I can see that." Mike glanced up at the sign that said Sinful Pleasures and gave a little chuckle. "Hi, Ruby. How's business?"

"Very good, thank you. The deep-fried Milky Ways are the big seller tonight."

Mike turned to Hannah. "Were you going to order one?"

"Of course she wasn't," Ruby covered for her. "Hannah was curious about the batter, that's all. How about you? Would you like one? It's on the house."

Mike shook his head. "I'd love to, but I gained a pound last week and I have to watch it."

A pound. He'd gained a pound and he was already dieting. Hannah gave a little laugh.

"What's so funny?" Mike asked, turning to her.

"You gained one pound and you're already dieting?"

"That's right. I figure it's like clearing the highways in the winter. They call out the plows when it starts to snow, because if they wait for it to pile up, it's a lot harder to get rid of."

Ruby looked interested. "So you don't want your weight to pile up?"

"Exactly right. If I gain a pound, I take it off before it can turn into two or three. I like to get a jump on it, you know? That's one of the reasons I weigh myself every morning."

"I see," Hannah said, settling for one of the most noncommittal comments she could make and squelching the urge to haul back and slap the face she found so incredibly attractive. She didn't start worrying about her weight until she gained at least five pounds. And since weighing in was such an ordeal, she'd been known to read the scale by peeking through her fingers, a technique left over from childhood for watching scary movies.

"So that would be a no on the deep-fried candy bar, then?" Ruby asked, winking at Hannah.

"Right. They do look good, though. And thanks a lot for the offer." Mike turned back to Hannah. "I need to talk to you."

"Officially or unofficially?"

"Officially."

"Then you're working?"

"I didn't even have time to get home before they called me in again."

"That sounds like something big."

"Big enough." Mike took her arm and walked her over to one of the unoccupied food tables. "There was a break-in at the Great Northwestern Rodeo and Carnival office."

Hannah sat down and unleashed the questions that flashed through her mind. "Somebody broke in? When did it happen? Was anybody hurt? Did they steal something, or was it vandalism?"

"If you get me a cup of coffee, I'll tell you all about it," Mike said, sliding into a seat across from Hannah. "I'd do it myself, but I'm beat."

It was rare that Mike asked for help, and

Hannah was up in a flash. She got two Styrofoam cups of coffee from the corn dog booth and carried them back to the table. "Here you go, Mike."

"Thanks. You probably just saved my life." Mike took a swig and made a face. "This coffee is worse than the stuff at the station."

"Do you want me to try another booth?"

"No. I just need it to wake up, and it's strong enough to do the trick. Sit down and I'll tell you about the break-in."

"I'm listening," Hannah said, sitting back down and leaning forward across the table.

"The secretary, Miss Vincent, locked up at six. That's routine. It's when the office closes every night."

"And all the employees know that?"

"Not just the employees. The hours are posted on a sign outside the door. She's new at the job, but she's been with the show for over a year. Before she took over as secretary, she worked at the ticket booth."

"Then she travels with the company?"

"Yes." Mike gestured toward the group of motor homes and trailers that were parked in the vacant lot behind the grove of trees. "It's the blue one just to the left of that arc light."

"I see it," Hannah told him, spotting it through the branches of the trees.

"Anyway, she got to her trailer at six-thirty, fished around for her keys to unlock the door, and realized that she'd left them in her center desk drawer at the office."

"So she went back to the office?"

"That's right. She got back there at a quarter to seven, but she didn't go in. She noticed that one of the windows on the side of the door was broken, and she did the smart thing. She walked to the gate and had them call for a security guard. That was . . ." Mike paused to flip open his notebook and refer to the notes he'd taken. "Mr. Roland Weiss. He's a retired Winnetka County Deputy. Mr. Weiss unlocked the door with his master key and went in to assess the situation, but the burglar was long gone."

Hannah caught Mike's use of the term. "You said *burglar.* What was missing?"

"Money. The cash box was full when Miss Vincent left. It had all the entrance fees for the rodeo contests, the gate receipts from yesterday and this afternoon, and the midway receipts. All told, it was over ten thousand dollars."

Hannah's mouth formed a silent **O** of surprise. "That's a lot of money," she said.

"I know, and it's all in untraceable cash. It would have been even more, but she'd already paid the hourly workers for the day."

"Where was it kept?"

"In the bottom right-hand drawer of Miss Vincent's desk. The drawer was locked, but the burglar pried it open."

"Then he knew it was there?"

"That's my assumption. Either that or he just got lucky. He didn't bother trying to open the cash box. That was also locked. He just took it with him."

Hannah shut her eyes and went over the information Mike had given her. One thing stood out. "You said Miss Vincent had yesterday's receipts. Why didn't she take them to the bank?"

"Their bank doesn't have branches here in Minnesota. They usually deposit the funds with a wire transfer, but the secretary's new and she didn't know how to do it. The owner was supposed to walk her through it this afternoon, but something came up and he couldn't get away."

"What came up?"

"I don't know. I'll find out as soon as I talk to him." Mike stopped speaking and stared at her. "Your eyes just opened wide and now you're frowning. Why?"

"Just a thought. If I were you, I'd want to find out what came up to keep the owner from transferring the money. And then I'd want to know if whatever it was could have been done deliberately to delay him."

"We're on the same wavelength. I figure maybe somebody wanted to make sure the owner didn't get that wire transfer done. And if I can find out who that someone is, chances are we've got our burglar."

Hannah was silent for a moment, and then she thought of another question. "You're sure the burglary took place between six and a quarter to seven?"

"We're positive. What's the matter? You're doing it again."

"Doing what?"

"Widening your eyes and then frowning. What is it this time?"

"You said Miss Vincent left the office at six and got to her trailer at six-thirty. Is that right?"

"That's right."

"And then you said that when she went back to the office to get her keys, she arrived at a quarter to seven."

"Right again."

"Well, that's fifteen minutes faster for Miss Vincent's return trip. So where did she stop on her way home?"

"Very good!" Mike reached over to pat her hands. "I should have known you'd pick up on that. Miss Vincent stopped right here at the food court for a Paul Bunyan burger.

She had them bag it, and she carried it back to her trailer."

"Okay."

Mike scratched his head as he stared at Hannah. "Hold on. You just widened your eyes and frowned again. What's wrong this time?"

"It's the Paul Bunyan burger!"

"But I checked it out. They remember putting one in a takeout bag for her."

Hannah shook her head. "Not Miss Vincent's Paul Bunyan burger. I was talking about *my* Paul Bunyan burger. Lisa and Herb gave me one for Moishe, and I left it at the Lake Eden Historical Society booth."

No sooner had the words left Hannah's mouth than the lights began to flicker on and off. It was the five-minute warning, the signal to let fairgoers know that their evening of fun was drawing to a close and the fair was about to shut down for the night.

"You're going to go back and get it?" Mike guessed, a pretty safe assumption since Hannah was now standing and she'd picked up her shoulder bag.

"I'd better see if it's still there. If I don't, Lisa and Herb will be very disappointed."

Mike gave what sounded to Hannah like an exhausted sigh. "Do you want me to go with you?" he asked.

Hannah thought about taking him up on his offer. She wasn't relishing the idea of bucking traffic and heading into the midway when most people were heading out, and Mike could clear a path for her. But then she remembered that he was pulling a double shift. He really did look as if he could use a couple of minutes' rest.

"I'll be fine," she said.

"Okay, but you'd better hurry," Mike said, yawning widely. "There's a bench right outside the gate. I'll wait for you there to make sure they don't lock you in. Do you want me to take that bakery box with me?"

"No, that's okay. I'll be back in a jiffy." Hannah reached out to scoop up the box with her Key Lime Pie. It was safer to take it with her. Mike was so tired he might cushion his head on the top of the box and fall asleep in the prizewinning pie.

CHAPTER ELEVEN

Hannah felt a bit like a salmon swimming upstream as she headed for the Lake Eden Historical Society booth. It was never easy bucking a crowd. Everyone seemed to be streaming toward the exit in a giant wave. She doubted that the bag with Moishe's Paul Bunyan burger was still where she'd left it, but she had to find out.

"Excuse me," Hannah said, resisting the urge to elbow three high school boys walking with their girlfriends six abreast. But they didn't even notice her, so Hannah stepped aside to let them past. This happened more times than she could count as she treaded water in the sea of humanity and darted forward against the surge of boisterous fairgoers whenever she saw an opening.

"Aren't you leaving?" someone shouted out, and Hannah turned to see Carrie passing her.

"Yes, in a second. Did I leave . . ." Hannah's voice trailed off. It was too late. Carrie had passed her in the opposite direction, and she couldn't possibly hear Hannah's question.

" 'Bye, dear," Delores hailed her. Hannah's mother and her two companions, Bernie "No-No" Fulton and Wingo Jones, were being carried along on the tide of people heading for the turnstile at the exit. If there'd been any doubt in Hannah's mind about the identity of the person who'd contacted the Triple A pitcher and invited him to visit the dunking booth, it was now erased.

" 'Bye, Mother," Hannah shouted back. No sense in asking Delores if her takeout burger bag was still at the booth. Her mother was already several booth-lengths away and there was no way Hannah could make herself heard over the din of the crowd.

Hannah considered her options. It was obvious that the Lake Eden Historical Society booth was closed since she'd seen both her mother and Carrie leaving. Finding the bag with Moishe's burger was unlikely, but she'd come this far despite the aggravation of opposing human traffic, and she might as well finish her quest.

She made good progress for several more feet, and then things came to a standstill. There was no way she could paddle upstream any longer. Hannah accepted the inevitable and moved laterally, heading for a handy booth where she could wait out the rush.

The Tri-County Dairy booth beckoned, and Hannah flattened herself against the shuttered front. She found an anchor of sorts, a giant milk bottle carved from wood and painted white. She held on as the crowd surged past her, hoping that no one would bump into her and knock her from her spot. She'd wait until the foot traffic had thinned, and then she'd set out for the historical society booth again.

Over the next several minutes, Hannah called hello to at least two dozen people she knew and the lights flickered several more times. At last the crowd thinned out, and Hannah set off for her mother's booth. It didn't take long to get there, and she met only one or two people walking rapidly in the direction of the gate.

By the time Hannah arrived, panting slightly, the lights had flickered on and off again. She was too late. The wooden shutters that served as counters were raised and padlocked shut. Hannah walked around to the side where the dunking stool was located and gave a dejected sigh. These counters were also locked into place, tightly shuttering the booth for the night. She should have known the futility of coming all the way back to the booth. If her mother or Carrie had found the bag when they were closing, they would have thrown it away.

"Trashed," Hannah muttered, wondering how she was going to explain this to Lisa and Herb. But then she realized what she'd said and looked quickly around for the nearest trash container. If no one had emptied the trash yet, Moishe could still be feasting on hamburger tonight.

A fifty-gallon drum painted red and labeled TRASH in big black letters stood only feet from the side of the booth. Hannah set her Key Lime Pie on the ground next to the trashcan, glad that she'd found a bakery box to put it in, and peeked inside the receptacle. There was a white bag right on top, and it certainly looked like the one she'd left on the counter.

Hannah sent up a silent plea for luck and good fortune, and then she opened the bag, hoping that it didn't contain any gross leftovers. She was almost afraid to look, but she did. And then she grinned from ear to ear. There was Moishe's Paul Bunyan burger, still neatly wrapped in waxed paper that was stamped with the green-and-white logo of the Burger Shack.

Hannah tucked the bag inside her shoulder bag and picked up the pie box again. She'd accomplished her mission, and now it was time to get back to the gate to meet Mike before he fell asleep on the bench and someone locked her in for the night.

As she walked, Hannah began to feel uneasy. Everyone else had left, and the only noise was the sound of her own footfalls. The thump of her rubber soles hitting the dirt was deafening in the surrounding silence, and she resisted the urge to tiptoe. There was something very unnerving about being alone on the midway at night.

She was just passing the Family Farms booth when everything went black. Hannah came to a standstill and reached out to steady herself against the mechanical bull. Rather than just a saddle and a mechanism that bucked and swiveled, this bull looked like a real Brahma bull and cost five dollars to ride.

For a moment Hannah just stood there gripping the bull's ear, feeling ever more apprehensive and wondering how she was ever going to find her way to the gate in the darkness. There were occasional flashes of heat lightning way off in the distance, but that provided no real illumination. She could hear a low rumbling, barely audible. Thunder? Whatever it was, it added to Hannah's growing apprehension.

She told herself not to panic. She'd just wait for her eyes to adjust and pick her way to Mike, lifting her feet high so she wouldn't trip over any ropes or cables. She was about to set out when there was a hollow clunk, as if someone had thrown the lever on a transformer, and a long string of dim lights went on overhead.

If Hannah hadn't been so nervous, she might have chided herself for borrowing trouble. Of course they had night-lights on the midway. It was a safety precaution, and it probably served to discourage kids from climbing the fence and sneaking in after hours.

Although the lighting was by no means bright, she could make out the rectangles of the shuttered booths and the looming, almost menacing shapes of the carnival rides. Hannah shivered even though the night was hot, and her skin felt slick with moisture. It wasn't good being here alone. It wasn't good at all.

As she made her halting way forward, Hannah kept to the center of the path, her eyes scanning the shadows for movement. Every bad horror movie she'd ever seen flashed through her mind, and she thought about what she might use for a weapon if someone, or something, emerged from the darkness. There was her shoulder bag. It was heavy enough to knock someone off balance, especially if she swung it in an arc. The Key Lime Pie she was carrying could be used to render someone temporarily blind. It was a terrible waste of a first-place-winning dessert, but if push came to shove, she wouldn't hesitate to use it. If she took it out of the box and shoved the sticky meringue directly in an assailant's face, it would take him a minute or so to wipe it from his eyes. By that time, she'd be well on her way to the gate to alert Mike.

Hannah walked on, but her mind was in turmoil. The old adage against borrowing trouble was warring with the advice to be prepared. The Boy Scout motto won, hands down. She stopped at the next trash can she passed and removed the pie, tossing the bakery box on top of the refuse the evening's fairgoers had left behind them.

Now she had a purse and a pie to use in her defense. Hannah gave a little sigh. Somehow that didn't seem like much. For the very first time in her life, she wished that she were wearing a pair of Andrea's stiletto-heeled shoes. Then she could slip one off and do real damage to anyone or anything that threatened her. Of course that was silly. If she'd been wearing a pair of her sister's stilettos, she wouldn't be in this position in the first place. There was no way she could walk in heels that high, much less fit into shoes that were four sizes too small for her.

She'd just passed the Tri-County Volunteer Fire Department's Red Hot Ringtoss booth when she heard a noise that couldn't be explained by the nonexistent wind or any small furry creature that made the fairgrounds its home. It was the sound of something heavy striking something composed of flesh and bone. Hannah wasn't sure how she knew that, but she did. And her blood ran cold.

"Is someone there?" she called out before she'd had time to consider the wisdom of speaking. And then she did, and she wished she could call back her words. Now the person who'd struck the blow she'd heard knew that he wasn't alone on the midway. And he also knew approximately how far away and in which direction she was.

Open mouth, insert foot, Hannah thought, but she didn't stand still to think about it.

She knew she had to get away fast, and that's exactly what she proceeded to do. But as she scurried away, her brain wasn't idle. She was almost certain the sound she'd heard had come from a booth across the path and around the corner, no more than three booths from where she'd been standing. If she remembered the layout of the midway correctly, that was where the shooting gallery was located.

But it hadn't been a gunshot. Hannah was sure of that. She tried to forget about the heavy object striking flesh and bone and considered what other things might produce a sound like it. It could have been someone kicking a hollow rubber ball with considerable force. Or someone striking a ripe melon with a baseball bat. Or a sledge hammer hitting . . . Hannah gave a little shiver. She didn't want to think about this now. Whatever it was, it was ominous. Right now she had to get as far away from the shooting gallery as possible!

Heart pounding hard and her senses on full alert, Hannah scuttled down the line of booths, keeping to the shadows and doing her best to move quickly, carefully, and silently. One misstep and he'd know where she was. She'd just reached the end of the row of booths when she heard a second thunk. Whoever it was hadn't moved, and that meant he hadn't heard her. Hannah took advantage of the moment to dart around the corner, putting even more distance between them.

She was at the side of the Strong Man booth, where fairgoers could win a Strong Man badge if they pounded a mallet onto a metal bed with enough force to make a ball scoot all the way up the vertical shaft to ring the bell at the top. Hannah took refuge behind several bales of hay placed there as a makeshift barrier to keep observers from getting too close to the prospective Strong Man and the mallet.

All was silent, perfectly silent. Hannah resisted the urge to slap at a mosquito that landed on her cheek and remained motionless. She crouched there for long minutes that seemed like hours, wondering if whatever or whoever she'd heard could hear her breathing or the rapid beating of her heart.

Was it safe to move yet? Hannah wasn't sure, so she didn't. Instead she swiveled her head slowly, examining her surroundings and committing every shape and shadow to memory. Mike had taught her that trick not long after they'd first met. He said cops on a stakeout got tired after a while and thought they saw things that weren't there.

He examined everything at the start so that his mind would sound an internal alarm if anything in his visual pattern changed.

As Hannah huddled there, trying to make as small a configuration as possible, her mind spun through the possibilities. Someone was here on the deserted midway with her. The noise she'd heard proved that. She didn't think it was another late fairgoer rushing toward the exit and tripping over a rope or a stake. If that had happened, she would have heard groaning or cries for help. She supposed it could have been a carnival worker locking up a little late or coming back to secure something or other he'd forgotten. But if it had been a carnival worker, he would have answered her when she called out. This person was up to no good. His silence proved that.

Hannah drew her breath in sharply. The Strong Man mallet was gone. When she'd walked past the booth earlier in the day, it had been on a chain next to the vertical shaft. The chain was still there. She could see it on the ground, glistening slightly in the dim glow from the string of lights. Had they locked the mallet inside the booth for the night? Or had someone taken it, used it to hit someone else, and begun the process of bringing it back so that no one would know . . .

And he was here! And it was too late to run! Hannah did what any strong, courageous, modern Minnesota-born woman might have done in the same circumstance. She shut her eyes and attempted to become one with the hay.

Of course it didn't work. There was no way she was going to huddle here waiting for him to find her and whack her with the mallet, too. Not only that, if she did escape his notice, she wanted to be able to give the authorities a good description.

Hannah opened her eyes, inched toward the side of the hay bale, and risked a peek. But the light was too dim. All she saw was a shadowy figure bending over the chain to reattach the mallet. She pulled her head back and listened for the sound of footfalls coming her way. She was almost positive that he hadn't spotted her, not unless he was a sideshow attraction and he had eyes in the back of his head. Still, it was better to be safe than sorry, and she readied the pie for action.

Long moments passed as she listened intently, alert for the slightest sound. She imagined that her ears swiveled independently like little satellite dishes, the way Moishe's ears did when he heard a mouse in the walls. The hair at the base of her neck prickled in apprehension, and she made her breathing shallow and almost inaudible. Except for the far-off sound of a dog barking in a neighboring farmyard, the muted swoosh of cars on the highway, and the faint rumble of thunder in the distance, all was deathly quiet.

And then she heard it. He was moving again. She held the Key Lime Pie in a death grip, ready to hurl it at the slightest provocation, but the sound grew fainter with each passing heartbeat. He was moving away from her, running away from her hiding place. He hadn't seen her! She was safe!

But where had he gone? The moment Hannah thought of it, she stood up and moved to the front of the booth. Her eyes scanned the midway for movement and found none. Had she been too slow? But then she spotted him disappearing around the side of the carousel.

It was safe for her to go now, and Hannah knew what she should do. She should head straight for the gate where Mike was waiting for her. She should tell him what had happened, and he could take over from here on out. He'd hammered that point home often enough. He was the detective, and she was not. The detective was an expert with credentials, and the nondetective should defer to the detective. If she thought something was wrong, she should tell Mike and he would take care of it. Her caution should win out over her curiosity.

Hannah leaned against the booth to let her breathing return to normal and her heartbeats slow to a reasonable rate. The moment she told Mike, he'd turn on the bright lights and investigate. But what if the sounds she'd heard had been perfectly innocent? What if everything was normal and nothing at all was wrong? She'd look like a first-class fool in front of a man she admired and could possibly even love.

There was only one thing to do. Perhaps it was the wrong thing, but that had never stopped her before. Hannah straightened up, stretched to relieve her cramped muscles, and headed off toward the shooting gallery. She'd check it out first, before she raised the alarm. And if she was right and something was wrong, she'd head for the gate and tell Mike immediately.

The sounds seemed magnified as Hannah headed down the row of booths. A slight breeze picked up, and she almost jumped out of her skin as the plastic flags fluttered over the face painting booth. They sounded as loud as the flock of crows that used to land in her grandfather's cornfield, the ones her Grandma Ingrid refused to chase off because she was partial to crows. Hannah's every instinct told her she was heading into trouble and she was likely to discover something she didn't want to find. She knew she should turn tail and run for Mike, but instead she forged ahead, each footstep deliberate and even, drawing her inevitably closer to the shooting gallery. She was like Moishe, who still occasionally pushed the cold water lever in the shower, even though he'd gotten drenched several times in the past.

When she arrived at the shooting gallery, Hannah took a deep breath. She was convinced it would be either or. Either she'd find something horrible, or she'd find nothing at all. In the dim light from the single string of lights high overhead, the teddy bear prizes lined up in rows inside the glass front of the booth seemed to be staring at a point just around the corner. Hannah rounded the corner, stopped short, and felt herself assume the same glassy-eyed stare. Someone was sprawled out in the dirt. It was a woman. Hannah could tell because she was wearing a dress. And she was perfectly motionless.

Hannah's mind spun. This was the time

to go after Mike, but of course she couldn't. What if this poor woman was injured and in need of immediate help? She knew CPR. She could even fashion a tourniquet if she absolutely had to.

Her need to help another human being in trouble drew her forward. The woman was facedown in the dirt, and Hannah was about to reach for her wrist to feel for a pulse when she saw the back of her head. This caused her to step back without taking her pulse or touching her. No aid she could give would make a particle of difference. This woman was quite dead, and Hannah hoped that it had been quick. Blunt force trauma didn't make for a kind demise.

The woman's skirt was pulled up a bit in back, a result of the way she'd fallen, and Hannah reached out to tug it down. It wouldn't make any difference to her now, but there should be dignity in death. And once she'd fixed the woman's skirt and straightened up again, Hannah had an awful realization.

"No!" Hannah gulped. She took one halting step closer and the pie dropped from her nerveless fingers. She'd seen and admired this dress before, no more than an hour ago!

Hannah stared down at the bits of meringue and Key Lime Pie filling that were scattered on the ground. She couldn't just stand here. She had to get moving and go after Mike. He needed to know about this.

"Hannah?"

Mike's voice rang out loud and clear, as if she had summoned him. It was a coincidence, a wonderful coincidence. And if she could only find her voice, she could answer him.

"Where are you, Hannah?"

"Here," Hannah answered, finding her voice at last. Of course her answer wouldn't do him much good. *Here* could mean anywhere. Her one-word answer wasn't descriptive enough.

"Where's here?" Mike asked, and his voice sounded closer.

Hannah had the insane urge to tell him he was getting warmer. It was almost as if they were playing her favorite childhood game, the one where someone leaves the room, the group hides something, the person comes back in, and the group directs them to the hidden object by telling them whether they're warmer or colder.

But this is no game, Hannah's mind told her. *It's all too real, and you have to answer him.* She took a deep breath and did what her mind had suggested. "I'm around the side of the shooting gallery," she said.

"You sound weird. What's the matter?"

Hannah opened her mouth to answer, but she was too busy wondering how he could run and ask questions at the same time. He didn't even sound winded! She certainly couldn't do it, but then she was at least twenty pounds overweight, and she'd been about to add to that total by ordering a deep-fried, cookie-battered Milky Way until he'd caught her standing in front of the booth.

"Hannah? I asked you what was the matter?"

Hannah sighed. He'd be here any second and then he could see for himself. But he'd asked and his question deserved an answer. "Dead," she said.

"Someone's dead?" Mike asked, rounding the corner with the speed of an Olympic hopeful. "Who?"

"Willa Sunquist." Hannah identified the victim for him before her legs gave way and she sank down to the ground to stare back at the glass-eyed teddy bears.

CHAPTER TWELVE

The phrase *through a glass darkly* floated in her mind. Nothing seemed quite real, not even the staring teddy bears or Willa's body lying crumpled only a few feet away. Hannah had the bizarre feeling that she was acting in a movie with no director, and she didn't know what she was supposed to do next.

"Hannah?" Mike's face loomed large, like a pale moon that floated over her. He must be bending down to talk to her. And that brought up a new thought. Why was she sitting on the ground?

"Let me help you up. Can you stand?"

Hannah considered that for long moments. Could she stand? She really wasn't sure. She wouldn't know until she tried, so she held out her hands and let Mike pull her to her feet.

"Yes," she answered, when she was actually standing.

"Yes, what?"

"Yes, I can stand. But I don't know how long."

"You're in shock," Mike said, tipping up her chin and shining his flashlight into her eyes.

"Oh. That explains the movie then."

Mike raised his eyebrows, but he didn't say anything. He just half-carried her over to one of the hay bales and pushed her into a sitting position. Then he stacked up two bales on the other side of her and three behind her so that she couldn't topple off his prickly makeshift chair.

"Nice," Hannah said, wondering how much longer she could have stayed on her feet. Her legs were trembling, and she felt a little dizzy. "It's better than the one-chair-fits-all in the secretary's office."

Mike made a little whooshing sound between his teeth and shook his head. "Just stay right there while I make some calls."

Hannah felt a wave of panic that started in her trembling legs and rose all the way up to her throat. She swallowed hard with a little gulp and tried to slow her rapid heartbeat. "You're not going to leave me, are you?"

"Never. I've got my cell phone. Just try to relax and let me get the crime scene team

191

over here."

Hannah nodded. Or at least she thought she nodded. She didn't seem to be able to completely control her own body. Her legs were still trembling even though she willed them to be still, and she felt terribly cold, so cold that her teeth were chattering. This was probably why each squad car was equipped with a blanket in the trunk. Hannah wished Mike would take his out and cover Willa. Of course he couldn't do that, not until the crime scene team was through. And his squad car wasn't here anyway. It was out in the parking lot.

"Here," Mike said, shrugging out of his sheriff's windbreaker and draping it over her shoulders.

"Thanks," Hannah said gratefully. The jacket was very comforting. It was lined with flannel and it was warm. There was also the fact that it belonged to Mike, and that made her feel warm all over. She pulled it closer around her and glanced down. The Winnetka County Sheriff's Department had adopted the Minnesota state colors, maroon and gold. Mike's windbreaker was no exception. It was maroon, only one shade darker than Reverend Knudson's pickled beets. Hannah imagined how Mike's jacket would look teamed with her red hair, and she started shivering again. "Don't look at me. Maroon's not my best color."

Mike gave a startled bark of laughter, and then he turned back to the phone again. Hannah half-listened as he contacted Doc Knight, the county coroner, and Andrea's husband, Bill, the Winnetka County Sheriff. She was just thinking about Delores and how upset she'd be that her eldest daughter had found another murder victim, when what Mike was saying into the receiver registered in her mind.

"Okay, Norman. Thanks a lot. I'll tell them to let you in."

Norman? In? Hannah wondered what all that was about. "Did you call Norman in to take crime scene photos?" she asked.

"No, I called him in to take you home. I don't want you driving in your condition."

"*What* condition?" Hannah was genuinely puzzled. "I haven't had anything to drink."

"I know that, but you're still in shock and I don't want to take the chance you'll get into an accident on the way home."

"But I'm perfectly capable of driving. And since I've got a valid license and I'm not under the influence of any substance that would negatively affect my driving ability, you can't stop me . . . can you?"

"Oh, yes."

"But how?

"It's simple," Mike said reaching into his pocket and holding up a key ring. "I've got the keys to your truck."

Hannah's mouth dropped open. "You took my keys?"

"Not exactly. I asked you to hand over your purse so I could have your keys, and you did. Don't you remember?"

"No," Hannah said, admitting defeat. Not only had she handed over her purse without question, she hadn't even noticed when he went through it and took out her keys. It was clear that her ladder wasn't reaching all the way to the top, she wasn't playing with a full deck, and she was several cookies short of a baker's dozen. Mike was right, and she was wrong. She was too distracted to drive safely.

"So you're okay with Norman driving you home?"

Hannah was about to nod when she thought of a rejoinder. "I am if *you* are."

Mike laughed. "You're at least halfway back," he said, reaching out to give her a little hug. "For a couple of minutes there, I was worried. It takes some people hours to recover from the shock of finding a victim of a violent crime."

Thanks for reminding me, Hannah said

under her breath.

"What was that?"

Hannah thought fast and then she said, "It's not like it hasn't happened to me before. Do you want to take my statement now?"

"Later. I'll be here for an hour or so, and then I'll drive out to your condo. I'll bring your truck. I can catch a ride back to the station with Norman."

Hannah might have been in shock, but she caught the implication of Mike's words. He didn't want Norman to stay at her condo any longer than he did. One way to ensure that was to arrange it so that both of them left in the same car at the same time.

"Why are you smiling?" Mike asked her.

Hannah considered her words carefully. Everyone, including her mother, always accused her of having no tact. "Oh, I'm just glad you're taking care of everything and all I have to do is ride home," she said, wondering if that qualified her to join the ranks of the tactful.

"He's got it in his mouth," Norman commented, watching Moishe as he passed by the back of the couch in Hannah's living room. "It's just the meat. He left the bun in the kitchen. He's going down the hall and

195

. . ." Norman craned his neck to see. "I think he's carrying it into your bedroom."

Normally Hannah would have been up and running, chasing after her feline so that he couldn't hide the burger under her bed. Tonight it was a different story, and she stayed put. Moishe was showing some interest in food for the first time in three days, and she wasn't about to do anything that might distract him.

"Do you want me to stop him? Or watch to make sure he doesn't drop it somewhere?" Michelle asked.

"Let him go. Maybe he'll eat it if we don't disturb him. It wouldn't hurt to check under your pillow before you go to bed, though."

"Would he put it there?" Norman asked.

Hannah shrugged. "I've found a couple of mouse parts under my pillow."

"Mouse *parts?*" Norman repeated, chuckling. "I don't think I want to know what that means."

They were quiet for a moment. Good smells were coming from the oven. Hannah had decided to bake right after Norman had brought her home. It always relaxed her and made her think more clearly. She'd no sooner slipped the pan in the oven than Michelle had come in from her date with

Lonnie. They'd taken seats in the living room and Hannah had told her the gruesome news.

"I still can't believe she's dead." Michelle shivered slightly. "Who'd want to kill Miss Sunquist?"

"That's what I've been asking myself ever since I found her. How about the girls in the beauty pageant?"

"But everybody adored Miss Sunquist. She was so helpful and nice. I don't think there was a single contestant who didn't like her."

Hannah's senses went on red alert as an interesting array of expressions crossed her youngest sister's face. At first Michelle was perfectly sincere, believing utterly what she'd just said. But then her eyes narrowed slightly, and a frown line appeared between her eyebrows. Her next expression was disbelief as she considered the thought she'd just had. And then there was denial, with just a hint of suspicion that lingered long after the denial had gone.

"What just crossed your mind?" Hannah asked, leaning forward.

"It's probably nothing. And I wouldn't want to get anyone in trouble. It's impossible, anyway. She really wasn't that upset."

"Who wasn't that upset?" Norman asked her.

"One of the other contestants. But I really don't think she'd actually do . . ." Michelle stopped speaking and looked terribly worried.

"She'd actually do *what?*" Hannah jumped in. "This is a murder investigation, Michelle. Somebody killed Willa in cold blood. She didn't pick up that mallet and bash in her own head."

Michelle looked sick. "I know that. But . . ."

"You liked Miss Sunquist, didn't you?" Norman interrupted what was clearly going to be more hedging from Michelle.

"Of course I did!"

Hannah seized the opportunity Norman had presented and took over the argument. "Then you owe it to Willa to tell us anything you think might be relevant to her death. That's *anything,* Michelle. Even if it's just a suspicion."

Michelle thought about that for a moment. "You're right. I don't owe Tasha anything."

"The blonde who wore the emerald green evening gown?" Hannah asked, remembering Michelle's fellow contestant from the first night of competition.

"That's right. She almost got me in trouble by asking me to cover for her. But I couldn't lie to Miss Sunquist, and I told Tasha that."

The oven timer sounded, and Hannah stood up. "Hold that thought. I'm going to get our popovers, and I want you to tell me everything when I get back."

It only took Hannah a moment or two to tip the popovers out of the muffin tins and into a wicker basket that she'd lined with a napkin. She picked up the tray she'd already assembled with fancy butters and jams. She set the basket in the center of the tray and carried everything out to the coffee table in front of the living room couch.

"Those smell really good!" Norman said, smiling at Hannah.

"They *are* good. Andrea got the recipe from Bill's cousin, Bernadette."

"Andrea makes these?" Michelle looked utterly astounded as she stared down at the golden popovers.

"Of course not." Hannah gave a little laugh. All three of them knew that the only cooking Andrea ever did was to microwave frozen dinners. "Andrea gave the recipe to me, and I make them for her whenever she wants them. We have to let them cool for a minute or two, and then we can dig in. And after that, Michelle can tell us everything she knows about Tasha."

BERNADETTE'S POPOVERS

Preheat oven to 450 degrees F., rack in the middle position.

Spray a 12-cup muffin pan with Pam or other nonstick cooking spray. You can also grease them with clarified butter, or lard if you prefer.

Hannah's 1st Note: Before I got this recipe, my popovers always looked as if they'd been run over by Earl Flensburg's tow truck. Now they're high, light, golden brown, and gorgeous.

4 eggs★★★
2 cups milk
2 cups flour (not sifted)
1 teaspoon salt

★★★ If you think your eggs might be too small or too large, you can easily check them by mixing them up in a measuring cup. Four eggs should measure approximately one cup. If

yours don't, adjust by adding more egg or pouring some out.

Hannah's 2nd Note: You should mix this recipe by hand with a whisk. If you use an electric mixer, it will add too much air to the eggs.

Whisk the eggs until they're a light, uniform color, but not yet fluffy. It should take no more than a minute or so.

Add the milk and whisk it in until it's incorporated.

Measure out the flour and dump it in the bowl all at once. Dump in the salt on top of it. Then stir for a moment or two with a wooden spoon until all the flour has been moistened and incorporated. You will still have lumps *(like brownie batter)* but that's fine. In this recipe, you actually want lumps!

Transfer the batter to a container with a spout *(I used a measuring cup.)* Pour the batter into the muffin cups, filling them almost to the top.

Bake at 450 degrees F. for exactly 30 minutes. *(Don't peek while they're baking or they'll fall!)*

When 30 minutes have passed, remove the pan to a cold burner or a wire rack and pierce the top of each popover with a sharp knife to release the steam.

Let the popovers stand in the pan for a

minute or two, and then tip them out into a napkin-lined basket.

Serve with sweet butter, salted butter, fruit butters, jams, jellies, or cream cheese.

Yield: 12 large popovers that everyone will love.

Hannah's 3rd Note: These popovers are also good at room temperature. I haven't done this yet, but I'm going to try filling them with egg salad, tuna salad, or salmon salad. If it works, it'll be a great dish for a brunch.

CHAPTER THIRTEEN

"Willa didn't say anything about disqualifying anyone," Hannah said, breaking open a popover and buttering one side with cashew butter and the other with honey butter.

"That's because she called us all together before the competition started tonight, and we agreed we wouldn't tell anyone the details. All we were supposed to say was that Tasha was no longer in the competition." Michelle looked a bit guilty. "I guess I'm breaking my promise."

"You made that promise when Willa was still alive. Circumstances have changed," Norman pointed out.

Hannah took a bite of her popover, gave a little sigh of contentment, and took a sip of coffee. "Okay. Tell us everything you know, Michelle."

"Tasha was thirty minutes late for the miniature garden show at the Ag-Hort Building on the first afternoon. She told

Miss Sunquist that her car broke down, but she told me that she was talking to her boyfriend in the parking lot and she lost track of time."

Hannah thought back to what Willa had told them about the grounds for disqualification. "Just being late once wouldn't be enough to do it, would it?"

"No. There were other things, too. We weren't supposed to use bad language while we were wearing our badges. Miss Sunquist explained why. But Tasha swore a couple of times backstage at the evening gown competition, and I know she got marked off for it."

"That's all?" Norman asked.

"I haven't gotten to the final thing yet," Michelle said, giving a little sigh. "I feel like a snitch, but that's not important, is it?"

"Not really." Hannah was glad her sister had her priorities straight. "Your feelings aren't the issue here. Willa's death is."

"Tasha was a no-show at the quilting demonstration this afternoon. She would have gotten another chance if she'd just been late, but she missed the whole event and she didn't call in to explain or anything. Miss Sunquist was really worried about her."

"When did she show up?" Hannah asked

the pertinent question.

"At six. Her boyfriend dropped her off for the swimsuit competition. And when Miss Sunquist asked Tasha why she wasn't at the quilting demonstration, she said she just didn't feel like sitting there for an hour and watching someone sew. Tasha didn't give Miss Sunquist a choice. She had to disqualify her."

"And Tasha was upset about being disqualified?" Norman guessed.

"Not really. I think she didn't show up on purpose so she'd get kicked out. I helped her pack up her things, and she told me she didn't want to be in the competition anyway."

"Do you think that was just sour grapes?" Norman asked.

"And you don't think that was bravado on her part?" Hannah added.

"No to both of you. She said she'd rather spend the time with her boyfriend, and I believe her. She never acted thrilled with the contest, not even when she took second in the evening gown competition."

"Then why did she enter in the first place?" Hannah wanted to know.

"She didn't. She told me her father filled out the entry form and sent it in. Tasha's only seventeen, so a parent can do that."

"I hear that happens a lot," Norman commented, knowing full well that Delores had signed the entry form for Michelle.

"I guess it does." Michelle gave a little laugh. "But I really don't mind being in the contest. It's kind of fun, in a way. And Lonnie *wants* me to be in the contest. He's the one who suggested it to Mother. Tasha's boyfriend thinks it's a waste of time."

"Even with that cash prize?"

"Tasha said he doesn't care about that. He wouldn't get any of the money anyway. Neither would she. Since she's underage, it would go to her father."

Hannah exchanged glances with Norman. Her glance meant, *Sounds like a motive for murder to me.* And his glance replied, *Sure does.*

"What's Tasha's last name?" Hannah asked.

Michelle was silent for a long moment, and then she gave a little shrug. "I don't think I ever heard it. Miss Sunquist called us by our first names, and that's all we had on our ID badges. Hers said Princess Tasha. I can probably find out for you, though. One of the other girls said she went to school with Tasha."

"Great. Ask around tomorrow and let me know right away."

"Does this mean you're not going to tell Mike about Tasha?"

Hannah thought about that for a split second, and then she shook her head. "All we have is her first name. There's no sense bothering Mike until we have more information to give him."

"And besides, you want to check out Tasha and her father by yourself," Michelle said.

"And present it to him as a *fait accompli*," Norman added.

"So you can prove you're a better detective than he is." Michelle gave her oldest sister a knowing smile.

Hannah laughed. They knew her too well to swallow the altruistic spin she'd attempted to put on it, and she'd better admit that it was true. "You're right. Now mum's the word. Mike ought to be here any minute. You both need to remember that for tonight, Tasha and her father belong to me."

"Here you go, Mike." Hannah carried out a piping hot basket of popovers and a refreshed tray of jams and fancy butters. "Just give them two minutes or so to cool and help yourself."

"You don't know what this means to me," Mike said, looking at her with what some people might call adoration. "I didn't have lunch, and once they called me in, I didn't have time for dinner."

"You could have had a deep-fried candy bar," Hannah couldn't resist saying.

"I know. I probably should have. When I'm working this hard I burn a lot of calories. But I just couldn't do that to my body."

"Right," Hannah said, watching him break open a popover and lather on both honey butter and peach jam.

"You ought to make these down at The Cookie Jar," Mike said, after his first bite. "They're great!"

Hannah just smiled. The complexity of serving piping hot popovers at The Cookie Jar for anyone who ordered them was ridiculous. But she was pleased that Mike liked them. It was a compliment.

"Hey, Norman," Mike hailed his rival for Hannah's affections. "Why aren't you having any popovers?"

"Because this is the second batch. And Michelle and I ate the first batch almost single-handedly. I might have one, though."

"Help yourself. I can't eat them all." Mike turned to Hannah again. "I thought you'd like to know that Doc Knight said death was almost instantaneous. The second blow was just window dressing."

Some window dressing! Hannah thought. She could have done just fine without hearing that. "So why did he do it?"

"To make sure she was dead?" Norman guessed.

"Bingo!" Mike pointed his finger at Norman and nodded. "The perp needed the comfort of overkill."

Hannah made a face that neither of the two men saw. Their conversation was gruesome. And they were still eating. How could they *do* that?

"Popover?" Mike held out the basket to her.

"No thanks." Hannah swallowed hard. It was a human being they were talking about here, someone she'd known and liked.

"Anything else you learned from Doc Knight?" Norman asked, reaching for the orange butter.

"Like what?" Mike broke open another popover and glopped on the raspberry jam. Then he passed the honey butter to Norman. "Try some of this, too. The butters are good together."

"Thanks, don't mind if I do. How about defensive wounds. Did she see he was trying to kill her and try to stop him?"

"Doc didn't think so," Mike said, wiping his mouth with a napkin. "She broke her right wrist, but he thinks it was the way she fell and not an attempt to defend herself." He turned to Hannah. "The victim was right-handed, wasn't she?"

"Yes," Hannah forced out her answer. How could he call Willa a *victim* so callously? They were discussing a real live person, at least she'd been alive earlier this evening, and there was something very wrong about going into details while they stuffed their faces.

"Doc thinks it was a man," Mike said. "Unless you know any woman who can lift a twenty-five pound mallet, bring it up over her shoulders, and smash open the head of a victim who was over five and a half feet tall, it had to be a man."

Hannah swallowed hard again. No way she could ask another question. Didn't Mike realize that she'd worked with Willa, laughed with Willa, and considered herself Willa's friend?

"Was there any maxillary damage?" Norman asked, looking much too interested to suit Hannah.

"Doc said it was extensive." Mike took another popover, broke it open, and infused it with strawberry jam. "A couple of her teeth were smashed."

"Which ones?"

"I don't know. I think Doc said it was thirteen and fourteen." He turned to Hannah. "Gee, these are good, Hannah."

Norman mulled it over. "It takes a heavy blow to smash a healthy bicuspid and a molar."

"Doc Knight thought her teeth were in pretty good condition, but he wants to consult with you."

"He does?" Norman looked very pleased. "I could drive out to the hospital now if he wants me to examine the teeth. And if the left side is intact, we could experiment with thirteen and fourteen's counterparts, three and four, to see how much force . . ."

"Out!" Hannah said, standing up and pointing toward the door. She'd had it with talk of victims, and crushed skulls, and broken wrists, and smashed teeth. This was a travesty! It was right that Mike did his job. That was a given. And it was right that Norman helped him if he could. But this wasn't how she wanted to mourn Willa!

"What?" Mike looked at her, utterly astounded. "You're asking us to leave now?"

"Yes! You're ghouls, both of you! You're talking about Willa as if she's just a . . . a *body!* She was more than that. She was pretty, and nice, and . . . and she was my friend!"

"I'm sorry, Hannah." Norman was the first to speak. "I didn't realize we were being so callous. I really do apologize."

Norman reached out to put his arm around her, but Hannah moved out of reach. No way she was going to make up with either of them right now. "Leave," she said, still pointing to the door.

"Okay. 'Nuff said." Mike stood up and looked down at the basket of popovers. "Is it okay if I take the rest of these?"

"Out!" Hannah shouted and clamped her mouth shut. The phrases that were running through her mind right now were far from complimentary.

"I'll call you tomorrow," Norman said, opening the door and stepping out. "I'm really sorry I was so insensitive."

Mike followed right behind Norman. When he cleared the doorway, he turned around to say, "Yeah. Sorry about that, Hannah."

When the door had closed behind them, Hannah shut her eyes for a moment and let the silence soothe her. Then she walked over to throw the deadbolt and double lock the door.

Something warm and furry rubbed against her ankles, and Hannah looked down to see Moishe. He must have sensed that she was upset and left Michelle's warm bed and the allure of his favorite butterfly coverlet to come out and comfort her.

Hannah scooped him up and buried her nose in the soft fur on the back of his neck. "Thanks, Moishe. You're a perfect roommate. You always come around when I need you, and you never say anything to make me mad."

"Rowwwwwr," Moishe gave a soft little yowl of acknowledgment. And then he turned his head and licked her nose. Hannah was so surprised, she came dangerously close to dropping him. She knew he loved her, but he wasn't this affectionate very often.

"Time for some shuteye," she said, carrying him off to her bedroom and placing him on the special goose-down pillow she'd bought especially for him. "Remind me of this in the morning in case I forget, but I think I just found out why I shouldn't marry either one of them."

Fancy Butters for Popovers

Hannah's 1st Note: Make these fancy butters the day before you plan to serve them. Take them out of the refrigerator an hour before serving.

Cashew Butter:

1/2 cup softened butter *(1 stick, 1/4 pound)*
2 Tablespoons *(1/8 cup)* finely chopped cashews *(measure AFTER chopping)*

Soften the butter and place it in a small mixing bowl.

Chop the cashews *(salted or unsalted — it doesn't really matter)* in a food processor with the steel blade until they're as close to a paste as you can get them. *(If you don't have a food processor, you can grind them in a food mill, chop them by hand and then crush them with a mortar and pestle, or grind them in a blender.)*

Measure 2 Tablespoons of crushed or finely chopped cashews. Mix the cashews with the butter, scrape the mixture into a small serving bowl, cover with plastic wrap, and refrigerate. When you uncover the bowl, place one perfect cashew on top of the cashew butter so everyone will know what it is.

Honey Butter:

1/2 cup softened butter *(1 stick, 1/4 pound)*
1 Tablespoon honey

Soften the butter and place it in a small mixing bowl.

Add the honey and stir until well blended. Scrape the mixture into a small serving bowl, cover with plastic wrap, and refrigerate.

Hannah's 2nd Note: I usually make a double batch of honey butter because everyone loves it so much.

Almond Butter:

1/2 cup softened butter *(1 stick, 1/4 pound)*
1 Tablespoon finely chopped or crushed blanched almonds *(measure AFTER chopping or crushing)*
1/2 teaspoon almond extract

Chop the blanched almonds in a food processor with the steel blade until they're as close to a paste as you can make them.

(If you don't have a food processor, you can grind them in a food mill, chop them by hand and then crush them with a mortar and pestle, or grind them in a blender.)

Measure 1 Tablespoon of crushed or finely chopped almonds. Mix the almonds with the butter.

Add the almond extract and mix well.

Scrape the mixture into a small serving bowl, cover with plastic wrap, and refrigerate. When you uncover the bowl, place one perfect almond on top of the almond butter so everyone will know what it is.

DATE BUTTER:

1/2 cup softened butter *(1 stick, 1/4 pound)*
8 pitted dates, finely chopped
1 teaspoon flour

Cut the dates into three pieces with a sharp knife and place them in the bowl of a food processor. Sprinkle them with flour and chop them with the steel blade until they're as finely chopped as you can make them. *(You can add a little more flour if they stick together too much.)* If you don't have a food processor, you can try this with a blender, or chop them with a sharp knife by hand.

Mix the chopped dates with the butter,

scrape the mixture into a small serving bowl, cover with plastic wrap, and refrigerate. When you uncover the bowl, place one pitted date on top of the date butter so everyone will know what it is.

Orange Butter:

1/2 cup softened butter *(1 stick, 1/4 pound)*
1 Tablespoon frozen orange juice concentrate
1 teaspoon orange zest*** *(optional)*
  *** *Orange zest is finely grated orange peel — only the orange part, not the white part.*

Measure out one Tablespoon of frozen orange juice concentrate and let it come up to room temperature.

Mix the orange juice concentrate with the softened butter. Add the orange zest if you decided to use it. *(It adds a lot!)*

Scrape the mixture into a small serving bowl, cover with plastic wrap, and refrigerate.

Lemon Butter:

1/2 cup softened butter *(1 stick, 1/4 pound)*
1 Tablespoon frozen lemonade concentrate
1 teaspoon lemon zest*** *(optional)*
  *** *Lemon zest is finely grated lemon peel — only the yellow part, not the white part.*

Measure out one Tablespoon of frozen

lemonade concentrate and let it come up to room temperature.

Mix the lemonade concentrate with the softened butter. Add the lemon zest if you decided to use it. *(It adds a lot!)*

Scrape the mixture into a small serving bowl, cover with plastic wrap, and refrigerate.

CHAPTER FOURTEEN

When Hannah's alarm clock went off the next morning at five-thirty, she was still mad at Mike. Norman wasn't fully back into her good graces yet, either, but he had apologized several times and she was sure that he was genuinely sorry. Mike didn't have a clue why she'd gotten angry with him. His apology had been perfunctory and an afterthought.

Hannah looked over at Moishe's pillow, but he wasn't there. There was a deep indentation where he'd stretched out and a few orange-and-white hairs on the pillowcase, but he'd obviously defected in the middle of the night. She crawled out of bed, stretched her back, and found her slippers under the bed. She was padding down the hallway in search of her morning infusion of caffeine when she smelled something wonderful.

The lights were on in the kitchen. Hannah's nostrils flared as she caught the scent again. Sausage. Eggs. Cheese. Onions. Had her fairy godmother arrived bearing breakfast?

"Morning," Hannah said, spotting her youngest sister at the table the moment she entered her gleaming white cooking and baking domain. She'd been too tired to clean up after making two batches of popovers last night, but Michelle had done it for her. The sink was empty of dirty dishes, the counters were sparkling after a fresh wipedown, and her mixer was spotless and denuded of bowl.

"Morning, Hannah." Michelle gestured toward the coffee mug that sat at Hannah's place. "I heard you get up, so I poured your coffee. Breakfast will be ready in . . ." She paused to look up at the apple-shaped clock that hung over the kitchen table. "Three minutes. It's just cooling now."

"Thanks," Hannah said, taking a huge swig of coffee that might, if she drank enough, render her capable of more than one-word sentences.

"It's a recipe one of my roommates gave me for a breakfast omelet. She said her mother always makes it for Christmas morning because you can put it all together the night before, refrigerate it, and bake it the next morning."

"Did you?" Hannah asked. Now she was up to two words. She reached for her mug of coffee again in the hopes of increasing her sentence length even more.

"I did."

Two words. Michelle must be catching it from her. Hannah took another big gulp of coffee and forced out her next question. "Where was it?" And then she drew a deep breath of relief. Three words. She was getting better.

"In the refrigerator."

She'd brought Michelle up to three words, too. Now it was time to do even better. "Down at the bottom?" she asked.

Four words! She was almost cured. All it took was concentration.

"In the meat drawer."

Hannah took a deep breath. Their morning conversation, if you could call it that, reminded her of trying to start an outboard motor. You gave it a yank and a little gas, and it gave you a couple of putt-putts. You gave it a harder yank and a little more gas, and it produced more putt-putts. Then, when you gave it all you had and the level of gas was just right, it actually started with a roar and it took you across the lake.

Without another word, Hannah got up

and refilled her coffee mug. She needed more gas. She drank it down despite the fact that it was piping hot, and her eyelids popped all the way open. "I don't have any meat in the meat pan, so that's why I didn't see it."

"I put it there on purpose. I wanted to surprise you, so I stopped at the Quick Stop on the way home and bought everything I needed. It's just a little thank-you for letting me stay with you. With her working all the time, it was a real drag at Mother's."

"Uh-oh," Hannah said, remembering that she'd promised Michelle she'd try to find out what was keeping their mother so busy every night in her office.

"What?"

They were down to one-word responses again, but that didn't worry Hannah. She knew that now she was capable of a string of words that made sense. "I forgot all about Mother's little secret," she admitted.

"That's not surprising after what happened last night."

"I know, but I can't help wondering what else I'm forgetting."

"Maybe you should keep a to-do list."

"I did that. I still do sometimes. But if I'm really busy, I forget to look at it, and that defeats the whole purpose."

Michelle laughed and got to her feet. She walked over to the counter to dish up two portions of the omelet she'd made and carried them to the table. "Why don't you get a cell phone with a built-in electronic notebook? All you have to do is program it for the time you want to be reminded of something, and it beeps."

Hannah made a face. "I really don't want to go that high-tech. Getting a computer was bad enough, and I only did it because I lost that bet with Andrea."

"I saw it in the living room. It's still in the box, and you haven't even set it up."

"That's right."

"Well, why not?"

"Because I don't have a cell phone with an electronic notebook that beeps to remind me," Hannah said, digging into the excellent breakfast that Michelle had served.

The sense of good humor her youngest sister had served along with her delicious omelet was short lived. Hannah had taken only three bites of her sister's delicious concoction when the phone rang.

Michelle glanced up at the clock. It was two minutes to six. "Who'd be calling at this hour of the morning?"

"Mike, Norman, Mother, Bill, or Lisa,"

Hannah answered, ticking them off on her fingers. "The only one it couldn't be is Andrea."

"Because she doesn't get up before eight?"

"You got it," Hannah said, standing up to reach for the phone on the wall. But just as her fingers were about to connect with the receiver, she happened to glance at Moishe.

His fur was puffed up to twice his normal size, and his back was arched in a classic Halloween cat pose. His tail was swishing back and forth like a scythe in a reaper's hands, and instead of a purr, a low growl emanated from his throat. He was staring at the phone with yellow eyes that were narrowed to slits, and he looked ferocious enough to leap through the air and puncture the wall with his claws.

Hannah pointed, and Michelle looked worried. "What's wrong with him?"

"He knows who it is."

"How can he know that?"

Hannah shrugged. "I'm not sure, but he's only been wrong once or twice. Maybe he's picking up some kind of cue from me, or maybe he's just extra sensitive. I'd better answer before he rips the phone off the wall."

"Good idea," Michelle said, still staring at Moishe with some alarm.

Hannah picked up the receiver and brought it to her ear. "Hello, Mother," she said.

In the ensuing silence Hannah could hear the sound of a clock ticking on the other end of the line. Then the clock began to strike the hour, a bell-like chiming that confirmed the identity of her caller. It was a gilded clock from the early eighteen hundreds that Delores had brought home from Granny's Attic to put on the shelf in her breakfast nook.

"What is it, Mother?" Hannah asked. "I know you're there."

There was an exasperated sigh and then Delores spoke. "I do wish you wouldn't do that, Hannah. It *turns me tip over tail.*"

"What?"

"Sorry, dear. It's a Regency term that means it upsets me. And speaking of being upset . . ."

Hannah took a deep breath and winked at Michelle. She knew exactly what was coming.

"I was just listening to Jake and Kelly on KCOW radio and they said that someone *coshed* Willa Sunquish over the head last night at the fair and killed her!"

"They said *coshed?*" Hannah was surprised. She'd catered enough cookies, coffee, and tea at the Lake Eden Regency Romance Club to know that *coshed* meant to strike a blow.

"Of course they didn't say coshed. They probably don't even know what it means. They just announced that a blow to the head killed her."

"I know, Mother."

"Then you were listening, too?"

"Not exactly." Hannah sent up a silent thank you to whoever had written the press release for not adding anything about how she'd found Willa's body.

"You weren't listening to Jake and Kelly, but you knew about it?"

"Yes, I knew."

It took Delores a moment, but then she gasped. "Don't tell me!"

"All right. I won't. Was there anything else you wanted, Mother?"

"Hannah Louise Swensen! This is no time to be flippant. It's not at all becoming. I don't know how you expect anyone to take you seriously if you insist on treating . . ."

"I'm sorry, Mother," Hannah interrupted what promised to be a lengthy lecture on improper behavior for a lady.

"That's better. Now tell me you didn't."

"I can't do that."

Delores groaned so loudly, it hurt Hannah's ear. "You have *got* to stop doing this, Hannah! It's bad enough that you trifle with the affections of those two perfectly lovely men. One of them cared enough to build you a house, you know."

"It's Norman's house, not mine," Hannah defended herself.

"Are you going to deny that you designed it with him?"

"No, but it was for a contest."

"Really, Hannah! You're acting as if you have *windmills in your head!*"

"What?" Hannah was genuinely confused. She hadn't heard that particular phrase before.

"It means confused. They used it all the time in Regency England. If you're half as bright as I think you are, you'll realize that the contest had nothing to do with Norman's real motivation. He wanted to build a house for you. And he did."

Hannah was silent. What could she say? Her mother could be right.

"If you have any doubt, go out and look at his den," Delores said. "But that's enough about Norman. Tell me everything about it."

"About what?"

"About Willa, of course. Bertie told me she had her hair done, and Claire mentioned that she bought an expensive dress. Do you think it was date rape gone bad?"

"Date rape?" Hannah choked out the words.

"Yes. You know what that is, don't you?"

"I know, but how do *you* know?" Hannah couldn't help asking.

"Dr. Love discussed it with a caller last week."

"You listen to Dr. Love?" Hannah was shocked. The advisor to the lovelorn on KCOW radio had a reputation for being outrageously outspoken.

"It's either that or the farm report, and I've heard enough about mastitis to last me for the next fifty years. The radio in the lounge only gets two stations, so we listen to Dr. Love while we're having lunch."

"Okay. I've really got to go, Mother. I haven't even taken my shower yet, and I'm due at work in forty-five minutes."

"Just a minute, Hannah! You haven't told me anything yet. Was it . . . bad?"

Hannah knew what her mother wanted. Delores expected her to couch her description of the murder scene in carefully chosen euphemisms. But Hannah didn't have the time or the patience to do that right now.

"Call me later," she said, standing to hang up the phone. "I'll tell you all about it then.

I'm running late and I have to get ready for work."

"Wait!" There was a frantic command from the other end of the line. "Just tell me where you found her. They didn't say that on the radio, and Bill won't tell me a thing."

It was clear that Delores wanted a juicy tidbit for the Lake Eden gossip hotline, something no one else but an insider would know. She'd obviously called Bill first and failed to learn anything she hadn't already known, and now she was trying her eldest daughter.

Hannah glanced at Michelle. Her youngest sister was holding Moishe in her lap while she chuckled silently. Michelle's whole body was shaking with mirth, and Moishe looked as if he wasn't sure whether he should bail or attempt to ride it out.

"Okay, Mother," she said turning back to the phone. "I'll tell you one thing that you didn't hear on the radio. Chances are, the police don't know it either. And when I tell you, I'm hanging up so I can get ready for work. Is that a deal?"

"Of course."

Delores sounded eager and Hannah rolled her eyes. She'd make this fast. "Willa was wearing the new dress she bought from Claire," Hannah said, "and she was also wearing new shoes she bought to go with the dress." And then, at the first squawk of protest, Hannah lifted the receiver from her ear and hung up.

Fifteen minutes later, Hannah looked back up at the clock and groaned. She'd just fielded two more phone calls. One was from Pam Baxter, who wanted to know if she should call Lisa at home to explain the situation and ask her to fill in on the judging panel. Hannah had told her yes, hung up the phone, and it had run again immediately. This time it was Lisa to report that Pam had called about taking Willa's place on the panel of judges. Lisa said she'd let Pam know by noon, but she wanted to ask some questions about it when Hannah got down to The Cookie Jar.

"I'd better hurry," Hannah said, glancing at the clock as she carried her dishes to the sink.

"Go take your shower and get dressed," Michelle said, reaching for the omelet pan and pulling it closer. "I'll catch the phone if it rings. I'm going to pick out some of this sausage for Moishe."

"Good idea. He's always loved sausage." Hannah headed for the kitchen doorway, but the phone rang as she passed by the table. "What is it about a ringing phone that I can't ignore?" she asked, reaching out to grab it. "Grand Central Station. This is Hannah speaking."

"Hi, Hannah," a familiar voice greeted her, and Hannah smiled. It was Norman, and he wouldn't try to probe her for more information about Willa's murder. "Do you have a minute?" he asked.

"For you I have two." Hannah sank down into a chair.

"Then I'll make it fast. First of all, I want to apologize again for being so insensitive last night."

"Apology accepted."

"Good. And I'd like the two of you to join me for dinner tonight."

"We'd love to, but we can't. Michelle has to be at the fairgrounds from noon until eight tonight."

"I didn't mean Michelle. I know she has a full schedule. I was talking about you and Moishe."

"You're inviting *Moishe* to join us for dinner?"

"Yes. I've got an idea for perking up his appetite. I know you want to see Michelle in the talent competition, so I thought we'd eat early. Bring the big guy out to my place at five."

"It sounds great, but I'll only have forty-five minutes. I've got a six o'clock meeting with Pam and whoever fills in for Willa at the fairgrounds. We have to go over the rules for judging."

"That's okay. I'll have everything all ready. I'll get takeout from Sally at the Inn, and we'll eat in my new den. It's the only room that's completely furnished. Then I'll take Moishe back to your place for you, and you can go straight to your rules meeting."

Hannah was about to beg off and ask him to make it another, less hectic night, when she remembered her mother's comment about Norman's new den.

"Okay. See you at five."

"Wonderful. Now there's just one other thing . . ."

"What?"

"I know Mike doesn't want any help from anybody, but you're going to investigate, aren't you?"

"Me? Investigate? How can I investigate when I'm not a licensed member of a law enforcement agency?"

Norman let out a yelp of laughter. "You're right, of course. See you at five with the big guy."

"What are we having for dinner?"

"Boneless leg of lamb with wild rice and

baby asparagus. Sally said it was one of your favorites."

"It is. I'll cut off a little piece for Moishe. I don't think he's ever had lamb."

"No need for that. I ordered a special entrée for him. If the big guy asks, you can tell him he's having mixed grill."

"That's really sweet of you, Norman." Hannah began to smile. Some men might be nice to their girlfriends' pets because it was politic to do so, but Norman really cared about Moishe.

Breakfast Omelet

Do not preheat the oven — this breakfast dish needs to be refrigerated before it can be baked.

Hannah's 1st Note: I didn't have the heart to tell Michelle that this dish wasn't technically an omelet. What's in a name anyway? It's like Shakespeare said, *Would a rose by any other name smell as sweet?* **— or in this case, as savory?**

1 1/2 pounds skinless sausage links or breakfast sausage patties
8 slices white bread *(white, sourdough, French, country, etc.)*
3/4 pound grated cheddar cheese *(approx. 3 cups, the sharper the cheddar, the better)*
1/2 cup chopped onion
1/4 cup finely chopped green peppers
6 eggs

1/2 teaspoon salt

1 1/2 cups milk

1/2 cup half-and-half, or cream

1 Tablespoon prepared mustard *(I used stone ground)*

1 can *(10 3/4 ounces)* condensed cream of mushroom soup, undiluted

1/4 cup sherry★★★

1 can *(5 ounces)* sliced mushrooms, drained
  ★★★ *If you don't have sherry, dry white wine will work just fine. Dry vermouth is also an option. If you don't want to use liquor of any type, you can simply add another 1/4 cup milk.*

Spray the inside of a 2-quart casserole dish with Pam or other nonstick cooking spray. A 9-inch by 13-inch cake pan will also work well for this recipe.

Cut the sausage links into thirds and sauté them until they're lightly browned over medium heat on the stovetop. If you used patties instead of links, cut each one into four parts and sauté them until they're lightly browned.

While your sausage is browning, cut the crusts from the slices of bread. *(You can either save the crusts to feed to the birds, or throw them away, your choice.)* Cut the remaining bread into one-inch cubes. Toss them into the bottom of your casserole or cake pan.

Drain the fat from your sausage. Put the drained sausage on top of the bread cubes in the casserole. *(Mother used to save the fat from sausage or bacon for Dad — he used it for frying eggs when he had one of his penny-ante poker nights.)*

Sprinkle the grated cheese over the top of the sausage.

Sprinkle the chopped onions over the cheese.

Sprinkle the chopped green peppers on top of the onions.

(Or, if you like things spicy, substitute 1/4 cup chopped jalapeños.)

Whisk the eggs with the salt, milk, half-and-half or cream, and prepared mustard in a bowl by hand, or beat them with an electric mixer.

Pour the egg mixture over the top of the casserole, cover it tightly with plastic wrap, and refrigerate it overnight.

(Michelle says that now you can sleep soundly because you know you've got break-fast almost ready to go in the morning.)

The Next Morning, 2 hours before you want to serve breakfast:

Preheat the oven to 350 degrees F., rack in the middle position

Take the casserole from the refrigerator and remove the plastic wrap. Place it on a baking sheet with sides, if you have it. A jelly-roll pan will work beautifully.

Mix the condensed cream of mushroom soup, the sherry *(or equivalent)*, and the drained, sliced mushrooms in a mixing bowl.

Pour the mushroom mixture over the top of the casserole.

Bake the casserole for 1 1/2 hours at 350 degrees F.

Remove the casserole from the oven and let it stand for 10 minutes to set up before serving.

Hannah's 2nd Note: Michelle told me that she once used some of her roommate's leftover champagne instead of the sherry and it was really good. I didn't ask her how her underage roommate got the champagne in the first place.

CHAPTER FIFTEEN

"But do you really think I'm qualified to do it?" Lisa asked, taking the last two trays of cookies out of the oven and sliding them onto the baker's rack.

"You're every bit as qualified as I am. You've been baking all your life."

"But so have you. And your life is a lot longer than mine." Lisa stopped and made a face. "That was tactless, wasn't it?"

"Don't ask me. I'm not exactly the guru of diplomacy, myself."

Lisa giggled and Hannah was reminded again of how young she was. Her partner was a study in contradictions. There were times when she was amazingly mature and responsible, especially when it came to the business, her recent marriage, and her father's care. But there were other times when Lisa still acted like the twenty-year-old she was. There had been several occasions over the past two years when Hannah had come in to find her partner dancing around the workstation with a broom as her partner, humming, *Some Day My Prince Will Come.*

"So you think I should do it?" Lisa asked again.

"I do. What does Herb think?"

"The same as you. Of course Herb thinks I can do anything, except . . ." Lisa paused and began to frown. "I was going to say that I'll be on the judging panel if you'll do a favor for me. But that's not really fair, is it?"

"Not really, but of course I'll be glad to do whatever . . ." Hannah stopped speaking in midpromise. The last time she'd promised a favor without knowing what it was, Andrea had tricked her into chaperoning a group of her high school girlfriends at a rock concert.

"You were about to make a blanket promise, but you changed your mind, didn't you?"

"Not exactly. I'll do it, whatever it is, as long as your favor doesn't involve a rock concert, or physical pain. And come to think about it, they could be the same thing."

Lisa laughed. "No rock concert and no physical pain. Unless . . . are you claustrophobic?"

"I don't think so. I can hide in a closet, no problem. I've done it a couple of times when I was snooping. And I've wiggled under my bed on my stomach to fish out one of Moishe's toys."

"Oh, good! Then you're definitely not claustrophobic," Lisa said, sounding very relieved. "I am."

"Claustrophobic?"

"Yes. I didn't know it until I volunteered to be Herb's assistant and then it was too late. I didn't want him to think I'd lost confidence in his ability to do the trick. It's just . . . the minute he closes that box, I'm absolutely terrified."

"You're talking about the lady in the box that the magician saws in half?"

"No. That one doesn't bother me at all, but it's really an expensive setup and we're still saving up for it. As long as my head's out, I'm fine. It's just the sword trick that gets to me."

"Hold on," Hannah said as a dreadful vision flashed through her mind. She pictured herself blindfolded and shackled in front of a wooden backdrop while an insane magician threw daggers at her. She could understand the terrified part, especially since Herb had never been able to hit the broad side of a barn when they'd played softball in high school. But that wouldn't make Lisa claustrophobic, would it? Perhaps she'd gotten her tricks mixed up.

"What?" Lisa asked, watching the expressions cross Hannah's face.

"You said *sword,* not dagger, right?"

"Right."

Hannah came close to sighing in relief, but she knew she wasn't safe quite yet. "Will you describe the trick for me?" she asked.

"The assistant gets in the box and the magician closes it up. It's like an old-fashioned wooden coffin standing upright, and it's called the magic cabinet. The assistant gets in the position that's printed on the inside of the lid. It's really easy, Hannah. There are little handholds and footholds and everything. You really can't do it wrong."

That remains to be seen, Hannah thought, but she didn't say it. "Then what happens?" she asked.

"Then Herb pokes these long swords all the way through the box. He leaves them in and by the time he's through, you think it's impossible for the assistant to survive. But she does, and that's because she gets into the right position before he starts poking in the swords."

"It's an optical illusion?"

Lisa shrugged. "I'm not really sure how it works. All I know is that every time I get inside and Herb shuts the door, I have to bite my lips to keep from screaming for him to let me out. I'm really relieved that he doesn't want me to do it for amateur night. But I promised I'd try to find him a replacement assistant."

"You said Herb doesn't want you to do it?"

"That's right. We showed the trick to Dad and Marge last night, and they said it would be better if Herb found someone else."

"Why?"

"I'm too little. It's a big coffin . . . I mean, *box,* and they thought the audience would be more impressed with Herb's act if we found a really big woman to be his assistant." Lisa stopped and gave a little groan. "I put my foot in it, didn't I?"

"You could say that."

"What I meant to say was that it would be more impressive if Herb had a *tall* assistant who filled out the box . . . heightwise, that is."

Hannah couldn't help but laugh. Lisa looked so chagrinned.

"Maybe I'd better rephrase that. What I meant was . . ."

"Stop!" Hannah held up her hand in the

universal gesture that meant halt in any language. "Don't make it worse. I'll do it."

"You will?"

"Sure. It'll give me more time to nose around at the fairgrounds."

It took Lisa a second, but then she nodded. "So you're going to try to find Willa's killer?"

"Of course. Willa was my friend. I can't just leave everything up to an official detective who calls her the *victim* instead of her name."

"Uh-oh. Somebody's in the doghouse." Lisa took one look at Hannah's angry face and changed the subject. "So when can you practice with Herb?"

Hannah countered with her own question. "When is the contest?"

"Tomorrow at five, right after the rodeo's over. It's on the same stage as the Miss Tri-County competition."

"Fine. I can practice this afternoon if we decide to close early, or . . ." Hannah stopped and started to smile. "If Herb can bring everything here, we can practice in the coffee shop. Any customers we have can be the audience. And if we don't have enough customers, we can recruit some from Bertie. She always has ladies waiting to have their hair done."

"That'll be fun. Let me call Herb and set it up. He can do it on his lunch hour if one o'clock is okay."

"It's fine. And then you can run up and tell Bertie. And stop in at Granny's Attic on your way back. Mother and Carrie are out at the fairgrounds, but I'll bet Luanne would like to come."

"How about the senior center?" Lisa asked, looking hopeful. "Dad's seen the act before, but the other seniors haven't."

"Sure. The more the merrier."

"Thanks, Hannah. You're the best friend ever!"

Hannah smiled, but when Lisa left to put on the coffee in the coffee shop and make her call to Herb, her smile slipped a bit. She hadn't exactly told the truth to her partner. She hated small, cramped spaces. She could endure them for a few minutes, but being closed up in something that looked like an old-fashioned coffin wasn't exactly her idea of fun.

"Oh, well," she said, shrugging slightly. Anything for her partner. And the trick would take only a few minutes, so there was really nothing to worry about, was there?

It was twelve noon when Mike came into The Cookie Jar. Hannah's heart leapt.

There was no other way to describe the sensation. It reminded her of the *kiss-me-quicks* her dad had driven over when she was a child. Hannah had no idea how the term originated, and the town of Lake Eden seemed evenly divided on naming them. Some, like Hannah's father, called them *kiss-me-quicks.* Others, like Lisa's family, called them *tummy-ticklers.* They were gradual rises in the road, small hills with a gentle rise and a steep descent. If you gunned the engine just right and backed off on the accelerator the instant you reached the top of the hill, the resulting drop left you with a sudden breathless feeling. It was the same feeling Hannah experienced every time she saw Mike.

"Hannah," he said, hanging his sheriff's baseball cap on the coat rack by the door.

"Mike," she replied, watching as he strode to the counter. How could any ordinary human being walk with so much assurance? He exuded self-confidence.

"Are you still mad at me?" he asked, taking a seat at the deserted counter.

You're the detective. You figure it out, Hannah thought, but of course she didn't say it. The customers scattered at the tables were staring at them, and all conversation had ceased the moment Mike had approached the counter. Every man and woman in the place was hoping to overhear something new about Willa's murder investigation.

"Well?" Mike prodded.

Hannah shook her head. The lie simply wouldn't pass her lips. And then she put on a smile for the benefit of her customers and said, "I know you like coffee, and I made a new batch of cookies I think you'll like. Do you want to try one?"

"Well, sure!" Mike smiled right back "What do you call them?"

"Cappuccino Royales. They're coffee cookies with milk chocolate chips." Hannah took two cookies from the display jar for Mike. "Let me know what you think."

Mike chewed thoughtfully, and then he started to grin. "I really like the strong coffee flavor. They'd be great on a stakeout. They'd also be a hit out at the station this afternoon."

"What's going on at the station?" Hannah asked.

"We're having a strategy meeting about . . ." Mike glanced around and he seemed to realize, for the very first time, that every other customer in the place was silent. "Um . . . police business. You know."

And Hannah *did* know. Mike was meeting with the other detectives to discuss a plan for solving Willa's murder. "I'll be happy to provide the cookies for your meeting. How many do you need?"

"There'll be six at the meeting, but I'll never hear the end of it if I don't buy enough cookies for everybody. And I'll *buy* them, Hannah."

"But I'll be happy to give them to you. I believe in supporting our local police."

"And this local detective believes in supporting you. I won't take no for an answer. I'm paying and that's that. I figure I can use four, maybe five dozen. Do you have that many?"

Hannah glanced at the display jar again. There were about a half-dozen left, and Lisa had brought them all out from the kitchen. "What time is your meeting?"

"Three-thirty, but don't put yourself out on my account. If you don't have enough of those coffee cookies, just give me what you've got and fill in with another kind."

Hannah debated the wisdom of that a moment, and then she shook her head. Mike hadn't said a word about the *victim,* and he was being very careful not to offend her. He deserved to be rewarded for good behavior. "I'll bake another batch for you."

"Will they be ready in time?"

"Absolutely. They might be slightly warm,

but that won't bother you, will it?"

Mike shook his head. "I bet they'll be even better that way."

"It's a deal, then. I'll drop them off at the sheriff's station no later than three-fifteen."

"Thanks, Hannah." Mike popped the last of the second cookie into his mouth, raised the mug of coffee to his lips and drained it, and stood up. Then he pulled some money out of his wallet and left it on the counter. "This should cover it. If it doesn't, just let me know. I'll see you at three-fifteen. If you're there a little early, I'll even buy you a cup of coffee."

Hannah shuddered. She still hadn't made up her mind where to find the worst coffee. The last time she'd cared to research it, it had been a three-way tie between Doc Knight's hospital vending machines, the pot that Jon Walker never washed in his office at the Lake Eden Neighborhood Pharmacy, and anything that was brewed anywhere within the confines of the Winnetka County Sheriff's Station.

"Thanks, but I have a lot to live for," she said.

"What?"

"Never mind." Hannah gave a wave as Mike retrieved his cap and headed out the door. And then she hurried to the kitchen

to mix up another batch of Cappuccino
Royales.

Cappuccino Royales

Preheat oven to 350 degrees F., rack in the middle position.

2 cups melted butter *(4 sticks, 1 pound)*

1/4 cup instant coffee powder *(I used Folgers)*

2 teaspoons vanilla

2 teaspoons brandy or rum extract

3 cups white *(granulated)* sugar***

3 beaten eggs *(just whip them up in a glass with a fork)*

2 teaspoons baking soda

1 teaspoon baking powder

3 cups milk chocolate chips

5 1/2 cups flour *(don't sift — pack it down in the measuring cup)*

*** If you prefer a sweeter cookie, roll the dough balls in extra granulated sugar and flatten before baking.

Melt the butter in large microwave-safe bowl at 3 minutes on HIGH. Or melt it in a saucepan over low heat on the stovetop.

Mix in the instant coffee powder, vanilla and rum or brandy extract. Stir it until the coffee powder has dissolved.

Add the sugar, beaten eggs, baking soda, and baking powder. Mix well.

Stir in the milk chocolate chips. Mix until they're evenly distributed.

Add the flour in one cup increments, stirring after each addition. Mix until the flour is thoroughly incorporated.

Form walnut-sized dough balls with your fingers. Roll them in a small bowl with granulated sugar if you decided you wanted them sweeter.

Place the dough balls on greased cookie sheets, 12 to a standard-size sheet. *(I used Pam to grease my cookie sheet, but any nonstick cooking spray will do.)*

Flatten the dough balls with the back of a metal spatula, or with the palm of your impeccably clean hand.

Bake the cookies at 350 degrees F. for 9 to 11 minutes. Let them cool on the cookie sheets for 2 minutes, and then transfer the cookies to a wire rack to complete cooling.

Yield: 12 to 14 dozen cookies *(depending on cookie size.)*

Hannah's Note: These cookies freeze well if you have any left over.

CHAPTER SIXTEEN

"What are you doing here, Mother?" Hannah asked, staring at Delores in shock.

"Did I ever fail to attend one of your school programs?"

"No, but this is . . ."

"I even showed up for the Chorale Club concert when you were in sixth grade," Delores interrupted her, "and I knew the music teacher had asked you to just pretend to sing."

"That was really good of you, Mother. But this isn't quite the same as . . ."

"Maybe I wouldn't have if Marge hadn't called me, but she was so excited about Herb's debut. And then I heard about you, so of course I had to come. I knew you'd see the light eventually, dear. Dithering between two perfectly acceptable men just isn't the smart thing to . . ."

"Mother!" This time Hannah got her interruption in first. "The audience is due here any minute, and I don't think we should be discussing something this personal in pub . . ."

"You're right, of course," Delores broke in. "I'm just so terribly grateful to hear you've finally come to your senses. Now you'll see for yourself that I'm right."

For one confusing moment, it was almost as if her mother were speaking in a foreign tongue. Hannah had felt like that only once before, when she'd tried to understand college trigonometry without first completing courses in geometry and algebra. It was a mind freeze, and all reason came to a screeching halt. The words her mother spoke were perfectly good words, and each one had at least one perfectly good definition. Together they formed perfectly sensible sentences, but the meaning of those sentences remained as elusive as the identity of Willa's killer.

"Mother? I really don't have the foggiest notion what . . ."

"Hush, dear. Bertie's about to come in the door, and you know what a big gossip she is. Did he tell you what you'll be having?"

"Having?" Hannah repeated dumbly, as if she'd never heard that particular verb before.

"For *dinner,* dear."

The entrance of the noun caused the light to dawn, and the glow it shed was clear, unsullied, even brilliant. Hannah hadn't lost her wits, and her mother wasn't speaking in code. Delores was talking about the dinner she'd agreed to have with Norman in the den of his new house tonight.

"Lamb," Hannah said, feeling in control once again. "He's picking up takeout lamb dinners from Sally at the Inn."

"Do you think you've got it?" Herb asked, looking every bit as nervous as the day he'd had to recite the witches' speech from Mac-Beth in English class.

"I think so. *Double, double, toil, and trouble.* You knocked 'em dead then, you'll knock 'em dead now."

Herb's mouth dropped open to match the little round silver moons on his purple velvet cape. "What are you talking about?" he asked, and then, a heartbeat later, he began to laugh. "I get it! High school English, Mr. Merek."

"Exactly right. No way you can be *that* nervous again. And you got the highest mark in the class."

"That's true." Herb looked very relieved. "Let's go over it one more time, just to be sure. What do you do when we walk on stage?"

"I just stand there, a little behind you. And you give your speech about magic."

"Good. And when I'm through, I command you to get in the magic cabinet."

"Command?" Hannah asked, bristling slightly.

"Sorry, wrong word. I don't command anything. I *suggest* that you get in the magic cabinet. And you do."

"And then I get into position while you say a few things about how dangerous this is, and how you really hope they'll be able to clean the bloodstains off the floor of the coffee shop, and how I'm the third assistant you've had this year."

"Right. All that is to build up the suspense."

"And then you ask me if I'm ready, and I call out that I am."

"Right again. That's the cue that tells me you're in position and I can start sticking in the swords."

"How many swords?"

"Twelve. I'll have the audience count when I stick them into the cabinet, and you'll be able to hear them."

"And then you'll pull them out again?"

"Yes. With difficulty. I'll pretend that one

is stuck. They always gasp when they think about *why* it might be stuck."

"Wonderful. And then you open the cabinet door?"

"Not quite. I give another little speech so you have time to get both feet down and you're ready to move. That speech ends with the words, *If you're still with us, Miss Swensen, give me a sign.*"

"Right. And I knock three times on the inside of the cabinet door."

"Exactly. And *then* I open the cabinet."

"And I step out, smiling and unscathed."

"I think you'll be perfect, Hannah. You've got it all down." Herb glanced at the old-fashioned pocket watch attached by a jeweled fob to his cape. "It's almost show time. Are you ready?"

"Absolutely." Hannah waited until they were ready to step out of the swinging door and enter the coffee shop before she said what she'd been thinking about all morning. "Don't worry, Herb. I'll be perfectly fine as long as you remember to use the collapsible swords."

Hannah pulled up in front of the one-story brick sheriff's station at precisely three o'clock. The magic show with Herb had gone perfectly, except for the slight bobble when her left ankle had almost gotten caught in the strap. She'd discovered that it did take some degree of agility to get into the position required to keep from being skewered by the blades, but some of the swords in critical places were indeed collapsible and would only go in as far as her stomach if she sucked it in.

Anything for my partner, Hannah repeated, her mantra for the next twenty-four hours. She'd promised to find an appropriate costume and meet Herb in the parking lot at the fairgrounds a half-hour early so that they could go over things one more time before the competition.

Once she'd pulled her cookie truck into one of the visitor parking spots at the front of the building, Hannah retrieved the cookie box from the back of her truck and walked to the front door. Someone had been busy decorating the walkway with summer flowers, and Hannah admired the perennials that lined both sides of the sidewalk all the way down to the employee parking lot. She was no flower expert, but they looked like nasturtiums to her. In any event, the orange, red, and yellow flowers were cheery and took some of the onus away from walking down this sidewalk to talk about a crime.

Hannah stepped inside the first glass door,

waited until it had closed behind her, and waved at the desk sergeant as she opened the second door. Most people didn't know it, but Bill had told her that the desk sergeant had a button to press that would lock the visitor midway between the two doors. It was a security precaution that had never been used, but if it was ever needed, it could be.

She stepped up to the desk and greeted the sergeant on duty, Rick Murphy. He was Lonnie's older brother and he was also a detective. "Hi, Rick. What are you doing on the desk?"

"Disability for two more weeks," Rick said, stretching out his leg and showing Hannah his cast. "I slid into home and got creamed."

"I remember." Hannah gave a little grin. The Cookie Jar fielded the only all-female softball team on the Lake Eden city schedule, and her catcher, Rose McDermott, had been as unmovable as a chunk of granite when she'd tagged Rick out.

"You want Mike?" Rick asked, grinning in a way that made Hannah bristle slightly.

Guys will be guys, she reminded herself, and did her best to curb the impulse to take him down a peg or two. "That's right," she said, smiling sweetly. "I'm delivering cookies for the detectives' meeting. I guess you won't be there, right?"

Rick looked disgruntled as he shook his head. It was clear he didn't like being chained to the desk, and Hannah took pity on him. She slipped several cookies out of the bakery box and placed them on his desk blotter. "Here you go. They'll never miss them."

"Thanks, Hannah." Now Rick was all smiles. "I think Mike's in his office. You know where it is, don't you?"

"Sure. Right next to Bill's," Hannah said, reminding Rick ever so nicely that she was the sister-in-law of his boss, the Winnetka County Sheriff, and he'd be wise not to treat her lightly. "I'll stop in to see Bill first."

"Okay. You can go on down. I'll page him and tell him you're coming."

Hannah walked down the tiled hallway and stopped at Bill's office. The door was open and she peeked in, but no one was inside. She went on to Mike's office, but before she could tap on the door to announce herself, she heard voices. Mike had someone in his office. It might be important and she wouldn't interrupt him. She'd just sit in Bill's office and wait for Mike's visitor to leave.

Bill's office was the biggest one in the

administrative wing, but that wasn't saying much. The county hadn't even come close to spending a fortune on accommodating its highest-ranking law enforcement officer. There was a two-window view of the parking lot, one window more than the other offices had, and there was room for three chairs in front of Bill's desk, rather than two. Since Bill's office was wider, there was room for an entertainment center with a television set and a conversational grouping of four barrel-backed chairs arranged around an octagonal table. The furniture wasn't new. When the sheriff's station was first built, Rod Metcalf had covered the grand opening in the *Lake Eden Journal.* Hannah remembered reading that every stick of furniture, office or otherwise, had been provided at no cost to the taxpayer. It had come from donations that had been refurbished by the inmates at the St. Cloud Correctional Facility.

As Hannah glanced around Bill's office, she saw the fine touch of her sister's hand in several places. A brass ship's lamp sat on the bookcase in the corner, casting a soft light in what would have been a shadowy corner. There was a photo cube on Bill's desk containing pictures of Andrea, Tracey, and Bethany. The windows were still outfitted with blinds to block out the glaring afternoon sun, but Andrea had hung curtains on either side of the two windows and tied them together with a valance of the same material. She was about to walk over to look at the framed picture on the wall, which looked like one that Tracey had drawn, when Bill's secretary, Barbara Donnelly, came in the connecting door.

"Hi, Hannah. Rick called me from the front desk to tell me you were here. Bill got held up in the parking lot. He's just giving the new class of checkpoint volunteers their letters of certification. They'll be out there this weekend, so don't drink and drive."

"I won't." Hannah opened the box of cookies and held it out toward Barbara. "Would you like a cookie before the guys eat them all?"

Barbara smiled and reached in the box. "Thanks. Bill ought to be back here before long. Do you want me to turn on the TV for you?"

"No, thanks. I've been talking to people all day, and I could use a little peace and quiet."

"How about some coffee?"

"I'd better not. I've been drinking it since five this morning, and I'm a little coffeed out."

"Okay. If you need anything, just open the door and stick your head in my office."

After Barbara had gone back to her office, Hannah took a seat in one of the barrel-backed chairs. It was more comfortable than she'd thought it would be and she leaned back and closed her eyes. That was when she heard voices from the office next door. Mike's office. The conversation had been inaudible only moments before, but now it was getting louder.

Hannah moved closer to the wall the two offices shared and took up a position by the bookcase. This could be interesting.

"I'm *not* going to take you off the case!" It was Mike's voice, and he punctuated the sentence with what sounded to Hannah like his fist thumping the top of his desk with considerable force. "You don't get to pick and choose the cases you work on. You'll do your job like everyone else!"

"But I went out with Willa a couple of times!"

Hannah began to frown. She wondered if that was before or after Lonnie had started to date Michelle.

"So what if you dated her?" Mike asked.

"Well, how would *you* feel?"

"I wouldn't feel. That's the difference between us. And until you stop empathizing with the victim, you won't make a good detective."

"But . . . how do I stop?"

"For one thing, you call her the *vic,* or the *victim.* And if that sounds too hardhearted to you, you call her Miss Sunquist. You never use her first name."

"What good will *that* do?"

"It'll help you to depersonalize her. Every time you feel those emotions welling up and attempting to cripple you from doing your job, you tell yourself, *The only thing I can do for her now is catch her killer and make him pay.*"

Hannah leaned against the bookcase, her heart beating hard. Had she accused Mike of being callous when all he was trying to do was depersonalize Willa so that he could do his job?

"That all makes sense," Lonnie said, after a long moment of thought. "But I don't know if I can do it."

"Sure you can. Stop concentrating on her, and start focusing on that lousy excuse for a human being who robbed her of the rest of her life."

"Yeah," Lonnie sounded thoughtful. "I can see how that'd work."

"Atta boy! You've got the ability to be good, Lonnie. All you have to do is put the empathy on hold and dial up the determination to catch the perp."

"Right. I think I can do that. There's just one other thing."

"What's that?"

"If you keep your emotions on hold all the time, don't you get kind of . . . jaded and cynical?"

"Absolutely. You've seen cynical cops, and believe me you don't want to be one! But I'm not telling you to keep your emotions on hold indefinitely. The only time you have to push that hold button is when you're working, or when you're thinking about how to run the case. I wouldn't be able to have any kind of personal life at all if I shut down my emotions all the time."

"Does that mean you felt bad about Will . . ." Lonnie stopped and cleared his throat. "Sorry. I forgot for a second. So you felt bad about the victim, too?"

"Of course I did! But I knew that if I got too empathetic while I was the only cop there, I wouldn't be able to assess the crime scene analytically and pick up on any clues that her killer might have left behind. Do you get it?"

"I think so."

"Do you know what I did when I finally

got home last night at four in the morning?"

"No. What?"

"I took my emotions off hold. I had to decompress, so I put on my favorite jazz album and I poured myself a brandy. I drank it down, and then I stood under a steaming shower until the hot water ran out."

"Did it help?"

"Yeah. I felt clean when I got out, almost like I washed away all the dirtbags and scum I have to deal with on a daily basis. And then I put on my sweats and walked barefoot to the living room and stared at the new picture I hung over my couch."

Hannah drew in her breath sharply. Mike had said he was going to hang *her* picture over his couch.

"It's a beautiful picture, and it makes me feel good to look at it," Mike went on. "And then I told myself, *There's good in the world. All you have to do is look and you'll see it.*"

Hannah swallowed hard. She'd never seen this side of Mike before.

"What's so interesting about my law enforcement books?" a voice asked, and Hannah turned toward the doorway. Bill was standing there, staring at her curiously.

"I was looking at this one." Hannah

grabbed a heavy book at random. "I've always been fascinated by . . ." She glanced down at the title, "Fingerprint analysis in the eighteenth century."

"Did you open it?"

Hannah shook her head. "Not yet. I was going to, but you came in, and . . ."

"Open it now. I want to see the expression on your face."

Hannah opened the book and frowned as she began to page through it. "But it's blank!"

"Right. Mike gave it to me when I was sworn in as sheriff."

"But why would Mike give you a blank . . ." Hannah stopped speaking and groaned instead. "There *was* no fingerprint analysis in the eighteenth century!"

"Right again." Bill glanced down at the box of cookies she'd set on his desk. "Are these for the detectives' meeting?"

"Yes."

"What kind are they?"

"They're Cappuccino Royales."

"Coffee and chocolate?"

"Yes. Mike tasted a couple at the coffee shop today. I think he's hoping they'll make his detectives energetic and euphoric at the same time."

"Will they?"

"I don't know, but Bertie Straub tried one and she said she got jazzed up from the coffee and happy from the chocolate. She was going to take some back to the Cut 'n' Curl, but she was afraid the chips would melt under the hair dryers."

Bill looked interested. "How many cookies are there?"

"A little less than ten dozen," Hannah answered, subtracting for the cookies she'd given Rick and Barbara.

"That should be enough," Bill said, opening the box and grabbing a sample cookie. "Since I'm the boss, I'd better taste one before I give them to my staff."

"Of course. Any caring boss would do the same."

Bill finished the cookie in three bites and reached for another. "Just to make sure they're all alike," he explained, eating his second cookie.

"That's very wise of you. Quality control is important."

Bill finished eating and picked up the box. "I'm going to go make sure everyone gets two cookies before I take the rest to the meeting. We're working five assault and batteries from a bachelor party that got out of hand, one stolen horse, two missing gerbils from a kindergarten classroom, three grand theft autos, two B and E's, and a murder. And that means we could all use a little energy and euphoria around here."

CHAPTER SEVENTEEN

"Here we are, Moishe," Hannah announced, turning into Norman's driveway. "You've never been invited to dinner before, have you?"

Moishe didn't deign to answer. She'd heard him prowling around in the back of her cookie truck, and he was obviously content to be riding, untethered, with her.

"Just in case you're interested, Norman ordered mixed grill for you," Hannah told him, not expecting an answer.

"Rrrrow?" Moishe surprised her by responding. And since the latter part of his yowl ended on a higher note than the beginning, she decided that it was a question.

"That's right. Mixed grill. Sally's making it for you. I've had it, and it's delicious."

This time there was no response, and Hannah concentrated on negotiating the rutted driveway. The spring rains had softened the hard-packed dirt under the gravel, and heavy trucks delivering building supplies had done the rest of the damage. Just as soon as the house was completely finished, Norman would have it graded and paved.

"Here we are," Hannah said, pulling to a stop as close to the front door as the circular driveway allowed. "You've never been here before, so come on up and let me put on your leash."

But before Hannah could coax her cat to move forward, there was a tap on the window. It was Norman. He must have been watching for her to pull up.

"I'll take the Big Guy," Norman offered, opening one of the doors at the back of her truck and scooping Moishe into his arms. "All dressed for dinner, I see," he said to the cat that was purring like thunder.

"What do you mean?" Hannah asked, totally confused. "He's not dressed at all."

"Yes, he is. He's wearing his harness and that's got a *black tie.*"

Hannah groaned all the way into Norman's foyer. "Great mirror," she said, noticing the oval glass that hung by the built-in coat rack they'd designed together.

"Of course it's a great mirror. You picked it out."

"I did?" Hannah was surprised. She didn't

remember looking through catalogues for mirrors.

"Remember the Bette Davis festival they were running on television?"

"Of course. We must have watched at least four films that night."

"Five including *Whatever Happened To Baby Jane,* but who's counting? But there was a mirror in one of the movies that you said would be perfect for the foyer of our dream house."

Hannah was impressed that Norman had remembered. But then she had a disturbing thought. "You didn't buy it from one of those expensive movie memorabilia auction houses, did you?"

"No, Luanne found it at an estate sale in The Cities, and the mothers gave it to me at cost. I had to have it resilvered, but it was worth it."

Hannah was smiling as she followed Norman to the den. Just being in the house they'd designed together made her happy. She was still smiling as she stepped into the den, but the moment she saw what Norman had done to furnish it, her smile increased by several hundred lumens.

"Gorgeous!" she breathed, taking in the total effect. Norman's den was elegance and coziness combined. It was comfort food for a weary soul who'd worked hard all day and wanted to relax in an oasis of ease. It was the kind of room that made you feel at home the moment you stepped through the arched doorway and onto the muted plaid carpet.

Once she'd experienced the total effect, Hannah took note of the individual touches. There was a beautifully polished oak bar that ran along one wall and barstools with dark green leather seats that resembled tall captain's chairs. There was a window behind the bar that would look out over the fruit trees that Norman would eventually plant.

The other end of the large room contained a home theater with a giant television screen that slid up when it wasn't in use. The television could be seen from the two leather recliners that were positioned as front row seats, the conversational grouping of six chairs in the main room, or the bar area at the opposite end of the room. Even though she wasn't a sports fan, Hannah could imagine sitting at the bar, eating snacks and watching the Vikings play.

"I ordered a couch to go under the windows," Norman gestured toward the series of tall, narrow windows that marched across one wall, "but it hasn't come in yet."

"This whole room is incredible," Hannah

said, not quite sure which area to explore next. And then she noticed that Norman was heading toward a spiral staircase that was built close to one wall. It was so narrow only one person could use it at a time and it rose up past a series of round windows that faced the side yard, leading to . . .

"The ceiling?" Hannah breathed, blinking hard. She really had to get a good night's sleep tonight. Norman had hired excellent carpenters with impeccable references. She must be completely exhausted to imagine that they had built a staircase rising to nowhere. She rubbed her eyes and took another look, but what she'd seen had been so. The staircase was attached at one end to the ceiling.

"What in the world is . . ." Hannah stopped speaking, so flabbergasted she couldn't even form the question, as Norman climbed the staircase with Moishe in his arms.

"Here you go, Big Guy," he said setting him down about halfway up, near a plate that had been placed by one of the round windows. "Dinner theater. You can dine on mixed grill and watch the grackles in the side yard."

It was a first for Hannah, two dawns in one day. And as the light rose for the second time, brilliant and clear, she realized that her mother was right. Norman had built this house for both of them. The spiral staircase didn't lead to nowhere. It led to marriage and a special place in their den for her cat!

"Whoa!" Hannah said under her breath. She knew Norman loved her, but she'd thought his proposal was a reaction to Mike's declaration, a defense against losing the time they spent together. Norman had seemed perfectly content to see her when it suited them both, but perhaps he hadn't been quite as complacent as she thought.

"Did you build that staircase for me?" she asked, the epitome of tactlessness.

"No, I built it for Moishe," Norman said with a smile. "It's working, Hannah."

"What's working?"

"The change of scene. The Big Guy's eating."

Hannah watched her cat take a morsel of something and swallow it. Then he turned toward the window and stared out at the birds that were strutting around in Norman's side yard, pecking at things in the grass. Moishe made several ack-ack noises in his throat, licked his lips, and turned back to the plate to take another bite. Norman had figured out a way to get her cat to eat. No doubt Moishe was imagining that he was crunching grackle bones along with the mixed grill Sally had made for him.

"Great plan, Norman," Hannah praised him. And then both of them watched Moishe eat for several minutes. Between the birds, the gourmet dinner, and the excitement of a new habitat, Moishe was having a wonderful time dining out. Hannah was just wondering how she could duplicate the same circumstances at her condo when she thought of something she'd forgotten. "Uh-oh!" she groaned.

"What?"

"I forgot to bring his litter box."

"That's okay. He's already found mine."

"Yours?" Hannah started to laugh.

"Well, it's mine in the sense that I paid for it. But I bought it for him."

"You didn't have to do that. You could have just called and reminded me to bring his. I know you had a busy day down at the clinic today."

"Oh, I didn't get it today. I bought it at the mall a while ago. I wanted it to fit in the nook by the utility closet, and I had to go to a couple of pet stores before I found one that'd work."

Hannah was amazed. Norman had planned this out long before he'd invited Moishe to come out to dine this evening.

Delores was right. Norman had been planning all along to ask her to marry him. Why else would he buy a litter box when he didn't even have a cat?

"Time to eat," Norman said, startling Hannah out of revelation mode. "The timer just buzzed."

"I didn't hear it."

"Of course you didn't. I've got it in my pocket, and it's turned to vibrate."

"I didn't know you could buy a timer like that!"

"It's not really a timer. It's a feature on my cell phone. Do you want me to take a picture of Moishe eating before I come down?"

"Sure. I'd like to show Michelle. Do you have your camera with you?"

"No, but I'll take it with my cell phone. The resolution's not quite as sharp, but it's good enough for our purposes."

Modern technology, Hannah thought as Norman pulled his cell phone out of his pocket, pointed it at Moishe, and took what must be a photo of her cat eating Sally's dinner. "Hold on a second, and I'll send it to Sally. She was wondering if her dinner would help."

"Send it to Sally?" Hannah repeated, feeling a bit like George Washington might have felt if someone had offered to airlift supplies to Valley Forge. "Are you going to print it out and fax it to her?"

"No, I'll just transmit it with my cell phone, and she'll see it on her cell phone. Let's text her. What do you want to say?"

Hannah wasn't completely unacquainted with technology. She watched the news, and she knew that people communicated with each other by pushing the appropriate letters that were teamed with the number buttons on their cell phones. "Just tell her thanks," she said.

When Norman was through sending Sally the picture, he came down the stairs and pulled out a stool for Hannah at the bar. Then he ducked behind the glossy surface to set two places with placemats and silverware. He opened the door of the small oven that sat behind the bar for making hot appetizers and pulled out two dinners covered in foil.

"Sally said to be careful of the steam," he said, lifting the corner of the foil to release a savory cloud of moisture and then removing the foil all the way. He set Hannah's dinner on her placemat and duplicated the procedure with his. And once he was seated on his own stool behind the bar, he filled two glasses with sparkling water and raised his in a toast. "To Moishe and the return of his appetite," he said.

"To Moishe," Hannah echoed. And then she added, "And to his best friend, Norman, who went to a lot of trouble to make both of us feel right at home."

Naturally they'd talked about Willa's murder and shed a few tears. Pam had known her the best, and she looked tired and drawn tonight. They'd decided that they couldn't do a good job judging if they were too busy feeling bad, so they'd agreed to table any thoughts of Willa until the first-place quick bread winner had been chosen.

"If I have to taste another piece of banana bread, I'm going to end up hating bananas!" Lisa declared, draining her coffee cup and heading for the sideboard to pour more from the thermos she'd brought. "Anyone else?"

Hannah shook her head. "Not me. I'm actually going to try to get a good night's sleep tonight."

"The caffeine in coffee keeps you awake?" Pam asked, slicing the next quick bread they were scheduled to taste.

"No, caffeine doesn't bother me at all."

Both Pam and Lisa looked puzzled, so Hannah explained. "It's all that liquid. Once

I start drinking coffee, I usually finish the pot. And then, when I have to get up during the middle of the night, I think of all the things I have to do in the morning and I can't get back to sleep."

"That used to happen to me when I was single," Pam confided.

Hannah was perplexed. "But it doesn't happen now that you're married?"

"That's right. All I have to do is listen to George breathing, and I go right back to sleep. It's so deep and rhythmic, like waves washing up against the shore."

"It's the same thing with me," Lisa said. "I used to spend a lot of sleepless nights before I married Herb, but now everything's changed. I think it's because Herb's a warm sleeper and I've always been a cool sleeper."

"What are those?" Hannah asked, a bit startled by this revelation. Lisa was a very private person, and she seldom discussed anything personal about her marriage to Herb.

"A cool sleeper needs lots of blankets and quilts or they shiver all night. I used to use a quilt, even in the summer. But a warm sleeper throws off the blanket and quilts because they're too hot."

"That sounds like real incompatibility to me!" Pam remarked, arranging the sample slices on the plates.

"But it's not incompatible at all. All I have to do is cuddle up next to Herb, and I'm warm again. He's like a cozy fire in the fireplace, or the warm air from a furnace. It only takes a minute or two, and I'm warm again. And then I go right back to sleep."

"Well, none of that works with me!" Hannah said, knowing full well that she'd shock Pam and Lisa. "Maybe you didn't know this about me, but I don't sleep alone."

"Moishe," Lisa said, giving her a smile.

"That's right. And sleeping with Moishe just doesn't do the trick. For one thing, he snores. Very loudly. Imagine a freight train going by right next to your ear. And for another thing, if I cuddle up next to him I get a nose full of cat hair."

Pam was smiling as she carried the three small plates to the table and Hannah was glad. She'd done her best to lighten the heavy mood Willa's murder and the ensuing investigation had created.

"This is another zucchini bread," Pam announced, "but this one has cinnamon topping."

"How many zucchini breads have we tasted tonight?" Hannah asked, frowning slightly.

"Seven. This one is the last one."

"The contestant left the peel on," Lisa commented, staring down at the dark green flecks in the bread. "I don't like the way that looks."

"Then give a lower grade for appearance," Pam advised.

Hannah tasted her slice. She wasn't wild about the cinnamon topping, so she marked the contestant off for that.

"One quick bread left," Pam said, as they handed in their scorecards, "and then we can declare the winner."

Lisa looked hopeful. "Tell me the last bread isn't banana."

"Or zucchini, or date-nut," Hannah added.

"It's not any of those," Pam informed them, slicing the quick bread and plating it. "This is Mango Bread."

Hannah and Lisa exchanged astonished glances, and Pam laughed. "It's true," she told them. "The contestant wrote a note on the back of the recipe saying that she wanted to try something different."

"It's different, all right!" Lisa said. "I don't think I've ever tasted a mango. Where did she get them?"

"She went all the way to The Cities to get hers. They have them at some of the specialty produce places in the summer. But she said that if you can't find mangos, you can use fresh or canned peaches."

"Really?" Hannah was intrigued. "Peach Bread is pretty unusual, too."

"Well, she baked both so that we could compare them." Pam carried the plates to the table. "The Mango Bread is on the left, and the Peach Bread is on the right. Let's try the Mango Bread first."

There was silence while all three of them tasted and Lisa was the first to break it. "I like the Mango Bread," she said.

"So do I," Pam agreed. "Hannah?"

"It's very good."

"Okay," Pam said, reaching for her scorecard. "Mark your scorecards and then taste the Peach Bread."

Again, the room was perfectly silent and this time it was Hannah who was the first to speak. "I like the combination of peaches and almonds. Did she use almond extract in place of the vanilla?"

Pam reached for the second recipe card and flipped it over. "Yes, she did. And I like it, too. Which bread do you like best?"

Lisa shrugged. "It's like comparing apples and oranges."

"Or mangos and peaches," Hannah quipped. "They both have their strong points, but I think I like the Peach Bread best."

"Mark your scorecards," Pam said, and all three of them wrote down their scores. Pam collected them and handed the calculator to Lisa, who added the scores while Hannah read them aloud.

It didn't take long with all three of them working and less than ten minutes later, they were through. Pam signed the final sheet and looked up to smile at them. "Want to guess which one came in first?"

"The Mango Bread?" Lisa guessed.

"No."

"Then was it the Peach Bread?" Hannah asked.

"Not exactly." Pam laughed at their puzzled expression. "It's a dead heat. We have a tie for first place."

"So we have to taste them again to see which contestant is the winner?" Lisa asked, obviously remembering the quick rundown Pam had given her on the rules.

Pam shook her head. "We already know which contestant is the winner."

It took Hannah a second, but then she nodded. "The Mango Bread and the Peach Bread tied for first place."

"Exactly right. And since both entries were baked by the same contestant, we don't have to do a thing. Now . . ." Pam turned to look at the sideboard filled with loaves of quick bread. "Who wants to take what home?"

Mango Bread

Preheat oven to 350 degrees F., rack in the middle position.

3/4 cup softened butter *(1 1/2 sticks)*

1 package (8 ounces) softened cream cheese *(the brick kind, not the whipped kind)*

2 cups white sugar *(granulated)*

2 beaten eggs *(just whip them up in a glass with a fork)*

1/2 teaspoon vanilla extract

1 1/2 cups mashed mangoes *(you can use fresh and peel and seed your own, or you can buy them already prepared in the ready-to-eat section at your produce counter.)*

3 cups flour *(don't sift — pack it down in the cup when you measure)*

1/2 teaspoon baking powder

1/2 teaspoon baking soda

1/2 teaspoon salt

1 cup chopped walnuts or pecans *(optional)*

Hannah's 1st Note: This is a lot easier

with an electric mixer.

Beat the butter, cream cheese, and sugar together until they're nice and fluffy. Add the beaten eggs and the vanilla, and mix them in.

Peel, seed, and slice the mangos *(or drain them and pat them dry if you've used prepared mangoes.)* Mash them in a food processor with the steel blade, or puree them in a blender, or squash them with a potato masher until they're pureed. Measure out 1 1/2 cups of mashed mangoes and add it to your mixing bowl. Stir well.

In another bowl, measure out the flour, baking powder, baking soda and salt. Mix them together.

Gradually add the flour mixture to the mango mixture, beating at low speed until everything is incorporated.

Mix in the walnuts or pecans by hand.

Coat the insides of two loaf pans *(the type you'd use for bread)* with nonstick cooking spray. Spoon in the mango bread batter.

Bake at 350 degrees F. for approximately one hour, or until a long toothpick or skewer inserted in the center comes out clean. If the top browns a bit too fast, tent a piece of foil over the top of the loaves.

You can also bake this in 6 smaller loaf pans, filling them about half full. If you use the smaller pans, they'll need to bake approximately 45 minutes.

Cool on a wire rack in the pan, loosen the edges after 20 minutes, and turn the loaf out onto the wire rack.

Yield: Makes two bread-sized loaves, or 6 small loaves.

Hannah's 2nd Note: This bread is also good toasted. Lisa took it home from the contest and tried it the next morning for breakfast. She said she liked hers plain, but Herb wanted butter on his.

PEACH BREAD

Preheat oven to 350 degrees F., rack in the middle position.

3/4 cup softened butter *(1 1/2 sticks)*
1 package *(8 ounces)* softened cream cheese *(the brick kind, not the whipped kind)*
2 cups white sugar *(granulated)*
2 beaten eggs *(just whip them up in a glass with a fork)*
1/2 teaspoon almond extract
1 1/2 cups mashed peaches★★★
3 cups flour *(don't sift — pack it down in the cup when you measure)*
1/2 teaspoon baking powder
1/2 teaspoon baking soda
1/2 teaspoon salt
1 cup chopped blanched almonds
★★★— You can use fresh and peel and slice your own, or you can buy them already sliced and prepared in the ready-to-eat section at your produce counter, or you can use canned

peaches.

Hannah's 1st Note: This is a lot easier with an electric mixer.

Beat the butter, cream cheese, and sugar together until they're nice and fluffy. Add the beaten eggs and the almond extract, and mix them in.

Peel and slice the peaches *(or drain them and pat them dry if you've used prepared peaches or canned peaches.)* Mash them in a food processor with the steel blade, or puree them in a blender, or squash them with a potato masher until they're pureed. Measure out 1 1/2 cups of mashed peaches and add it to your mixing bowl. Stir well.

In another bowl, measure out the flour, baking powder, baking soda and salt. Mix them together.

Gradually add the flour mixture to the peach mixture, beating at low speed until everything is incorporated.

Mix in the almonds by hand.

Coat the insides of two loaf pans *(the type you'd use for bread)* with nonstick cooking spray. Spoon in the peach bread batter.

Bake at 350 degrees F. for approximately one hour, or until a long toothpick or skewer inserted in the center comes out clean. If the top browns a bit too fast, tent a piece of foil over the top of the loaves.

You can also bake this in 6 smaller loaf pans, filling them about half full. If you use the smaller pans, they'll need to bake approximately 45 minutes.

Cool on a wire rack in the pan, loosen the edges after 20 minutes, and turn the loaf out onto the wire rack.

Yield: Makes two bread-sized loaves, or 6 small loaves.

Hannah's 2nd Note: This bread is also good toasted. Mother loves it toasted with honey butter on top.

CHAPTER EIGHTEEN

By the time Hannah arrived home, all she could think about was climbing into bed and shutting her eyes. Unfortunately, she'd promised Herb and Lisa that she'd find an appropriate outfit for being a magician's assistant, and she had less than twenty-four hours to do it. She seemed to remember that she'd once bought a midnight blue skirt with the constellations of the winter sky drawn in glitter. She'd planned to wear it to the astronomy club Christmas party because she was dating an astronomy major at the time, but they broke up a week before the party and she'd never worn the skirt. Now would be the time to find it. If she'd kept it, and she probably had, it would be with the other clothes that she no longer wore but were too good to throw away and were stored in the guest room closet.

Now would be the time to find it. Michelle wasn't there, so she wouldn't disturb her.

She'd noticed that their mother's car hadn't been parked in the garage. Since Lonnie was working the case with Mike, Michelle had probably gone to see some of the girls she'd hung around with in high school.

Hannah unlocked her condo door and prepared to catch Moishe in her arms, but no furry medicine ball of a cat hurtled out to greet her. He was perched on the wide, carpeted ledge that attached to the living room windowsill. Michelle had picked up two at the pet store, one for the living room and one for the guest room, so that Moishe would be more comfortable.

"Hey, Moishe," she said, walking over to give him a pat. "I see Norman turned on the television for you. You had fun at his house, didn't you?"

"I think he did."

Hannah whirled to see Norman coming in from her kitchen, carrying a cup of coffee. "He acted really disappointed when I tried to leave, so I decided to stay until you got home. I hope you don't mind."

"Of course not."

"How about a fresh cup of coffee? I made some."

"That sounds good. I've got some date bread from the contest."

Hannah turned back to her cat to give him

a scratch under the chin. Moishe responded with what Hannah interpreted as a kitty smile with slightly open mouth and narrowed eyes, and then he licked her hand once, rather perfunctorily in her opinion, before he swiveled his head to look out the window again.

"I don't know what's so fascinating about Clara and Marguerite's living room window, but you go right ahead and enjoy. I'm going to have coffee with Norman, and then I have to look for something to wear in the magic cabinet tomorrow."

Once Hannah and Norman had finished their coffee and date bread, he got up to leave. But he stopped at the door and turned back to her. "Did I hear you say something about going through your guest room closet?"

"Yes. I'm looking for something to wear for the amateur magician contest."

"You do magic?"

"The only magic I do is make food disappear. I'm just helping Herb with his show."

Norman chuckled. "Seems to me the last time you looked in that closet, somebody was trapped in there because the pole came loose."

"That's right."

"Did you get a new pole?"

Hannah shook her head. "I just moved some things around so the weight was more evenly distributed."

"And now you're going to move things around again?"

Hannah gave a little nod. Norman was right. "Yes, I guess I am."

"Then you'd better let me help you. I don't want you to be trapped in that closet until Michelle comes home."

"Maybe I should just buy something," Hannah said, her voice muffled by a coat she hadn't worn since high school. "It's just that I know it's here somewhere, and now I don't want to give up without finding it."

"I understand." Norman stood just outside the closet, his arms piled high with formal dresses.

"But it's a lot of trouble for you."

"That's okay. I don't mind."

"Okay, if you say so. I've been promising myself I'd go through all this stuff anyway. I just tossed it in here right after I moved in, and I haven't looked at it since. The dresses you're holding are going to go to charity. Who knows? Somebody might actually want them."

With that prediction, Hannah emerged

from the recesses of the closet. Her face was flushed and her hair was a mass of disorderly red curls made even more unmanageable.

"Your hair," Norman said, chuckling.

Hannah reached up and attempted to pat it down, but she could tell that nothing short of a shampoo followed by gobs of conditioner would do it. "I guess I had too many *clothes encounters,*" she quipped.

"Don't say things like that when my arms are full," Norman warned her.

"Hold on a second," Hannah reached back in the closet and plucked out another dress to add to his pile. It was a pink satin dress in a shade of pink that someone with her hair color should avoid at all costs. "Another one for the Helping Hands Thrift Shop."

"Very fancy," Norman said, glancing down at the dresses in his arms. There was a purple taffeta, a Kelly green silk, a white dotted Swiss with a full lavender lining to match its dots, a turquoise voile, and a bright yellow chiffon. "You must have gone to a lot of dances."

"Weddings," Hannah told him, not repeating the old adage her mother spouted every time Hannah was included in a bridal party, even though *Always a bridesmaid, never a bride* seemed to apply to her unmarried state. She'd worn close to a dozen brides-maid gowns that had been expressly de-signed to make the bride look lovely in comparison.

"And you don't think you'll wear any of these again?" Norman asked, referring to the colorful pile he was holding.

"Over my dead body," Hannah said, giv-ing double meaning to the old cliché. She ducked back into the closet, rummaged around for a few moments, and gave a vic-tory yell. "I found it!"

"The skirt?" Norman asked, shifting the dresses in his arms so that the orange satin flower wasn't tickling the side of his neck.

"No, my red mitten. It's been missing since the day I moved in. I'm afraid the skirt's a lost cause. I must have given it to someone. Just toss those dresses on the bed and grab Moishe, will you?"

Norman did as she asked, capturing the orange-and-white tomcat before he could attempt the jump he was contemplating, from the floor to the upper shelf of the closet.

"Rowwww!" Moishe complained, eyeing him balefully and purring at the same time.

Norman held him in one arm and closed the closet with the other. "I know you're disappointed, but there wasn't anything on that shelf you'd want. Mackerel don't swim in closets."

"He must have been after the dust mice," Hannah joked, and she was pleased when Norman laughed. "I wonder when Michelle will be . . ." Her question was interrupted by a knock at the door, and she hurried to answer it. "That must be Michelle now. I hope she didn't lose her key."

But it wasn't Michelle. It was Andrea, and she looked very worried.

"Hi, Andrea," Hannah said, holding the door open. "Come in. Do you want coffee?"

"No, I came after you. I figure it's going to take both of us because she has three brothers."

It took more than a couple of minutes to explain things, but once they were on the road, they didn't waste time. Hannah drove, Norman sat in the passenger seat at Andrea's insistence, and Andrea got in the back.

"I'm really glad we're going to get her," Andrea said, leaning forward so they could hear her. They'd decided to take Hannah's cookie truck. It was almost a decade older than Norman's sedan or Andrea's Volvo, and less desirable to car thieves. The parking lot at the Eagle, the dive that most of its patrons called the *Illegal,* was known for its high incidence of stolen vehicles. The rundown bar, twelve miles from the Winnetka county line, was also famous for barroom brawls, resulting in the use of plastic beer mugs and glasses and lighting so dim the owner could claim that he'd misread the birth date on a minor's driver's license.

"Have you ever been to the Eagle before?" Norman asked.

Hannah shook her head. "Not me."

"Mother would have locked us in our bedrooms for the rest of our lives if we'd ever even planned to go," Andrea explained. "The Eagle's got a really bad reputation. Bill says it's a real dump and a hangout for convicts and preconvicts."

"What did Bill say when you told him that Michelle was at the Eagle?" Norman asked.

"I didn't tell him."

Hannah gave a little chuckle. "And I bet you didn't tell him that we were going out to get her, either."

"Of course I didn't. If I had, he would have made me promise not to go. And since I don't ever want to break a promise to my husband, I didn't tell him."

"There's a certain logic to that," Norman mused.

"I know. I learned it from Hannah."

"You did?" Hannah was surprised.

"Yes, you do it with Mother all the time. I call it *Don't go there.* If you don't mention it to them, they won't think to ask."

"Is *Don't go there* a Swensen sister trait?" Norman asked Hannah.

"Probably. I haven't noticed Michelle doing it yet, but if she hangs around with us long enough, she'll probably pick up on it."

They were silent for a moment as Hannah navigated the washboard road. The windows in the cookie truck were rolled down to let in the slightly cooler night air, and so far they were outrunning the mosquitoes. Every once in a while one would get lucky and dive-bomb through the window when Hannah slowed for a particularly deep rut, but both Andrea and Hannah were Minnesota born and bred, and they had learned the ability to accurately judge their location by the sound and swat mosquitoes on the fly.

"What did Bill say about Tasha's brothers?" Norman asked.

"He didn't. I asked Grandma McCann after I put the kids to bed, and she told me how bad they were. Except she didn't say *bad.* You know how nice Grandma McCann is. She never says anything negative about anybody."

Hannah knew Andrea's live-in nanny was

the sweetest soul on the face of the earth. "If she didn't say *bad*, how do you know Tasha's brothers are bad?"

"She used the word *unfortunate*. And *misguided*. And to make it even worse, she said they got it from their father!"

"Then they must be awful, all right." Hannah hugged the side of the road as a motorcycle came roaring toward them. The driver was wearing leathers, and he looked like he might have been a member of a motorcycle gang several decades ago. His passenger, a hard-looking woman well past her prime with overdone makeup and hair many shades removed from her natural color, gave them one less finger than the peace sign and laughed shrilly as they sped by.

"Delightful," Hannah said. "If the rest of the clientele look like that, Michelle's going to stick out like a sore thumb. Are you one hundred percent positive she's out here?"

"I'm positive. Lucy Dunwright's husband comes right past here on his way home, and he said he saw Mother's car parked right under the light in their parking lot. And then Lucy called me to ask me what Mother was doing in a dive like the Eagle."

"And you're sure she's talking about the Hicks brothers?"

"I'm sure. I saw her right after the contest

tonight, and she said to tell you that Tasha's last name was Hicks. And then she said she was going to try to talk to Tasha's brothers to see where they were on the night Willa was murdered."

"You must be right," Hannah said as she turned into the parking lot and pulled up right next to her mother's car. She looked up at the neon sign that buzzed and blinked on and off in an irregular pattern, and gave a long sigh.

"Look at that," Norman said, getting out of the truck and pointing at the sign. "They spelled *Eagle* wrong!"

"You're right," Andrea said, looking up at the sign. "They left out the *A*."

Hannah gave a little laugh as she double-checked to make sure her truck was locked up tight. "With the exception of Michelle, I'll bet there's not one single person inside who knows that it's spelled incorrectly."

CHAPTER NINETEEN

Norman opened the door, and the noise and music, Hannah wasn't sure which was which, blared out to assault their eardrums. The racket was accompanied by a smell Hannah wasn't sure she wanted to analyze but that probably had something to do with spilled beer, the heat of a Minnesota summer, and perfume that didn't put more than a dent in a five-dollar bill. All it took was one look at the rickety tables and the unswept floor, and Hannah knew it wasn't the sort of place where someone hurried over to greet you and lead you to a table.

"Come on," Andrea said, motioning to Hannah and Norman since they couldn't hear her over the din, and pushing through the crowd to an empty table.

Once they were seated on wooden chairs that were sticky with multiple coats of varnish, Hannah turned to her sister.

"Where did you learn how to do that?"

"Do what?"

"See an empty table, push through a huge crowd, and get it before someone else does."

"Shopping."

"Shopping?"

"That's right. I always go to the mall for their giant Labor Day Weekend sale. The stores are wall-to-wall people, and if you spot something you want, you have to push everybody else out of the way to get to it first."

Hannah made a mental note never to come within five miles of the Tri-County Mall on Labor Day weekend, and turned to Norman. But Norman wasn't there. "Where's Norman?"

"I don't know. He was right here a second ago. Maybe he went to the little boys' room."

"Do you see Michelle?"

"Not yet, but it'll be easier to look for her when they stop dancing."

"Dancing?"

"Over there." Andrea pointed to a heavily populated area where couples were shuffling around and embracing. The space was no bigger than the area rug that covered the center of the hardwood floor in their mother's living room.

"That's the dance floor?"

"I hope so. Either that, or . . . uh-oh!"

"Uh-oh what?"

"There's Michelle."

"Where?"

"On the dance floor. See the guy that looks like Clark Gable on steroids? He's got the mustache and everything."

Hannah squinted through the haze of blue smoke that clouded the place. Someone was grilling hamburgers behind the bar without adequate ventilation, but nobody seemed to mind.

"I see him. But I don't see Michelle."

"She's just to the left of him, dancing with the guy that's trying to look like Elvis. She's wearing . . ." Andrea stopped and groaned slightly. "Where did she get that outfit?"

"What outfit? I don't see her."

"She's wearing skintight jeans and a sleeveless shirt that's tied halfway up her chest. And I'm pretty sure she's not wearing anything under it, if you get what I mean."

Hannah took a deep breath and asked the question foremost in her mind. "Is she . . . decent?"

"Yes, barely. But I've seen worse. And now somebody's cutting in, and it's . . ." Andrea stopped speaking and gasped. And that was the moment that Hannah finally spotted her youngest sister.

"It's Norman!" Hannah gulped. "Norman's cutting in."

"I know. And the guy who looks like Elvis isn't happy."

"Uh-oh!"

"Uh-oh is right. I can't look." Andrea gave a little moan and held her hands over her eyes. "I like Norman, and I don't want to see him get trashed."

"Hold on." Hannah could barely believe her own eyes. "It's okay, Andrea. Norman's not getting trashed."

"He's not?"

"No. The Elvis not-so-look-alike just gave him a pat on the back, and now he's making a quick retreat."

Andrea took a look, and then she turned to Hannah in absolute amazement. "But . . . why did Elvis back off?"

"I don't know. Whatever Norman said to him worked. And now Norman's got Michelle's arm and he's bringing her over here to us."

It took a couple of minutes for Norman and Michelle to get to the their table. The crowd was milling around, and there were raucous shouts as the lights flickered.

"Here she is," Norman said when they arrived at the table. "Mission accomplished, so let's get out of here."

"Great idea!" Hannah agreed, standing up and grabbing her purse. "Let's go."

Andrea followed in their wake and they made their way to the door. Their progress was slow. There were simply too many people crowded into the place. It reminded Hannah of the time she'd watched two dozen guys from a fraternity try to get into a Volkswagen Bug.

The lights flickered several times on the way, and despite telling herself that the same thing couldn't happen twice, Hannah was reminded of the way the lights had flickered last night when she'd found Willa. "I wonder why the lights are flickering," she said, not really expecting an answer.

"I don't know," Norman responded, glancing at his watch. "It's not time for last call. They've got an hour and fifteen minutes before they have to close."

"Before they have to close *legally*," Hannah reminded him.

"Right," Andrea chimed in. "This is the sort of place that turns off all the lights, calls itself a private club, and stays open for anyone who's already inside until they stop buying drinks and leave by the back way."

"How do *you* know about things like that?" Michelle asked, looking slightly shocked.

"She's married to the sheriff," Hannah answered what could have been an embarrassing question for her sister. "Andrea knows all the inside stuff."

"Right." Andrea shot her a grateful glance.

"Well, I know why the lights flickered," Michelle said. "Elvis told me."

Hannah laughed. "You nicknamed him the same thing we did."

"No, I didn't. His name really *is* Elvis. He said his mother was crazy about The King and she wanted to pay tribute."

"What some mothers won't do to their kids!" Andrea said, giving an exasperated sigh. "He might have turned out all right if his mother hadn't practically dictated his personality by naming him after a famous person."

"I doubt it. I think he'd be a jerk no matter what." Michelle turned to Hannah again. "Do you want to know why the lights flickered?"

"Yes. There they go again. Why?"

"They're having a drawing for a pony."

"You mean . . . a little horse?" Andrea asked.

"No, a pony of beer. It's a half-keg."

Hannah started to frown. "How do *you* know that?"

"Everybody in college knows that. It's what you buy when you're having a party because it's cheaper than bottles or cans. You have to pay a deposit, but they refund it when you bring the pony keg back."

"I hope you're not ignoring the law. You can't buy liquor if you're underage."

"I know that. It's why I was drinking ginger ale tonight. It looks like a mixed drink, so I fit right in."

"We made it," Norman said, opening the door and shepherding them all out to the parking lot and over to the two vehicles they'd driven. "Do you want me to ride with you, Michelle? Or are you okay to drive home by yourself?"

"I'm fine. I was drinking ginger ale, remember? I'll see you at the condo, then."

"Not so fast," Andrea said, grabbing her sister's arm. "I want to know where you got that outfit. You look like . . . well . . . I'm not going to say what you look like in polite company."

"These are jeans that shrunk in the washer. And I ruined a perfectly good shirt by ripping off the sleeves in the car before I went inside."

"Why did you do that?" Hannah asked.

"I watched the girls that came out and I knew I'd never fit in if I didn't have that biker chick look. There wasn't time to go back and change, so I improvised."

"You should have taken one look at those girls and gone home," Andrea said, frowning.

"But I knew Hannah was investigating, and I wanted to do my part. Once I knew Tasha's last name and I found out where her brothers hung out, I just had to go there."

"I appreciate that," Hannah said, "but you could have been killed! Or worse!"

Michelle looked puzzled. "What's worse than being killed?"

"I don't know, but I'm willing to bet that something is. That's not important right now. What's important is that you don't take foolish risks that compromise your safety."

"You mean like the times you confronted killers alone without a weapon?"

"Exactly. But I'm older than you are, and you have your whole life ahead of you."

"What does being older have to do with it?"

"Never mind that." Hannah knew her logic was falling apart, and she thought fast. "The whole point is, I'm your older sister and you're obligated to listen to me. And I'm telling you not to take foolish chances. I'd never forgive myself if something happened to you."

Michelle looked properly chastised. "You're right. But I really wasn't taking chances. I had my cell phone programmed for a one-button call to the sheriff's department, just in case."

"Okay," Hannah said, willing to let the subject drop for the moment. "Let's get out of here before something bad happens. And I've got the feeling that something bad happens here every ten minutes or so."

"Give," Hannah said, putting on the most determined expression she could muster. "Michelle doesn't know what you said to Tasha's brother, because she couldn't hear you over the music. Tell us what made him back off like that."

Norman reached for another Spicy Dream and dunked it into his fresh cup of coffee. Andrea had found the cookies in the back of Hannah's truck on the way home, and only threats of imminent death had kept her from eating them all by herself. "These are really good, Hannah."

"I know. Lindy finally got around to sending me the recipe."

"Lindy Frank?" Andrea asked, taking another cookie for herself.

"Yes. She made them for the Fourth of

July picnic two years ago. She was going to give me the recipe then, but her husband got transferred, and in all the excitement of moving and everything, she forgot."

"They really are good, especially with coffee," Norman said.

"And you're really good at changing the subject," Hannah shot back. "Tell us what you said to that Hicks brother."

"It's really not that important."

"Yes, it is. I may die of curiosity if you don't tell me, and so will Andrea and Michelle."

"Right," Andrea confirmed it.

"Absolutely," Michelle agreed. "Right before you came up and tapped him on the shoulder, he was trying to get me to come out to the parking lot with him so he could show me his truck."

Andrea's mouth dropped open. "You didn't believe that tired old line, did you?"

"Of course not. I wasn't born yesterday. I figured it wasn't going to be easy to get rid of him, but Norman just said a couple of words to him and he backed right off."

"It was nothing," Norman gave a little shrug, but his eyes were crinkling at the corners and Hannah could tell he was enjoying himself.

"Give," Hannah repeated, grabbing the

plate with the cookies and pulling them over to her side of the table. "No more Spicy Dreams for you if you don't tell us what you said."

"Okay," Norman agreed, capitulating with good grace. "All I said was, *Hey, buddy. There's a sheriff's deputy over there, and I think he's looking for you or one of your brothers. He said something about a warrant, so I figured I should tell you.* And I didn't say any more than that because by then he was leaving. Really fast."

"But . . ." Andrea looked confused. "There aren't any warrants outstanding against the Hicks brothers, are there?"

Norman shrugged. "I don't know, but I figured it was like that old saying my grandmother used. It was, *Lecture your children every day. You may not know what they did wrong, but they do!*"

Hannah laughed, although she was sure that Norman wouldn't lecture his children the way his grandmother had advised. All the same, it had worked with the Hicks brothers and gotten them out of the Eagle without any trouble, and that was something.

"Thank you, Norman!" Michelle sounded very grateful. "I don't think I was in over my head, but that's the trouble about being in over your head. You never think you are. That place was horrible. I'm really glad that all of you came to get me."

"You're our little sister. Of course we came out to get you," Andrea said, giving Michelle a little hug.

"That's right," Hannah told her. "But don't be running off on your own again without telling someone where you're going."

"I promise I won't. But I found out where the Hicks brothers were last night."

"Where?" all three of them asked, almost in unison.

"At the Golden Wheel Speedway. One of their friends was in a demolition derby and they went to watch him. And on their way home, they were stopped by the highway patrol for speeding." Michelle turned to Andrea. "Bill can check out that alibi, can't he?"

"You bet he can."

"And when he confirms it, I can cross three suspects off our list," Hannah said, smiling at her sister. "Good work, Michelle, And now you'd better get some sleep. You've got a full day tomorrow."

When Michelle had left for the guest bedroom, Andrea stood up. She said her goodbyes and got ready to head down to the garage.

"Hold on, and I'll go with you," Norman said, giving Hannah a quick kiss and walking to the door with Andrea. "I know this complex is safe, but it's almost one in the morning and you shouldn't be walking anywhere alone."

Hannah saw them to the door, closed and double-locked it behind them, and settled back down on the couch to flick through the cable channels. Moishe came to sit beside her, but after a few pats, he jumped up to the carpeted ledge by the window again.

The food channel was doing something with ramps, and since Hannah had no idea what they were, she watched. It turned out that ramps were simply wild leeks that grew in the southern United States. They'd been around for years, but the food channel had made them a desirable item that a lot of grocery stores were now carrying. It was almost the same as Chilean sea bass. In the nineteen-seventies, it was called the Patagonian tooth fish and nobody wanted it. It was sold mainly for fish sticks. Then a marketing firm was hired to promote the tooth fish, and they gave it another name, Chilean sea bass. Hannah had tasted it out at the Lake Eden Inn, and it was delicious. It was also expensive because its sudden popularity caused it to become overfished, and it was heading for the rare fish section of the ichthyic phylum.

Once the scalloped potatoes made with ramps had been served on a gorgeous platter that would have cost Hannah a day's receipts at The Cookie Jar, she switched off the television and got up. She was about to head for the bedroom when the doorbell rang.

Andrea, who'd forgotten something? Norman? He might have come back for some reason? Or Willa's killer, who'd found out she was sleuthing and had ferreted out her address and come here to kill her?

Hannah walked to the door and looked through the peephole. As usual, she couldn't see her caller's face, but she did recognize the insignia over the breast pocket of the Winnetka County Sheriff's Department windbreaker. Mike, or Bill, or Lonnie. Unless they were here to cite her for some silly health board infraction, she was safe.

"Hi, Hannah," Mike greeted her when she pulled open the door. "I didn't want to wake you, but your lights were still on so I knew you weren't in bed."

"Right. Come in, Mike. There's coffee left in the pot if you want some."

"No, I'm on my way home. And I'm hoping that I can get some sleep tonight. I just stopped in to tell you that the cookies were delicious, and I hope you're not still mad at me for calling Miss Sunquist the victim."

"I'm not. I know you have to depersonalize things," Hannah repeated what she'd overheard him say at the sheriff's station. "It's okay, Mike. Really."

"Good. My world's not right when you're mad at me."

And with that said, Mike pulled her into his arms and kissed her so hard, it almost bruised her lips. And then he gave her another hug and a much gentler kiss. With a wave, he let himself out the door and was gone before Hannah could do more than gasp for breath.

When she recovered enough to move, Hannah double-locked the door. Less than twenty-four hours ago, she'd written Mike off, banished him from that special corner of her heart, and decided that Norman was the man for her. And then she'd overheard Mike talking to Lonnie, and she understood why he'd appeared to be so uncaring about Willa. And now he'd come to apologize again, something she never thought he'd do, and he said his world wasn't right without her. That put him right back in the running, tied for prospective fiancé with Norman again.

It was impossible for her to go to bed now, not when Mike had left her this unsettled. Hannah sat back down on the couch and patted the spot beside her, hoping that Moishe would leave his perch and come to sit on the couch with her.

For once, her cat came immediately. He settled down in her lap, gave her hand a lick, and began to purr contentedly. Hannah smiled as she stroked his soft fur and scratched him behind his ears. Moishe was her only constant, the one male in her life that she could rely on to give her unconditional . . .

"Ouch!" Hannah gasped as her normally accommodating pet let out a tigerlike growl, dug his claws in, and leapt from her lap. Another leap and he was on the carpeted ledge that Michelle had bought for him, staring out the window into the darkness.

"Whatever got into *you?*" Hannah asked, not expecting an answer. And then she massaged both thighs where eight separate claws had punctured her jeans. It was clear that Moishe was on his own mission, staring out the window at something she couldn't see but that totally fascinated him.

"Maybe it's nature of the beast," Hannah

muttered, heading off to her bedroom. "Just when you think you've got the male of the species all figured out, they go and change the rules on you."

SPICY DREAMS

Preheat oven to 350 degrees F., rack in the middle position.

Hannah's 1st Note: This recipe is from Lindy Frank and I'm glad she finally sent it to me. Her cookies disappear faster than a Popsicle on a hot day. Lindy calls these cookies "Ginger Cookies," but since we already serve a cookie by that name down at The Cookie Jar, we've renamed these "Spicy Dreams."

Hannah's 2nd Note: Lindy says to tell you that she makes these cookies festive by using colored sugar for holidays, i.e., pink for Valentine's Day, orange for Halloween, green for St. Pat's Day, etc.

1 cup soft butter *(2 sticks, 8 ounces, 1/2 pound)*

1 lb, 6 oz white granulated sugar *(2 2/3 cups)*

3 eggs

1 cup molasses

2 Tablespoons vinegar *(white will do just fine)*

2 Tablespoons baking soda

4 teaspoons ground ginger

1 teaspoon ground cinnamon

1 teaspoon ground cloves

1 teaspoon ground cardamom

1 lb, 12 oz all purpose flour *(6 cups — not sifted)*

1/2 cup powdered *(confectioner's)* sugar, for rolling★★★

★★★ In her original recipe Lindy used white granulated sugar for rolling. Lisa and I use powdered sugar so that we won't get the Spicy Dreams mixed up with the Molasses Crackles when we serve them on the same day down at The Cookie Jar.

Mix the butter and the sugar together and beat them with a mixer or a spoon until they look nice and fluffy. *(That's what the phrase "cream the butter and sugar" means if you see it in another recipe.)*

Add the eggs one at a time, mixing thoroughly after each addition.

Mix in the molasses and the vinegar. *(I always spray the inside of my measuring cup with Pam or another nonstick cooking spray before I pour in the molasses. Then it glops right out without sticking to the sides.)*

Lindy sifts the flour, baking soda, ginger, cinnamon, cloves, and cardamom together before she mixes them in with the wet ingredients. *(She also weighs the flour and the sugar the way a true pastry chef would do.)* That means she's probably a better baker than I am, because I don't do any of that. I just mix in the baking soda first, and then the spices. I stir everything up thoroughly, and then I add the flour in one-cup increments, stirring after each cup is added.

Use your hands to roll the dough into walnut-sized balls. If the dough is too sticky, put it in the refrigerator a half-hour or so — that'll make it easier to roll.

Put the powdered sugar in a small bowl and roll the balls in it. Place them on a greased cookie sheet (I used Pam) 12 cookie balls to a standard-size sheet. Press them down just a bit when you place them on the sheet so they won't roll off when you carry them to the oven. You don't have to flatten them. They'll spread out all by themselves while they bake.

Bake the cookies at 350 degrees F., for 10 to 12 minutes. *(Mine took only 10 minutes.)*

Let the cookies cool for a minute or two on the cookie sheet and then move them to a wire rack to finish cooling.

Yield: Approximately 10 dozen, depending on cookie size.

CHAPTER TWENTY

"More coffee to get us thinking straight?" Lisa asked, bringing the carafe to the back table and pouring them all another cup. They were having a strategy meeting at The Cookie Jar, and they had less than an hour before the first customers would arrive. Hannah had called the meeting so that they could go over the suspect list.

Norman had called in to cancel. He was whitening Bertie Straub's teeth before her first appointment at the Cut 'n' Curl. It was an old-fashioned barter. Norman whitened Bertie's teeth, and Bertie gave Carrie a special treatment guaranteed to give her hair a glorious sheen.

"Thanks, Lisa. I can use this." Andrea took a sip of her coffee and smiled. "I'm not used to getting up this early. And I didn't get to bed until almost two. I don't have bags under my eyes, do I?"

Michelle leaned over to take a look. "No bags."

"Let me see," Hannah said, looking deeply into her sister's eyes. "Michelle's right. No bags. Your eyes are a funny shade of red, but other than that . . ."

Andrea let out a shriek that would have raised the dead and jumped up. "Call Jon at home. He's just got to open early so I can get some eye drops. Tracey and I have to be on stage at two for the mother-daughter judging, and we're not going to win if I've got a case of redeye!"

"Relax." Hannah pulled her sister back down. "Your eyes are fine. I was just kidding."

"Don't *do* that. It's mean!" Andrea said petulantly. But then she started to laugh. "The last time I said that, I hit you with a pillow."

"I remember. It broke open and the feathers flew all over."

"And we had to clean it up and try to sew it back together before Mother got home from the grocery store."

"Did you make it?" Michelle asked.

"No," Hannah answered. "Andrea didn't know how to sew yet, and I was terrible at it. We ended up dumping all the feathers in a garbage bag and tying it shut. We put that in the pillowcase, and I had to sleep on a pillow that crinkled every time I moved my head."

Lisa looked a little wistful. "My sisters were all grown up by the time I was born. Two of them were married, and the other one had her own apartment and a job in Minneapolis. It must have been wonderful growing up with sisters."

Hannah turned to Andrea. "Did you ever notice how people who didn't grow up with sisters are the ones who think it would have been wonderful?"

"Right. And those who did grow up with sisters don't say anything at all?"

"Well, nobody has better sisters than I do. Last night proves that." Michelle turned to Andrea. "Did Bill check out those alibis?"

"First thing this morning. The highway patrol officer who stopped them remembers Elvis. He said he'd never seen a pickup with pictures of naked women painted on the bottom of the truck bed before."

Michelle made a face. "What a creep! And he wanted to show me his truck! But at least we know they're not murderers."

"Right." Hannah opened her steno notebook, the type she habitually carried in her large leather shoulder bag, and flipped to the suspect list. "Tasha's brothers. I guess I can fill in the names now, just so I can cross it out."

"It pays to be thorough," Michelle said. "Something might happen to make the Hicks brothers suspects again."

"They were thirty miles away from the scene at the time of Willa's murder," Andrea reminded her. "What could possibly make them suspects again?"

"I don't know, but there could be something."

They were getting nowhere fast, and Hannah knew it. It was time to take charge of the meeting. "Listen up," she said, glancing at the three women around the table. "Let's go over the motives and see if we can think of any more suspects."

"Good idea," Lisa said, giving Hannah a glance that said she understood. "Why don't you read us the motives?"

"Motive number one," Hannah didn't waste any time jumping in. "Willa's murder and the burglary are connected. Either Willa was a witness to the burglary, or she found out who did it. And she was killed before she could notify the authorities."

"So if we find the burglar, we find Willa's killer?" Lisa asked.

"If the motive is the correct one, we do."

Michelle looked thoughtful. "Then we're

running two investigations. Willa's murder and the burglary."

"Right. And we haven't even started working on the burglary yet. Are you ready for motive two?"

Everyone nodded and Hannah went on. "Motive two. There's no sense reading this one. We've already eliminated it."

"Read it anyway," Andrea suggested. "It might make us think of something else."

"Okay. Willa disqualified Tasha Hicks from the beauty pageant. And Tasha comes from a family known for violent retribution. We eliminated her brothers, but . . ." Hannah turned to Michelle. "Didn't you say her father entered her in the contest?"

"That's what she told me."

"Can you find out more about their father from Grandma McCann?" Hannah asked Andrea.

"I can try, but it'll be like pulling teeth. She's the one person in Lake Eden who doesn't gossip."

"I can do it," Lisa spoke up. "Marge knows everyone around here. And if she doesn't know the Hicks family personally, she'll know someone who does."

Hannah turned back to her notebook again. "Okay. Lisa's going to take care of that one. Let's go on to motive number three. It's something I found out from serving on the judging panel with Willa."

"Go on," Andrea said, leaning closer.

"Pam Baxter flunked a male home ec student on Willa's recommendation. Let's find out who he was and whether he's the type to take revenge."

"That one's mine," Michelle said. "Some of my friends have younger brothers and sisters that are still in school. I'll ask around."

" 'Good." Hannah made another note in her book. "Motive four. Willa gave Mrs. Adamczak's cinnamon bread a low grade, and now she can't win the baking sweepstakes again this year."

Andrea's mouth dropped open. "You think Mrs. Adamczak killed Willa?"

"Not really, but it's a motive. And we won't be doing our job if we don't check it out."

"Okay." Andrea looked dubious, but she nodded. "I'll see what I can find out from Mrs. Adamczak. I have to drop off some real estate flyers on her street anyway. What's next?"

"I don't really have a motive for the next one, but I do have a suspect. Unfortunately, we don't know who he is. It's Willa's boyfriend."

"What boyfriend?" Lisa wanted to know.

"The one she got all dressed up for," Andrea explained. "That dress she was wearing was expensive, and so was her new hairdo."

Hannah nodded. "Pam asked Willa whether there was a man involved and Willa said, *Isn't there always?* And then, when I walked out of the building with her after the judging, she told me she was meeting someone."

"That means we need to find out more about her personal life," Andrea said.

"Maybe you should go over and search her apartment," Lisa suggested. "I can hold down the fort here, if you want to do it now."

"Good idea," Andrea said. "I'm sure Mike and Lonnie have already done it, but they could have missed something. I'll call Pam right now and set it up."

While they waited for Andrea to complete her call, Lisa refilled coffee mugs. Hannah replenished the cookie platter, and they were all ready to continue when Andrea came back.

"She'll be home all morning," Andrea reported. "We can go over there right after we finish our meeting."

Hannah glanced down at her notes again.

"That's it, at least for now. I couldn't think of any other motives, except for the common one, of course."

"What common one?" Michelle wanted to know.

"Willa was killed by some unknown person for some unknown reason."

"That should be simple to check out," Lisa said, and they all shared a laugh.

"There's one more thing . . ." Hannah frowned slightly. "Maybe it doesn't have anything to do with her murder, but I think Willa had a secret."

At the word *secret,* all three women leaned closer.

"What secret?" Andrea asked.

"It wouldn't be a secret if I knew it," Hannah said. And after she'd gotten the groans she expected, she went on. "When we were judging the baked goods, Willa talked about a couple of things did that didn't fit with her personality . . . at least as I knew it. And Pam, who certainly knew Willa better than I did after a whole year of working with her, seemed totally surprised, too."

"Can you give us an example?" Michelle asked.

"Yes. Willa said something about picking cherries. She seemed to know all about it, and Pam asked her why. Willa said she worked in a cherry orchard for a while in Washington State."

Andrea shrugged. "Okay. I guess it could have been a summer job or something like that."

"That's true. But then she said something about working as a waitress down in Florida and how she'd served key lime pie. And she also said something about California."

"So she must have traveled," Lisa came to the obvious conclusion. "Maybe her family moved a lot when she was in high school."

Michelle shook her head. "I don't think so. One of the contestants was all upset because her parents were selling their house and moving to a condo when she went off to college. Miss Sunquist told her to take lots of pictures and that would keep the memories alive. She said she knew how hard it was to lose the house where you grew up, because she had to sell her family home a couple of years ago when her parents died, and it was really hard to leave it."

"So she must have traveled *after* high school." Andrea was clearly not ready to give up her theory. "Maybe she took the money she got from selling her parents' house and used it to see America, or something like that."

Lisa looked puzzled. "But it sounds like

she worked her way across the country. Why would she do that if she had all the money from selling her family home?"

"Maybe there were outstanding bills," Andrea suggested. "She might have cleared only a few thousand or so, especially if her parents had medical problems and they needed special care."

"But if they were old enough, they'd be on Medicare," Lisa pointed out.

"There are things that Medicare doesn't cover. And maybe her parents weren't old enough to be on Medicare."

"Enough speculation." Hannah held up her hand and everyone turned to her. "Here's what we have to do. Andrea and I will go through Willa's apartment to see if we can find out something about her background. There may be photos that could give us a clue, or papers of some kind. We'll also see if Pam has any background information on her. I'm sure the college forwarded something when Pam agreed to be Willa's supervising teacher."

"While you're gone, I'll call Marge about Tasha's father," Lisa offered.

"Good. We'll get that ball rolling."

"If we can find out Willa's address when she was in high school, I'll go through the sales records and see how much the house sold for," Andrea told them. "And I can also check to see if there were any liens against the property."

"Good. Don't forget Mrs. Adamczak," Hannah reminded her.

"I won't. I'll go see her right after we get back from searching the apartment. What kind of ribbon did she win again?"

"White. That's just an honorable mention. It's bound to be a letdown for her."

"Would she know it was Willa's fault that she didn't win?"

"I don't know. I didn't say anything, and I don't think Pam did either, but Pam hands in our scorecards to other people. It's possible that Mrs. Adamczak knows Willa was the one who kept her from being in the finals."

"Okay. I'll find out how mad she is that she didn't win."

"I still have a couple of hours before I have to drive out to the fairgrounds," Michelle said. "Is there anything else I can do?"

"Yes."

"What is it?"

"You can deliver the cookies to the Cookie Nook booth when you go out to the fairgrounds. And if you go early, you can help me with something else."

"I'll go early."

"Great. Do you know where you can get a picture of Willa?"

"Sure. There's one in the front of the program. We all have our pictures in there."

"Take a program with you, and stop by the 4-H building. There were some kids wearing 4-H shirts standing around when I said goodbye to Willa on Tuesday night. It's a long shot, but maybe one of them noticed where she went or who she met."

"Any idea which kids were there?"

"Not really. It was getting dark and I didn't notice. Just make the rounds with the photo and see what you can come up with."

"I will."

"How about me?" Lisa asked. "All I'm doing for you is asking Marge about Tasha's father. Can't I do anything else?"

Hannah laughed and held up her fingers as an aid in counting. "Let's see . . . you came in early to start the baking this morning, you're finding out about Mr. Hicks, you're running The Cookie Jar while Andrea and I go off to search Willa's apartment, you made some great suggestions at our meeting . . . isn't that enough?"

"Not in return for all you're doing for me!"

Hannah was puzzled. "What am I doing

for you?"

"You're saving me from a giant panic attack by taking my place as Herb's assistant."

Hannah groaned. She'd forgotten all about her costume, and time was definitely running short.

"Uh-oh!" Lisa said, looking worried. "You *are* going to be Herb's assistant, aren't you?"

"Of course I am. Absolutely. It's just that I haven't found a costume yet. I looked for one last night, but I couldn't find the skirt with the stars on it that I bought in college. And I can't go like this." Hannah looked down at her bright blue T-shirt that said EAT DESSERT FIRST in black block letters.

"That's okay. When I call Marge, I'll ask her to go through the clothes at Helping Hands Thrift Shop. There's bound to be something you can use, and Dad just loves to go there. Don't worry about a thing. They'll take care of it."

Hannah was even more worried, but there was no way she'd say so. Lisa adored her mother-in-law and either didn't realize or totally ignored the fact that Herb's mother favored a style of clothing that Hannah secretly thought of as "visually-impaired gray-haired Hippie." Instead of addressing that problem, she said simply, "Not red."

"I'll tell her. Just go on with Andrea and

leave your costume to us."

"All right, I will," Hannah said, already regretting it. But she'd only have to wear the costume for an hour at the most, and then she'd never have to look at it again. How bad could it possibly be?

CHAPTER
TWENTY-ONE

"Find anything yet?" Andrea asked. She was sitting at Willa's desk, going through the drawers while Hannah tackled the small kitchen that was built into an alcove.

"Yes."

"You found something?"

"Yes, but not what you think. I found three boxes of macaroni and cheese, and a two-pound can of coffee. Those were the only consumables in her kitchen cupboard. For a home economics teacher, Willa didn't do much cooking."

"Pam probably invited her to eat with them every night."

"That could be. Did you find anything?"

"A couple of things. Come and take a look."

Hannah ducked out of the alcove and pulled a chair over to join Andrea at the desk. "A diploma?" she asked, taking the paper from Andrea.

"From high school. It's got the year, and that means I can start researching the sale of her parents' house."

"Great. Anything else?"

"Yes. Willa was a romantic."

Hannah took the hardcover volume that Andrea handed her. "A copy of *Gone With The Wind* makes her a romantic?"

"I think it does. But look inside and you'll be really convinced."

Hannah flipped the book open and discovered a flower pressed in a small cellophane bag. "Is that an orchid?"

"Yes. Read the card."

There was a florist's card under the flower and Hannah pulled it out. It read, *Yesterday and Today, Tomorrow and Forever.* "Do you think it's from her high school prom?"

"Maybe. Or it could be from some other special occasion. She saved it, so it must have been important to her."

"Very important, especially since she didn't save anything else." Hannah glanced around her. They'd searched every nook and cranny of Willa's apartment, and the pressed flower and card were the only two personal items they'd found. "Let's go up and talk to Pam. I want to find out if Willa ever brought any friends here."

■ ■ ■ ■

"Not really," Pam responded to Hannah's question and filled her coffee cup at the same time. "I didn't think we were ever going to meet Gordon, but finally she agreed to bring him to dinner."

"Gordon?" Hannah pulled out her steno pad.

"Gordon Tate. Professor Gordon Tate. He's head of the archaeology department at Tri-County College."

"And Willa was dating him?" Andrea asked.

"Yes. He was a bit older than she was, but that didn't seem to matter. They were both loners, and they got along really well together. George and I were absolutely delighted when she told us he'd asked her to marry him."

"Whoa," Hannah said, frowning. "You didn't tell me Willa was engaged."

"That's because she wasn't. She told Gordon she couldn't marry him, and they broke up two months ago."

"Was it a bad breakup?" Andrea asked.

"No. If you ask me, there wasn't enough passion in their relationship for it to be bad. The only thing either of them were passionate about was riding."

"Riding?"

"Gordon had a place with a stable, and they went riding almost every weekend. Willa was a real cowgirl on her days off."

"What about after they broke up?" Andrea asked.

"Oh, she still went out to his place to ride. They even dated for a while after she turned down his proposal. It was just that Willa really didn't want to marry him. She said Gordon was much too set in his ways."

"How do you mean?" Hannah wanted to know.

"He had a rigid schedule. Willa told me about it once. He had toast and orange juice for breakfast every morning, he read the paper from the front page back and never sneaked a peek at the comics first, and he washed the car every Thursday. That type of thing."

"Sounds deadly dull," Hannah commented, sighing a bit and wondering if she could use a little less passion and a little more dullness in her own love life.

"Well, Gordon *was* a bit of a stuffed shirt. He's a very nice man. Don't get me wrong. But Willa had so much more life in her. George and I weren't too upset when they called it off, and Willa didn't seem that upset either."

"But was *Gordon* upset?"

"Upset enough to have taken revenge?" Andrea followed Hannah's question with one of her own.

"Oh, no," Pam waved off that suggestion. "Gordon would never do anything like that! I'm absolutely positive of it. And even if I've completely misread his personality, Gordon *couldn't* have done it."

"Why's that?" Hannah asked her.

"He's been out of the country for at least a month, and he's not coming back until fall semester starts at the college. He's taken six of his best students to a dig in Mexico."

"Do you know where in Mexico?"

"No. Sorry. But you could probably check with the college. Whoever's filling in for him at the department should know."

Hannah was thoughtful on their way back to The Cookie Jar. Pam had always been a good judge of character, and Gordon didn't sound like the type to murder Willa over a rejected proposal, but Hannah wasn't willing to let it go. It was *possible* that Gordon had done it. People flew back and forth to places like Acapulco all the time. Until she'd eliminated that possibility, Gordon would remain on her list.

Hannah stared down at the pile of formal dresses that Marge and Jack Herman had placed on the work island in her kitchen and mouthed the words that the little girl in *Poltergeist* had exclaimed. "They're back," she said, under her breath.

"What was that?" Marge looked puzzled.

"Nothing. Where did you get all these?"

"From Helping Hands. They let us bring all of them. You choose the one you want, and we'll bring the rest back."

"Great," Hannah said, because the first phrase that occurred to her would have shocked everyone.

"I really like the pink satin, but you probably won't want to wear it with your hair," Marge went on. "The Kelly green silk is nice, though. And the dotted Swiss with the lavender lining is just darling."

"I like the purple," Jack offered his opinion. "It'll match Herb's . . . whatchamacallit."

Marge turned to him with a smile. "You're right, Jack. It'll match Herb's cape perfectly."

"That's it, *cape*." Jack returned her smile. "I'm surprised I forgot that word. Especially since we just watched that latest Superman movie. Which dress do you like, Lisa?"

"The turquoise voile. Or . . . maybe the yellow chiffon. Either one would look nice on you, Hannah."

"I like the yellow, too," Marge said, "but I'd take off that orange flower. It looks a little shopworn."

"Right," Hannah said, glancing at the huge orange flower that adorned the neckline of the yellow dress. Unfortunately, it covered a plunging neckline, and removing it would expose a whole lot more of her than she wanted to expose. If only Norman weren't quite so efficient. He'd obviously dropped off her dresses at Helping Hands this morning, and now they were haunting her. She hadn't expected him to keep them in his trunk forever, but another twenty-four hours would have been nice.

"Do you want to try them on?" Marge asked.

"No, that's okay. They look like they'll fit."

"So which one will you wear?" Lisa asked after a long moment passed and Hannah hadn't reached out to take one.

Hannah felt like a condemned man ordering his last meal and discovering that his only choices were foods he hated. As far as the dresses were concerned, they were equally bad. She told herself that she'd worn each of these outfits once, and she could make everyone happy if she wore one of them again. It wasn't too much to ask.

"The purple?" Jack looked hopeful.

"Definitely the purple," Hannah said, earning a huge smile from Jack. "I think it would be good if I coordinated colors with Herb, don't you?"

"It'll be perfect," Lisa said.

"That's very sweet of you, Hannah," Marge said, and Hannah suspected that Marge had guessed the real reason she'd chosen the purple dress.

"Let's take the rest of these back," Jack suggested, carefully removing the purple taffeta from the pile and handing it to Hannah. "You're coming, aren't you, Marge?"

"Of course I am."

After Marge and Jack had gone out the back, carrying the dresses, Hannah went to hang the purple taffeta in the bathroom so that she could change before she left for the fairgrounds. When she came out, she found Lisa waiting for her.

"Thanks, Hannah," Lisa said, giving her a hug. "You made Dad really happy. But are you sure you really want to wear that dress? It'll look horrible with your hair."

Hannah shrugged. "That's okay. It's only

for fifteen minutes or so, and then I'll change clothes. It's not like I'm going to wear it forever, you know."

Hannah glanced at the clock. It was almost two, and they hadn't had a customer in forty-five minutes. Everyone was out at the fairgrounds, and it was a waste of time and energy for them to stay open. "How about closing at two?" she asked Lisa.

"That's fine with me. Herb's getting off at two-thirty, and we're going out to the fair early with Marge and Dad. And that reminds me, you can cross Mr. Hicks off your suspect list. Marge knows the family, and he's been in a wheelchair for months. He broke his leg in a bar fight."

"Thanks, Lisa." Hannah took out her notebook and crossed off Tasha's father. "I saw Willa's killer running away, so it couldn't possibly have . . ."

"I've got to go to the kitchen right now," Lisa said. "Tell me later."

"But we're all through with the baking. Why do you have to go to the kitchen now?"

"Because Mrs. Rhodes just pulled up out front, and your mother's getting out of the car."

Hannah glanced out the plate glass window. Lisa was right. "And you're deserting me in my hour of need?"

"Yes, but it's for my own safety. Your mother might be looking for more volunteers. Herb and I saw that piece Wingo Jones did on KCOW television about No-No Fulton. If your mother asked me, I'd probably say yes, and I don't want to get dunked."

Hannah laughed and waved her away. She certainly couldn't blame Lisa for that. She didn't want to get dunked, either!

"Hello, dear," Delores said, coming through the doorway as if she owned the place. "Carrie and I just got back from lunch. She's going to check in with Luanne at the store, and I stopped in to bring you a kitty bag."

"Don't you mean doggy bag?"

"No, it's for Moishe. We had the trout at that new fish place in the mall. It was so good, I ordered takeout for Moishe. There's coleslaw in there, too, if you want it. He doesn't eat that, does he?"

"Not usually. Thank you, Mother. That was very sweet of you."

"You're welcome." Mother and daughter were both silent for a moment, and then Delores cleared her throat.

Here it comes, Hannah thought. Her mother hadn't come all the way into town simply to deliver food for the grandcat who'd shredded a half-dozen pairs of her pantyhose.

"You're looking into Willa Sunquist's murder, aren't you dear?"

"Yes, Mother. Unofficially, of course."

"Of course. I'm not certain, but I may have some information you'll find useful."

"Really?" Hannah's ears perked up. Delores was a charter member of the Lake Eden gossip hotline, Hannah's name for the group of women who could spread a rumor ten times faster than a billboard in the center of town. Although Delores insisted that she never repeated gossip, the tidbits she'd divulged to Hannah in the past had helped to solve several murder cases.

"You know I don't like to gossip, don't you, dear?"

"Yes, Mother."

"This may not be important, but Willa came into Granny's Attic on Tuesday morning, right after she got her hair done. Luanne was working and she said Willa seemed quite *Friday faced.*"

"Friday faced?"

"Sorry, dear. I've been stuck in Regency mode lately. What I meant to say was that Willa appeared to be depressed."

"Any idea why?"

"Yes, she came right out and told Luanne. She said she found a dress she adored at Claire's shop, but she couldn't afford it. And then she asked Luanne if we ever bought old silver."

This was getting interesting. Hannah poured her mother a cup of coffee and brought out the cookies. "And Luanne told her you did?"

"That's right. Willa said she'd be right back, and she was, about fifteen minutes later, with a cardboard box full of silver. She said she'd been lugging it around for ages and she couldn't bear to unpack it."

"Did she say why?"

"Yes. It was from her parents' house, and looking at it made her miss them too much."

"I guess I can understand that."

"Really? Is there something of mine that would make you miss me too much?"

It was a trick question, and Hannah knew it. Whatever she said would be wrong. But she had to say something, so she simply blurted out the truth. "It wouldn't be any sort of special object, Mother. I think that just waking up in the morning and remembering that you weren't there would make me miss you every day."

"Oh, Hannah!" Delores looked perfectly astonished. "I didn't know that you were so sentimental."

"I didn't either," Hannah said, surprising herself by blinking back a tear. "Don't tell anyone, okay?"

Delores used her napkin to wipe her eyes. "All right. I won't."

"Thank you, Mother. I don't want to ruin my reputation for being pragmatic. So did Luanne buy the silver from Willa?"

"Yes. She opened the box, and the first thing she saw was a three-tiered filigreed candy dish, circa nineteen forty. And since one of our decorators is looking for a candy dish exactly like it and she's willing to pay a hundred and fifty dollars, Luanne knew how valuable it was. And right next to the candy dish was a pair of silver candlesticks that must have belonged to Willa's grandmother."

"Valuable?"

"Yes. At least a hundred dollars, perhaps more. Luanne asked Willa how much she wanted for the silver, and Willa said she was hoping it would be worth a hundred dollars."

"So Luanne paid her a hundred dollars?"

"No, dear. That's not the way we do business at Granny's Attic. After all, we have to live in this community. It's different at an auction. Then we get the best bargain we can. But this was a purchase from someone right here in Lake Eden. No one would ever patronize us again if we cheated our neighbors."

"So Luanne offered Willa two hundred and fifty dollars?"

"Two hundred. We're entitled to make a profit."

"And Willa was happy with that?"

"She was delighted, and she went right off to buy her dress. Luanne put the box in the back, and she didn't get around to going through it until this morning." Delores frowned slightly. "I'm meandering like the Serpentine, aren't I, dear?"

Serpentine. River in London. Delores was back in Regency mode again. Hannah just smiled. "That's okay, Mother. Just tell me what Luanne found."

"Several other nice pieces, but nothing outstanding. It turned out that two hundred was a fair price."

"And . . ." Hannah encouraged her mother to go on.

"Way down at the bottom of the box was another box. It was one of those gift presentation boxes lined with blue velvet. Do you know what I mean, dear?"

"Yes. You gave me some silver salt and pepper shakers in a box like that last year.

What was inside Willa's presentation box?"

"Two crystal champagne glasses in silver sleeves, the kind a bride and groom use to toast each other at weddings."

"And they were from her parents' wedding?"

"No, dear. They couldn't have been. I looked up the history of the company that made them, and they've only been in business for three years."

CHAPTER
TWENTY-TWO

"I'll be right back. I need something cold to drink." Herb fanned his face with the schedule they'd picked up at the box office. They were standing outside the stage door to the auditorium, and getting there hadn't been easy. Hannah and Herb had carried the magic cabinet, which had turned out to be surprisingly heavy. "Do you want me to bring you something?"

"Yes."

"What?"

"A glass of water and three strong guys. Seriously, Herb . . . I think we're going to need some help getting the magic cabinet inside."

"You're right. I'll look around for someone to recruit. Stay by the cabinet, okay? It was expensive, and Lisa and I saved up for a month to buy it."

Hannah stood there for a few moments, watching the crowds pass by. And then she heard someone call her name. She turned to see Eddy and Ginger Eilers rushing toward her. Both Ginger and Eddy were 4-H Club supporters, and their nine-year-old son, Kenny, had joined the moment he was old enough.

"Kenny, tell Miss Swensen what you told us." Ginger motioned him forward, and Hannah had the distinct impression that if Kenny had failed to move, both parents would have grabbed him by the arms and shoved him up to face her.

"Okay. I just didn't want to . . . you know," Kenny said, gulping a little.

"He's afraid he won't be able to show his calf if he tells you what he did," Eddy explained. "Kenny broke the rules."

Hannah was puzzled. "But . . . I don't have anything to do with the livestock judging."

"That's what I told him. And I also said that maybe you wouldn't have to say where you got the information."

"What information?" Hannah asked.

"I know something about the lady that was killed," Kenny said, "but I didn't want to say anything because I was sneaking into the barn after it was all locked up to make sure that Boomer was okay."

"Boomer's his calf," Eddy explained.

"This is Kenny's first 4-H competition."

"He thought Boomer might be lonely in the barn with all those strange calves," Ginger added.

"I see." Hannah turned to Kenny. "Then I think it would be best if you tell me what you saw in confidence, and I won't use your name. Is that okay with you?"

"Okay!" Kenny looked very relieved. "I didn't know it was important until Princess Michelle came around with the picture. She passed it around, and I recognized that lady. Do you want to know all about when I saw her?"

"That would be a good place to start."

"Okay. The first time I saw her was on the first night, and she was with a rodeo cowboy. They were fighting, you know . . . arguing about something. I didn't hear what it was, but she looked really mad. And then he said some stuff and they made up."

Hannah took a deep breath and prepared to address what could be a delicate subject. "How do you know they made up?"

"I saw them hugging. They hugged for a long time. And then he walked her out to the parking lot."

"What did he look like?"

Kenny shrugged. "Like all the rest of the rodeo cowboys."

"Describe him, Kenny," Ginger broke in. "Tell Miss Swensen what he was wearing."

"Oh. Okay, Mom. He was wearing cowboy boots. They all wear cowboy boots. And jeans and a snappy black shirt."

"He means a shirt with snaps instead of buttons," Eddy clarified.

"And he had on a cowboy hat. That's why I don't know what color his hair is or anything like that. It was one of those big hats."

"You said Monday night was the *first* time you saw them."

"Yeah. I saw them again the next night. It was late and I was checking on Boomer again. They started turning the lights on and off, and I knew I had to get back to the dorm with the other kids."

"They stay overnight in the dorm building," Eddy explained. "The parents take turns chaperoning them."

"She was with that cowboy again," Kenny went on. "Leastwise I think it was the same cowboy. It was dark, and it was kinda hard to tell. They were just walking past the barn when I saw them."

"Which way were they going?" Hannah asked.

"Towards the Ferris wheel. And I was going the other way towards the dorm. And then the lights flickered again, and I started to run so I could get in before they locked the door."

"Was that the last time you saw them?" Hannah asked.

"Yes."

"Thank you for telling me, Kenny," Hannah said. "You helped me a lot. And don't worry. I won't tell anyone we talked."

After Ginger, Eddy, and Kenny had left, Hannah leaned against the magic cabinet and thought about what she'd learned. On Tuesday night, right after the judging, Willa had told her she was meeting someone. Was that someone the rodeo cowboy that Kenny had seen? She was just wondering how things tied together when she overheard a snatch of conversation.

"Tucker sure messed up with that Brahma," one man said. "I've never seen him get thrown so easy before."

"Yeah. Makes you wonder, don't it?"

"Wonder what?"

"Wonder if he did it on purpose. Darn near killed Curly getting that bull sidetracked so Tucker could get out. Hope he's gonna be okay."

Hannah risked a peek around the corner. Just as she'd suspected, two rodeo cowboys were headed her way. If they saw her, they'd stop talking so candidly, and she was very interested in what they had to say, especially since she'd just learned that Willa had met a rodeo cowboy on the night that she was killed.

"Poor Curly. You saw him right after. Do you think he's gonna be all right?" the second cowboy asked.

"I don't know. He was tore up pretty bad. And Tucker didn't act right about it, you know?"

"Why? What did he do?"

Hannah couldn't wait any longer. Their voices were getting louder as they approached, and there was no cover she could take to keep from being seen, except . . .

The moment she thought of it she was moving, opening the door of the magic cabinet and stepping inside. She closed the door, latched it from the inside, and peeked out through one of the slots for the swords as the two cowboys came around the corner.

"Most guys that come over that top rail look like they saw a ghost. They're real scared. Tucker wasn't. He was grinning until he saw I was watching him."

"That's real bad if you're right about it. But why'd Tucker want to hurt Curly?"

Their voices had sounded familiar, and now that she'd seen them Hannah knew why. They'd been a part of the group of rodeo cowboys giving the trick roping demonstration the first morning of the fair. Had Willa known one of these cowboys? Had seeing him again been such a shock that Hannah and Pam had mistaken Willa's reaction for sunstroke?

And then another question jumped front and center in Hannah's mind. Was one of these men the rodeo cowboy that Kenny Eilers had seen with Willa shortly before she was murdered?

Hannah expected the two cowboys to walk on by. When they did, she planned to step out of the cabinet and try to hear more of their conversation as they walked away. But they stopped right next to the magic cabinet, and one of them leaned against it with a thump.

"There's bad blood between those two," the second cowboy explained. "Curly was sweet on Brianna, and they were going out almost every night before Tucker joined up with the show."

"I know that, but Tucker's got no reason to kill Curly. He beat Curly out fair and square. Brianna's gonna marry Tucker. He gave her a ring and everything."

"A ring don't mean it's over."

"What do you mean?"

"Gals change their mind all the time. It's not over until Sam walks Brianna down the aisle and she says *I do* in front of a preacher."

"You mean Curly might win her back?"

"Anything's possible. The way I hear it, Curly's been asking questions about Tucker's background. I think he's trying to dig up something to keep Brianna from marrying him. And that could be why Tucker tried to do him in today. Could be that Curly's getting a little too close to the truth."

"What truth?"

"I dunno. Say . . . are you going to the roundup dance Saturday night? Some of these local gals look pretty good to me."

"Me, too. But there's that new little barrel rider. She's cute."

"You're better off with the local girls. You have a little fun, and then you can leave town. If you go for the barrel rider, she's with you for the whole season."

"You got a point. And that reminds me . . . we're gonna get paid, aren't we?"

"You mean because of the robbery?"

"Yeah."

Burglary, Hannah mentally corrected them, but she didn't make a sound. She didn't dare move, either, although she was getting more than a little cramped.

"I asked Riggs, and he said not to worry

about it. Sam's got plenty put away."

"Hannah?" a familiar voice called her name. And then again, a bit closer, "Hannah?"

Hannah remained perfectly silent and perfectly motionless. It was Herb calling her, but she couldn't answer. If she made a sound, the two cowboys would know she'd been eavesdropping on their conversation.

About the time Hannah didn't think she could stand being confined a moment longer, she saw Herb come around the corner. He looked worried and she was sorry about that, but there'd be time to explain everything later.

"Hi, guys," Herb greeted them.

"Hey," one of the cowboys answered. "You must be the magician, huh?"

"That's me. Did you see a woman around here, tall and a little chubby with frizzy red hair?"

There would also be time to make Herb pay for that chubby remark later, Hannah promised herself. Right now silence on her part was essential.

"Nope," the second cowboy answered. "Haven't seen anybody like that, and we've been standing here talking for a couple of minutes or so."

"Lose your wife?" the first cowboy asked.

"No, my assistant. And I can't do my trick without her. But since you guys are here, I wonder if you'd do me a little favor."

"Sure, as long as you're not gonna pull us out of a hat," the second cowboy said with a laugh.

"It's nothing like that. I have to get this cabinet inside and ready to go out on stage. It's heavy, and I can't do it alone. Do you think you could help me carry it?"

"We can do that," the first cowboy said with a grin. "How'd you get it this far anyway?"

"My assistant helped me carry it."

"Tall and chubby with frizzy red hair *and* muscles?" the second cowboy turned to his friend. "Sounds like your type."

"Maybe. Be a lot better than that gal from Fargo." The first cowboy flashed a grin. "Where do you want us to grab this, Houdini?"

"See the handles on the sides?"

"Yeah. I see 'em."

"You take one side, your buddy can take the other, and I'll get the handle on the end. Ready?"

There was a breathless moment when Hannah felt herself lifted, and tilted so that she was on her back with her feet higher than her head. Then everything changed and they set her down. Hard.

"Whoa!" one of the cowboys exclaimed. "This thing's heavy! You say you and your assistant carried it all the way here?"

"That's right. This probably sounds crazy, but it didn't seem this heavy then. Maybe we need more muscle. Do you think we should look for a fourth guy to help us?"

"Nah." The first cowboy shook his head. "We lift heavier than this when we strike the show. We'll get this dang thing inside for you or die tryin'."

Hannah took a deep breath and tensed for what might be a rough ride. The back of her head felt slightly sore, and she hoped they wouldn't set her down hard again.

What a terrible pickle! she thought, using one of her father's favorite expressions as she was jolted and jounced and bumped inside. Then the cabinet came to rest, upright, thank goodness, and Hannah took a grateful breath.

"Thanks a lot, guys," Herb said, and Hannah watched through the sword slit near her head as Herb shook their hands. "I'd better go look for my assistant before they call my name."

Hannah watched Herb walk away, presumably to go look for her. The two cowboys stood there for a moment and then they left, too. Hannah moved her head to look out of another slit. There was no one around.

After a second check of all the slits she could use as peepholes, Hannah inched the door open and stepped out. She shut the door behind her and was just dusting herself off when Herb rushed up to her.

"Where were you?"

"Not that far away."

"But I looked all over for you and I couldn't find you. I thought you were going to stay with the magic cabinet."

"I had it in my sight the whole time," Hannah insisted, not mentioning that her sight had been from the *inside* of the cabinet. "Those two cowboys were pretty good lifters, weren't they?"

"I'll say!" Herb wiped his forehead and took a deep breath. "Sorry, Hannah. I shouldn't have yelled at you. We're up next, and I guess I'm nervous."

"You'll do fine. Really you will."

"I sure hope so! Lisa's got all her old girlfriends from high school out there to cheer me on. Do you think we can get the magic cabinet out on stage by ourselves?"

"Absolutely."

"But it's really heavy."

"Just leave it to me. I'm used to lifting fifty-pound sacks of flour and sugar down at The Cookie Jar." Hannah thought it wise not to mention that the magic cabinet would be more than a few pounds lighter when they moved it on stage. "All you have to do is stick the right swords in all the right places at all the right times, and we'll be just fine."

CHAPTER
TWENTY-THREE

"Come on, Hannah. They're calling for us!"

Herb was beaming from ear to ear as he took her arm and escorted her onto the stage. Hannah was beaming, too. They'd won the competition. Herb had been judged the best magician in the show.

Her smile stayed in place until there were several flashes and she realized that Norman was standing up in front of the audience, taking their picture. Her picture. In the awful purple taffeta bridesmaid dress!

Another few minutes of handshaking with the judges and bowing to the audience and they were through. Hannah walked offstage and into the wings with a huge sigh of relief.

"Congratulations!" Norman said, rushing up to Herb to shake his hand. And then he turned to Hannah. "You were just perfect, Hannah. I knew it was a trick, but I still got nervous when Herb asked you to knock three times if you were okay, and he had to ask twice before you did it."

"I think that's what really impressed the judges," Herb said. "Hannah's sense of timing was just great. I knew she was fine, but I was still starting to get a little worried about her."

Me, too, Hannah thought, but she didn't admit it. She wasn't about to tell anybody that her leg had gone to sleep and she was so busy massaging it, she hadn't even heard Herb's question the first time he asked it.

"Rod said to tell you he's writing a feature story about the contest and he's going to run a picture of the two of you in the *Lake Eden Journal* on Sunday."

Hannah gave a weak little smile. Her picture. In the awful purple taffeta bridesmaid dress. Her own words had come back to haunt her. *It's not like I'm going to wear it forever, you know,* she'd told Lisa. But now it appeared she was. She'd be frozen forever in the archives of their local newspaper, wearing the awful purple . . .

"What is it?" Norman asked as Hannah suddenly started to smile.

"Nothing." Hannah gave a little shrug, but she felt more like whooping, hollering, and dancing. Rod only published one color picture a year, and that was at Christmas. The rest of the year all photos were in black and white. In the picture that Norman had just taken, she'd be wearing a black dress. She was saved! This wasn't the worst day of her life, after all!

"Too bad we won't be in color," Herb said, frowning slightly. "Lisa really likes the way I look in this purple cape."

Norman thumped the side of his head with his hand. "I was so excited about your winning, I forgot to tell you. Rod's pulling out all the stops for this feature. He's even going to publish your picture in color right under the banner on the front page."

"It's really nice of you to drive me, Norman." Hannah was grateful, due in no small part to the cool air that was blowing from the vents in Norman's sedan. Although she had air-conditioning in her cookie truck, tepid was the word that best described the lowest temperature it reached. "And thanks for letting me call Doc Knight from your nice, cool car."

"That's okay. You need one."

"A car with good air-conditioning?"

"No, a cell phone. It's a good thing to have in case of an emergency. It could even save your life."

"Maybe you're right, but think of all the calls I'd get from Mother. It would be like wearing an electronic leash."

Norman thought about that for a moment. "Then don't turn it on unless you want to make a call."

"But doesn't that defeat the whole purpose?"

"Not really. It would be there for your convenience, not your mother's. Think of it as the miniature phone booth you carry in your purse. Instead of putting in money to make a call, you just turn it on and punch in the number."

"That's worth considering," Hannah said, warming to the idea. "I promise I'll think about it."

"Good. Only two miles to go, Hannah."

Hannah glanced at her watch. "I think we're going to make it. Doc Knight promised he'd delay as long as he could before he put Curly under."

"I sure hope he's okay. He's my favorite rodeo clown."

"You know him?"

"A little. I talked to him before the rodeo this afternoon, and I took his picture."

"When he was saving Tucker from the bull?"

"Before that. They needed a few photos for flyers to advertise the show, and I volunteered."

Hannah smiled. Norman was a very generous man. "That was nice of you, Norman."

"Maybe. But I had an ulterior motive."

"What?"

"When I was a kid, I loved rodeos. I guess it sounds silly now, but I always wanted to be a rodeo star."

"It doesn't sound silly to me. I always wanted to be a prima ballerina, but I have lousy balance."

"Same here. Not the ballet part, but I'm a lousy rider so I knew I couldn't be a rodeo cowboy. That's when I started noticing the clowns and I realized that their job was more important and a lot more dangerous than any rodeo star out there."

"I never came to terms with the ballet thing," Hannah admitted. "I skipped school one day, took the bus to Minneapolis, and bought myself a pair of Capezios. I thought that if I had the right shoes, I could be a ballerina."

"That's sad." Norman reached out to squeeze her hand.

"No, that's stupid. But I still put on *Swan Lake* sometimes, and dance around the living room."

Norman pulled up in the parking lot and shut off the engine. "Do you think Curly can shed any light on Willa's murder?"

"I don't know. The whole thing is like a jigsaw puzzle, the kind that doesn't have a picture on the cover. I've got a lot more pieces in place right now than I did when I started, but so far all they're doing is making me realize how many other pieces are missing."

As they pushed open the door to the lobby at Lake Eden Memorial Hospital, a familiar scent hit Hannah's nostrils. It was the smell she always associated with hospitals, a combination of antiseptic floor soap, talcum powder, and coffee that had warmed in a pot for too long. There was a mirrored wall that had been designed to make the waiting area seem larger, and Hannah winced as she caught sight of her reflection. She was still wearing the purple taffeta dress. She hadn't wanted to take the time to change.

"Nobody at the desk," Norman said, walking up to the deserted reception area and stating the obvious.

"That's okay. Doc Knight told me which room. Come on."

Hannah led the way down the corridor to one of the rooms Doc Knight used for pre op. She opened the door, expecting to see Doc Knight and a nurse hovering over

Curly, but the only person in the room was the cowboy.

"Hi, Curly," she said, walking over to take the chair by his bed. "I'm Hannah Swensen. Did Doc Knight tell you I was coming?"

Curly nodded, which was all he could do. It was obvious that he'd taken a turn for the worse since she'd spoken to Doc Knight. Curly was now on a ventilator.

"I realize you can't speak, so I'll only ask questions you can answer with a yes or a no. Do you think that Tucker deliberately tried to kill you this afternoon?"

Curly's eyes widened. He was clearly startled by the question, and Hannah hoped she hadn't shocked him too much. Then he sighed and gave a nod.

"One of the other cowboys said you've been asking questions about Tucker's background. Is that true?"

Curly gave another nod, a little weaker this time. Hannah knew she had to hurry. He was fading fast.

"Did you find out anything that might have caused Tucker to try to kill you?"

Curly tried to move his head, but it didn't happen. He blinked his eyelids as if they were too heavy to keep open, and then they fluttered shut. Hannah glanced at the IV stand next to his bed. Something in a bag was slowly dripping into Curly's veins and Hannah concluded that Doc Knight had ordered a pre-op sedative.

"Hannah?" It was Doc Knight, and Hannah moved over as he walked to the bed and made an adjustment to Curly's IV. "That's it. I have to get this young man patched up."

"Okay, Doc." Hannah turned back to Curly. He looked as still as death, and she hoped it was just a metaphor.

"Good luck, Curly," Norman said, reaching out to touch his arm.

"Yes, good luck," Hannah echoed, and then she turned to Doc Knight. "Is he going to be okay?"

Doc Knight motioned them out into the hallway. "I can't make any promises," he said. "He's young and he's strong, and he was in good health before that bull got to him. That's in his favor. And I'm going to do my best. That goes without saying. The only thing is, I'm not going to know how much damage there is until I open him up."

"So it could go either way?" Norman asked.

"I'm afraid so. Times like this make me wish I'd gone into dermatology."

"Not exactly a balanced meal," Norman

said, smiling as he dug into his Corn Dog Combo. Since they'd gotten back to the fairgrounds forty minutes before the Miss Tri-County Competition was scheduled to start, and changing clothes had taken Hannah only a couple of minutes, they had time to stop at the food court for sustenance.

Hannah glanced down at his plate. "Looks balanced to me. You've got a corn dog balanced on top of a pile of baked beans."

"I like the way you think," Norman said, glancing over at her plate. "How's that Big Blue Ox burger?"

"A little heavy on the blue cheese, but a lot better than I thought it would be."

Hannah and Norman were silent for a few moments while they hurried through their meals. Norman was the first to finish, and he stood up. "What do you want for dessert?"

A deep-fried candy bar, Hannah thought, but she didn't say it. They'd passed the Sinful Pleasures booth on their way in, and someone else had been taking Ruby's place. Hannah assumed that she was at the hospital with Riggs, since Curly was one of his rodeo clowns. She'd wait to indulge in that particular calorie-laden treat until Ruby was working again.

"Just coffee," Hannah said, although she

was already tasting the gooey confection in her mind. "We're judging cakes tonight so I'll have plenty of dessert later."

"Okay, I'll get the coffee. Which booth is best?"

"The Cookie Nook. Mayor Bascomb's staff makes a mean cup of coffee."

Once Norman had headed off to fetch their coffee, Hannah glanced around at the other tables. There was no one she knew except . . . "Mary?" she called out, spotting Mary Adamczak several tables away.

"Yes?" several women chorused, and Hannah felt like a fool. Mary was a very popular name in the Tri-County area.

"Sorry," Hannah apologized to all the women who were staring at her. "I thought I saw Mary Adamczak."

"Here I am," Mary Adamczak called out.

"And here I am," her younger companion added.

Hannah felt her mind clutch as she walked over to their table. "What's going on? *Both* of you are Mary Adamczak?"

"That's right," the older woman, the Mary Adamczak Hannah knew, answered her. "I'm Mary *Lou* Adamczak, and I'd like you to meet Mary *Kay* Adamczak, my son Ronnie's wife."

Hannah laughed. "You really had me go-

ing there. Glad to meet you, Mary Kay."
And then she noticed that Mary Lou's right
arm was in a sling. "What happened to your
arm?"

"I pulled a tendon last week. That's why
Mary Kay had to make my cinnamon bread
this year."

"That was you?" Hannah turned to Mary
Kay.

"Yes, and it's the first time in my life I've
ever baked anything. I couldn't believe I
won a ribbon!"

"And she did it without any help from
me," Mary Lou said, sounding very proud.
"Ronnie took me in to see Doc Knight, and
when we came home, she'd baked two
loaves."

"Are you moving here to Lake Eden?"
Hannah asked Mary Kay.

"No, we're just visiting until the end of
the month. That's when Ronnie goes back
to work. He's an assistant basketball coach
for the Badgers."

University of Wisconsin Badgers, Hannah
recited to herself, remembering how she'd
once memorized all the university team
names in a five-state area to impress a college baseball player she'd wanted to date.
That had never happened, but she still
remembered the team names.

"I think that man over there wants to get your attention," Mary Kay said, gesturing in Norman's direction.

"You're right. He went to get us some coffee, and he's back. Nice seeing you, Mary Lou. And nice meeting you, Mary Kay. Congratulations on your success in the competition."

As Hannah hurried back to the table and the hot cup of coffee that awaited her, she mentally crossed Mary Lou Adamczak off her suspect list. And then she mentally congratulated herself for giving Mary Kay's cinnamon bread a high enough score to win an honorable mention.

"I'm not surprised Michelle won tonight," Norman said as they made their way out of the auditorium. "She gave an excellent answer to the question about world hunger, and it was a tough question."

"I know. She's always been good at thinking on her feet, and she's well informed about social issues. I thought it helped a lot when she interjected a little humor into the question about nutrition."

"It cracked everybody up, including the judges." Norman gave a little chuckle. "And I know where she got that answer."

Hannah assumed a guileless expression.

"Can I help it if she picks things up from me?"

Norman stopped at the steps to the Creative Arts Building and put his arm around Hannah's shoulders. "Do you mind if I wait for you to get through with tonight's judging? I'd like to follow you home and check in with Moishe."

"With Moishe?"

"Yeah. I'm still worried about the Big Guy. I thought I'd run over to the mall while you're judging and pick up some treats from the pet store."

"That's really nice of you, Norman." Hannah smiled. Norman really was a great guy. "Moishe always loves to see you. But I do have to make it an early night. I've been up late three nights in a row, and I need to turn in early and sweat myself to sleep."

Norman laughed appreciatively. "I know what you mean," he said, "but the weatherman said it's going to cool down by midnight."

"Which weatherman?"

"Rayne Phillips on KCOW."

"Then it's going to be hot all night. Rayne Phillips is always wrong. I'm really glad the former owners put a window air conditioner in my bedroom."

"And I'm really glad you thought to put

central air in our dream house."

"It's *your* dream house, Norman."

"Whatever. I'm glad you suggested it."

"You mean you actually installed it?"

"Of course. You're surprised?"

Hannah nodded. Air-conditioning had been a part of the plans they'd submitted for the contest. But when Norman had decided to build the house they'd designed together, she hadn't expected him to actually install it for the week or two it was needed every year. "It was a big expense."

"I know, but it's like you said when we drew up the plans. You don't need air-conditioning very often in Minnesota, but when you do, a fan blowing over a bowl of ice cubes just won't cut it."

CHAPTER
TWENTY-FOUR

When Hannah walked out of the judging room with Lisa and Pam, she was in a marvelous mood. They'd made quick work of sampling everything, and an incredible orange cake, entered by Sue Plotnik, Hannah's downstairs neighbor, had taken first place.

"So did you learn any more about poor Willa?" Pam asked, her voice breaking slightly.

"A couple of things. She sold Luanne a box of silver that supposedly belonged to her parents."

"Supposedly?" Pam picked up on the word right away.

"Most of it probably did, but there was a pair of silver champagne glasses that were only a couple of years old."

"You mean the type they use at weddings?" Lisa asked.

"Exactly. Mother thinks that maybe Willa

was married."

"That doesn't make sense," Pam said. "She never said anything about a husband, and she didn't wear a ring. And her name is the same as it was on her high school records. There's got to be another explanation."

"Maybe her parents got the champagne glasses as a gift for a special occasion," Lisa suggested. "Or maybe they bought them intending to give them to a bride and groom, but the wedding was called off or something like that."

"Possible," Hannah said, filing the suggestions away for further consideration. "One of the 4-H kids said he saw Willa with one of the rodeo cowboys on Monday and Tuesday nights."

"Which one?" Lisa asked.

"I don't know yet."

Pam sighed as she locked the door behind her. "That could explain the new hairdo and dress, especially if she was really interested in him. And it's entirely possible she was. After she broke up with Gordon, Willa was lonely. Of course she never told me that. Willa kept pretty much to herself. But she'd been seeing Gordon every night, since they were on the same campus and all. Even if she didn't love him, she was bound to miss the time they'd spent together."

Hannah made a mental note to follow up on Gordon Tate. Even if he wasn't directly involved in her death, he might know something about Willa's background that could point them in the right direction.

"Did Willa have a best friend at college?" Lisa asked Pam. "Or maybe someone on the staff at Jordon High that she confided in?"

"Not really. I think I was probably closer to her than anyone else, but I really didn't know that much about her. She never talked about herself."

"Do you know if Willa had a safe deposit box? Or a storage locker somewhere?" Hannah asked.

"I'm almost sure she didn't. The only other place she kept things was . . ."

"Where?" Hannah asked, as Pam stopped speaking.

"Her desk at school. I forgot all about it! Do you want to search it?"

"Absolutely. Something could be there."

Pam opened her purse and pulled out a key ring. She snapped off a key and handed it to Hannah. "This opens the delivery door in my classroom. I always go in that way, so I don't have to carry two keys. You know where it is, don't you?"

"Yes. I used it when I taught that night class for you."

"Right. Willa's desk is the one in the back of the room between the windows. You might have to break the lock. She was always careful about locking it before she left, and she had the only key."

"And they didn't find her keys?" Lisa asked.

"No. Mike warned us to re-key the locks to the apartment, and George did that right away. But I never even thought about the key to my classroom and the one to her desk."

They parted company at the end of the corridor. Pam went out the back door to turn in their results at the judging office, and Hannah and Lisa went out the front.

"See you tomorrow, Hannah," Lisa said. "I'm meeting Herb at the food court."

"Tell him congratulations again for me."

"I will. And thanks again. You were just wonderful."

When Lisa left, Hannah glanced at her watch. It was only eight forty-five, and Norman wasn't picking her up until nine. She had fifteen minutes to kill, and she was going to spend them right here.

It was a good vantage point, and Hannah sat down on the top step to watch the crowd pass by. Three teenage girls sauntered past, eating snow cones and giggling. Right behind them were three teenage boys, swaggering a bit and talking loudly. It was clear that the boys were interested in the girls, and Hannah wondered if any of them would work up the courage to actually say anything directly to them.

A young mother pushing a stroller stopped outside the 4-H building. She glanced at her watch and then she leaned down to wipe her baby's face with a washcloth she removed from her diaper bag. Hannah heard the baby start to whimper, but the mother took out a bottle of water, gave the baby a drink, and then plugged in a pacifier. A moment or two later, five stair-step kids came rushing up. They were called stair-step kids because if you lined them up from shortest to tallest and looked at the tops of their heads, they'd rise upward like a staircase.

The oldest girl, around twelve Hannah thought, handed her mother something in a cup, and then she moved behind the stroller. She said something to her older brother, but Hannah was too far away to hear, and he shouldered the diaper bag. The three younger children held hands, and the family set off for the exit with the young mother looking much less tired than she had only moments before.

The little slice of life unfolding before her eyes made Hannah think about her own family and how she'd helped to take care of Michelle. She'd helped with Andrea too, although there were only four years between them. Maybe she was cut out to be a mother. Or maybe she didn't have to be a mother because she'd already been a stand-in for her own mother. There were times when Michelle seemed like her own child. And then there was Andrea, and . . . here she was!

"Hi, Andrea," Hannah said as her sister climbed up the steps. "What are you doing here?"

"I came to report on the house. And I've only got a couple of minutes because I have to drive home to put Tracey to bed. She hates to go to bed without her stories."

"That's good, Andrea. What book are you reading to her?"

"Oh, I'm not. I tell her stories. Tracey just loves the ones about Tracey and the Widget."

"The Widget?" Hannah started to grin. She'd told Andrea stories about Andrea and the Widget when Andrea was about Tracey's age.

"It's your Widget. I still remember the

stories. And if I forget something, I just make it up. I thought it would be good if we continued the family tradition, you know? Anyway, Willa got next to nothing for the house. It was mortgaged to the hilt, and the agent I talked to thought the money went to pay lawyer's fees."

"Willa's parents were being sued?"

"I asked him. He didn't know. But all Willa cleared on the estate auction and the sale of the house was about six thousand dollars."

Hannah filed that information away to write down later in her notebook. "When did Willa sell the house?"

"Over two years ago, right before she started college at Tri-County. Bill accessed her records for me. She transferred in from another college, but I don't remember which one."

"I can find out. Pam probably knows." Hannah patted the top step. "Sit down for a minute and I'll tell you what I learned to-day."

"I can't."

"You don't have a couple of minutes?"

"It's not that. I can't sit."

"Why not?"

"My pants are too tight."

"Too tight?" Hannah asked, grinning at

her sister.

"Yes. When you have two children, you add an inch or two to your waist. And that's *not* funny!" Andrea stopped and looked at Hannah intently. "You don't think I'm getting fat, do you?"

"I should be so fat!"

"Oh. Okay. I just worry about it sometimes, you know? I mean, look at our family history."

"Mother's been a size six all of her life. She could probably get into the clothes she wore in high school."

"I know, but I still worry. Dad wasn't exactly a lightweight. I don't want to get fat, Hannah. Bill might leave me if I get fat."

"Bill will never leave you. He loves you."

"He might not love me so much if I'm fat. The only thing I've got going for me is my looks, and they're going to fade when I get older. I've got a good figure, but I've got to work to keep myself in shape. It's different with you."

"How so?" Hannah asked, expecting a massive blow to her ego.

"You've got so much more than I have. You're smart, you're funny, and you're just plain good. I . . . well . . . the only thing I've got going for myself is that I look good."

Hannah had the urge to run down the

steps and out into the crowd. She really didn't know what to say. But Andrea was reaching out to her and she had to respond. So she decided to wing it and hope for the best.

"You're an idiot, Andrea," Hannah said. "You're putting yourself down, and I don't like it."

"No, I'm not."

"Yes, you are! I don't have anything more going for me than you do. You're right about being good-looking, but you're also smart. And you're a good wife and mother, and you're creative, and you're the best sister in the world. And I love you."

"Oh, Hannah! That's so nice of you to say!"

"Well . . . don't take it seriously. I might change my mind tomorrow. Now hurry home to Tracey and Bethie, and I'll tell you everything I found out later."

After Andrea left, Hannah watched the crowds for a few moments, and then she glanced at her watch again. Norman should be arriving in five minutes or less. It couldn't be soon enough to suit her. She wanted to go to the school to search Willa's desk, and there was no way she wanted to go alone, especially since Willa's keys hadn't been recovered. She was just wondering if she had time to walk over to the 4-H building and take a look at Kenny's calf when she saw Mike round the corner.

"Hannah," he said, running up the steps. "I just found out something interesting. In cases like this when we don't have many leads, we usually run the vic's . . . uh . . ."

"It's okay," Hannah jumped in before he could apologize again. "Do you want some cake? It's the winning entry for tonight, Kitty's Orange Cake."

"Sure. I love orange cake. I haven't had it since . . ." Mike stopped and swallowed hard.

"Well, I think you'll like this one," Hannah said, jumping in so that Mike didn't have to explain. She was certain he had been about to say that his wife had baked orange cake.

"Thanks, Hannah." Mike took the slice that Hannah handed him and tried it. "Mmm . . . this is good. And it won first place?"

"Yes. It beat out an excellent chocolate sauerkraut cake and a really good coconut spice. Another piece?"

"Yeah, but that better be it. I skipped lunch, but I still have to lose another pound."

Hannah cut another slice, making it a bit larger than the last, and covered the plate again. "You said you usually run the victim's what?"

"Background. We run the fingerprints and do a background check. And something came up about the . . . Miss Sunquist. Did you know that she was married?"

"No," Hannah said, not mentioning the fact that Delores had come to the same conclusion when she'd found out about the silver champagne glasses. "When did she get married?"

"Three years ago. Her husband was Jess Alan Reiffer, and they got married on June eleventh. She didn't tell anybody about him, not even Mrs. Baxter. I just called her on her cell phone to ask."

"Where's Willa's husband now?"

"Nobody knows. But here's the thing . . ." Mike sat down next to her on the step and put his arm around her shoulders. "The bride spent four months in jail when her new husband, Jess Reiffer, used her as a lookout in a convenience store robbery."

Hannah's jaw dropped. She felt it go, and she quickly snapped her mouth shut again. She was right! Willa *did* have a secret! "Where was this?" she asked, angling for more information.

"Oregon. A town called McMinnville. It's only about forty-five minutes or so from Portland. The day she was arrested, she got her one phone call and she used it to call her parents. They drove all the way to Oregon to line her up with a good attorney. But while her parents were in Oregon, they had a fatal auto accident, and both of them were killed."

"Good heavens!" Hannah could barely believe her ears. Just when she was sure the story couldn't get any worse for Willa, it did. "And Willa was still in jail?"

"That's right. But her lawyers pulled out all the stops, and the charges against her were dropped. They convinced the judge she thought her husband had just gone inside to use the phone and she had no idea he was planning to rob the place."

"What happened to her husband?"

"Oh, he was convicted. But since it wasn't much money and he hadn't used a weapon and no one was hurt, he was sentenced to only two years in jail."

"So he's out now?"

"That's right. Actually, he's been out for a while. He got his sentence reduced for good behavior, and he was released after fourteen months."

Hannah thought about that for a moment.

"Did Willa know he was out?"

"I have no idea. And I can't question him, because nobody knows where he is. He served his time, and he's a free man. He's not accountable to anyone, so he could be anywhere."

"Do you think Jess Reiffer is the man who killed her?" Hannah posed the question that was flashing like a beacon in her mind.

"Why would he kill her? She had a reason to kill *him* for nearly ruining her life, but he didn't have any reason to kill *her*."

"But . . . what if she tried to kill him and he killed her defending himself?"

"That didn't happen. Doc Knight found no wounds to indicate a scenario like that. She wasn't physically engaged with anyone that night, and Doc Knight's conclusions go even further. He didn't find any evidence of anticipation on her part."

Hannah gave a little sigh. Why couldn't they come right out and say it in plain English? But just in case she was misinterpreting what Mike had meant, she decided to ask for clarification.

"Are you saying that Willa didn't know she was in any danger from her killer?"

"That's right. The first blow came from behind, and it was fatal. The other blow, the one from the right side, was extraneous."

Hannah shivered slightly. "So you were right."

"About what?"

"On Tuesday night when you were talking to Norman at my place, you said you thought the second blow was just for insurance."

"That's right. At that point, she was already . . ." Mike stopped and sighed deeply. "She was already gone. At least she didn't see it coming and she didn't have time to be frightened. This guy is scum, Hannah. I really want to get him."

"Me, too," Hannah replied, letting him take that response any way he wished. It really didn't make any difference to her which one of them caught Willa's killer as long as he was tried, convicted, and spent the next hundred years or so in jail.

Kitty's Orange Cake

Preheat oven to 350 degrees F., rack in the middle position.

1 box yellow cake mix *(1 pound, 2.25 ounces)*
One package *(3 ounces)* orange Jell-O powder *(NOT sugar free)*
1 cup orange juice
1 teaspoon orange extract
1/2 cup vegetable oil
1 teaspoon orange zest *(optional — if you like it super orangey)*
4 eggs
1 cup semi-sweet mini chocolate morsels★★★ *(6-ounce package — I used Nestles)*
★★★ These are miniature chocolate chips. If you can't find them in your area, you can use regular size chocolate chips and cut them in halves, or quarters. If you use them as is, they'll sink to the bottom and make your cake hard to remove from the pan.

Grease and flour a Bundt pan. *(I sprayed*

mine with Pam and then floured it.)

Hannah's 1st Note: You can make this cake without an electric mixer if you have a strong arm and determination, but it's a lot easier if you use one.

Dump the dry yellow cake mix in a large mixing bowl. Mix in the orange Jell-O powder. Add the orange juice, orange extract, vegetable oil, and the orange zest *(if you decided to use it.)* Mix all the ingredients together until they are well blended.

Add the eggs one at a time, mixing after each addition.

Beat 2 minutes on medium speed with an electric mixer or 3 minutes by hand.

Fold in the mini chocolate morsels by hand.

Pour the cake batter into the Bundt pan.

Bake at 350 degrees F. for 45 to 55 minutes or until a cake tester inserted into the center of the cake comes out dry.

Cool on a rack for 20–25 minutes. Loosen the outside edges and the middle, and tip the cake out of the pan. Let the cake cool completely on the rack.

When the cake is cool, drizzle Orange-Fudge Frosting over the crest and let it run down the sides. *(Or, if you don't feel like making a glaze, just let the cake cool completely and dust it with confectioner's sugar.)*

ORANGE-FUDGE FROSTING:

2 Tablespoons chilled butter *(1/4 stick, 1/8 cup)*

1 cup semi-sweet chocolate chips *(6-ounce bag)*

1 teaspoon orange extract

2 Tablespoons refrigerated orange juice

Place the butter in the bottom of a 2-cup microwave-safe bowl. *(I used a glass one-pint measuring cup.)* Add the chocolate chips. Heat on HIGH for 60 seconds.

Stir to see if the chips are melted. *(They tend to maintain their shape even when melted, so you can't tell by just looking.)* If they're not melted and can't be stirred smooth, heat them on HIGH at 15-second intervals until they are, stirring to check after each 15-second interval.

Add the orange extract and stir it in.

Add the orange juice Tablespoon by Tablespoon, stirring after each addition.

Pour the frosting over the ridge of the cake, letting it run partway down the sides. It will be thicker on top. That's fine. *(And if it's not, that's fine, too — you really can't go wrong with this cake.)*

Refrigerate the cake without covering it, for at least 20 minutes before serving. That "sets" the frosting. After the 20-minute refrigeration, the cake can be left out at room temperature, if you wish.

Hannah's 2nd Note: When I bake this cake for Mother, I use both the orange extract and the orange zest. Mother adores the combination of orange and chocolate. Come to think of it, Mother adores ANY combination that includes chocolate.

CHAPTER
TWENTY-FIVE

"Are you sure you have time?" Hannah asked Norman once they got back to her condo and Moishe had sampled her mother's trout dinner and Norman had given him the realistic-looking mouse filled with fresh catnip that he'd picked up at the pet store. "I can search Willa's desk alone if you want to hurry home to print the pictures you took today."

Norman shook his head. He was staring down at Moishe and frowning a bit. "I'll go with you. I've got the time, and you'll need me to break into Willa's desk."

"That's true. Do you have a dental pick with you?"

Norman laughed. "It's not something I carry around in my wallet. But I've got a Swiss Army Knife. There's bound to be something on there I can use."

"Okay." Hannah filled Moishe's water dish with fresh water and tossed him a couple of salmon-flavored kitty treats that he probably wouldn't eat. "Are you ready to go?"

"I'll be ready as soon as I give you this and plug it in." Norman pulled a box from the bag he'd carried into the condo and presented it to Hannah. "Here's your new cell phone. I activated it at the store for you."

"But . . ."

"No buts," Norman interrupted her protest. "I'll put it in the charger and plug it in, and it'll be ready to go tomorrow morning. All you have to do is turn it on to make a call."

Norman plugged in the phone and then he walked over to scratch Moishe behind the ears. As usual, Hannah's feline roommate was sitting on the carpeted ledge Michelle had bought him, staring out the living room window. "He's definitely losing weight, Hannah. I can almost feel his ribs. He took only one bite of your mother's trout."

"I know. And he's not interested in treats or catnip, either. He batted that mouse for less than a minute, and then he went back to the window again."

"I don't think he really wanted to play with the mouse at all. He was just humoring me." Norman waited for Hannah to lock the door behind them, and then he followed her down the outside stairs and took her arm as they walked down the path to the visitor's parking lot.

Once they were in Norman's car and headed toward the exit to her condo complex, Hannah picked up their discussion of Moishe. "I don't think he's sick. Dr. Bob says his blood work is just fine. Moishe's just . . . preoccupied. He's focused on something, and I can't figure out what it is."

"I tried to find out for you. I stood there and stared at the place he was staring the whole time you were changing clothes. And I didn't see a thing except your neighbor's windows. The shades were down, and absolutely nothing was happening."

"Do you think there's something out there?"

Norman considered that for a moment. "Call it a hunch, or instinct, or whatever, but I do. And whatever it is must be a lot more intriguing than trout or a catnip mouse."

The school parking lot was eerie at night in the glow from the halogen lights that were stationed at intervals to protect the cars of teachers who were working late. Nothing was moving, but there was a large cluster of cars parked at the far end by the football field.

"What are all these cars doing here?" Norman asked, pulling up next to the back door to the home economics classroom.

"They're resurfacing Gull Avenue tomorrow morning. And since it's going to be blocked off from midnight tonight until midnight on Saturday, Mayor Bascomb arranged for the residents to use the school parking lot and drive out the back way."

"How do you know all that?"

"Lisa told me. Herb's going on patrol at midnight to knock on doors and ticket any cars on the street."

The school loomed large and dark as they approached. Hannah gave a little start as they walked past the motion sensor and the high-wattage light mounted over the back door to Pam's classroom went on. "Thanks, Norman," she said.

"Thanks for what?"

"For being here. There's no way I'd enjoy doing something like this alone. I keep thinking about all the bad thrillers I've ever seen on television, with big empty buildings and homicidal stalkers."

"I wish you hadn't said that."

"Me, too." Hannah drew a deep breath

and waited for Norman to unlock the door. He'd just started to push it open when she heard what sounded like a crash from inside.

"What was that?" she gasped, grabbing his hand to hold him back.

"What was *what?*"

"Didn't you hear that noise?"

"I heard something, but maybe it was just the air conditioner kicking in."

"Jordan High doesn't *have* air-conditioning."

"Oh. Well . . . this door leads to the pantry, right?"

Hannah nodded, although she knew he couldn't see it. "That's right. It's the door Pam uses for deliveries."

"Maybe someone stacked something wrong and it fell."

"Possibly," Hannah said, even though she knew that things didn't fall without provocation. It was one of the principles of inertia. She was sure that Norman knew it, too, but he was trying to reassure her. "Do you think we should go in?"

Norman considered that for a moment. "Yeah. I'll go first, and you come right behind me. We'll leave the outside door open, and if there's something wrong, you turn and run straight to the car. Take my keys."

Hannah was about to object when Norman pressed the keys into her hand. She opened her mouth to tell him that there was no way she'd leave him to face any kind of threat alone when she reconsidered. He wanted to protect her. His ego was at stake.

"Okay?" Norman prompted for an answer.

"Okay," Hannah said, bowing to the centuries-old tradition of letting someone who wanted to be stronger take the lead. And if she were being completely honest with herself, she felt pretty good about it. Norman wanted to protect her. That was the important thing. Whether she needed protection or not was another matter for another time.

"Lights are to the right of the door," Hannah said, remembering Willa's instructions.

"Okay."

With Norman leading the way, they entered the pantry. Once the lights were on and the area was illuminated with a burst of pseudosunlight from the fluorescent bulbs overhead, Hannah glanced around at the pantry shelves. Everything was lined up just the way she remembered. The spices were at the end, the canned goods arranged by food group on the shelves, and the bulky items like flour and sugar stored at waist height at the other end.

"Everything looks all right to me," she told Norman.

"Me, too."

"Let's go in, then." Hannah moved up behind Norman as he approached the door to the classroom. "Lights are on the left."

"Got it." Norman flicked on the lights in the classroom, and both of them immediately saw the reason for the noise that Hannah had heard. One of the chairs near the door to the hallway was tipped over on its back.

"Somebody was here," Norman said.

"Somebody or something," Hannah added. "Hold on."

Since she'd used this classroom only months ago for her adult class, Hannah remembered where the kitchen utensils were kept. She pulled open a drawer near the first kitchen pod, pulled out a rolling pin, and handed it to Norman. A moment later, she had a second rolling pin in her hand. "Okay. Let's make sure we're alone in here."

With both of them walking the rows of desks, it didn't take long to discover that they were, indeed, the only occupants of the home economics classroom. The intruder, if there'd been one, had left.

"All clear," Norman said, putting down

his rolling pin. "We don't need these anymore."

"Not right now, but I think I'll keep mine
handy until I go shut that outside door."

"I'll do it."

"Okay. Take your rolling pin with you. On
your way back, you can drop it off on the
counter in kitchen number one."

While Norman shut the outside door,
Hannah checked the classroom door to the
hallway. It was shut, but not locked. She
opened it, rolling pin at the ready, and went
out to look down the hallway. Even by the
dim lights that were left on at night, she
could see that it was completely deserted.
By the time she went back in and closed
and locked the door behind her, Norman
was back and they headed for the desk that
Willa had used under the windows.

"Let me see what kind of a lock it is," Norman said, tugging on one of the drawers. It
slid open, almost knocking him back, and
both of them just stared at it.

"Pam said Willa always locked her desk,"
Hannah said.

"Well, it's not locked now." Norman
pulled out the drawer beneath the one he'd
opened, and then he tried the drawers on
the other side. They all slid open, even the
long, shallow center drawer.

"Do you think someone broke in?"

"Doesn't look like it. I don't see any scratch marks, and all the wood is intact."

"But Pam told me there was only one key. And Willa had that."

"Where is it now?"

"I don't know. Mike told Pam to change the locks on her basement apartment because Willa's keys weren't recovered from the crime scene."

Norman thought about that for a moment. "Then I guess we can assume that the killer has them, the killer threw them away and someone else has them, or someone found Willa before you did and took her keys."

"You forgot one."

"One what?"

"One other possibility. Willa could have lost her keys earlier in the day and someone found them."

"But how would that someone know to come here and look through her desk?"

That stymied Hannah for a moment, but then she recovered. "Maybe Willa's name was on her key ring. Or maybe someone *stole* her keys from her purse for some reason."

"What reason? She wasn't wealthy, there probably wasn't anything valuable in her desk, and why would they go to the trouble of snatching her keys without taking her whole purse? It's a dead end."

"It's a cul-de-sac," Hannah corrected him. "You just turn around and go back to something you passed by before."

"And that is. . . . ?"

"The killer or the person who found Willa's body before I did."

"My money's on the killer," Norman said.

"Mine, too. Let's search the desk and get out of here. I'm getting a really bad feeling, and it's getting harder and harder to convince myself that it's all in my imagination."

They were silent for long moments as they went through the desk. Norman started with the drawers on the right side, and Hannah took the drawers on the left. Norman found Willa's college transcripts, some lesson plans she'd written for Pam, and a whole folder of recipes. Hannah found printouts of e-mail messages from Gordon Tate, confirming meetings at the campus coffee shop, dates for dinner, or simply *hello-how-are-yous.* The tone of the messages was more friendly than intimate, and Hannah could understand why Pam had doubted the passion in Willa and Gordon's relationship.

They reached for the center drawer and

smiled as they met there. They'd both finished their side drawers at the same time.

"Only one place left," Norman said.

"I know. So far, we've struck out. Let's hope there's something here."

And there *was* something. They both saw it at the same time. Sitting in the exact center of the otherwise empty center drawer was a small album with a red enamel cover. The cover had a word stamped in gold on the front, and both of them bent down to read it. It said, "Photos," in script so fancy it was almost indecipherable.

"After you," Norman said.

"Thanks." Hannah reached for the album and opened it. The first photo was a picture of an older couple leaning against the fence of a corral. "They're probably Willa's parents," Hannah said.

"And that must be a favorite horse," Norman guessed when Hannah turned the page.

"Right," Hannah said, flipping to the next picture. It was Willa astride what appeared to be the same horse. There were several similar pictures, one of the older man they'd identified as Willa's father on another horse, and one of the older woman standing in front of a stove.

"Nice ranch," Norman commented as Hannah flipped through several photos of the house, pastures, and horse barn. And then they came to the last photo.

"What in the world . . . ?" Hannah stared down at the picture of Willa in what she assumed was her wedding dress. There was no veil, but it was certainly fancy enough to wear to a wedding. It was a professional photo of the happy couple, and Willa did look happy. But the groom who had stood at her side was missing, cut cleanly off with a scissors.

"Do you think this was a picture of Jess Reiffer?" Norman asked.

"Yes," Hannah answered. She'd told Norman everything she'd learned from Mike on their way to the school.

"And do you think the noise you heard before I opened the door was Jess Reiffer cutting himself out of this picture?" Norman took things a step further. "Or is that too far-fetched?"

"I guess it could have been Jess Reiffer, but that doesn't make a whole lot of sense. He had no reason to kill Willa. And why would he track her down just to cut himself out of their wedding picture?"

"Good point. But you still think the noise you heard was Willa's killer searching her desk?"

"That's my guess. And if he took something, it's gone. And since we don't know what was in here in the first place, we can't even guess what it was." Hannah dropped the photo album in her shoulder bag and stood up.

"Ready to go?" Norman asked.

"Oh, yes." Hannah picked up her rolling pin and gripped it tightly. "Get your rolling pin on the way out, okay? I can return them to Pam tomorrow."

"Good idea. It never hurts to be ready."

Hannah did her best to keep from wondering how much damage a rolling pin could do to a determined killer and gave Norman a smile. "That's right. You never know when you'll have to roll out a piecrust."

Hannah locked her door and buckled her seatbelt. They'd seen absolutely nothing out-of-the-way in the parking lot, and they'd arrived at Norman's car without incident. "He's probably long gone."

"Probably. If you're right and he got whatever he came for, there's no reason for him to stick around."

Not unless he thinks I'm closing in on him, Hannah thought, but she didn't say it. It would be counterproductive to make the driver nervous. They'd been in Pam's classroom for at least twenty minutes. Willa's killer was probably across the Winnetka County line by now.

"Home?" Norman asked, pulling out of the parking lot and onto Gull Avenue.

"Yes." Hannah took a deep breath and prepared to ask for another favor. "I know you're really busy and you want to print those photographs tonight, but do you think you'll be on your computer?"

Norman laughed. "I *have* to be on my computer. That's where I download the photos. And that's how I print them."

"Oh. Well . . . do you think you might be able to e-mail someone for me?"

"I can do that. And then I can hook up your computer this weekend so that you can discover the joys of cyberspace for yourself."

Hannah gave a little groan. "I'm sorry, Norman. I should have hooked it up weeks ago. It's just that I've been so busy, and I'm trying to decide just where to put it, and . . ."

"You're resisting," Norman interrupted her. "Some people have to be dragged kicking and screaming into the twenty-first century."

"It's the twenty-first century?" Hannah acted shocked. But then, before their good-natured kidding could go on, she noticed headlights in the rearview mirror. "There's a car behind us, and it's coming up fast."

"I know. I've been watching it for a couple of blocks, now. Is your seatbelt fastened?"

"Yes."

"Good. I want you to hang on. We're going to make a few sharp turns."

Hannah braced herself as Norman took a hard left onto Third Street. She'd never been in a car that went around the corner on two wheels before, and she did all she could do not to scream. But just when she was recovering from the first turn, Norman made another hard left onto Maple.

Hannah felt the breath whoosh from her lungs. Her life hadn't quite flashed before her eyes, but it was close.

It was the screeching left onto Fourth Street that did it. Hannah was sure she was going to die in a fiery wreck. And then Norman took another hard left that put them back on Gull Avenue, and before Hannah had even caught her breath, he pulled into someone's driveway, cut the engine, and flicked off the lights.

"What are you . . . ?" Hannah gasped out.

"Duck." Norman reached over and pushed her down in the seat. "He missed that first turn, so it'll take him a minute to catch up."

"You . . . you mean the . . . the car that

was following . . . ?"

"Yes." Norman interrupted her attempt to ask an intelligent question. "He should be coming around the corner of Fourth and Gull any second now."

Hannah's window was down an inch or so, and she listened for the sound of a car. For a breathless moment, all she heard was the sound of crickets in the grass next to the driveway and two cats yowling somewhere in the distance. She was about to tell Norman that they must have lost him when she heard the sound of an engine.

"There he is. Stay down," Norman warned her. "If we're lucky, he'll think he's still behind us and keep on going."

Hannah shut her eyes and did her version of positive thinking. *Keep on going, we're ahead of you. Keep on going, we're ahead of you,* she chanted in her mind. And then she risked a glance. Her silent suggestion must have worked because the car kept on going right past the driveway where they were hiding and on down the street.

"Did you see him?" she asked Norman, wondering if he'd also risked a peek.

"Yes. Lone driver. Looked like a man to me," Norman said, turning on the engine and backing out of the driveway. "Is that what you saw?"

He knows me too well, Hannah thought. But she said, "What makes you think I looked?"

"We both put our heads up at the same time. I saw you. It's a good thing he wasn't looking at my car."

"You're right," Hannah said, agreeing completely. "And I saw the same thing you did. Do you think we ought to tell Mike?"

"Tell him what? That we think someone followed us from the school, but we don't have a description or a license plate?"

Hannah thought about that for a moment. "Guess not," she concluded, and then she changed the subject. "You know how people who're about to die say that their lives flash before their eyes?"

"I've heard that."

"Well, mine almost did."

Norman was silent for a moment and then he reached out to take her hand. "You were never in any danger, Hannah. There's no way I'd risk your life."

"I wasn't?"

"No. Every turn I made was carefully calculated."

Hannah wasn't sure that made her feel any better, but she nodded. "Okay. I believe you. How did you learn to do that?"

"Do what?"

"Drive like that. You took those corners at just the right speed. Any faster and we would have wiped out. Any slower and he might have caught up to us."

"Oh, that," Norman said, shrugging slightly. "I used to race when I was in college."

"You mean . . . professionally?"

"Yes. It was only two years, though. When I started out, I was on the pit crew. Did you know that I can change a tire in ninety-three seconds flat?"

"No . . ."

"Well, I can. I'll show you if we ever have a flat. You don't mind if I take you back to the condo by a different route, do you? I think it might be safer, just in case he's still out there."

"I don't mind at all."

The moon was almost full, and Hannah stared at Norman all the way back to her condo. A racecar driver! Norman was full of surprises. Just when she thought she knew him as well as anyone could know anyone else, he threw her a curveball.

Chapter
Twenty-Six

"Will you be all right alone?" Norman asked, standing just inside the door to the condo.

"I'll be fine. Nobody can drive in without a gate card."

"Unless they drive through that flimsy plywood arm at the entrance. Or park outside and walk in on foot."

"True, but no one followed us here. You checked."

Norman stood there for a moment, clearly undecided. And then he sighed. "Okay. But turn on the alarm system after I leave. It'll make me feel a whole lot better about leaving you here."

"I will. I promise," Hannah said, wondering if she remembered how to do it or whether she'd have to look for the instruction sheet.

"All right, then. I'll see you in the . . ." Norman stopped speaking and started to frown. "Look at Moishe! He sees something outside that window. I'm sure of it!"

"Me, too. Or maybe he just hears another animal or a person. Whatever it is, it's out there and he's reacting to it."

They moved together to the window. Hannah stared out into the darkness, but she saw nothing moving. "Do you see anything?" she asked.

"No, but maybe it's something small that we're not noticing, like a field mouse or a snake."

"That must be it," Hannah agreed, moving away from the window again and leaving her cat to keep watch.

"Where were we?" Norman asked her, walking to the door again.

"You were about to kiss me goodnight."

"I was?"

"Oh, yes. At least twice."

Norman chuckled and pulled her into his arms. And then he exceeded her suggestion by at least a half-dozen kisses. When he let her go and opened the door, Hannah swayed slightly on her feet. Norman definitely knew how to kiss!

Hannah stepped out onto the landing with him, and they were just sharing a final kiss when she heard voices below.

"Sorry," Michelle called out. "We didn't

mean to interrupt you."

Hannah turned to see Michelle coming up the stairs, followed by Andrea. Both of them were grinning, and Hannah knew they'd seen her kissing Norman.

"I was just leaving," Norman said, heading down the stairs. "I've got pictures to print tonight."

"Will you let me know how the one you took of Tracey and me turns out?" Andrea asked.

"It'll be great. You're remarkably photogenic, and so is Tracey. And that one of you should be really good, Michelle. You're photogenic, too."

Perhaps her two sisters weren't aware of the omission, but Hannah was. As Norman went down the stairs and her sisters climbed up, Hannah gave a little sigh. She was always the odd sister out. If there was something she was not, it was photogenic, and everyone who'd ever tried to take her picture knew she was about as far from camera-friendly as a person could get. The picture Norman had taken of her at The Cookie Jar, the photo that had won first prize in the photography exhibit and now hung over Mike's couch, had been nothing short of remarkable, a stroke of good fortune that might not happen again in her lifetime.

As she opened the door and ushered her sisters in, Hannah thought about the picture of her that Norman had taken this afternoon. It would also be remarkable, but in the negative sense of the word. The purple dress would clash spectacularly with her red hair.

"What's wrong, Hannah?" Michelle asked, as they entered the living room.

"Just thinking," Hannah said, leaving it at that. There was absolutely nothing she could do to change the picture of her that Rod would run on the front page of the *Lake Eden Journal* on Sunday. The deed was done. The dress had been worn. And if she could somehow rewind her day to the point where Marge, Jack, and Lisa had spread all the dresses out on the work island and asked her to pick one, she'd probably choose the purple taffeta all over again. It had been worth it to see the smile on Lisa's dad's face.

"So there was something out there, after all!" Hannah gave Moishe a scratch behind his ears and a chicken-flavored treat for hearing Michelle and Andrea drive in and watching for them to come up the stairs.

"He heard us?" Michelle sounded amazed.

"He heard something, and that's good

enough for me. Coffee?"

It was a silly question to ask a family of coffee drinkers, so Hannah didn't wait for an answer. She just went to the kitchen and put on the coffee. Then she sliced the rest of Sue Plotnik's orange cake, arranged it on a plate, and carried everything out to the living room, where Andrea and Michelle were waiting for her.

"So what brings you out tonight?" Hannah asked Andrea.

"You said you'd tell me everything you found out later. This is later."

Hannah took a huge swig of her coffee, even though it was only a few degrees short of scalding. She was too low on sleep, too high on caffeine, too much had happened today, and her brain was spinning too fast. She needed a minute or two of downtime to recover, or she'd never be able to keep things straight.

"Give me just a minute," she said, putting her coffee down and heading for the bathroom sink. Splashing cold water on her face might help. It wouldn't help as much as a full eight-hours' sleep, but it might be enough.

The cold water was a shock, and she relished it. Perhaps she should have offered to take the late shift at the Lake Eden

Historical Society Booth tonight. Then Bernie No-No Fulton could have pitched at the bull's eye and dunked her awake.

"Are you okay?" Michelle asked when she came back into the living room.

"No, but I'm better. I haven't seen you since this morning, is that right?"

"That's right."

Hannah turned to Andrea. "And I haven't seen you since right after the judging, but you didn't have time to talk then. Is that right?"

"That's right."

"Okay. Here's what I learned today that neither one of you knows about."

Hannah started at the beginning and told them about climbing in the magic cabinet and overhearing the two cowboys talking.

"And they really thought Tucker tried to kill the clown?" Andrea asked.

"They sounded as if they meant it to me! According to them, it's a rivalry over the owner's daughter, Brianna. She used to date Curly, the clown, before Tucker joined the show."

"I heard that one of the clowns was hurt at the rodeo," Michelle said. "But the girl who told me about it thought it was an accident."

"That's because it *looked* like an accident.

It happened during the Brahma bull riding competition. The two cowboys thought Tucker got thrown on purpose to put Curly in danger."

Andrea began to frown. "But wouldn't that be hard to do?"

"I don't know enough about rodeos to know. But they sounded so convincing, Norman and I went to see Curly in the hospital."

Both sisters put down their coffee mugs and leaned forward. "What did you find out?" Michelle asked.

"I asked Curly some questions, but he was on a ventilator so he couldn't talk. I had to use questions he could answer by nodding and shaking his head. He nodded yes when I asked him if he thought Tucker tried to kill him. And he nodded yes again, when I asked him if he'd been looking into Tucker's background. Then I asked him whether he'd found anything that would make Curly want to kill him, but the sedative Doc Knight gave him knocked him out before he could answer."

"You have to talk to him again." Andrea looked worried. "If Tucker tried to kill him once, he'll try again."

"*If* Tucker tried to kill him," Michelle pointed out. "We don't know that for sure.

All we know is that Curly thought he did."

"You're both right. Doc Knight said he'd call me when Curly's out of surgery, and I'll go right out there to talk to him again. But that's not all that happened today. After Norman and I came back from the hospital, we went to the food court to grab a bite to eat. I saw Mary Adamczak there."

"Oh, good!" Andrea said, looking relieved. "I went to her house this afternoon, but she wasn't home."

"Right. Well, both Marys were at the food court."

Andrea looked puzzled. "Both Marys?"

"Mary Lou Adamczak and Mary Kay Adamczak. Mary Lou is the one who won all the first place ribbons. Mary Kay is her daughter-in-law. Since Mary Lou hurt her stirring arm, Mary Lou used her recipe and entered the baked goods contest for the first time this year. She won an honorable mention, and they're all delighted about it."

"Cross her off the list as a suspect?" Michelle asked.

"That's right. And we can cross off Mr. Hicks, too. Marge Beeseman knows the family, and Mr. Hicks has been in a wheelchair for the past two months. He broke his leg, and he still can't stand on it. Since I saw Willa's killer running away, there's no way it could have been him."

"It's not Lyle Mortsensen, either," Michelle said.

"Who?" both Hannah and Andrea asked, a half-beat apart.

Michelle laughed. "You two sound like you have an echo. Lyle Mortensen is the home ec student Willa flunked."

"Right." Hannah pulled out her notebook and wrote down his name. "And where was he when Willa was killed?"

"In Minneapolis watching Toxic Thompson trounce the Racine Ripper."

"Huh?" Hannah just stared at her youngest sister.

"It's professional wrestling. Lyle's dad works with Toxic's father, and they go to every match. The kids went along this time. There's no way Lyle could have killed Willa. They didn't get back here until midnight."

Hannah looked down the list of suspects and zeroed in on another name. "I'm waiting for more information, but I think Gordon Tate is out."

"Who?" Michelle asked.

"Willa's former boyfriend. He's an archaeology professor at Tri-County, and he's been on a dig in Mexico. Norman's trying to communicate with him by e-mail."

"So he's out of the country and he

couldn't have done it?" Andrea asked.

"I'm waiting for confirmation on that. He's not eliminated, not until we know for sure he didn't fly back here, but it's really unlikely."

"So who do we have who's still in the running?" Michelle asked.

"The new boyfriend we don't know about, the one she got all dressed up for," Hannah said.

"But who *is* he?" Andrea asked.

"I don't know. And then there's the burglar, the one who broke into the office at the fairgrounds."

"And we don't know who *he* is either," Michelle reminded them. "I talked to Lonnie about it tonight, and he told me there's been no break in the case. How about the picture I showed around this morning to the 4-H kids? Did any of them tell you anything?"

"Yes. One of the kids came to see me today with his parents. I can't tell you who they were, because I promised to keep it confidential. It seems the boy saw Willa with a cowboy from the rodeo on Monday night and again on Tuesday, shortly before she was murdered. Unfortunately, he didn't get a good look at the cowboy's face."

"Do you think the cowboy is the boyfriend

she got all dressed up for?" Andrea asked.

"Could be," Hannah said, squelching her desire to correct her sister's sentence structure. "Or it could be the boyfriend is someone else entirely. That's still up for grabs."

"How about Willa's apartment?" Michelle reminded them. "Did you find anything interesting there?"

Andrea sighed. "Not much. The only thing was a florist's card she saved. It said, *Yesterday and Today, Tomorrow and Forever.*"

"It was stuck in a hardcover copy of *Gone With The Wind,* along with an orchid that probably came from a corsage," Hannah added. "It must have been important to her, or she wouldn't have saved it."

"I ran into Pam and she said she gave you the keys to the school so you could search Willa's desk," Michelle said. "Do you want us to help you do it?"

"It's already done. Norman went with me." Hannah made a unilateral decision not to tell them about the car they'd outrun. They'd only worry, and that would do no one any good.

"The only thing we found that was the least bit interesting was a little photo album," she went on, retrieving it from her purse and handing it to Michelle.

"I've got one exactly like that, except it's

black," Andrea commented, looking over Michelle's shoulder.

Hannah bit her lips to keep silent. Now was not the time to point out that one thing could not be *exactly* like another with a difference. "Take a look at the last picture."

"There's Willa in a white satin gown," Michelle identified it. "It looks almost like the one I wore for the evening gown competition. But it's only half there. Somebody cut off Willa's date. You can see his arm around her, but the rest of him is missing."

"Willa probably did it," Andrea said, sounding very certain.

"But why would she do that?" Michelle asked.

"It's simple. Remember when I went to the Junior prom with Benton Woodley?" Andrea waited until they nodded, and then she continued. "After we broke up, I cut him out of our prom picture. Willa could have done something like that."

"I agree," Hannah said, "but I think it's her wedding picture and she cut off Jess Reiffer. I certainly couldn't blame her for that!"

The total shock on both of her sisters' faces made Hannah groan. "I didn't tell you that Willa was married?"

Two heads shook in tandem, and Hannah went on. "And you don't know that she sold

Mother the silver champagne glasses from her wedding?"

Again the two heads, one blond and one light brunette, shook in tandem.

"Or that Willa spent four months in jail in Oregon?"

The heads started to shake again, but then Michelle spoke up. "When did you learn all this?"

"Today. If one of you will get me another mug of coffee, I'll tell you all about it."

CHAPTER
TWENTY-SEVEN

"Tell me why we're doing this again," Hannah said as Andrea pulled up in front of "Digger" Gibson's mortuary.

"We're doing it because the flower shop at the mall is closed," Andrea explained. "And if we come in without flowers, they'll think we're just trying to pump them for information about the identity of the cowboy who was seen with Willa on the night she was murdered, and whether Tucker really attempted to kill Curly or not."

"We *are* trying to pump them for information."

"I know that and you know that, but we don't want *them* to know that."

"And what happens if they ask us who the flowers are for?" Hannah posed another question.

"We'll have a name by that time." Andrea sounded very confident as she opened her car door. "Wait here. I'll be right back."

"I just don't believe she's doing this," Hannah groaned, watching as her sister walked up the sidewalk and rang the bell to Digger's apartment over the mortuary.

"Neither do I. You know what to do when we get to the hospital, don't you?"

Hannah nodded. "You and Andrea will keep the charge nurse busy, and I'll get a look at the patient list. Lake Eden isn't that big. We're bound to know somebody in the hospital."

"Right. And then?"

"We carry the flowers to the waiting room and pretend we're waiting to see someone. And then we do what we came for in the first place, which is to pump whoever's there for information about Curly and Tucker."

"Right. Here comes Andrea with Digger." Michelle stared out the window. "It looks like he's laughing! I don't think I've ever seen Digger laugh before."

"That's because the only time you see him is at funerals. I'm sure he laughs in private."

"Really?"

Hannah thought about the dour-faced undertaker and shrugged. "Well . . . maybe not. But he could be like the concert pianist who moonlights on a keyboard in a rock band. For all we know, Digger's a standup comic in his off-hours."

They'd just gone over the plan again when Andrea came back to the car. "Hold these, will you?" she half asked, half ordered, thrusting a small vase filled with flowers into Hannah's hands.

"Very pretty," Hannah said, glancing down at the bouquet.

"We took one stem from each arrangement," Andrea explained as she slid in behind the wheel. "Digger didn't want anyone to suspect that we'd taken part of the funeral flowers."

"No lilies, I see," Hannah noted.

"No. Digger thought maybe that would raise some questions. He said lilies were traditional funeral flowers. Except on Easter, people don't usually bring lilies to patients in the hospital."

Andrea drove out of town and soon they were on the road to Lake Eden Memorial Hospital. In less than ten minutes they were pulling up in the section reserved for hospital visitors.

"Looks like Curly has some friends here," Michelle said, pointing to the car next to them. "That car's got a Great Northwestern Rodeo and Carnival sticker on the window."

Hannah glanced at the pickup truck on the other side. It also had a Great Northwestern sticker. "This truck has one, too. Does everybody know who to zero in on?"

"I take the owner's daughter Brianna, if she's here," Michelle said. "I'm closer to her age and she might talk to me. I'll try to get her alone and away from Tucker."

"And I'll take Tucker," Hannah said. Then she turned to Andrea. "You'd better take Brianna's father, Sam Webber. He owns the show."

"Okay. What shall I ask him?"

"Find out if he thinks there was bad blood between Tucker and Curly. That's what the two cowboys said. That might be hard to do."

"Yes, but I'll figure out a way. Anything else?"

"Try to find out if any of his cowboys knew Willa. That'll probably be tricky. And if you finish that, ask him questions about the show. That ought to distract him from what Michelle and I are doing."

"Got it," Andrea said.

"Me, too," Michelle agreed, opening her door and getting out. "Are you still tired, Hannah?"

"Oh, yes. Actually, I now know for sure that I'm a couple of light years past tired."

"How do you know that?" Andrea asked.

"I know because this whole crazy plan is

starting to make perfect sense to me."

"Three choices," Hannah told them as they walked down the hall. "Calvin Janowski's in for a tonsillectomy, Ed Barthel is having a hip replacement, and Dot Truman Larson's in labor with her first baby."

"Not Calvin," Andrea said. "Nobody would believe we came here at almost eleven at night to visit a first grader."

"Good point. Ed Barthel? His wife is in Mother's quilting club."

"That's a possibility," Michelle agreed.

"I vote for Dot Truman Larson. If it's her first baby, it could take a while."

"You're right," Andrea said.

"My vote's for Dot, too," Michelle agreed. "All three of us know her, and we went to her wedding last summer."

"There's only one problem," Hannah reminded them, heading down the hall to the large waiting room.

"What's that?" Michelle asked.

"There's a separate maternity waiting room. If we came to see Dot's first baby, why aren't we there?"

"Because her husband's there with all his relatives, and it's crowded," Andrea offered a possible explanation.

"Good enough for me," Hannah said,

rounding the corner and stopping so suddenly her two sisters nearly plowed into her.

"What is it?" Andrea asked.

"The cowboys I overheard this afternoon are in the waiting room."

"What's wrong with that?" Michelle asked.

"They might recognize me."

"Hold it." Andrea took Hannah by the arms and pulled her back a couple of paces. "I thought you were in the magic cabinet at the time."

"Oh, I was."

"And you didn't say a word, or make any noise?" Michelle asked.

"That's right."

"Then how could they possibly recognize you?" Andrea questioned her.

Hannah shook her head like a dog coming out of Eden Lake. Logic seemed to have deserted her, and she wondered whether she'd be able to question Curly. "Coffee?" she asked.

"We passed the alcove with complimentary self-serve coffee. I'll go back and get you some." Michelle hurried off. Several moments later she was back with a Styrofoam cup of coffee. "Drink this," she said. "It'll help."

Hannah took a sip and grimaced. Although she seriously doubted that anything that tasted like paint thinner could deliver the necessary caffeine to her exhausted brain, she drank it down in three gulps.

"Okay," she said. "Let's go."

"Did it help?" Andrea wanted to know.

"I think so. My eyelids felt as if they were weighted down with quarters before, and now the quarters feel like dimes."

"That's good enough for me," Michelle said.

"Me, too," Andrea agreed. "I'll take the flowers. You might drop them."

"Do you want to interview Tucker?" Hannah asked, something she never would have done if she'd been less exhausted.

"No. You're better than I am with guys who swagger and think every woman out there will fall in their laps if they snap their fingers. I'd slap him silly if he said anything sexist to me."

That remark caused Hannah's eyelids to experience an unscheduled lift. "Do you know him?"

"Not personally, but I saw him at the rodeo that first afternoon. Tracey wanted to go, so I took her. She didn't like Tucker, either. She said, *That cowboy's really full of himself. He thinks he's something and that means he's not.*"

Hannah was impressed. Her eldest niece

was a good judge of character. For that matter, so was Andrea. "Okay. I'll take Tucker."

"Good." Andrea gave her a little hug. "Give him your best shot, and Michelle and I will let you sleep all the way home."

The coffee had done it. Or perhaps it was the sludge in the bottom of the cup. Hannah didn't even want to think about how that had tasted, so she crooked her finger at Michelle to follow her and headed straight for the long row of chairs that held the youngest couple in the room.

"Do you mind if we sit here?" Hannah asked, not even considering what she'd do if they said they'd mind. But they shook their heads, and Hannah and Michelle took up their positions. Hannah sat next to the cowboy, and Michelle sat down next to the girl who was the very picture of youth and innocence.

"I hope you're not here for something really serious," Hannah said to the cowboy, knowing full well why he was here.

"Serious enough," he said, sighing a bit. "I'm from the rodeo. One of the clowns was injured, and we're all here waiting for news."

"He's in the operating room," the young girl explained. "The doctor said somebody would come out and tell us how Curly was doing, but we've been here for an hour, and nobody's told us anything."

"Then let's go try to find out something." Michelle stood up and held out her hand. "I'm just here because my friend's having a baby, but I know some of the nurses. Maybe they'll tell us something."

"That'd be great!" the girl said, practically jumping to her feet. She turned to the cowboy Hannah assumed was Tucker. "Do you want to come along?"

"Better not," Hannah told him.

"Why not?"

"Because the nurses aren't supposed to give out any information, and they'll clam up if too many people ask. They don't want to get in trouble, you know?"

"Oh. Well . . . go ahead then, Bri."

As the girl she'd pegged for Brianna bent down to kiss the guy she'd nailed as Tucker, Hannah gave a little smile. She might be exhausted and not thinking straight, but so far she was batting a thousand. Even though the waiting room was crowded, she'd correctly identified their two interview subjects.

She waited until Michelle had left with Brianna, and then she turned to Tucker. Andrea and Tracey had described him perfectly. Although he was sitting, Hannah knew he'd swagger when he walked, and he looked about as full of himself as a man could get. He had a face that was movie cowboy handsome, tousled blond hair that looked as if he'd just ducked his head under the pump in front of the bunkhouse to wash off the dust of the trail, and a twang in his voice that would make *Howdy, Li'l Lady* sound authentic. She could see how someone like Willa, who'd had the same air of innocence about her as Brianna did, would be attracted to someone excessively self-assured like Tucker.

"Is something wrong?" Tucker asked, startling her out of her thoughts.

"No. Just thinking about how nice it would be if they'd put cots in here instead of chairs."

"Oh, yeah?"

Hannah saw his face brighten and realized that he was looking at her appraisingly. She'd really put her foot in her mouth with that remark! She could try to explain herself, or she could let it go.

"I think I saw you at a roping demonstration the other day," she said, going for the second option.

"Could've been me. I go along with the other guys sometimes."

"I'm almost sure it was you. You did an incredible thing jumping in and out of a loop you were twirling, and the 4-H students were absolutely amazed."

Tucker began to smile. "I figured they thought I was good. I got more applause than the other guys."

He was just as conceited as Andrea had thought, and she decided to lay it on even thicker. "Oh, you were good all right! They all want to be cowboys, you know, especially famous rodeo cowboys like you. You're Tucker Smith, the star of the show, aren't you?"

"That's me. But I wouldn't say I was the star of the show. Maybe on a good day, but not all the time."

You're so egotistical, you think that's being humble, Hannah thought, but all the while she managed to keep the admiring smile on her face. She was getting a lot better at duplicity. Perhaps it had something to do with practice. "Did you know the clown who was injured?"

"Yes." Tucker put on an appropriately serious expression. "He's my best friend."

That's not what I heard, Hannah thought. But she said, "It must be awful sitting here waiting to see if he's going to be all right."

"It's the hardest thing I've ever done. Curly and I are close. Real close."

And the lies are getting deep in here. Real

deep. Hannah took a deep breath and plunged in. "Everything that's happened makes you wonder if some places are just plain unlucky, doesn't it?"

Tucker looked puzzled. "What do you mean?"

"I mean the Tri-County Fair has been plagued by misfortune this year. First it was that poor woman killed on the midway, and now it's your best friend winding up here in the hospital. I bet you'll be glad to move on."

"Yeah. You could say that."

"Did you know the woman who was killed?"

Tucker looked startled. "How would I know her? She wasn't with the show."

"I just thought maybe you ran into her. Her name was Willa Sunquist, and she was a judge on the baked goods panel."

"Oh. Well . . . I might have seen her, but I don't remember."

"She was also the beauty contest chaperone."

"Maybe I did see her, then. Some lady brought the girls over to the arena to pose for pictures with us."

Hannah knew she was spinning her wheels. If Tucker had known Willa, he wasn't about to admit it. She'd try another tack. "I really hope your friend is going to be all right."

"Me, too."

"I'm almost glad I didn't get to the rodeo this afternoon. It must have been awful. Did you see what happened?"

Tucker nodded. "I saw it. I was the cowboy riding the Brahma bull."

"You mean . . . you were right there when it happened?"

"That's right, Li'l Lady. I got thrown, and Curly put himself in harm's way to protect me from the bull."

"Oh, my!" Hannah pretended to be shocked. "I'll bet you feel terribly guilty about it."

"Oh, I do. I really do. I wish it had never happened. You don't know how many times I went over it in my mind, wondering if I could have done something to help him. It was horrible, just horrible!"

Hannah did her best not to react. As far as she was concerned, Tucker was about as phony as a six-dollar bill.

"I've never had anybody protect me like that before. I know rodeo clowns are supposed to protect the riders, but Curly went that extra mile for me. I want everyone to know what a wonderful man he was . . ." Tucker stopped and looked stricken. "What a wonderful man he *is*. I've got to think positive on this, Li'l Lady. Curly's going to be all right. He just has to be!"

Their conversation deteriorated from that point on. Hannah asked him how he came to join the rodeo, and he told her about growing up in Wyoming and how his dad had taught him to ride. He was just talking about the first time he competed in a rodeo when a familiar voice interrupted them.

"Well, well, well. Look who we have here."

Hannah turned to see Mike walking over to them. "Hannah Swensen. And there's Andrea over there. What are *you two* doing here?"

Hannah's heart dropped down to her toes. She'd been caught in the act of interrogating a suspect by the very person who'd told her not to get involved. But she did have a cover story.

"Hi, Mike," she said. "We came over to see if Dot had her baby yet."

"Then shouldn't you be in maternity?"

"We were, but the waiting room was too crowded. All of her husband's relatives were there."

"I see," Mike said, but he didn't look convinced. "And you're here talking to . . ." Mike turned to look at Tucker, ". . . Tucker, isn't it?"

"That's right. And you're . . . ?"

"Detective Mike Kingston of the Winnetka County Sheriff's Department."

Tucker gave a little gasp. "Is Curly all right? I mean . . . he didn't . . . *die,* did he?"

"Oh, no. I'm here about the burglary at the fairgrounds. You didn't see anything suspicious between six and six forty-five on Tuesday night, did you, Tucker?"

"Can't say as I did. That's the time I usually eat, so I was probably in the food court, or maybe at Bri's trailer."

"Bri?"

"Brianna Webber, my fiancée. She's trying to learn how to cook, and I'm her guinea pig. I was probably with her, but you can check to make sure."

"And I'll find Brianna where?"

"Somewhere around here. She left with . . ." Tucker turned to Hannah. "What was her name again, darlin'?"

Mike gave Hannah a long, hard look. "Let me guess. Michelle, right?"

"That's right," Hannah jumped in quickly. "Michelle went to school with Dot."

"And she came out here with you because Dot's having a baby. You told me already." Mike glanced down at the coffee table in front of the row of seats. "You don't have coffee. Let me go get you some."

"Oh, well . . ." Hannah started to say she didn't want any more coffee, but Mike had already started for the door. She turned back to Tucker. "I guess I can drink one more cup. How about you?"

"I'm always up for coffee. Say . . . you don't think he thinks I had anything to do with that robbery, do you?"

Burglary, Hannah mentally corrected him. "I don't think so," she said. "If he suspected you, he would have asked you more questions."

"Well, good! Because I didn't have anything to do with it."

Hannah caught Andrea's eye and motioned her over. She'd pushed Tucker as far as she could, and more questions would just put him on guard. Andrea caught her signal, and she brought Sam Webber over to join them.

The conversation was trivial from that point on. Hannah was just getting sleepy again, when Mike came in carrying a tray with coffee.

"Here you go," he said. "Sorry about the cups, but all I could find were these plastic ones. I thought I'd better use doubles since the coffee was really hot."

That made sense. Hannah reached for a cup. But before she could offer it to Tucker,

Mike passed him the tray. Tucker took a cup, sipped it, and made a face.

"This is almost as bad as chuck wagon coffee," he said, putting his cup down on the table.

"You must have gotten the gunk at the bottom of the pot," Mike told him. "Here. Take another one."

Tucker did, and he sipped it. "This is better," he said. "Thanks."

"I'll go get rid of this one," Mike said, picking it up by the rim and heading for the trash can.

Mike had just resumed his seat when Michelle and Brianna came in. Brianna rushed to Tucker and gave him another kiss on the cheek.

"Good news?" Tucker asked.

"The best. Curly's out of surgery, and the doctor thinks he repaired all the internal damage. He upgraded his condition from critical to stable."

"Can he talk yet?"

"Not yet. The doctor put him in a drug-induced coma. He'll be out cold for two days, and then they'll wake him up and reassess."

"But . . . he'll be all right eventually?"

"The doctor thinks so, but he warned me that Curly's not out of the woods yet."

"I'm so glad for you," Michelle said, giving Brianna a hug and then glancing at Mike. "We'd better go see how Dot's doing. The nurse said she's almost ready to go to the delivery room."

Hannah didn't wait for a second invitation. She stood up, said her goodbyes, and they were out the door. On their way down the corridor, Hannah glanced behind her to see if Mike was following, and then she turned to Michelle. "Is Dot really in the delivery room?"

"I don't know. I just said that so we could leave. Do you want to check on her?"

"I think we'd better. If we don't, Mike will find out about it."

It only took a minute to check on Dot. And it only took another two minutes to drop off the flowers in her room. They took a quick peek at Baby Girl Larson in the nursery, and then they headed for the exit.

"Wait," Hannah said, as they passed the alcove with complimentary coffee.

"You want more coffee?" Andrea sounded incredulous.

"No, I just want to check something out."

Hannah ducked into the alcove while her sisters waited. There was a thirty-cup coffee pot, similar to the one they used at The Cookie Jar, and baskets of sugar, artificial sweetener, and coffee creamer in packets. A box of straws and plastic spoons sat next to the coffee pot, and there were stacks of Styrofoam cups for coffee and plastic cups for water. From sheer force of habit, Hannah poured herself a cup of coffee and walked back to join her sisters.

"I thought you didn't want coffee," Andrea said.

"I don't, but now that I've got it, I'll drink it. Waste not, want not. Come on, let's go."

Hannah didn't see the look her younger sisters exchanged on their way out the door. She was too busy wondering what reason Mike had for claiming they'd run out of Styrofoam coffee cups when they hadn't.

CHAPTER
TWENTY-EIGHT

She was on a sailing ship, and the sun had crossed the yardarm. Whatever that meant. Even though she was right there, she still didn't know precisely what a yardarm was. A warm breeze kissed her cheek, and salty spray kicked up like sandpaper against her skin. Except salty sea spray didn't feel like sandpaper. The only things that felt like sandpaper were sandpaper itself, and a cat's tongue.

"Moishe?" she asked, opening her eyes to see two unblinking yellow orbs staring into hers. She blinked, but Moishe didn't. She'd lost the staring contest.

"What time is it?" she asked, sitting up in bed and noticing that light was streaming in her western exposure window. Of course Moishe didn't answer, but one glance at the alarm clock on her bedside table told Hannah that it was ten after two in the afternoon. She'd forgotten to set her alarm! She was late to work, extremely late to work! Why hadn't anyone called to wake her?!

She was just starting to enter full-scale panic mode when she saw a note propped up by the clock. It said, *Don't you dare come to work today! We're closing at two, and that gives me plenty of time to get out to the fairgrounds. I don't have to be there until three today. I'll be helping Lisa, and Andrea is doing the deliveries. Don't worry, I won't let her bake.* And it was signed, *Michelle.*

There was an old saying about not looking a gift horse in the mouth, and Hannah decided it had merit. There was no point in dressing and driving to town. The Cookie Jar was already closed for the day. She had absolutely nothing to do until seven this evening, when she'd watch Michelle at the Miss Tri-County competition. After that, she'd judge tonight's baked goods entries, and then she'd be through for the day.

The smile on her face stayed with her all the way to the kitchen. Michelle had left the coffee all ready to go, and Hannah poured in the water. While she waited for it to drip down, she sat down at the kitchen table and found herself staring at her new cell phone.

It was no longer attached to the charger. Michelle must have unplugged it, because there was another note on the kitchen table.

It read, *I don't know if this is important — Bri showed me her engagement ring, and it had an inscription. It said, "Yesterday and Today." Didn't the card you found in Willa's apartment say something like that?*

Hannah stared down at the note in shock. The florist's card they'd found in Willa's apartment had started in exactly the same way! There was a connection between Tucker and Willa and this proved it!

Mike should know. Hannah was reaching for the phone when she thought of all the questions he'd ask her. Who had thought of the inscription for the engagement ring? Did Brianna tell the jeweler what she wanted? Or was it Tucker's idea? Was *Yesterday and Today, Tomorrow and Forever* a common phrase? Or was it unique and therefore did it tie Tucker to Willa in some way?

Hannah went to pour herself another cup of coffee and sat back down at the table. Unless she wanted to look like an idiot, she needed more information before she alerted Mike.

Her new cell phone was on the table. Hannah flipped it open, pressed the button marked ON, and immediately heard a burst of tinny music. It appeared that she was up and running. She'd call Norman to thank him for her new phone. She punched in his number, but when nothing happened and she wasn't connected, she knew she'd done something wrong. She was about to hang up and try again when she spotted another button with a phone receiver in green.

Her Grandmother Ingrid used to say that if at first you didn't succeed you should try, try again. Hannah pressed the green button and heard a ringing tone. There was another ringing tone, and then Norman's voice came on the line. "Hello?" he said.

"Hi, Norman. It's Hannah. I just wanted to thank you for this phone. I'm using it right now."

"Did you dial my number?"

"Isn't that what I'm supposed to do?"

Norman laughed. "You can if you want to, but there's an easier way. I'm number one."

"Of course you are," Hannah said, and paused while he laughed again.

"Thanks, but I meant that I programmed your phone for speed dial and my cell phone is number one. Just turn on the phone, punch in a one, and hit the green phone button. The phone will do the rest."

"That's great," Hannah said with a smile, wondering what other numbers, if any, Norman had programmed. "If you're a one, who's a two?"

"I am. That's my home number."

Hannah grinned. She was beginning to see a pattern here. "And three is your number at the dental clinic?"

"That's right."

"How about four?"

"That's Andrea's cell phone number."

"Five?"

"Michelle's cell phone."

"Six?"

"Your mother's cell phone."

Hannah blinked. Surely she hadn't heard him correctly. "Did you say that *Mother* has a cell phone?"

"Yes. She just got it a couple of weeks ago."

Hannah groaned. As usual, she was the last person in the family to embrace new technology. "I suppose your mother has one, too?"

"Of course. She had hers first. I'm pretty sure that's why *your* mother got one."

"Keeping up with the Joneses? Or in this case, the Rhodeses?"

"Could be. I'm really glad you called, Hannah. I heard from Professor Tate."

"He called you?"

"No, he e-mailed me. They're in a remote area, but a truck comes to pick them up every two weeks and take them to the nearest place to replenish their supplies and pick up their messages. In their case, it's a village without an airstrip."

"So he couldn't have flown back here to kill Willa?"

"That's right."

"Hold on a second," Hannah said, reaching for her purse. She pulled out the short-hand notebook she thought of as her murder book and flipped it open to the list of suspects. "Okay. He's an ex."

"An ex?"

"That's ex-suspect. I crossed him off my list. I must be getting close to solving this case, because I've only got three suspects left."

"How many were there?" Norman asked.

"Thirteen. I had Tasha's three brothers, Mr. Hicks, Mrs. Adamczak, the high school boy Willa flunked, Professor Tate, Jess Reiffer, the old boyfriend who may or may not be Jess Reiffer, and the new boyfriend who may or may not be the cowboy someone saw with Willa on the night she was killed."

"Okay. Who else is on the list?"

"The burglar."

"The one who broke into the office at the fairgrounds?"

"Right. He's not crossed out yet. It could be a case of Willa's being in the right place at the wrong time. But there's something else that just came up."

"What's that?"

"It's that florist card Andrea and I found in Willa's apartment. It's the only personal thing she saved, other than the little photo album we found in her desk. I told you about it, didn't I?"

"If you're talking about the card that said, *Yesterday and Today, Tomorrow and Forever,* you did."

"That's the one. Michelle got a look at Brianna's engagement ring last night when we went back to the hospital."

"You went back to the hospital after I left?" Norman sounded concerned. "How much sleep did you get?"

"Fourteen hours, but I'll tell you about that later. Anyway, Brianna is the owner's daughter, and she was there with her fiancé Tucker Smith."

"The cowboy who tried to kill Curly?"

"Yes, if that's really what happened. He's a real piece of work, Norman. Slick and handsome, with a grin that he thinks will melt any woman's heart."

"And you're thinking Willa knew him in the past and he's the one who gave her the flowers?"

"Could be. Do you think you could find

out anything about that phrase on the Internet? I'd like to know if it's a common one."

"I'll give it a try." Hannah heard paper rustle, and she knew that Norman was making a note. "Anything else?"

"Not really."

"Okay. I'll get back to you on that. One last thing. You mentioned twelve suspects so far. Who's the thirteenth?"

"The wild card."

"The wild card?"

"Yes. I add him to every one of my suspect lists. He's the unknown person who kills for some unknown reason."

"Which makes him impossible to find."

"Right." Hannah shut her notebook with a snap. "Are you going to the Miss Tri-County competition tonight?"

"I wouldn't miss it. How about you?"

"I'll be there. Do you want to come over after?" Hannah asked the question, and then she laughed at the way she'd lapsed into regional Minnesota dialogue.

"Sure. Do you want to drive? Or shall I drive and you can come with?"

Hannah cracked up. Norman was quick on the uptake, and he'd wasted no time throwing another Minnesota phrase back at her. "I'd better drive."

"Okay. See you later."

"You bet. Norman?"

"Yes, Hannah."

"I really like this phone."

"I'm glad."

"There's only one thing . . ."

"What's that?"

"Can you tell me which button I should press to hang it up?"

It was six hours later, and Hannah couldn't remember the last time she'd felt so good. Norman had used his most powerful search engine, and he'd gotten over eight million hits on the words *Yesterday and Today, Tomorrow and Forever.* That meant the phrase was a lot more common than any of them had guessed. While the popularity of the phrase didn't rule out her hunch about Willa's knowing Tucker in the past, it was a lot less likely. She supposed she should be depressed, but she wasn't. Fourteen uninterrupted hours of sleep had put things into perspective, and she felt she was thinking clearly for the first time since Willa's death.

Michelle had done very well in tonight's dance competition. Since live partners weren't permitted, she'd appropriated the decorative scarecrow from the side of the stage and danced to *Turkey in the Straw.*

She'd brought down the house and come in second. The first-place contestant had studied ballet for eight years and performed with a professional ballet company in Minneapolis.

They'd all gathered outside the auditorium after the competition to congratulate Michelle. Even Lonnie and Mike had been there, taking a break from their official duties to catch Michelle's act. Hannah had congratulated her youngest sister, exchanged a few words with everyone who was there, told Delores that she agreed the ballet dancer had an unfair edge, and then headed for the Creative Arts Building with Lisa to judge the cookies.

As they'd tasted the sugary treats, they'd talked about Willa's marriage. Pam still couldn't believe that the classroom aide and student teacher she'd befriended had harbored such a painful secret.

"No wonder she turned Gordon down," Pam said, taking a bite of the last entry, a soft molasses and raisin cookie that Hannah thought smelled a lot better than it tasted. "After being married to Jess Reiffer, poor Willa was probably afraid to trust any man again."

Lisa gave a little nod. "I can understand that. Even though he wasn't directly responsible, Willa's parents would still be alive if she hadn't gotten mixed up with him."

Now was not the time for a discussion about time and consequence, and Hannah knew it. She just took another bite of her cookie and washed it down with the coffee Lisa had brought. "Maybe the reason Willa turned Gordon down was because she was still married."

There was a moment of silence as both Pam and Lisa turned to her in surprise. "You think?" Lisa asked.

"I don't know. Do you think I should ask Andrea to check it out? It might be mentioned in the real estate papers when she sold her parents' house."

"Ask her," Lisa said.

Pam nodded. "Yes, do. It probably doesn't have anything to do with her murder, but I'd really like to know." She glanced down at her master sheet and then back up at them. "We've tested all the entries. Fill out your last scorecard, and we're done for the night."

Hannah filled out her scorecard and handed it to Pam. A moment later, so did Lisa. Once the scores were tallied, Pam completed the judge's master sheet. "Do you want to guess which cookie won?" she asked.

"I thought the Chippers were the best," Lisa said.

"Agreed," Hannah offered her opinion. "The Chippers were absolutely delicious."

"That's what I thought, too," Pam said, signing the sheet. "You'll be happy to know that they won, hands down."

"Who baked them?" Lisa asked.

"Let's see . . ." Pam flipped the entry card over, read the name, and turned to Hannah. "It's Regina Todd. That's Andrea's mother-in-law, isn't it?"

"Yes. I'll tell Andrea and she can break the news. It might win her points. And if you don't mind, I'll take the rest of those Chippers to Mother."

"You're forging a peace between Delores and Regina?" Pam asked.

Hannah laughed. "I think it'll take more than blue ribbon cookies to do that! The last time they got together at Andrea's house, Mother asked Regina if she was gaining weight, and Regina asked Mother if she was trying out a new hair color."

CHIPPERS

Preheat oven to 350 degrees F., rack in the middle position.

1 1/2 cups softened butter *(3 sticks, 3/4 pound, 12 ounces)*
1 1/2 cups white *(granulated)* sugar
2 egg yolks
1/2 teaspoon salt
2 teaspoons vanilla extract
2 1/2 cups flour *(no need to sift)*
1 1/2 cups finely crushed plain potato chips *(measure AFTER crushing)*
1 1/2 cups finely chopped pecans *(measure AFTER chopping)*
1/2 teaspoon finely grated lemon zest *(optional) (zest is just the colored part of the peel, not the white)*
1/3 cup white *(granulated)* sugar for dipping approximately 5 dozen pecan halves for decoration
Hannah's 1st Note: Use regular potato

chips, the thin salty ones. **Don't use baked chips, or rippled chips, or chips with the peels on, or kettle fried, or flavored, or anything that's supposed to be better for you than those wonderfully greasy, salty old-fashioned potato chips.**

In a large mixing bowl, beat the butter, sugar, egg yolks, salt, and vanilla until they're light and fluffy. *(You can do this by hand, but it's a lot easier with an electric mixer.)*

Add the flour, crushed potato chips, chopped pecans, and lemon zest *(if you decided to use it.)* Mix well.

Form one-inch dough balls with your hands and place them on an UNGREASED cookie sheet, 12 to a standard-sized sheet.

Place the sugar in a small bowl. Spray the bottom of a glass with Pam or other non-stick cooking spray, dip it in the sugar, and use it to flatten each dough ball. *(Dip the glass in the sugar for each ball.)* Place a pecan half in the center of each cookie and press it down slightly.

Bake at 350 degrees F., for 10 to 12 minutes, or until the cookies are starting to turn golden at the edges. Let them cool on the cookie sheet for 2 minutes and then remove them to a wire rack to cool completely.

Yield: Approximately 8 dozen, depending on cookie size.

Hannah's 2nd Note: Mother loves these when I use orange zest instead of lemon zest. Since the orange flavor isn't as strong as the lemon, I use one whole teaspoon of orange zest when I bake Chippers for her. I also substitute one teaspoon orange extract for the vanilla.

CHAPTER
TWENTY-NINE

Hannah and Lisa had just stepped outside the Creative Arts Building when Andrea and Michelle came running up the steps.

"I thought you'd *never* get through!" Andrea exclaimed, grabbing Hannah's arm. "I tried to call you, but there's something wrong with your cell phone. Let me have it."

Hannah reached into her purse and handed her sister the phone. "Here, but there's nothing wrong with it. I just didn't turn it on."

"But what if there'd been an emergency?"

"Then I *would* have turned it on. Why were you trying to call me?"

"They caught him," Michelle explained, obviously the calmer of the two.

"Willa's killer?"

"That's right." Michelle turned to Lisa with a smile. "Your *husband* is the one who caught him! He's down at the sheriff's station right now, watching Mike and Lonnie interrogate him."

"Herb caught Willa's killer?" Lisa was clearly astonished. "How did he do that?"

"He was standing right where we are now, waiting for you to finish judging," Andrea took over from her younger sister. "He was just staring out over the crowd, and he noticed a cowboy hanging around the office building. At first Herb thought he was waiting for somebody, but he didn't look at his watch or anything, the way you'd do if somebody you were supposed to meet was late."

Michelle picked up the thread. "So Herb was about to walk over and ask him what he was doing when the cowboy glanced around to see if anybody was watching him."

"He didn't see Herb because Herb wasn't on ground level," Andrea interjected.

"And when the cowboy thought no one was paying any attention to him, he snuck around the corner." Michelle stopped and turned to Hannah. "Is that *snuck,* or *sneaked?*"

"It's *sneaked,* but it doesn't matter. Go on."

"So Herb ran down the steps and over to the building. He went around the same corner, and he saw the cowboy halfway through one of the office windows."

Lisa's eyes widened. "What did Herb do?"

"According to Bill," Andrea took over, "and Bill's the one who called to tell me about it, Herb grabbed the cowboy by both legs, pulled him backwards really fast, and dumped him on the ground on his back. Then he flipped him over, pinned him down, and called for security. Roland Weiss, he's the retired deputy that discovered the break-in, came to put the cuffs on."

"Wait a second." Hannah was confused. "Did this cowboy confess to killing Willa?"

"No, but he's the one who stole the box-office receipts on the night Willa was killed. He didn't confess to that either, but Mike sent Lonnie to search his motel room, and Lonnie recovered the money bags the secretary used for the box-office receipts."

Hannah just shook her head. "And this guy came back to the same place to steal more box-office money?"

"That's right." Andrea gave a little laugh. "Of course he was severely impaired at the time."

"Drugs? Or booze?"

Michelle shrugged. "Lonnie wasn't sure. He said the guy was either drunk as a skunk, high as a kite, or both. Doc Knight came in to draw blood for a tox screen, but that'll take a couple of hours."

Hannah was silent for a moment, putting together the pieces. "You said this guy was a cowboy. Was he with the rodeo?"

"He was until Tuesday night. That's when the manager fired him."

"Let me guess," Hannah said. "They marched him down to the office and had the secretary pay him off, right?"

"That's right. And *that's* how he knew exactly where the money was kept. He just stuck around and broke in."

Hannah began to frown. "But that was between six and a quarter to seven. And Willa wasn't killed until after the carnival closed at ten."

"Maybe he was the cowboy Willa was dating," Lisa proposed. "If he was, he probably stuck around to wait for her. Maybe he was stupid enough to show her the money and invite her to go off with him for the weekend, or something like that. Willa could have known about the robbery by then and put two and two together."

"So you think he killed her to keep her from talking?" Hannah asked.

All three women nodded. Hannah thought about it for a moment, and then she had an idea. "It all makes sense," she said, "but let's take it even further. Let's say that the cowboy Herb caught isn't who he says he is. His real name is Jess Reiffer."

"Willa's husband?" Andrea asked, staring at Hannah in surprise.

"Exactly. We know that Willa liked to ride. Pam mentioned it, and the album Norman and I found had all those pictures of horses. Jess Reiffer might have liked to ride, too. That could be how they met. And if he was a good rider, he could have changed his name when he got out of jail and joined the rodeo circuit."

"And he was in the roping demonstration, and that's why Willa looked so shocked?" Michelle asked.

"Yes. Willa recognized him. And maybe, despite all the grief he caused her, Willa was still in love with him."

"You could be right," Andrea agreed, "especially if he managed to convince her that he'd learned his lesson in jail and he promised her he'd never break the law again."

"And then, when he met her on Tuesday night, he suddenly had lots of money. And Willa had heard about the break-in at the carnival office and the box-office money that was stolen."

"So her husband killed her because she

guessed what he'd done," Lisa said with a sigh.

Michelle sighed, too. "Willa died because she loved the wrong man."

There's a Country-Western song here, Hannah thought, but she didn't say it. "It all ties in with the photo album," she said instead.

"You're right," Michelle said with a nod. "Jess Reiffer used Willa's keys to open her desk to make sure she didn't have anything to identify him. He found their wedding photo and cut himself out of the picture so that no one would recognize his face."

All four of them were silent for a moment, thinking about Willa's unlucky fate. "At least they've got him," Hannah said at last.

"That's right. There'll be justice for Willa." Andrea turned to Lisa. "I'll give you a ride out to the sheriff's station."

"Thanks. That'd be great."

"It's on our way. Michelle and I are going to Mother's. She asked us to stop by the mall to pick up an ink cartridge for her printer. Do you want to come along, Hannah?"

"No, thanks. You can take these cookies to her, though. They're Regina's Chippers, and they won first place in the cookie competition." Hannah thrust the package of cookies into Michelle's arms and turned to Andrea. "You can call and tell Regina that she won."

"I'll call her when I get to the sheriff's station. Then Bill can congratulate her, too. Are you heading home now, Hannah?"

"Just as soon as Norman gets here."

"Uh-oh." Michelle looked guilty. "I forgot."

"You forgot what?"

"I forgot to tell you that we ran into Norman and he said to tell you he was going straight to the condo. I hope it's all right that I gave him my key to get in."

"It's fine, but I thought he was going to meet me here after the judging."

"He was. And we were supposed to tell you about the change of plans. In all the excitement about catching Willa's killer and everything, I just plain forgot."

"That's understandable. So Norman's at the condo right now?"

Michelle glanced at her watch. "He should be. He wanted to see if he could figure out what's bothering Moishe. He told me he thought that maybe if he was alone with Moishe and there wasn't anything else going on, he could spot whatever it is."

"It's certainly worth a try." Hannah was slightly disappointed that Norman wasn't meeting her until she remembered one important fact. As soon as her sisters and Lisa left, she'd be by herself, and the food court was still open. That meant she could dash over to the Sinful Pleasures booth and get a deep-fried Milky Way at last!

"I've got something to wrap up here," she said, not saying that what she was planning to wrap was her mouth around a gazillion scrumptious calories. "I'll see you at the condo later."

Once Michelle and Andrea had left with Lisa, Hannah headed for the food court. But her great escape into carbohydrate nirvana was cut short by the appearance of Ruby herself.

"Ruby!" Hannah called out, causing the candy bar chef to stop in her tracks and whirl around.

"Hi, Hannah. I hope you didn't want a deep-fried Milky Way tonight. I closed a little early."

Hannah was about to say that was exactly what she wanted, but then Ruby might feel bad. "That's okay. I was just coming to tell you that they caught the guy who stole the box-office money."

"They did?" Ruby looked absolutely delighted. "I'll tell Sam. I'm going over there now. He's driving Brianna and me to the hospital to take Curly some flowers."

"Curly's awake?"

"Not yet, but the doctor upgraded his condition to good, and he's going to wake him up tomorrow morning. He's almost positive that Curly's going to be all right. We want Curly to see our flowers first thing and know that we were there."

"That's nice. I'm really glad he's going to be okay."

"Me, too. About the robbery . . . do you know if they recovered any of the stolen money?"

Hannah shook her head. "The only thing I know for sure is that the thief was a rodeo cowboy who was fired on Tuesday."

"Buck Jones," Rudy said with a frown. "I knew he was trouble the second I set eyes on him. He gave Sam a hard luck story, and Sam hired him to help with the setup and do some of the roping demonstrations. I gotta say he was good with a rope, but Riggs caught him taking shortcuts with the setup for the Brahmas."

"What do you mean?"

"There's supposed to be a barrel every fifteen feet and a stand between the barrels. That's to protect the clowns. The barrels are reinforced and they're heavy, and Buck wasn't bringing them all out the way he should."

Hannah's mind spun into high gear. "How about when Curly was hurt? Were all the barrels in place?"

"I'll have to ask Riggs. But that was yesterday, and Buck was already gone."

"I know. I was just wondering if he could have gotten rid of some barrels so he wouldn't have to roll them out. And maybe the guys that did the setup yesterday didn't know how many there were supposed to be."

Ruby's eyes narrowed. "That would explain a lot! Curly's fast on his feet, and he's great at diving in those barrels with a bull hot on his heels. But if a barrel wasn't where he expected it to be, it could have thrown him way off."

"My thoughts exactly," Hannah said. "Let me know what Riggs says, will you? They might be able to charge him with . . ." Hannah stopped short. "I don't know what the charge would be, but I'm sure there's something."

"I'll let you know. If that lazy little twerp had anything to do with Curly's accident, I'll take him down myself."

CHAPTER THIRTY

There was no way she should be hungry, but she was. Hannah got her order in right before the lights started flickering for the five-minute closing warning. She headed for a deserted table, sat down, and wolfed down the funnel cake. She was just starting in on her coffee when she spotted a familiar swagger heading her way. It was Tucker Smith.

"Hannah," Tucker said, grinning his gal-winning grin. "Mind if I join you?"

Hannah was tempted to say no. Tucker wasn't the killer, but that didn't mean she had to like him. At the same time, it would be rude to refuse. "Pull up a bench," she said, hoping she sounded more welcoming than she felt.

"I'm glad I caught you." Tucker stepped over the bench with an ease Hannah could only admire, and sat astride it, like a horse. "Somebody told me you were investigating the murder, and I wanted to see how you were doing."

"Why?"

Tucker shrugged. "I guess I was just curious, being that it happened right here at the fair and all. You *are* investigating, aren't you?"

"No."

"No?"

Hannah shook her head. "I *was* investigating, but I'm not investigating now."

"Why not?"

"Because they caught him."

"No kidding! Well . . . that's good news. Did you catch him yourself?"

"Not me. Our local marshal picked him up trying to break into the Great Northwestern office again tonight."

"You mean . . . the guy who broke into the office is the killer?"

"It looks that way."

"No kidding!" Tucker exclaimed again, causing Hannah to wonder if he had a limited vocabulary. "Did you think he was the killer all along?"

"Not exactly," Hannah said, deciding that the truth was in order. "If you must know, I thought that *you* were the killer."

"Me?!" The lights flickered for the second time as Tucker leaned closer. "Why did you think *that?*"

"It's a long story," Hannah said. "Do you have an hour?"

"I've got all night for something like that," Tucker shot right back.

"Unfortunately, we've only got three minutes or so," Hannah said. "I don't want to get locked in."

"Oh, you won't. I can let you out the back way." Tucker jingled the ring of keys in his pocket. "You didn't tell anybody else what you thought about me, did you?"

"No. And now that they caught the real killer, I'm glad I didn't."

"Me, too." Tucker gave a little chuckle. "Why did you suspect me anyway?"

The lights flickered again and Hannah took another sip of her coffee. She really wanted to head for the gate with the crowd, but she owed Tucker an answer. "Because one of the 4-H kids saw Willa with a cowboy and I thought it was you," she explained. "And because when Willa walked past the roping demonstration with me, she almost passed out cold from shock. I thought you were her husband, Jess Reiffer."

"Her *husband?*" Tucker looked completely mystified. "But I'm not married. I'm engaged to Brianna."

"I know that. And I realize that if anyone was Willa's husband, it's Buck Jones."

"Hold on." Tucker held up his hand as the lights flickered for the fourth time. "Buck Jones is the bum we fired right after the rodeo on Tuesday. Sam said Riggs caught him slacking off on the setup."

"I know. Ruby told me about it. We think that's what happened when you got thrown and Curly got hurt. Ruby's almost sure there were supposed to be more barrels. She figures Buck hid some so he didn't have to move them all out."

Tucker's mouth dropped open. "So *that's* what was different! I knew something wasn't right, but I couldn't figure out what it was. What do you think Buck did with the barrels?"

"I don't know. You'll probably find them when you pack up the show."

"Probably." Tucker glanced up as the lights flickered again. A moment later, there was a hollow thunk and then the dim strings of nightlights went on.

"I'll take you out the back way," Tucker said, looping his leg over the seat and standing up.

"Okay," Hannah agreed taking a bit longer to extricate herself from the picnic-style table with the attached seat. "What really threw me off was the engagement ring."

"You mean the one I gave Bri?"

"That's right." Hannah followed him past the deserted food booths and onto the midway. "It was the inscription inside."

"Yesterday and Today," Tucker repeated. "And her wedding ring is gonna have, *Tomorrow and Forever.* What's wrong with that?"

"Those same words were written on a florist card that Willa kept. That's why I thought she was tied to you somehow."

"You don't know?" Tucker asked, grinning his engaging grin.

"Know what?"

"It's from a Country-Western song. Somebody big sang it. I forget who. You must not listen to Country-Western music."

"Not often," Hannah admitted. She was about to ask him the name of the song so that she could tell Norman, when she heard the first two bars of the *William Tell Overture* and they seemed to be coming from her purse. "What's that?"

"Sounds like a cell phone."

Hannah reached in to grab it. "Oh, great! Andrea must have turned it on. I hate these things. Hold on a second and I'll shut it off."

In the dim glow from the strings of nightlights all the icons looked alike and it was impossible to tell the green phone from the red phone. Hannah pressed buttons at random trying to find the right one and dropped the phone in her purse again. They'd just started to walk down the midway when she heard her sister's voice. It was muffled from inside her purse, but it was perfectly audible.

"Hannah? We were wrong about Buck Jones. He stole the money, but he didn't kill Willa. Are you there?"

She really didn't need to hear this now. Hannah hoped that Andrea would assume she wasn't there and hang up. But her sister's voice continued to resonate from the depths of her purse.

"Hannah? I'm just hoping you're hearing this and it didn't go to voice mail, because they checked out his alibi and it's good. Buck Jones was at the Corner Tavern when Willa was killed, eating a sixteen-ounce porterhouse and a rock lobster. Nick Prentiss remembers him because he had too much champagne and he tried to dance with Albert, the grizzly. Anyway, call us back. We're getting worried about you."

Buck Jones hadn't done it. And that meant every one of her suspicions about Tucker were still valid. Hannah turned to glance at him and swallowed hard. His boyish, gal-winning grin had turned into a nasty gal-

slaying grin. And he was grinning it straight at her.

"Uh-oh!" Hannah breathed. And then she was off and running as fast as she could, down the midway heading for . . .

She didn't know what she was heading for, but that didn't slow her pace. She'd stop at the first place she found to hide. It had worked before when she'd hidden behind the hay bales from Willa's killer. And now he was after her. And nobody knew she was here at the fairgrounds in danger!

Hannah shut off her mind and concentrated on making her feet move. Left, right, left, right, as fast as she could go. She didn't turn to look, but she could feel that Tucker was behind her and that made her run faster. She rounded a corner, hurtled a fence with the grace of an elephant and found herself in the enclosure that housed the tilt-a-whirl.

Hide, Hannah's mind said. And she did. Before anyone could say *There's a psychopathic rodeo cowboy killer after you, and you should take cover,* she was huddled in one of the tilt-a-whirl carts, hoping against hope that Tucker hadn't seen her tumble in.

CHAPTER
THIRTY-ONE

Hannah huddled on the floor of the round orange cart. She could see the moon above her through the double bars of the safety handle, a thin sliver of pale blue-white. Not a full moon. That was in her favor. And the fact that the string of dim nightlights was not directly over her cart was in her favor, too.

Footfalls pounded past her on the dirt path and Hannah held her breath. Would he find her hiding place and kill her? But the sound receded and Hannah realized that he'd run past the tilt-a-whirl and around the corner.

She wasn't out of the woods yet, but perhaps she could stack the deck in her favor. Without even realizing that she'd generated two clichés in a row, Hannah rummaged in her purse for her cell phone. Norman was number one. She'd call him and tell him to send Mike out to the fairgrounds to save her. At full speed in his powerful cruiser Mike could be here in ten minutes.

There was a clinking sound and Hannah felt her hold on reality slipping. Tucker was doing something two rows over, and she thought she knew what it was. He was taking the chain from the strong man mallet. Mike might be able to be here in ten minutes, but she could be dead in five!

She had to think of some way to delay Tucker if he found her. She'd kept killers talking for longer than that in the past. They seemed to like to tell her about their exploits, to explain why they'd done what they'd done. Perhaps it was ego. Perhaps it was stupidity. Whatever it was, she'd take it.

Hannah's fingers punched in a one, and then the button she thought contained the green phone icon. And then, wonder of wonders, the phone started to ring.

"Call Mike!" she gasped when Norman answered. "I'm hiding. Tilt-a-whirl. Tucker killed . . ."

And that was when it happened. Her phone went dead. Hannah heard it go with two clicks and a beep. The dying swan had gasped its last breath and Hannah could only hope that she wasn't in the same boat.

That was when she heard it, a squad car

with siren screaming in the distance, racing down the highway that led to the fairgrounds. But she also heard something else and that was the sound of someone running straight for her. Hannah looked down at her choice of weapons. Nothing. And then she looked down at her means of defense. All she had was her saddlebag purse and while it might deflect one blow from the strong man mallet if she was very lucky, it couldn't last forever.

Frantically, she looked around her for ammunition, anything that she could use to thwart a killing blow. There was nothing, unless a piece of grape bubblegum sticking to the safety handle counted. She'd have to depend on her wits to save her. And at that moment, she felt quite witless.

The night wind picked up, blowing down the midway and kicking up debris from the trash cans. They were in for another summer storm. A crumpled Dixie cup zipped past Hannah's cart, closely followed by several scraps of paper.

She heard rather than saw him coming. The sound of his boot heels hitting the dirt was like thunder. Hannah did her best to emulate a piece of flat cardboard in the bottom of the cart and prayed that Mike would get here soon. She no longer heard the siren. Perhaps it hadn't been a police cruiser after all. It could have been an ambulance, or a fire truck, or . . . Hannah deliberately stopped thinking of other vehicles with sirens. She had to believe that it was a police cruiser and help was coming. The alternative was unthinkable.

And that was when it happened. Something she'd never expected. Opportunity dropped in her lap. It occurred quite literally as a black plastic raincoat someone had left on the seat of the cart just above her was blown up and out. It hovered in the air for a moment, looking like a huge black bat, and then the wind ceased and it dropped down to land in her cart. Some would call it fate, providence, perhaps even divine intervention. Whatever the origin, it was incredible timing. The coat spread over her like a welcome blanket only seconds before he walked through the opening in the fence and stepped up to her cart.

The raincoat was directly over her face. It was nearly suffocating her, but she dared not move. Through the narrow slit of one buttonhole, she could see him looking down at her and she held her breath and fought her urge to scream. Was this how a mosquito felt a split-second before a giant human palm came down to flatten it into oblivion?

If that were true, she'd never kill another mosquito as long as she lived!

Several thoughts ran through Hannah's mind so fast they seemed simultaneous. Was the plastic raincoat thick enough to camouflage her shape and render her nearly invisible in the dim light? Had she told her family that she loved them lately? Would Norman take Moishe after she was gone? Would it hurt when Tucker killed her? Would Lisa manage to work the quirks out of the recipe for Black Forest Cookies that had her stymied?

And then he was turning away. The raincoat had worked! She was saved! But a second later, it was snatched away and he was grinning down at her. "Did you really think I wouldn't see you?"

It was too late for hiding, but perhaps she could buy a little time. "I was hoping," she said.

"And now you're going to try to keep me talking until your boyfriend gets here, right?"

"Which boyfriend?" Hannah asked, the reply coming to her lips almost automatically.

"That deputy in the hospital."

"Mike Kingston," Hannah said his name, half-hoping he'd magically materialize. Of course that didn't happen, so she went on. "I thought maybe you meant Norman Rhodes."

"A gal like you has got *two* boyfriends?" Tucker Smith, or Jess Reiffer, or however the man who meant to kill her thought of himself, gave an ominous little chuckle. "That's enough talking from you. This'll be over in a second."

"Did Willa know it was coming?" Hannah asked, shuddering as he bent over to pick up the strong man mallet.

"Naw. I got her in the back of the head. I'm gonna have a little trouble with you, being as you're inside that tilt-a-whirl cage. Might take me two or three tries."

"Wait!" Hannah called out as he reached out for the mallet. "Why did you kill Willa? She wasn't any threat to you."

"Two million dollars. That's why I killed her. That's how much money I'm gonna inherit when I marry Bri and Sam dies. But I couldn't marry Bri when I was already married, could I?"

"What was wrong with divorce?" Hannah asked.

"Willa didn't want a divorce. She said she was still in love with me. And if I hadn't played along, she would have said something to somebody about that time I spent in jail.

And then . . ."

"Were you driving that car that was behind us when Norman and I left the school?" Hannah interrupted him.

"Yeah, that was me. The guy you had with you is some driver. I still don't know how I lost you."

Hannah sent a silent thank-you to Norman, along with a silent plea for someone, anyone to do something to save her. "And right before we got to the school, you went through Willa's desk and cut yourself out of your wedding picture?"

"That's right. Didn't want anyone to recognize me. Now stop talking, sister, and sit real still. I don't want to hurt you any more than I have to."

"I thought you were a good rider," Hannah said, hoping his vanity would distract him.

"I *am* a good rider."

"It didn't look like it in the arena. Unless . . . did you let that bull throw you on purpose?"

"Of course I did."

"Then it all makes sense. And because you're such a good rider and you made it look so real, nobody suspected that you set Curly up."

Tucker was smiling as he took a step

closer to her cart. "You know, you're pretty smart. Too bad it won't do you any good."

"I'm not *that* smart," Hannah retorted. She had to keep him talking. "I still haven't figured out why you tried to kill Curly."

"That one's easy. Curly found out who I really was, and he gave me an ultimatum. He said if I didn't leave town right after the rodeo was over, he'd tell Brianna and Sam."

"So you tried to kill him?"

"Yup. And I'll finish the job right after I take care of you. Now you just stay there nice and still and it'll be over real quick."

Hannah raised her purse to block his blow, but he grabbed it out of her hands and dropped it on the ground. "That's just gonna delay things."

Hannah watched the mallet rise up in his arms. It hovered overhead and was just starting its whizzing descent when she flew forward, then, backward, then around in a circle.

For a second, she thought she was dying. People who'd described near-death experiences talked about walking into the white light, but she'd never heard anyone mention a whirling wind tunnel. She was aware of the wind blowing against her hot cheeks, she could see the sliver of moon flashing by overhead, she could hear calliope music playing loudly, and she could feel her stomach churning. Since there was no way throwing up to the strains of *Yankee Doodle* could be a part of anyone's journey to the hereafter, she must be still alive. And someone had turned on the tilt-a-whirl to whisk her away out of danger!

Hannah struggled to lift herself off the floor. It took some doing, but after several attempts, she managed to scramble onto the bench seat and grasp the safety handle. As the cart whirled crazily, she looked down to see Mike fighting with Tucker.

Mike was alone! And while he was strong and fit, so was Tucker. Hannah watched as she whirled past. On the first whirl, Mike was on top, but on the second, Tucker had the upper hand. Then it was Mike, Tucker, Mike, Tucker . . . she had to do something to give Mike an edge!

She could help Mike if she were on the ground, but the tilt-a-whirl was going too fast for her to jump out. She'd never make it. She couldn't even stand up in the cart without being thrown back into her seat. If her phone was working, she could call for backup, but it was as dead as she would have been if Mike hadn't flipped the lever to start the tilt-a-whirl. What could she do with a dead phone besides throw it away and . . .

That was it! She'd throw the phone to distract Tucker. Hannah tried to stand up, but she was thrown back when the cart began its dizzying descending whirl. She couldn't even lean out to throw. The centrifugal force pinned her against the back of the seat like a bug on a moving windshield. She was about to throw the phone anyway and hope for the best when she noticed something.

Most of the time, the cart whirled madly this way and that, alternating between left swirls and right swirls. But there was one place, just as it reached the apex, when the cart hovered for a moment, caught between two equal forces, one from the left and one from the right. If she threw the phone then, she might actually hit something that would distract Tucker so that Mike could finish him off.

The music played gaily as Hannah's cart whirled. *Yankee Doodle went to town, riding on a pony. Stuck a feather in his hat and called it* . . . She reached the apex on the third syllable of *macaroni,* raised her arm and let loose with all the force she could muster. And then the dizzying whirl began again and she had no idea if she'd succeeded, or not.

"Way to go, Hannah!" she heard Mike yell. "You hit him in the head!"

And then there were other voices yelling over the sound of the calliope. There were several deputies with Mike now, and she thought she heard Norman calling her name. She was about to shout out for someone to put an end to her newest least-favorite carnival ride when the music ceased and her cart slowed and stopped at the very bottom.

"Thanks," she said, as Norman took her arms and helped her out. "What are *you* doing here?"

"I jumped in the car the second after you called me. They patched me through to Mike and I talked to him on my way out here. He was already halfway here."

"But if you hadn't called him yet, how could Mike have been halfway here?" Hannah asked, congratulating herself for regaining her powers of logic. Unfortunately, she hadn't yet regained her powers of locomotion, because she felt as wobbly as one of Winnie Henderson's newborn foals.

"I ran Tucker's fingerprints and I got a hit for Jess Reiffer," Mike arrived just in time to answer her question. "Come on, Norman. You take one arm and I'll take the other and we'll walk her to your car. I'll bring her truck by later."

"Hold it," Hannah said, digging in with both feet as they rounded the corner by the box office. She was still shaky and a bit woozy, but what Mike had said didn't make sense.

"Come on, Hannah." Mike pulled her forward. "You know you're in no condition to drive. You were on that tilt-a-whirl for at least five minutes and you're still dizzy."

"I'm not arguing about that." Hannah let them walk her forward again. "I want to know how you got Tucker's fingerprints without arresting him."

"I lifted them from his coffee cup at the hospital."

"Of course you did," Hannah said, mentally chiding herself for not figuring it out on her own. She'd caught Mike's lie when he'd said that there were no more Styrofoam cups, but she hadn't guessed the reason he'd substituted a double layer of slick plastic cold drink cups. "What I want to know is why you checked on Tucker in the first place."

Mike looked as if he didn't want to answer her question, but he felt he should. "It's like this. Sometimes a cop will operate on a hunch and I had a hunch about him. I just knew he was no good."

"What did he do to give you the hunch?" Hannah persisted.

Mike opened the passenger door of Norman's car and practically shoved her in. "I didn't like it when he called you *darlin'*. Nobody's supposed to do that except me."

Norman cleared his throat pointedly, and Mike turned to look at him. "Okay. You're right. What I meant to say was nobody's supposed to do that except me. And Norman. Is that all right with you, Hannah?"

"That's fine with me," Hannah said, snapping on her seatbelt before Mike could do it for her and taking her purse from Norman's hand.

"Okay. See you later," Mike said.

Hannah waited until he'd closed the door and walked away, and then she turned to Norman. "You were right."

"About what?" Norman started his car and drove out of the lot.

"About that cell phone you gave me. It's not exactly how I thought it would happen, but it did save my life."

Hannah was just starting to relax when Norman pulled up in her extra parking spot and parked directly in back of Michelle. "This is all right, isn't it?"

"I'm sure it's fine. I don't think Michelle's going out. Lonnie will be tied up with Mike."

"I think I've got Moishe's problem narrowed down to a specific unit," Norman said, getting out of the car and coming around to open the door for Hannah. "It's the one directly across from you. I was sitting there in the dark watching out the window with Moishe, and I swear I saw the curtain pull back and a little face peek out."

"A little face?"

Norman nodded. "It looked like a cat to me, but it was dark and I couldn't really tell. It could have been a small dog, I guess."

"It couldn't have been either one. That's where the Hollenbeck sisters live and they don't have any pets. Clara's violently allergic to cats and dogs. I can't even go over there to see them unless she takes an allergy pill first."

"She's allergic to you?"

"No, to Moishe. And since he lives with me, I've got dander and cat hair practically imbedded in everything I wear."

"So they couldn't possibly have a cat," Norman said, staring off into the distance at something Hannah couldn't see.

"That's right."

"Okay. Get out of the car, Hannah. I want

you to see something."

Hannah got out of the car and turned to look. "What did you want me to . . ." she stopped speaking as she saw Marguerite Hollenbeck carrying something to the dumpster.

"Is that a litter box?" Norman asked, when Hannah's voice trailed off.

"Looks like one to me. And that would explain absolutely everything. Let's go find out if we're right."

Marguerite was standing by the dumpster, tying off the litter box liner and preparing to drop it inside. Hannah was about to greet her when she saw that tears were running down her neighbor's cheeks.

"Marguerite!" Hannah said, putting her arms around the older woman. "What's wrong?"

"It's Cuddles. It's breaking my heart, Hannah. I love her so much and I've got to give her up."

Norman took care of the litter while Hannah took care of Marguerite. After a few moments of sobbing on Hannah's shoulder, she finally wiped her eyes and drew a deep breath.

"I know I've got to be strong, but it's just awful. I've wanted a cat for so long. Clara and I really thought we had her allergies under control, but it's just not working. Clara's miserable and Doc Knight can't give her any stronger medication. She's just as upset as I am. She loves Cuddles every bit as much as I do. But we're going to have to find a new home for her!"

"Right here," Norman said, stepping up to the plate with a speed that amazed Hannah. "I'll take Cuddles and you can come out to visit her any time you want to."

"You will?" Marguerite looked as astonished as Hannah felt. "Just like that?"

"Just like that. And if Cuddles gets along with Moishe, I'll bring her over here to visit a couple of times a week. Then you won't have to drive all the way out to my place."

And that means you'll be here to visit a couple of times a week, Hannah thought, admiring Norman's tactics. But she wasn't at all upset. Norman was welcome at her condo anytime.

"Oh, Dr. Rhodes!" Marguerite gave him a hug.

"You'd better call me Norman since I'm going to be your cat's foster father," Norman said, earning a big smile from Marguerite.

"All right . . . Norman. You're the answer to our prayers! Would you like to meet Cuddles now?"

"I'd love to. Do you have a cat carrier?"

"Why yes. I do."

Norman turned to Hannah. "If it's all right with you, I'll go meet Cuddles. And then Marguerite and I will bring Cuddles over to meet Moishe. Will that work?"

"Perfectly," Hannah said, smiling at both of them. Her problem was solved because Willa's killer was behind bars. And Moishe's problem was solved because he'd been pining away, hoping to meet Cuddles. Everything was coming up roses except for the purple taffeta dress she'd be wearing on the front page of the *Lake Eden Journal,* the dunking she was bound to get at Bernie No-No Fulton's hands at the Lake Eden Historical Society booth, and the fact that she had yet to experience the sinful pleasures of a deep-fried Milky Way.

CHAPTER
THIRTY-TWO

The curtain was about to come down. Hannah shifted slightly on the dunking stool in the Lake Eden Historical Society booth and did her best to smile pleasantly. Mike and Norman had promised not to dunk her, but Bernie No-No Fulton hadn't.

"Time?" she asked Michelle, who was standing by with a towel.

"Ten minutes until closing. And Andrea hasn't seen him come in yet," Michelle gave her report. Andrea and Tracey had taken up a position near the entrance, and they were all hoping that No-No wasn't coming to the Tri-County Fair tonight. Michelle had been crowned Miss Tri-County tonight, and they'd planned a celebration at the Lake Eden Inn at ten-thirty, a half-hour after Hannah's shift was over. There wouldn't be time for her to go home and change, so she'd brought another outfit with her. But her hair would be another matter. Once dunked, it would resemble a bright red plastic pot scrubber, and she wouldn't have time to wash and condition it.

Five minutes passed, and Hannah counted the seconds off in her mind. In the interim, three people tried to hit the bull's-eye. Drew Vavra, the new coach of the Lake Eden Gulls, was the first to make the attempt. He'd pitched for the Gulls baseball team when he was in high school, but Mike whispered something in his ear and the three balls Drew threw missed the target by a country mile.

Florence Evans was up next, and she told Hannah that she was just showing her support by eating up the time. Florence wore glasses and everybody knew she was terribly nearsighted. But there was the phenomenon of beginner's luck to consider, and Hannah held her breath until Florence's last ball had fallen harmlessly several feet in front of the target.

The third pitcher was Doc Knight, and Hannah thought she might be a goner. He was a crackerjack surgeon, and surgeons had to aim carefully or they'd take out somebody's gall bladder instead of their appendix. But Doc wasn't wearing his surgical greens, and he winked at Hannah before his first throw. That tipped her off that he was

missing deliberately, but he came satisfacto-
rily close to hitting Delores with his third
throw, which went wild.

The clock had almost run out. There were
only two minutes to go when Michelle's cell
phone rang. She listened for a moment and
then she approached Hannah's stool. "No-
No's on his way," she said. "Sorry, Hannah."

Oh, well, Hannah thought. She'd survived
a lot in her life, and one dunking wouldn't
kill her. Actually, she should be grateful that
she was here to be dunked. She could have
been killed in the tilt-a-whirl if things had
turned out differently. She'd had a series of
near misses and she should be grate . . .

Near-misses, Hannah's train of thought
hit a junction and went off in a new direction. Didn't near mean that the goal hadn't
been achieved? If something was a near-
success, that meant it wasn't a success at
all. It was the same as if someone said, *He
nearly made it.* That meant he hadn't, but
he'd come close. So was a *near-miss* a miss?
Or was *near-miss* a hit because it had nearly
missed?

These and other similar thoughts engaged
Hannah's mind until she caught sight of a
grinning baseball player wearing a Twins
uniform. "Hi, No-No," she said, accepting

the inevitable.

"Hi, Hannah. Guess what? I'm going to the show!"

Hannah knew a bit of baseball lingo. Her father had followed the Twins for years and he'd never tired of talking baseball to his daughters. "They moved you up and you're pitching for the Twins now?" she asked.

"That's right. But I'm really worried about you."

"What do you mean?"

"I heard you struck out a killer last night and I've never done that. I figured that maybe I should let you have a shot at the best rookie pitcher the Twins are ever gonna have."

"You mean . . ." Hannah didn't dare voice what she was thinking. It was almost too good to be true.

"That's right. I want to take your place and have you throw three balls at me. If you dunk me, you're the best amateur pitcher in the state. And if you don't, I'll take a crack at you. Fair enough?"

Hannah glanced out over the crowd. There was Wingo Jones and his cameraman. Delores would love this publicity for the Lake Eden Historical Society. And that gave her a really great idea.

"Sure," she said, giving a big grin for the

camera, "but I'm not the best amateur pitcher around."

No-No looked surprised. "You're not?"

"Oh, no. My mother is. She's Delores Swensen, the president of the Lake Eden Historical Society, and she told me all about it. She used to play softball when she was in high school, and she was terrific. If my mother can't dunk you with three pitches, you can have a crack at her. Is that a deal?"

"It's a deal," No-No said, and Hannah almost laughed out loud as she caught sight of her mother's shocked face. Delores was caught, and she knew it. If she refused to honor Hannah's bet, she'd fail to support her favorite cause. And if she did honor Hannah's bet, she'd probably get dunked, but she'd also get a lot more airtime to promote the Lake Eden Historical Society. Hannah figured she'd done what a good daughter should do and helped her mother achieve her goal. Delores deserved it. Oh, boy, did she ever deserve it!

"Did you wait until the third ball on purpose?" Andrea asked, when one of Sally's waitresses had served their entrees.

Delores shrugged. She'd gotten at least three minutes of airtime on KCOW television, and she was pleased. And to make her

500

time on camera even sweeter, she hadn't been dunked. "Of course I waited until the third ball," she said. "I had to build up the suspense. That's very important in the television world."

Hannah, who was sitting between Norman and Mike again, despite her protests that she felt like the mustard in their ham and cheese sandwich, just smiled. Her mother had dunked No-No fair and square and it would probably become a family legend. And when it came to family legends, she had one she had to correct.

"You can stop eating oatmeal," she said, leaning across the table to speak to Andrea. "You fooled me when you were a kid, and I was just getting even."

"I know."

"You do?"

"I knew that day. But I felt guilty for fooling you, and I figured it was my penance."

"Well, you don't have to be penitent any longer."

"Thanks, but I think I'll still eat oatmeal."

Hannah stared at her for a moment and then she began to smile. "Don't tell me . . ."

"That's right," Andrea interrupted. "I discovered I really like it!"

"Hannah?" Lisa motioned to Hannah and Hannah leaned back to talk to her behind

Mike's back. "I just wanted to tell you I really like your earrings. They match your pendant perfectly."

"Thank you," Hannah said and left it at that. The earrings had arrived that morning, a special delivery from the jeweler who'd designed her pendant. They were a gift from Ross Barton, the producer of *Crisis in Cherrywood.* There had been little gifts, or flowers, every week since he'd been gone. When they'd spoken on the phone, he'd told her that he was "fanning the flames to keep them alive."

"So how's Cuddles?" Michelle asked Norman. She was sitting between Norman and Lonnie, but Hannah was willing to bet that she didn't feel like anyone's sandwich.

"She's great." Norman passed her the picture he'd taken of the gray tabby curled up with Moishe in their father's desk chair. "Cuddles adores Moishe, so we're going to let them visit at least three times a week."

Hannah glanced at Mike. He didn't look happy.

"So . . ." he said. "Do you think they'll have any kids? I've been thinking about getting a kitten."

Good heavens! Hannah thought. She had to end this before Mike and Norman tried to out-feline each other.

"Cuddles is spayed," Hannah explained. "She can't have kittens. And even if she could, Moishe's been neutered."

"Oh, Hannah! How could you?!" Mike looked horrified.

"I didn't," Hannah told him. "He was already neutered when he arrived on my doorstep. But if he hadn't been, I would have taken him to the vet. It's part of being a responsible pet owner. There are too many homeless dogs and cats."

"But . . ." Mike floundered in the face of Hannah's determination, but he was given a reprieve as Delores began clinking her fork against her champagne flute.

"Could I please have everyone's attention?" Delores asked. It was designed in the form of a question, but given the force of her personality, of course she had it in no time flat.

"First of all, Lisa and Herb need our help," Delores said, startling Hannah and causing her to almost stab her napkin instead of the anchovy on her salad.

"I knew I should have told you first," Lisa said, leaning back to talk to Hannah around the rear of Mike's chair. "It was just that you were so busy. And all I asked her was if she'd let some of my relatives rent her cabin on Eden Lake for the last week in August."

"Lisa and Herb are having a family reunion," Delores went on, "and they need places to rent on Eden Lake. You can help them with that, can't you, Andrea?"

"Of course," Andrea said, pulling out some kind of an electronic device and making a note. "The last week in August?"

"Right," Lisa said, glancing over at Herb, who nodded. "We thought that might be a good time because it's right before school starts."

"I'll take care of it for you. How many people are coming?"

Lisa looked at Herb, and Herb looked at Lisa. Hannah thought both of them seemed a little stunned that their plans were being made so public so soon.

"Maybe three dozen?" Lisa ventured. "We're doing RSVPs so we can let you know."

"And maybe a dozen or so more," Herb added. "Lisa comes from a big family, and so do I."

"That's okay. I can handle it. Most people are shutting their cabins down about that time, and they'll be happy about the extra rental. I can probably get you a deal."

"In any event, we'll start the ball rolling for you," Delores said, smiling at Lisa and Herb. "And now, I'd like to propose a toast to my daughter Michelle for winning the Miss Tri-County Beauty Pageant."

"Thanks, Mom," Michelle said, clinking her glass with her mother's. "And I'd like to propose a toast to Andrea and Tracey, who came in first in the Mother-Daughter contest."

"And I'd like to . . ." Tracey paused and turned to her mother. "What did Grandma call that?"

"Propose a toast," Andrea said.

"Right. I'd like to propose a toast to Bethany, who would have come in first in the Beautiful Baby contest if she hadn't pulled off the head judge's hair."

"It was a toupee," Andrea explained. "Everybody there thought it was really funny, but Bethie got disqualified for misbehavior."

Delores shook her head. "They should have given her an award for good taste. It was the worst toupee I've ever seen. He must have gotten it used from Digger."

"Mother!" Hannah gasped, laughing in spite of herself.

Delores laughed right along with her daughters. "I'm a little giddy tonight because I finally finished the project I've been working on for months."

"Tell us about it," Hannah said, hoping

that her mother would reveal what she'd been doing every night in her home office.

"Not quite yet, dear. It's something I've been wanting to do for years, and we'll have another family celebration if it actually flies."

Orville and Wilbur beat you to it, Hannah thought, but of course she didn't say it.

"I'd like to congratulate Norman for winning first place in the photography exhibit," Delores went on, "and Herb for being the best amateur magician. And I want to thank Mike for saving Hannah from that dreadful man. I'm through talking now. Let's have dessert!"

The waitress must have been listening, because the dessert cart appeared immediately. There were Hannah's Blonde Brownies to celebrate the fact that Willa's killer was behind bars, and a round silver platter that was totally empty.

"Here, Hannah," Norman said, passing a second photograph to her.

Hannah glanced down at the photo, and a broad smile spread across her face. "It's perfect, Norman. How did you *do* that?"

"With my photo program. That's the beauty of digital photography. I could have changed your dress to any color, but I thought dark green looked better with your hair."

"It *does* look better," Hannah uttered the understatement of the year and gave silent thanks to whoever had designed Norman's photo program. "Is this the picture that's going to be in the paper tomorrow?"

"Yes."

"Thank you, Norman," Hannah said, already thinking of other ways she could show her appreciation. And then the waitress approached her, and Hannah noticed that empty silver plate again.

"Why do you have . . . ?" Hannah started to ask, but she stopped as she saw Ruby walking up to their table with a plate liner to fit that silver platter. The glass liner contained at least a dozen deep-friend goodies.

"Milky Ways are on the left, and Snickers are on the right," Ruby said, placing the liner on the silver platter and smiling at Hannah. "Your mother arranged it, and Sally let me make them right here."

Ruby left the platter and came around the table to give Hannah a big hug. "Thank you for saving Brianna from making the biggest mistake of her life!"

Hannah hugged her back and accepted the deep-fried Milky Way that Ruby put on her plate. As she took her first bite and came very close to moaning in pleasure, she thought about how lucky she was. It was wonderful to be here with her family and friends, enjoying a once-in-a-lifetime treat. And then she caught her mother's eye. And she wondered exactly what project her mother had finished. And whether that secret project was going to affect all of their lives.

Blonde Brownies

Preheat oven to 350 degrees F., rack in the middle position.

4 one-ounce squares white chocolate *(or the equivalent — 3/4 cup white chocolate chips will do fine.)*
3/4 cup butter *(one and a half sticks)*
1 1/2 cups white *(granulated)* sugar
3 beaten eggs *(just whip them up in a glass with a fork)*
1 teaspoon coconut extract *(or vanilla)*
1 cup flour *(pack it down in the cup when you measure it)*
1/2 cup pecans
1/2 cup coconut
1/2 cup white chocolate chips *(I used Ghirardelli)*

Prepare a 9-inch by 13-inch cake pan by lining it with a piece of foil large enough to flap over the sides. Spray the foil-lined pan with Pam or other nonstick cooking spray.

Microwave the white chocolate and butter in a microwave-safe mixing bowl for one minute. Stir. *(Since chocolate frequently maintains its shape even when melted, you have to stir to make sure.)* If it's not melted, microwave for an additional 20 seconds and stir again. Repeat if necessary.

Stir the sugar into the white chocolate mixture. Feel the bowl. If it's not so hot it'll cook the eggs, add them now, stirring thoroughly. Mix in the coconut extract.

Mix in the flour and stir just until it's moistened.

Put the pecans, coconut and white chocolate chips in a food processor. Chop them all together with the steel blade. *(If you don't have a food processor, you don't have to buy one just for this recipe — just chop everything up as well as you can with a sharp knife.)*

Mix in the chopped ingredients, give a final stir, and spread the batter out in your prepared pan.

Bake at 350 degrees F. for 30 minutes.

Cool the Blonde Brownies in the pan on a metal rack. When they're thoroughly cool, grasp the edges of the foil and lift the brownies out of the pan. Put them facedown on a cutting board, peel the foil off the back, and cut them into brownie-sized pieces.

Place the squares on a plate and dust

lightly with powdered sugar.

Jo Fluke's Note: I developed these Blonde Brownies for Laura Levine's party when she launched the third book in her Jaine Austen mystery series, Killer Blonde.

RUBY'S DEEP-FRIED CANDY BARS

Oil for deep-frying *(I used Canola)*
6 or more assorted chocolate-covered candy
   bars***

   ***— **Milky Way, Snickers, Mars Bars,
or Almond Joy work well. You can use
regular size candy bars (approximately
2 ounces) or the miniatures you buy in
a bag to give out at Halloween. Ruby
uses the regular size. If you choose to
use the miniatures, they won't take as
long to fry as the larger size.**

   Buy the candy bars the day before you
intend to make these and chill them in their
wrappers in your refrigerator overnight.

   An hour and a half before you want to
serve, mix up the batter from the following
ingredients:

1 2/3 cups all-purpose flour *(not sifted)*
1/4 teaspoon salt
3/4 teaspoon baking soda

1/2 teaspoon cream of tartar

2 Tablespoons white *(granulated)* sugar

1 egg

1 cup whole milk

Combine the flour, salt, baking soda, cream of tartar, and sugar in a medium-sized bowl. Mix it all up together.

In a separate small bowl *(I used a 2-cup measuring cup)* whisk the egg with the milk until it's nice and smooth.

Dump the milk and egg mixture into the bowl with the flour mixture and stir until there are no lumps. *(The resulting batter is about twice as thick as pancake batter.)*

Cover your bowl and chill it in the refrigerator for at least an hour. *(Two hours is okay, but no longer than that.)*

Hannah's 1st Note: You can use a heavy pan on the stove to deep-fry these sinful treats as long as you have a reliable deep-frying thermometer. If you do this, you'll have to keep a sharp eye on the temperature of the oil. It should remain at a fairly constant 375 degrees F. A deep fryer that regulates its own temperature is really preferable, but you don't have to run right out and buy one just to try this recipe. If you use a deep fryer, DO NOT use the basket. The battered candy bars will stick to it and

you'll never get them loose.

Prepare for deep-frying by heating your oil to 375 degrees F.

Prepare a cooling and draining surface by setting a metal rack over a pan lined with paper towels.

Hannah's 2nd Note: You will fry these candy bars one at a time and serve them the same way. That's to keep them from sticking together in the hot oil. You'll probably find that eager dessert eaters will line up in the kitchen to receive their treats.

Take out a candy bar, unwrap it, and dip it in the chilled batter. Make sure it's completely covered by the batter. Slide it gently into the hot oil with your batter-covered fingers *(or with two forks)* and fry it for approximately two and a half minutes, or until nicely browned. Use a slotted metal spoon, or a pair of tongs to remove the candy bar from the hot oil.

Set the candy bar on the rack to drain and leave it there for at least a minute to cool. Then transfer it to a dessert dish or plate and serve.

When all the candy bars have been fried and eaten, you may have batter left over. If you do, dump it into a plastic bag, cut off the end, and squeeze it into the hot oil in a circular pattern. If you haven't guessed by this time, you're making funnel cake. Once the funnel cake is nicely browned, remove it from the oil, set it on the rack to drain, and then sprinkle it with powdered sugar. Yum!

WARNING: NEVER LEAVE HOT OIL OR FAT UNATTENDED!!!

BAKING CONVERSION CHART

These conversions are approximate, but they'll work just fine for Hannah Swensen's recipes.

VOLUME:

U.S.	Metric
1/2 teaspoon	2 milliliters
1 teaspoon	5 milliliters
1 tablespoon	15 milliliters
1/4 cup	50 milliliters
1/3 cup	75 milliliters
1/2 cup	125 milliliters
3/4 cup	175 milliliters
1 cup	1/4 liter

WEIGHT:

U.S.	Metric
1 ounce	28 grams
1 pound	454 grams

OVEN TEMPERATURE:

Degrees Fahrenheit   325 degrees F.
Degrees Centigrade   165 degrees C.
British (Regulo)   3
  Gas Mark
Degrees Fahrenheit   350 degrees F.
Degrees Centigrade   175 degrees C.
British (Regulo)   4
  Gas Mark
Degrees Fahrenheit   375 degrees F.
Degrees Centigrade   190 degrees C.
British (Regulo)   5
  Gas Mark

Note: Hannah's rectangular sheet cake pan, 9 inches by 13 inches, is approximately 23 centimeters by 32.5 centimeters.

INDEX OF RECIPES

ABOUT THE AUTHOR

Joanne Fluke was born and raised in a small town in rural Minnesota, but now lives in sunny Southern California. She is currently working on her next Hannah Swensen mystery and readers are welcome to contact her at the following e-mail address, Gr8Clues@aol.com, or by visiting her website, murdershebaked.com.